CROOKED TRACKS

BY

BARRY NEMETT

PRAISE FOR *CROOKED TRACKS*

"**I**magine an adolescent Jewish boy growing up in New Jersey during the turbulent mid-1960s. Imagine that this boy, who is afraid and defiant, writes poems about paintings, which say as much about his growing pains as they say about their subject matter. Say these pains include death, drugs, desire, flights of the imagination, hero worship, embarrassment, and a family that feels rightfully displaced—the classic itches.

Such writing would require an author who is sensitive to the language of youth, its harsh epithets and regretful mortifications, and to the non-verbal mysteries of art. It would be quite a feat to pull this off, Houdini-like, which is exactly what Barry Nemett does in his first novel, *Crooked Tracks*. The author's empathy for his troubled characters, their painful pranks, explosive anger, and revealing tics, always remind us of the frantic sparkle of growing up."

John Yau
Art critic and author of *The United States of Jasper Johns*

"**A**rtist Nemett paints—draws really—a boy's life as he gropes to come to terms with tragedy, grandfather, parents, sex, sports, peers (his friend, English, belongs in *Hairspray*), and paintings. 'Lines linked them. Smudges and erasures did too.' Sweet, funny, brave, inspired."

Alan Armstrong
Author of *Whittington,* a 2006 Newbery honor book

"**B**arry Nemett's first novel is a wise and courageously imaginative story about love and forgiveness: love and misunderstanding between generations of the Schaech family; inspired first love between Stephen and his student teacher; and love of great art. Old Master and contemporary paintings serve Stephen as resonant arenas for the drama of his relationships, which lend the narrative characters that come vividly to life. By way of the story, Nemett (a painter) helps us dive into great art with abandon. He also deeply understands the nuances of childhood and adolescence and creates relationships with an emotional intimacy that rings resoundingly true."

Ted Leigh
Author of *Material Witness: The Selected Letters of Fairfield Porter*

Crooked Tracks

by

Barry Nemett

Library of Congress Cataloging-in-Publication Data

Nemett, Barry.
Crooked tracks / by Barry Nemett.
p. cm.
ISBN 978-0-9715402-6-2 (alk.paper}
I. Title.

PS3564.E4799C76 2007
813' .6—dc22   2007006931

Printed in the United States of America

Barnhardt & Ashe Publishing, Inc.
Miami, Florida 33131
800-283-6360

For my parents, who first taught me to navigate life's crooked tracks, and my wondrous wife and children, who give joyous meaning to the journey and guide me, always.

LIST OF ILLUSTRATIONS

Part I

PICTURES AND POEMS I

A Sunday on La Grande Jatte
by
Georges Seurat

Georges Seurat, French, 1859–1891, *A Sunday on La Grande Jatte-1884*, 1884-86, oil on canvas, 81 3/4 x 121 1/4 in. (207.5 x 308.1 cm), Helen Birch Bartlett Memorial Collection, 1926.224. Combination of quadrant captures F1, F2, G1, G2. Reproduction, The Art Institute of Chicago, Photography © The Art Institute of Chicago.

1

ASYLUM

Sookie DiMaeoli jammed his foot in my crotch and said, "Disappear like piss on sand, Dave," but I didn't. He also said, "I don't give a shit," when I told him my name wasn't Dave. Then his leg snapped in three places.

That was about two hours ago in Jersey, at a place called Take Five. Now I'm leafing though one of my grandfather's art books, called *Seurat's Dots*, and before I know it, I find myself strolling through the crowded shade of a Parisian park where the grass never needs mowing, every leaf remains loyal to its branch, and a Frenchman belches tug-stack notes from his fancy toy French horn. Parasols and tobacco smells and chimpanzees on leashes. De-Stephened, I have nothing on my nineteenth-century, middle-aged mind but the top hat on my head, spectral dots before my eyes, a cigar between my fingers, and at my side, a corseted woman and her colossal rump. With each squishing step, monkey dung cakes the heel of my left shoe. My father, the seldom-seen Jacob Schaech, is as comfortably visible as a pipe smoker in a sleeveless T-shirt, and my brother, Howie, is still alive.

I'm not just *imagining* myself inside Seurat's painting, that's where I am—*in* it—every part of me, breathing colored specks, feeling the sun's heat on the back of my neck. I never know how long I actually remain inside these pictures. Hell, one time I trekked for so many hours across an English landscape painting that my big toe pushed a hole through one of my shoes. That was several years ago, right around the time when I first discovered my skill, or gift, or curse (I'm still not sure what to make of it) of losing myself inside a painting. Since then I've found that it's often there when I need it, like now in my grandfather's New Jersey apartment, looking at Seurat's dots.

Most paintings are calming places for me to play, hide, or get lost within—asylums—where I'm protected from my Howie memories, which I do my best to keep out of my sixteen-year-old gut. Today, those memories won't let go.

2

EARLOBES, SOLDIERS, AND SNEEZES IN THREES

People used to say I looked just like Howie and that both of us looked like our mother's father, Grandpa Oscar. Our family likenesses skipped a generation, which never bothered me any.

I like the way I look now, distortions and all, when I see myself reflected in my grandfather's glasses. I inherited his dark brown eyes, eyebrows, and near-blond, curly hair, as well as the bend of his nose, and his thin, bony frame. If it weren't for the length of my sideburns, which extend below my ears, his mostly bald head, and a sixty-five-year difference between us, we could be brothers. I wonder if I'll lose my hair and grow to be six feet tall like the old man, and if someday I, too, will need glasses (or, as Grandpa Oscar calls them, spectacles) with lenses thick as the headlights of my parent's Oldsmobile.

My grandfather's apartment is filled with time, and I can slip into any part of it. In this apartment I can still feel my four-year-old finger-tips stroking Grandpa Oscar's long earlobes, wrinkled like used Saran Wrap. I can still remember wanting a haircut with a hole in the middle—like my father and grandfather, my mother saying no. If I want to, I can picture myself with Howie staging battles, dark green miniature soldiers spread strategically across the living room's braided throw rug. In their tiny tins, waiting to be scooped like M&M's into Howie's chubby and my skinny fingers, are green bugles, tents, hand grenades, bayonets, and belts of bullets destined for khakied infantrymen who can stand in place forever, killing.

I still dream of Howie and I playing, frozen in time like the soldiers. Our battles over, Grandpa Oscar reads us stories about wonderlands and mushrooms bearing large, blue caterpillars sitting so high up above the ground that little girls in party dresses have to stand on their toes to see them. I can still recite the *You are old, Father William* lines the caterpillar directs Alice to repeat after she complains about not remembering things as she used to. Howie and I know every word by heart. Why shouldn't we? Grandpa Oscar read us the cherished lines a thousand times. And the three of us would act out the poems—our own Jewish trinity: grandfather, grandson, and soon-to-become holy ghost.

Certain numbers remind me of Howie. Like three, that's how many times I could count on him to sneeze, fast, like firecrackerings—*hacubtz, hacubtz, hacubtz*. Always a trio of sneezes. He couldn't help it, just like my father couldn't prevent the bottom of his shoe from "God blessing" into Howie's shin right after the sneezes. Without fail, hard—two, three, sometimes four times—it was a knee-jerk reaction, literally. In those days, my father was mostly invisible—at least that's how he often referred to himself, and I think he was right—so we wouldn't even know he was in the room with us 'til his hard-hitting heel would tip us off. Maybe one time Howie couldn't stop sneezing and my father's foot accidentally surprised him, which got Howie's sneezing to stop. It would've been the closest Jacob Schaech ever got to "healing," only you'd have to spell the word with two e's.

I try to keep memories of Howie like these to a minimum because they have a way of squeezing all the juice out of my day. But not thinking about my brother doesn't mean I can't think about my father, or the curse of his invisibility, which disappeared, like piss on sand, three years ago.

Invisibility. If it was a skill or gift, Jacob Schaech didn't deserve the freedom it gave him. I think of ways to give him what he deserves. Something like DiMaeoli got. Or maybe something even better.

3

TAKE FIVE

Fall, friendless, 1964. The beginning of my fourth week at Garrison City High School. I'd just moved from Marchwood, several weeks after my sophomore year had already started. Though I dreaded the isolation I knew would walk through the door with me, I'd been wanting to go to Take Five, the after-school hangout I'd heard everyone talking about. It took me a month to get up the courage.

Silent, I was carried through the door to Take Five on a wave of clamoring voices. The room had cramps, swelling and contracting with each new invasion of fresh bodies. Trapped cigarette smoke, mixed with steam hissing from the grills, and the sizzling smell of soggy-french-fry grease spitting at no one in particular, made my eyes and nostrils sting. I could feel the thick air pressing against my forehead. Each breath hurt.

Only one of the overhead light fixtures was working. The little sunlight available recognized the futility of trying to come indoors through the thick wall of bodies blockading the room's one closed window, which was about the size of a face. Piles of crumpled coats scaled the wall to the left of a jukebox. Bordering the other side of the jukebox was a poster of Smokey the Bear, from whose mouth someone had drawn a line that circled a neon sign flickering a command to unwind: "T-A-K-E F-I-V-E, t-a-k-e f-i-v-e, T-A-K-E F-I-V-E!" Each sprawling turquoise and orange letter played its part, bursting color across everything and everyone in its path. Even the gray, slow-motion smoke in the room convulsed within spasms of hot orange and ice blue. "T-A-K-E F-I-V-E," "t-a-k-e f-i-v-e," "T-A-K-E F-I-V-E." The neon sign belonged in the room, but the bear looked as out of place as me.

There was nowhere to stand without being in the midst of someone's conversation, each competing with Frankie Valli and the Four Seasons's observation about big girls not crying. I could just about make out the song bouncing through the clamor of the room. . . *"Who said they don't cry? My-y girl said good-bye-yi-yi. My, oh my. My-y girl didn't cry. I wonder why."*

I recognized many but not all of the people I saw there as students I had seen in the halls at school. Some of them were in my classes, but I wasn't comfortable enough to go over and talk to anyone. I almost approached one guy I had seen at the nurse's office a few days before, but when he saw me he turned and whispered something into the ear of the girl standing beside him.

As I walked toward the counter, Sookie DiMaeoli, a senior at Garrison City High, stuck his leg out onto the empty seat of a chair next to him, to block my way. I was surprised at how pointy and unscuffed DiMaeoli's shoes looked. "You. Where you goin' to?" The way he said it.

"The counter."

"To get me a Coke?"

"To buy a burger. . . for me."

As he asked my name, DiMaeoli rubbed his thumb against the long, pointed collar of his shirt. I looked around and noticed all the other guys in the room wearing the same style shirt. My collar was short and buttoned down, which suddenly heightened my feeling of being out of place. Me and the bear. . . only I couldn't prevent forest fires.

"Stephen."

DiMaeoli waited. Stephen wasn't enough.

Noticing a part of the chain sticking up from beneath the collar of my shirt, he asked what I was wearing around my neck. "A cross?"

"It's a Star of David. A Jewish star."

"Get me a Coke, Dave. A large."

"My name is Stephen. Stephen Schaech." Despite my attempt to sound tough, I said it into the top button of my shirt.

"Shake, huh? Rhymes with break, which is just what I'm gonna to do to your face, right in half, if you don't get me that Coke."

I didn't move.

"What'd'ya think you're a badass or somethin'? I don't give a shit what you think your name is. You hearin' what I'm saying to you, David Starberg?"

"Stephen. Stephen Schaech."

My eyes were teary from all the smoke trapped in the room. I hoped no one noticed—and if they did, I hoped they wouldn't think the teariness had anything to do with this conversation.

"Give'm a break, Sookie," intervened a girl wearing heavy eye makeup. A thin line of black fuzz rimmed the area just above the girl's dead-white lipstick. Her chocolate-colored hair had the proportions of a tall layer cake iced into position with six cans of hairspray. The girls in Marchwood didn't look like this. Even if they did, I would know what they looked like with their hair regular because I would've grown up with them. I couldn't picture this girl ever being in elementary school.

Ignoring the girl and keeping his eyes locked on mine, DiMaeoli shoved his foot into my crotch and said, "Plus which, I don't even know what you're doin' in here."

Suddenly, I didn't know either. Placing his foot back onto the chair next to him, he added, "You can stay and get me the Coke I'm wantin', and then I'm lookin' for you to disappear, like piss on sand, Dave." He spit out the name Dave, crushing his tongue into the roof of his mouth.

I could feel the whispers of the room pelting the back of my short-collared shirt. Then the conversations surrounding us stopped. At that moment I wanted nothing more than to disappear like the prick blocking my way had just directed me to, but I couldn't. I couldn't move.

Sookie DiMaeoli was good at getting the attention he wanted, and he wanted this attention. Besides being two years older, he suddenly grew twenty feet taller and two hundred pounds heavier than me. Since moving to Marchwood, guys fell into one of two categories for me: ones I thought I could take in a fight and ones I knew I couldn't. This kid definitely belonged with the ones I knew I couldn't.

"I'm waitin' on it, Starberg," DiMaeoli said as he rubbed his leg against my knee. The back of DiMaeoli's shoe rocking slightly against the sticky seat sounded like paper tearing. He smiled. It was a fake, perfectly controlled, mocking smile, a chapped-lip smile—too big—like the mouth of an old woman who paints her lips past the edge. The smile brought my attention to a gob of Clearasil next to the left side of

DiMaeoli's mouth. Just above his upper lip was a dark, sandpapery arc that, I realized, could've been a mustache if this pointy-shoed, pointy-collared, pointy-smiling son of a bitch had let it grow. I was still waiting for the day I would need to start shaving.

"C'mon, Sooks," said the girl with the eye makeup and the hair.

"Now, Asswipe!" DiMaeoli shouted at me. "You own a bank or somethin'?"

"No." One word was all I could do.

"Then you must work in one of them delicatessen stores, selling bagels and whitefish and corned beef and shit. You oughta be good at getting food. That what you're good at, *yidberg?*"

I could feel my face collapse. Several beads of sweat made their way down my spine, not all at once but in slow stages, so that I intermittently felt them, then I didn't, then I felt them again. I was doing my best to look cool, but my back was dripping. Ice cubes with holes in their center plinked against one another and against the Dr. Pepper fizz hitting the slippery insides of a plastic cup. Inside the jukebox, a teardrop escaped from one of Frankie Valli's big girls who didn't cry.

I stared into DiMaeoli's eyes, waiting, trying to prepare myself. More and more conversations near the back of the room were breaking off in the middle of sentences.

"C'mon, Sookie, give him a break, why don'tcha?" the girl repeated.

DiMaeoli stared hard at the girl. "What's the matter with you, anyhow? Your hair too heavy on your brain or something? For a skank, you got a lotta fuckin' opinions, don'tcha?"

The girl suddenly reminded me of someone I knew in third grade.

DiMaeoli's was the only conversation going on now. Even the grease-hissing grills had shut up.

"But your opinion don't matter nothin', does it? Matters less than toad shit, is how much. What's mattering right now is I'm thirsty and this skinny piece of Jew toad shit here is gonna learn how to be a waiter."

I looked down at the leg blocking my way. "No," I said. The syllable shook.

Except for the jukebox, the room was wordless. "*Shame on you, your momma said. Silly girl. Shame on you, you cried in bed. Shame on you, you told a lie. Big girls do cry. Big girls do-on't cry-yi-yi. . .*"

"No? No what?"

I heard the song playing in the jukebox more clearly than ever before. Before I heard the beat, not the words. Or maybe because I had heard this sad song so many times, it'd been stripped of its sadness. I wondered how many times Smokey the Bear, hanging on the wall next to the jukebox, had heard the song, and whether he, too, had become numb to it.

"No, I'm not getting you any Coke. I'm not getting you anything."

DiMaeoli smiled again. This time it was a fuck-you smile. "What'd you say, Badass? I thought you said 'no' at me."

"I did. You finally got something right. What's wrong? Your new shoes too tight? Your feet hurt so bad you can't walk over to the counter and order for yourself, Douchebag?"

Somewhere in the room the legs of a chair moved. Otherwise the room made the agonizing kind of silence that only a room jammed with people could make, people who had suddenly stopped what they were doing to witness humiliation, pain—someone else's humiliation, pain.

I braced myself for DiMaeoli's fist in my face. Whatever I did now was going to help me out of this as much as my pee would help put out a forest fire. I just stood there.

Frankie Valli and his friends stopped singing. Someone lit a match; it sounded loud.

Then Sookie DiMaeoli overwhelmed the match and all the rest of the world with a single, searing sound. . . a wail. It was a head-turning wail, a wail that brought him the absolute and immediate attention of the few remaining patrons at Take Five who were still into whatever they were into before I tried to make my way to the counter to get myself a hamburger. It wouldn't have surprised me if the drivers passing by outside pulled over to the side of the road to make way for the speeding fire engine they mistakenly believed was trying to get by, so piercing was DiMaeoli's cry.

He wailed at the same time his knee popped.

Besides DiMaeoli and, in the periphery, the girl with the layer-cake hair, I thought I was alone. It had not occurred to me that others surrounded us, just as it had not occurred to me to drive my foot into DiMaeoli's knee; at that moment my thoughts, eyes, and legs were frozen in fear. And even if I wasn't scared, driving my foot through someone's knee—even this guy's—would have creeped me out more than getting my nose broken.

"Your feet hurt so bad you can't walk over to the counter and order for yourself, Douchebag?"

Had I said that? The words had escaped without my even knowing my lips were moving. And "Douchebag." Where had that come from?

DiMaeoli's smile was gone and so was the color in his face. As he squirmed on the floor, Mike Dumbrowski pressed his knee into DiMaeoli's throat, picked off one of the salty, ketchup-soggy french fries that had fallen onto his shirt, ate the fry, wiped the salt and ketchup off his fingers onto DiMaeoli's face—making a point to avoid the wad of Clearasil—and whispered something in his ear. Then he took a large cup of Coke that had been sitting on a nearby table and spilled it over the crotch of DiMaeoli's pants. "Here, Sookie. This what you wanted? Had a hard-on for some Coke, didja?" A girl mumbled something about "piss on sand, Coke on pants," and laughed. Two of the middle fingers of DiMaeoli's left hand twitched weakly in the smoky air like the tiny, upside-down legs of a fallen bird.

Mike asked me my name, and I told him, adding that I'd just moved to Garrison City three weeks ago. "I'm in your gym class," I said. I looked down at DiMaeoli.

Mike's eyes followed mine. "Don't let that here chickenshit bother you. Likes to play tough with guys he's sure he can take. . . guys like you—but he's nothin'. Take my word for it. You'll see it yourself, plenty, after you been here a while." Later on, Mike told me that although I looked to him like I'd be too small and skinny to be much good in a fight, I definitely had balls. . . and, just as important, there was something squeezing them. That's what he liked about me.

"I'm glad it's him down there, not me," I said. I could smell the blood-colored ketchup Mike had smeared near DiMaeoli's mouth. "Sheesh, that was fast. Hey, you think he'll be okay?" I asked. "I think you broke his leg."

My new friend looked down again at Sookie DiMaeoli, lying there, alone. "I give a fuck" is all he said before wrapping his arm around my shoulder and leading me to a crowded table located beneath a sign firing off its grizzly advice to "take five."

 4

X, Y, AND Z

The tail end of the alphabet brought Felix Ybañez and me together.

"These yours?" I asked a husky Puerto Rican kid as I stooped to pick up a batch of loose-leaf papers strewn across the school hallway. No answer. Felix was on his knees, carefully scraping his fingernail under a page stuck to the tiled floor. He got all his fingers in the act, but the lined piece of paper refused to budge. The page contained a portrait that looked pretty much like him: long black hair, thick eyebrows, dark sunken eyes, and a meager high-school mustache. Although I couldn't make the name out clearly ("J" something), the signature sprawled across the bottom definitely wasn't "Felix" or "F" with a last name attached.

After securing the drawing, I followed his glance to the overturned notebook and noticed his full name scribbled across the top of one of the homework assignments. "You're Felix, right? I'm in your English class."

Felix looked up. "*Shalom*," he said. I waited to see where he was going with that, but he didn't take it anywhere. "Met you at 'Take Five' yesterday, right?" I nodded. "DiMaeoli'd've kicked your ass," he added. "Lucky for you Dumbrowski came in on it. Don't hafta worry about DiMaeoli no more. He's not gonna be kickin' nothin' for a while."

"You spell your last name with a 'Y'?" I asked. I didn't want to talk about my ass getting kicked.

"What, you got a problem with how I spell or something?"

"It's just that you're the only person I ever met who has an X, Y, and Z in his name. Lots of people have Ys in their names. Hardly anyone has an X or a Z. I bet you're one of the only people in the world with all those letters. It's got to be a one-in-a-million shot!"

Felix hesitated. Then he smiled. "That's right, *kemo sabe*. You noticed. Not too many people notice that."

From then on, Felix and I were friends.

5

NAKED

Upon a shallow blackboard ledge, Diane Adamsohn crammed a naked baseball player between a desolate landscape with drooping, blue-faced clocks and a ragged group of blind men. The ball player immediately bumped into a dusty eraser and two sticks of chalk. Like a Gold Glove shortstop, the first-day student teacher caught the eraser but she missed the chalk, which broke into half a dozen pieces and then broke again when the blind men and the clocks fell on top of them. Stooping to pick up the pieces of blind-sided time and chalk, the young teacher knocked her pocketbook off her desk at the front of the room, which brought with it a five-legged clay rabbit that Mrs. Bilheimer, the supervising teacher, had placed there the first day of class. Two broken legs, but the animal survived. By the time order was restored, her face was the color of the drooping clocks.

Reading off our names from her attendance sheet (probably more to regain her composure than to see who was in her class), she mispronounced my name like most teachers do when they first say it.

"Shack," she called. Then "Shek." "Schaech," I corrected her. "Like break."

The student teacher was from Baltimore. Apparently, she had an aunt in Garrison City and had arranged to live with her while she did her student teaching. I wanted to call her aunt and offer to mow her lawn for free. When Miss Adamsohn told the class she was attending a school in Maryland called Goucher College, Ryan Sugar, who was sitting next to me, shouted out, "Bumfuck Hicksville is where you're from."

"Towson, Maryland is not the sticks. It's right next to Baltimore," she answered. She said it with confidence and authority.

"Bawlamer? Bawlamer is the sticks too," Ryan said. "And it's a kind of pruny purple. Like a squirrel, only without the fur. You wish you was from Garrison City. New Jersey. It's bright orange." Ryan's frontiers of geography extended little past the forty-eight cutout shapes that pieced together his little brother's brightly colored jigsaw puzzle of the United States. New Jersey was orange, Maryland, a furless, squirrely purple. Oklahoma was his favorite. It was silver, and looked like a meat cleaver. "Or New York."

The student teacher's forehead crimped as she smiled and asked, "And what color is *Noo Yawk*?" which embarrassed Ryan, who, thereafter, remained quiet.

Felix asked me what I made of the three pictures leaning against the blackboard. "I don't get it. What's clocks got to do with blind guys and baseball?" Felix didn't know a whole lot about most things, and for some reason he thought I did, as if what he missed he missed because it went my way instead of his.

"Yo, see that picture with the blind dudes?" Felix asked me. (He pronounced it *pitcher*.) "If there was another picture of what comes next. . . you know, like in comic strips or somethin', the fuckin' guys'd be all broken and shit, and they'd be piled on top of each other like one a them mile-high Bacon Derby sandwiches they make over at Take Five."

Meanwhile, Miss Adamsohn tried to get us going with this assignment she thought up. "Open your imagination to what you see in one of the reproductions I brought in, and write about it," she said. "A poem, an essay, a few sentences, whatever you want. You'll have the whole period to work on it." When she added that she hoped we'd like the assignment, her face turned red, and her fingers twitched, gracefully. I say gracefully because there was nothing clumsy about how she moved any part of her body, even when she first came into class, tripping all over her first-day nerves.

If we liked writing about the pictures, she'd bring in other ones throughout the semester for us to write about. All different types of artworks. According to her, it was a way for us to project ourselves into worlds of all kinds, places we've never been before; we could even imagine ourselves traveling to past times. . . times before we were even alive, or maybe back to an earlier period in our lives. We could look at the pictures however we wanted; there were no rights or wrongs.

Sounded good. Right up my alley.

Miss Adamsohn looked over toward her supervising teacher for approval. Then she printed "PARABLE OF THE BLIND MEN by PIETER BRUEGEL" above the first picture, "PERSISTENCE OF MEMORY by SALVADOR DALI" over the landscape, and "TRYOUT by SIDNEY GOODMAN" over the painting of the baseball player.

Ryan turned around toward me and whispered, "I got one. Wanna hear?"

I wasn't interested, but Felix was.

Turning toward me, Ryan recited: "Roses are red, violets are blue, that limp dick with the bat looks sorta like you."

"*Buenisimo*, Booger," Felix cheered. "I got one too. Want it?"

Ryan smiled. He was pleased Felix had chosen him to try his poem out on.

"I'll sing it. It's your theme song, Snotrod."

Sugar's smile disappeared.

Booger's always doin' it, doin' it, doin' it. . .
Pickin' his nose and chewin' it, chewin' it, chewin' it. . .
He thinks it's candy. . .
but it's sssnot!

Ryan Sugar had earned the nickname Booger Sugar as a five- or six-year-old, when he couldn't keep his finger out of his nose. The nickname stuck, just like his finger used to. I guess to some degree all nicknames (good or bad) stick. Some hang on to your emotional skin like brand-new Band-Aids, never fully scarring over, even when you outgrow them or find a way to bravely rip them off. Mercifully, some disappear on their own, dying natural deaths along with the forgotten reasons that gave them birth. The worst ones live on.

Several months after we met, Felix dubbed me Shakespeare when I made the mistake of admitting in English class that sometimes I wrote poetry at home, just for the hell of it. He turned Shakespeare into "Shakes" because he got it in his head that I "Made 'em quiver" whenever I talked to the girls in class. "New kid's got the moves," is what Felix told everyone.

I used to call my father Poppa PJ, or Poppa J, because he wore his pajamas under his clothes. He'd come home from work, take off his shirt and pants, and there he was, ready for bed. But my father left his pj's behind in Marchwood, and I don't call him much of anything these days. That's the only good thing about growing up in one place and

Parable of the Blind
by
Pieter Bruegel

Bruegel, Pieter (1525–69), Parable of the Blind, 1568. Tempera on canvas, 34˝ x 66˝, Galleria Nazionale, Naples. By kind concession of the Photographic Library of the Special Superintendence of the Polo Museale Napoletano

The Persistence of Memory
by
Salvador Dali

then moving to another: You get to leave behind what you don't want anymore. I wonder how long it'll take Ryan Sugar to get his six-year-old finger out of his nose.

At the top of my paper, just below the name Bruegel, I wrote:

Game—follow-the-leader gone wrong. Only follow-the-leader isn't a game here, it's how these blind guys live.

Group fall,
One of them goes,
There go them all.

Barely noticeable flock of birds ringing-around-the-rosey church steeple far in distance. Good detail. Birds not bumping into church. That's something. Otherwise, pretty depressing picture. I wonder if they know that, if they've ever talked with each other about their lousy luck—having gotten stuck living out their lives in such a depressing picture, or worse yet, being like this in real life and having someone paint them the way he saw them.
They're blind; are they mute, too?

I saw *Persistence of Memory* as not only depressing but creepy as well, like watching your cat eating its own throw-up. Below my notes for Bruegel's painting, I scribbled:

Dali

What to make of all those drooping, blue-faced watches besides "Time makes no sense"? Time distorted—bent to will of artist. Parched time. Blue time. Time, dangling from dead branch. I know the feeling, a second dangling like an hour, a day, a year. Happy Blue Year! How come the seconds you wish would last never do, while the ones you wish never came, won't go away?
Persistence of Memory—good title. I get the feeling the memory pictured in this painting has more to do w/the future than the past.
Two and a half kinds of time: Willie Mays time, time on the baseball field, and time everywhere else.
Or, two times: alive time and dead time. Dali's painting is about dead time. But it's not altogether grim. I wouldn't mind swimming in the bay by the cliffs. Other parts of the painting may be polluted, but the water's clean. And the watches aren't broken, just waterlogged. And bent. Sometimes I wish life could have a little more "not-broken, just-bent" parts. Maybe that's what most pictures are about when you get right down to it, just a whole lot of wishful thinking. . . brightly colored strokes of "if only."

The painting I liked best was the naked baseball player, so that's the one I wrote about for the assignment.

October 19, 1965

English Class: Mrs. Bilheimer/Miss Adamsohn
"What do you see when you look at this painting?"

"FINAL OUT"
(based on *Tryout* by Sidney Goodman)

"Is that you, watching?" the naked ballplayer bays
in his barely hearable way. Sandwiched beneath
the watcher's owly eyes and scores of snapdragons
following-their-leader around drooping, blue-faced bases,
linedrive inquiries light up the stadium.

"Are you there? Still watching?
This one's headed for the upper deck," boasts the batter.
"Count on it," he brags, even as he thinks,
"Gotta sit down," his skin reflecting dreams
sweating along the veins of his shivering crotch.
But seats are for sissies, for cowards who can't stand
to stand any longer. Gripping the most primitive of weapons,
he keeps his crouch, willing time to his bend.

A branch breaks, bending time to its will.
Each second dangles like a day,
defeating the boy with the wooden club,
who collapses into a chair. An "Aha!" hits the hitter,
who barely hears the call of the distant pitcher,
or feels the trauma of the toss. Other "Aha's!"
Then, "Batter up!" and again, "Batter up!" "Batter up!"
more high pitched, as if from a flying bird
who's never warmed a perch.

No matter.
Sitting on his pitch, eyeing the mound and the outfield owl,
the batter knows the game is over.
So do all the fans. That's why they've all gone home.
This batter can always be counted on
to make the last out.

—Stephen Schaech—

Tryout
by
Sidney Goodman

Goodman, Sidney; Tryout, 1965. Oil on canvas, 24 3/4˝ x 35˝, private collection. Courtesy of ACA Galleries, Inc., New York

6 ❖

GIL MCDOUGAL, CLOTHED

The last thing I wrote was the poem's first words: the title. Making the second out in the middle of a game, or even at the end, that wasn't so bad. But being the last one up and blowing it, that mattered. Everyone remembers what happened last. And who was responsible for making it the last thing remembered.

Howie and I loved sports, especially baseball. Everything about the game mattered to us. Nothing about any sport mattered to my father. Sports bored him. He was allergic to them. Especially baseball. He hardly ever came to our games. "Just my luck I'll get bitten by a spider or some such," was his defense. He was deathly afraid of anything that crawled and had more legs than he had. He never got over his near-fatal allergic reaction to some kind of bite he suffered while picnicking with my mom before they were married. He claimed his life was on the line every time he stepped foot on a field of grass.

The only baseball memory I have of my father is the time he got an autograph from Gil McDougal, my favorite Major League player. Such an unPoppa PJ thing to do. Still, spotting a Yankee shortstop pulling out of the stadium parking lot and following him for ten miles after a rained-out night game, flashing his high beams, honking, running traffic lights, riding the ass of cars before passing them, until, on a residential street, when the shortstop stopped short behind a double-parked rental truck with three guys unloading a pottery wheel, telling me and Howie to wait in the car while he burst out of it to bang on the ballplayer's window and stick a pen in his face—probably scaring the living shit out of the guy. That's something I'll never forget. McDougal could've pulled off an unassisted triple play that night and it wouldn't've been as memorable! I can still see the soggy bottoms of my father's pajamas sticking out of his trousers when he returned, his face gleaming, and in his hand a drenched scorecard sporting a scrawl you could hardly read which, for all I know (now that I think about it), could've come from Poppa J's own pen after he realized that the guy he'd been following was an accountant from Secaucus or a proctologist from Poughkeepsie.

That one's a good memory. I have others, though.

Brothers
by
Ben Shahn

Ben Shahn, American, 1898–1969; *Brothers,* 1946; tempera on paper mounted on fiber-board mounted on wood mounted on fiberboard; 38 15/16 x 25 15/16 in. (98.5 x 65.8 cm). © Hirshhorn Museum and Sculpture Garden, Smithsonian Institution, Gift of the Joseph H. Hirshhorn Foundation, 1966. Photographer, Lee Stalsworth

7

SECRETS

I looked again at the picture of the isolated batter in the empty stadium. I was only looking; I didn't actually *enter* the painting as I could've if I wanted to. I didn't want to, not here in class.

Except for the few (too many) occasions when it just *happened*, I kept my "shahning" to times when I was by myself. And I kept it *to* myself.

I got shahning, the term I coined to describe this experience of being inside painted worlds—smells, sounds, and all—from the artist Ben Shahn, who made the first picture that I lost myself within. I'd never heard of him before, but when I looked him up I liked what I read.

I shahned for the first time several weeks after Howie died. I was looking at a reproduction of two brothers, lit by darkness. They were embracing, their heads joined as if they made one head. Suddenly, I was the guy on the right. I could smell my companion's breath. He smelled like Howie, only worse, so I made sure not to inhale too deeply. Each of us had only one nostril, and we were mashed together so tightly my skin turned purple and the bone beneath my eyebrow ached from the pressure. Don't get me wrong, it wasn't only smelly and painful; the hugging felt good. But I didn't know what was happening, who was holding on more tightly, me or him, and if it was him, whether he was ever going to let me go.

Even Grandpa Oscar didn't know about my transporting thing. I'm pretty sure he couldn't shahn; the old man loved looking at paintings, but he never said anything to me about physically being inside any of them. Like everyone else, he was content to look. But unlike everyone else, what my grandfather saw when he looked at pictures was *connections*—worlds, both intimate and grand, made up of closely related parts—which is what, and how, he taught me to see. The more than trance-like—more like transporting—part he didn't teach me. That was all mine.

I can't always control when I do it, or for how long, but I usually like it when I shahn, except for the rare times when I get stuck in the absolutely wrong place, like finding my sun-blistered, seasick, absolutely starved self adrift on a raft called Medusa, or when I can't stop doing something that a picture gets me started with, like once when I trekked so far across a Corot landscape that my ankles turned purple.

I didn't tell anyone about my special way of connecting to pictures. And I didn't tell anyone in Garrison City about my brother. Or my father. Keeping certain secrets can help keep you sane, so I saved some of them for my most personal stories and poetry.

Here in class today I had written a poem about a painting. First time. So obvious, bringing together two of my greatest interests—poetry and painting; why had it never occurred to me before that they might like to meet one another, that they might really hit it off? Individually, they were often right in front of me, but they never played together, except maybe hide and seek, with the seeker never, ever finding the hider. Until now. It took a shy, pretty, gracefully awkward student teacher to play blackboard matchmaker, presenting the coupling of word and image as something far greater than any game, as something no less than, as far as I was concerned, what was at that moment the single most important act in the universe to perform.

My grandfather took me to museums ever since I was little. Even before Howie died, my grandfather and I—just the two of us—went all the time to look at what he called, "illusions, colored illusions, more mysterious than magic." He loved looking at paintings and talking to me about them, and I loved being with him and hearing him talk. And he liked reading my poems and talking to me about them, too.

I looked again at Goodman's strange painting. First I thought, What is this lunatic doing without any clothes on in the middle of an empty baseball stadium? But that quickly changed to, Who am I kidding? What's so strange? I bet we've all got "naked" stories in one form or another shivering just beneath our smiles.

 8

THROUGH THE EYES OF AN OWL

Poem completed. Waiting for class to end. My body is at peace, but not my mind, which takes me back to third grade.

Actually, the batter in Goodman's painting took me there.

It was the beginning of June 1957, shortly before the end of the school year. I had agreed to help Howie campaign for Marchwood Junior High School student council treasurer.

"Jeez, Stevie, what's so darn hard? I'd do it for you." All I had to do was go "OOOOH Howie!" like an owl each time one of my friends stood up to ask his question.

"Yeah sure, Howie. That'd be the day."

"Yeah, well I would if you were ever running for an office. C'mon Stevie. Let me hear it. Break my eardrums. Just one solid 'OOOOH Howie!' C'mon, Stevie, why'd'ya have to make such a big deal about everything?"

"OOOOOOOOOOOOOOHHOOOOOOOWIIIEEEEEEEEEEEEEEEE," I screeched as if, famished, I had just bared my spiky claws, and swooped onto what was about to become dinner.

Howie was thrilled.

My scream scared my mother, who came running into the room.

"What's going on?"

"Me and Stevie are working on my campaign speech for the assembly, Ma." Howie's voice was bouncing. "He's gonna be an owl."

"An owl?"

"Stevie's gonna plant some of his friends in different parts of the auditorium," Howie explained, "and just before I come out, he's gonna set me up by getting Richie, and Stuart, and Kevin, and maybe some of his other friends, to stand up in the audience, and then this one guy'll say something like: 'Who's the most responsible person at Marchwood Junior High?' and Stevie'll be all dressed up in this owl's costume and. . ."

"Why the owl costume?"

"Because, Ma, you know, the wise old owl. . ."

"Oh. I get it."

"And then after Stuart or Richie or whoever it is gets up and asks his question, Stevie's gonna go 'OOOOHHOOOWWIIIIEEE!' you know, long and drawn out."

My mother said it sounded like gargling.

Howie insisted it sounded like an owl, a smart one.

Like an owl gargling, my mother conceded.

"Ma." It was one of those long, hilly syllables.

"A very *wise,* gargling owl," she added.

"See, Mom likes it." Howie looked at me. "So?"

I blew air through my closed lips. "Everybody'll laugh," I whined. "At me."

Hardly anyone would know who I was, Howie insisted, since I'd be covered up by the costume. Besides, it was supposed to be funny. "C'mon, Stevie. I'd do it for you. You can be my campaign manager."

When I finally agreed, Howie started running in place and raising his arms like a boxer who'd just knocked his opponent unconscious. With no hint of the potential ill whims of a win, and certainly no predictions of loss for victors who indulge in victory rituals, his triumphant dance lasted until his fist accidentally crashed into my ear.

Two weeks later, I slipped my head through a hole Howie cut into a cardboard carton from an RCA television set. We painted the carton and added extra cardboard strips for wings and a tail. The carton extended only from my shoulders to the middle of my thighs, so I took my pants off and Howie painted my legs with the same colors and patterns he had used for covering the cardboard. The hairs of the paintbrush tickled my knees and the back part of my calves around my ankles. Otherwise I liked the soft feel of the brush and the coldness of the paint against my skin. While he painted my legs I rolled a torn piece of cardboard, no bigger than a pencil point, between my fingertips. Rolling a string or wad of paper, or better, wedging something between fingernail and flesh, always had a settling effect on me. My mother and Howie did it, too. A calming family trait.

Getting the carton on took careful maneuvering, but getting it off was easy. Howie had cut the back of the box and sewn in a string which, when untied, would permit the carton to fall straight down around my knees. For the owl's feet, we decorated the turquoise rubber flippers I wore for swimming. After removing the flippers, I could step out of the carton, flitting from bird back to boy. One final touch, the owl's face: a brown paper bag with two holes cut into it so I wouldn't trip over anything on my way toward center stage.

Shortly before we completed the costume, mom told me that Gil McDougal telephoned to say he was proud of me for helping out my big brother. I knew there was no such call. Nonetheless, I liked that she said it. It was the kind of line my mother had been using on me ever since my father had gotten his autograph. The signed scorecard still rested atop the headboard of my bed. McDougal was still my favorite ballplayer, but I had reached the age where (mostly) I saw through the Gil McDougal stories. After all, why did I never get to talk to the Yankee shortstop myself? Why was it always my mother who answered the phone that I never heard ring? *"Stevie, Gil McDougal just called from the dugout and said you should eat all the liver on your plate before it gets cold."*

The morning of the student council elections, Mom took Howie and me aside to tell us how happy it made her, watching us work on the owl project. It reminded her, she said, of when Howie and I used to play together so perfectly she thought of us as one child. "At night," she said, "I used to imagine both my sons dreaming the same dream. The two of you were like this," she added, pressing the palms of her hands together like she was praying. "Maybe you could start playing together again more. . . like you used to."

"Yeah, Ma," Howie agreed, "but only if Gil McDougal thinks we should."

9

A MUMMY, A TUTU, AND HOPALONG CASSIDY

"Is that you? Are you there? Still watching?" In my poem, the naked batter is full of questions. Just how I felt as an eight-year-old owl, waiting in the wings to hoot out Howie's name to the entire sixth, seventh, and eighth grades.

I wished I wasn't there. I hoped no one would be watching.

Working on the costume with Howie was great, but being inside it at school felt ridiculous, and the smell of the recently painted cardboard was bothering my stomach. Howie hadn't said anything about how hot it was going to be inside the box.

"Is that you, Stevie?" asked a mummy.

"Yeah. I guess. Who're you?"

"It's me, Abby." Hanging in front of Abby Lentz's linen-wrapped chest was an oak tag sign stenciled with large, multi-colored letters. The sign read:

Don't be a fool.
Add new life to your school.
LONG LIVE Marsha Lentz,
the best of Presidents.

"How'd you know it was me, anyways?" I asked, momentarily flustered because Howie had convinced me I'd be unrecognizable in my costume.

"Heard you talking to your brother. Recognized your voice. Are you a television set?"

"No."

"A robot?"

"I'm a owl."

"Oh."

"What're you, a mummy or something?" I asked.

"Uh huh." Then, pointing with her chin toward three silver paperclips securing the end of one of the strips of bed sheet wrapped around her body, she explained while floating in and out of view that her sister Marsha was going to pull a strip on her costume while she kept twirling until she unraveled herself. Then she would dance in her tutu across the stage like a butterfly. Her crisscrossed arms were bound tightly against her chest, and her legs were bound tightly together. The girl looked like a caterpillar on a pogo stick. I couldn't understand why she wanted to look like a butterfly. It was her dad's idea, she said. Something about mummies being dead. "And," she added, "if Marsha's elected president, she'll breathe life into cocoons and they'll wake up different the next day just like all the kids in school will too, and me, too, after she unravels me. There was something else too, but I forget."

I had no idea what she was talking about, and she probably didn't get it any better than I did, but what did that matter? Mainly, we both would be satisfied if we made it through our routines without throwing up.

"Wait'll you see my tutu. Underneath. It's pink!"

The word "pink" escaped like a hiccup from behind Abby's wrappings, winging its way inside the paper bag covering my head. Pink! The mummy pronounced the color with her whole body. She made the word smell like a flower. Clearly, as long as there was a part where Abby could dress up as a ballerina and pirouette around the stage, it didn't matter if the sheet skit made sense or not. Through myopic paper bag squints I noticed that, besides me and Abby, no one else's little sister or brother had been led from the safety of ancient Egypt or the untamed kingdom of birds and beasts to wear pink, or dance, or gargle wisely on the stage of Marchwood Junior High.

"OUR NEXT CANDIDATE RUNNING FOR THE OFFICE OF STUDENT COUNCIL TREASURER FOR THE CLASS OF '58 IS HOWARD SCHAECH," the principal announced. There was a little applause, then Howie appeared. That was my cue.

"Gotta go," I whispered to Abby.

"Good luck, Stevie."

"You too. I bet your tutu's pretty," I said, which made the mummy's lips curve.

There was some laughter when I entered the stage, but no more than Howie had predicted. Then the audience quieted down as the final wicshp, wicshp, wicshp, wicshp of flapping rubber flippers slapped against the wooden floorboards.

Howie was right, my costume kept me out of sight. What a hiding place! Smack in front of everybody, and no one could even see me. I was more right than I knew; most of the overhead spotlights in front of me were either missing or broken, leaving me silhouetted. A brotherless owl backlit by a row of 1,000-watt stars.

"What's that supposed to be?" students asked one another. The principal's staticky voice resounding over the microphone explained. "MAY I HAVE YOUR ATTENTION PLEASE? I HAVE A BRIEF ANNOUNCEMENT. I WAS JUST INFORMED THAT A BRIEF QUESTION

AND ANSWER PERIOD WILL PRECEDE HOWARD SCHAECH'S CAM-PAIGN SPEECH. PLEASE DIRECT YOUR QUESTIONS TO THE WISE OLD OWL PERCHED ON STAGE. THANK YOU." The announcement clarified some of the confusion. "Oh, I get it. It's supposed to be an owl. A black one." "With duck feet," someone else contributed.

The owl presentation came off pretty much as planned. My friends came through, and my "OOOOOHHOOOOOOOOOWWWIIIIIEEEEs!" got better and better as I settled into my role. Leaning against the wall at the rear of the auditorium, my mother watched with joy as Howie approached center stage to make his campaign speech.

"Okay, Stevie. You did good," he whispered to the ear hole, placing his hand on the part of the box covering my shoulder. No one could see it beneath my costume, but I could feel my chest swell. Howie would never forget my performance and the office of treasurer it was bound to win for him.

I was comfortably perched.

"Go on, Stevie. I gotta do my speech." I didn't move. "Stevie!" Howie said again, less of a whisper this time. There was some laughter in the audience, but none on stage. Still, I didn't move. I don't remember ever being more proud of myself or happier about having done something to help out my older brother.

"C'mon, Stevie," Howie implored. "You're gonna screw everything up. Don't be such a pig ass. You did great. Now beat it, willya?!"

"I-ay am-nay ot-nay a-ay ig-pay ass-aye. I'm an owl."

My Pig Latin threw Howie off, just like his calling me a pig ass did to me. He blanked on the opening lines of his campaign speech. I could feel him groping for something to roll between his fingertips.

"You're right, Stevie. You're an owl. So c'mon and fly the fuck away!" The owl's wings stayed by its sides. "Move it!" Howie screamed as quietly as he could.

I didn't move. Howie's finger found the string that held together my cardboard body. First he fidgeted with the string, then he wedged it into the space behind his fingernail.

What was he getting so excited about? I had single-handedly won him his election, hadn't I?

That's when it must've occurred to my brother. It was right there, thin and twisted, and utterly available.

Hundreds of eyes were on Howie, looking up to him, waiting. He was in charge. His next move could bring uncontrollable laughter from an auditorium of friends, admirers, voters. At this moment, all his, Howie Schaech could bestow upon them something they would always remember, something far greater than his forgotten speech.

He could give joy. He could be a hero. He could pull the string.

He pulled the string.

The first pull didn't do anything. The second one did.

The cardboard box slipped in one motion down to my elbows and stopped. Then more slowly it continued its fall, rubbing against my hairless arms and wrists until it caught the bony projection on the left side of my pelvis, which is where it stayed, dangling diagonally for one second, then another, while the rest of the world remained perfectly still. The top of the box see-sawed gradually, stopped, and see-sawed once more. Howie sneezed. It was a soft, clipped sneeze followed by two more, identical to the first one. The third sneeze coaxed the box off my hip. Then I heard, along with Howie and every sixth-, seventh-, and eighth-grader of the Marchwood Junior High School, the soft tap of cardboard against the stage floor.

Phluut.

A seventh-grader in the front row buried her face in the collar of Richie's shirt. Stuart bit the insides of his cheeks. On the other side of the room, all the way in the back, Kevin's mouth gaped; the rest of his body went dead. My mother's spine became a straight metal rod. Then it bent. When she squirmed against the wall her shoulder accidentally hit a light switch.

In one pop, the sun rose upon the audience. I could no longer smell the paint on my cardboard costume, nor the witching-hour air on stage. I was temporarily senseless.

And front lit.

A freckled, blue-legged, skin-and-bone, joyless, featherless, spurless, horseless, hatless, six-gunless cowboy, I wore nothing beneath my costume except underpants—pee-stained and torn Hopalong Cassidy's that I had begged my mother to buy me to match my hat-and-holster set when I was in first grade. Sure I had long ago outgrown these underpants, but it's not easy turning your back (or littler parts of your anatomy, for that matter) on the coolest, most hard-won acquisitions of your youth, just because they no longer fit.

I was paralyzed. Beneath the paper bag, my sad, forest-fire eyes burned slits through my owl face onto a stand of faceless owl-haters.

The moment lasted, taking me out of time.

Frantically, and mercifully, my mother turned off the auditorium lights. She could do nothing about the lights on stage, even when she saw how harshly they glared down at her sons.

For one dangling moment I shivered, until my shivers shook me out of my paralysis. My right hand went for the six-gun that once upon a time hung at my hip. Involuntarily, I twitched, my twitches becoming more rapid by the second. My arms began to flap, up and down, up and down, more like a stranded, bloodied car-wreck survivor desperately trying to get help from a passing motorist—any passing motorist—than a wounded owl trying to get airborne. Saliva gurgled against the muscles of my throat, intermittently choking me and dribbling out the side of my mouth. With each rapid heave of my chest, the lines of my ribs grew bolder and bolder beneath my goosebumped skin.

A shrill soprano squeal escaped from my flimsy brown-paper beak: "HOOOOOOOOOOOOWWWWWWWWIIIIIIIIIIIIIIIIIIIIIIIEEEEEEEEE! OOOOOOOOOOHHHOOOOOOOOOOOOOOOOWWWWWWWWWW WWWWWWWWWWWWWWWWWIIIIIIIIIIIIIEEEEEEEEEEEEEEEEEEE!"

Inside the owl's head, twinges stabbed the upper lip and below both eyes of the unwise campaign manager who, without meaning to, or wanting to—even without knowing I was doing it—started running in circles upon a stage that tottered miles above a crowded auditorium. My flippers slapped mutely against the floorboards. Flailing more and more out of control as I whirled round my brother, the sensation of cold air rising inside my chest to my throat told me that the stage and I were making our way back down to earth. Shadows from my raw-boned frame flew wildly into the crowd.

Complete pandemonium filled the auditorium. Vibrations from the laughter and foot stamping shot from the soles of my seven-year-old owl's swim-finned feet to my hairless, Hopalong groin, the screaming and laughter echoing endlessly within the paper bag. "OOOOOOOOOOOOOOOOOOOOHHHHHHHHHHHHHHHHHHHHHH HHHHHOOOOOOOOOWWWWWWIIIIIIIIEEEEEEEEEEEEEEEEEE!"

The principal's amplified voice appealed to the audience to settle down. "RIGHT NOW!" the voice demanded. Then, static. Then, "THIS INSTANT!"

The students had filed into the auditorium in minutes. It took them years to leave.

I stopped running in circles. Howie hadn't moved. He tried to take my hand and lead me off the stage, but I wouldn't let him. A fizzle, like air from a broken balloon, seeped through his lips before he slithered off, leaving me alone, sadly spent yet also oddly exhilarated, to look out upon endless rows of empty metal chairs and a sole spectator standing stunned at the rear of the auditorium with her elbows crushed into the wall.

Backstage, a mummy aged, and a butterfly was never born.

Gilles
by
Jean Antoine Watteau

Watteau, Jean Antoine (1684–1721). *Gilles,* ca. 1718-1719. Oil on canvas, 184.5 x 149.5 cm. MI 1121. © Erich Lessing/Art Resource, N.Y.; Photo credit: Erich Lessing/Art Resource, N.Y; Louvre; Paris, France. Réunion des Musées Nationau/Art Resource, New York

October 20, 1965

English Class: Mrs. Bilheimer/Miss Adamsohn
"What do you see when you look at this painting?"

LOOK AT ME
(based on *Gilles* by Antoine Watteau)

In the limelight I'm suspended
without strings,
masquerading in white,
shoes laced with pink, pants too short, sleeves too long,
all those dribbling buttons—
each concealing a secret or protecting a lie.

But don't just dwell on my costume; it's only an act.
Beneath my chin, a smile of ruffles
completes the circle of a devil's halo hat.

> *Roses are red, violets are blue*
> *that clown in white looks just like you.*

Look, please, beyond the masquerade,
until you see who I am. Then tell me,
that I may see too.

—Stephen Schaech—

Part II

WHISPERS AND A WAIL

10 ❖❖

ENGLISH

"Just like Sputnik. You should've seen it. It just kept hanging up there," English Otis maintained. "Okay, not exactly *Sputnik*, but almost. Pretty much like it, I swear, like that Strato Ship ride at Palisades, no. . . more like Sputnik, only shooken up more. . . like it's writing something into the air or something." Overhead, English fluttered his long, thick fingers as if trying to get the spelling right. "It was like the guy hit it so hard," English explained, his head bobbing up and down, "it got sucked right into one of them black holes in outer space that once you get sucked into you get trapped forever inside of 'cause gravity don't work in black holes, so things like baseballs just keep hangin' up there 'cause there's jack-all pulling them back down to earth. Shit man, I never seen nothing like that before. Hardly ever."

At home he was Eddie, but his friends called him English. It came from shooting pool. He put English on everything, no matter how simple the shot. Hitting the cue ball in the center was against his religion. For Eddie Otis, spin constituted equilibrium, which, in English's case, defied not only gravity, but a mess of other laws, as well. He didn't mean to put on spin; it came naturally.

English kept talking, but we were only half listening. Rapt beneath closed eyelids, Jerry Eppers, the artist of the group, was tracking the journey of a cypress tree that twisted into one of those glorious, way-above-ground hells Vincent Van Gogh called sky. Jerry told me that this is what he'd often see when he'd close his eyes after shooting up. Thousands of ink-black hatchings would pull on his mind, as he'd visualize Van Gogh's swirls of moon and stars suspended above the nightmares of a sleeping town. Maybe English's story had thrown a soaring baseball into the mix, and Jerry was trying to catch it.

Mike Dumbrowski, legs outstretched, back hunched, was using his cigarette to burn lines of some sort into the floor. If he was spelling out a word, I couldn't read it. He looked up from his burning just long enough to tell English to cut the bullshit. "Can't noboby hit a ball that hard. You hit a ball—really connect with one, maybe it's got some hang time. . . four, five, six seconds. Then it comes down. Every time. It's got to. It's like science or math or something. *Sput*-nik."

"I'm just saying, Mike. The guy, I know he was. . ."

"You don't know what's fucking what, English, 'cause you're a fuckin' melvin is why. He was in your head is what he was. And that's the only thing he was."

English's head was yo-yo-ing double-time, the opposite of Jerry's, who's head was hanging so still a glass of water could have balanced on the back of his neck. "I swear. I was there! I seen it! And that's after he fouled off about fifty hundred pitches before, seemed like. Maybe three hundred. Four. One after the other. Even the bad pitches. Thing is, he could've walked a hundred times, but the guy, he keeps swinging. At everything. Don't matter where it's throwed. He hits it, or tips it. Never misses. Never gived up. Even the bad pitches, he'd doink 'em. I swear. Just about everyone else leaves 'cause it gets boring, but not me. No way. It wasn't boring even a little for me. It was like the guy, he steps barefoot right out of the world everyone else is stuck inside of and I was there straight with him. I never seen nothing like it before, 'cept maybe one time I. . ."

English was on a roll. When he was like this it was hard to stop him. Though for the moment the subject was a baseball, he could go off on anything.

But balls, what is it about them, anyway? My grandparents have a reproduction hanging in their living room of an acrobat balancing on a ball that I look at a lot whenever I'm over there. I don't know why I'm so moved by the picture, but I know that the ball is a big part of it. Funny though, how different the one in that painting is from English's. One ball never leaves the ground, the other is all about the sky.

"So then this guy," English went on, "This guy, you could tell he finally got the pitcher where he wanted him at, and he hits one fair. . . way up there. You should've seen it, it just keeps going up, and when it stops going up it just hangs there. Levitatening. It. . ."

"Waitaminute!" I whispered all in one syllable. "I think I heard something."

Mike held his hand up, his palm close enough to English's mouth to feel his breath. Dumbrowski's hands were small, like a girl's, nothing like what you'd expect if all you knew about him was what you'd heard.

"I mean, he must've caught it on the sweet part of the bat, maybe a fraction off the sweet part, less than a fraction, no, definitely the sweet part, right clean on it, 'cause. . ."

Mike smacked English on the back of the head. "Someone's coming."

Jerry yanked himself out of the swivels of Van Gogh's clouds and listened. Pushing back loose strands of his red hair in order to see better, he picked up the flashlight he had brought with him to the empty apartment and shined it toward the burnt wooden floor near Mike. Pungent smell. No sound. "There's nothing there, bro," Jerry declared. "Nothing."

Upstairs, in apartment 11B, all I could hear was the night air momentarily whir as two cars on the street below passed each other.

"Me either," English agreed, his words suddenly coming out slowly. "Only thing I hear is our man Schaech Shit here murderin' my bug. I can still hear it if you wanna know. Besides that, I don't hear Jack Shit." Slowed by the hit of heroin he had taken earlier in the evening, English remained seated alongside Jerry with his back pressed against the wall. For a few minutes he stopped talking. Finally.

English was the only guy I knew who didn't slow down from heroin. Mostly, he'd be his normal self—wired. Only for brief periods would it get to him, and then he'd nod out. For the past half hour, English had been intermittently complaining about my misstep. "Even if you're only sixteen years old so you don't know how to watch where you're putting your feet," he argued, "I'm not countin' that as a good enough excuse for you murderin' something I cared about. Or was going to care about if I'd've ever got a chance to." English was only a year older than me, so I could never figure why my age should piss him off so much, but it did. "Not Jack Shit," he repeated, "'cept Schaech. I don't hear nothin'."

"All Shakes cares about is his own self," English continued. "Every time he moves his foot I hear crackling." Looking at me, he added, "Least you could do is clean off your fuckin' shoe. I was keepin' my bug, goddamnit. I was gonna train it. That's what I was gonna do, you know. I was gonna train it to do lots of shit, like roll over and make a noise when someone's trying to sneak up on me, and I was gonna feed it sundaes and different kinds of desserts, and find other bugs so it could have bug sex when it got horny, and shit like that.

"You killed it before I even got to know if it was a girl or boy bug, but I was gonna figure that out and if it was a girl I was gonna sprinkle horse on her so she could dance around high like a bride in a snowstorm, and there'd've been millions of straight little beetle cocks humpin' after her to get a taste. What'd you go and kill it for anyways, Shakes?"

What could I say?

"I didn't even get to name it," English complained, his head bobbling like a pigeon's. "I was gonna call it 'Bug' 'cause. . ."

Mike cut him off, pointing out with friendly frustration that he didn't give a fat rat's ass what English was gonna call his "Superbug." "Call it 'Dead,' 'cause sure as shit, that's all it is now." Mike's voice was calm, but with him you never knew when his frustration might infuriate his friendliness, and draw blood.

English sat perfectly still. Mike's comment drained all the joyful innocence that normally colored his face. Even in the dark you could feel the drain. Reflexively, he placed the fingertips of his left hand against the palm of his right, each straightened digit of the one hand touching the palm of the other. That was English's (open) secret, his shame—his fingertips were all the same length. No one else had a pinkie or thumb the same size as a middle finger. He should know; it was always the first thing he checked out when he met someone new. He was grateful that no one had ever noticed his handicap—a term he believed was invented just for him since the word, no matter how hard it tried to end on a high note, started out by pointing right to his particular shortcomings. Neither Jerry nor I noticed his fingers being so different from everyone else's, but English was convinced they were.

Mike looked back at English. "Eh, who knows?" Mike's voice was soft, his hand jerking outward like he was dealing cards. "It probably ain't completely dead anyways, the bug. It's probably up there in the sky, hanging out with that baseball that never came down, or even higher up in that outer space that never shuts up with you."

English's eyes cleared. "You think?"

"Yeah, sure," Mike said, even more softly. "Why not?"

 # 11

MIKE

The room was so dark, Mike's straight, dead-black hair could've been curly like mine, or red like Jerry's, you couldn't tell. Glow from his cigarette painted a swollen orange frown across his mouth.

The oversized beetle that I accidentally stepped on earlier in the evening didn't die right away; it just writhed on its back until I stepped on it again. "What'd you want me to do, English? I had to put it out of its misery." Half the beetle was still stuck to the sole of my shoe; the other half, glazed in a thick, green ooze, caked the wooden floor.

English had adopted the bug and housed it beneath a cellophane wrapper he'd ripped off a pack of Lucky Strikes. "See, how I'm gonna take care of my pet bug is I'll hear the crinkling of the cigarette wrapper if it tries to skip out or, you know, crawl back home or anything, or if I don't hear it, one of you guys will and you'll say, 'Hey English, your bug's getting away, want me to save it?' and then I'll say, 'Nah, I will,' and I will, 'cause bugs are people too, you know, and then I'll make sure it stays safe under the cellophany wrapper that I'll make into a kind of barn with a big window for a roof so's my bug can look at stuff and still move around 'cause the wrapper's not heavy like real glass'd be, only see-through like glass in a skylight, but a skylight that couldn't break and slice my bug in two, and that's more better." After English said this he waited for one of us to praise his ingenuity, but none of us did.

"What'dja go and kill my bug for?"

English wouldn't quit. "Go on, tell me, Shakes," he taunted. "Afraid he'd've killed you if you didn't get him first 'cause you knew his stinger was full of poison and it'd just be a matter of time before you pissed him off and. . ."

"*Jezu Chryste!*" Mike screamed. "He told you he didn't mean it." Ingredients of Abbot and Costello often ground their way through the blender of Mike and English's interactions. I was never sure which part had the sharpest edges, English's lunacy or Mike's sanity. "*Jezu Chryste!*" Mike repeated. "*Masz srake zamiast mózgu!*" Like no one else, English had a way of dragging his friend's limited Polish vocabulary kicking and screaming away from Aspidistra Avenue, where it usually stayed with his parents, his dog, Vujo, and the other Polish family who lived a few houses away.

Neighbors. Mike had fewer of them than anyone else I knew. Besides Mike, everyone I had ever hung out with, both in Marchwood and Garrison City, lived in apartment complexes, each unit a wall's, floor's, or ceiling's width away from next door. In Marchwood, Caleb Aram lived in a corner apartment with windows facing not only the clothesline out back, but the laundry room and playground on the side as well. I always envied Caleb for that. Mike did Caleb one better.

One of the reasons I saw Mike Dumbrowski as richer, smarter, stronger, a few inches taller, and justifiably more cocksure of himself than anyone else I knew, was because he lived in a *house*, a house that not only featured a metal deer on the front lawn and a hedge that turned bright yellow in the spring, but, better still, enjoyed a strip of grass and two pavement borders on the remaining three sides that effectively separated him from his neighbors.

"Christ, English, you don't quit, do ya?"

"Yeah, but," English protested.

Mike shifted his approach. "I ain't hardly kidding, you fuckin' yamadoo. You lip flap one more time about that bug and you're gonna be eatin' what's left of it off the bottom of Schaech here's shoe. Schaech didn't squash it, I woulda."

English left the bug alone, but went back to the ball. "Anyways, there's no one comin', no one's there, just like after a while the ball field's empty where the guy I was tellin' you about kept fouling off pitches at. The fuckin' guy he just stands there up at bat for I don't know how long, like an hour or two hours, or maybe not two, but so long that everyone ups an' leaves."

Mike remained silent as he looked at English, who made a face to no one in particular. He wanted to get back to his story, but his friend's silence said shut up—about the bug, about the ball, about everything—so he did. English's look of annoyance disappeared; oddly, his face took on an expression of concentration, like he was trying to figure out a math problem in his head. English could infuriatingly stay on the same track long after he had reached his destination, but he could also shift gears like no one else I had ever met.

"No one say nothin' 'til we make sure no one's comin'," Mike commanded.

Mike Dumbrowski had been left back three times, which made him the oldest student at Garrison High. His age stood upon authority, menace, and might, making him, maybe not in inches, but at least in one sense, the tallest kid in the school. The fact that he had just spent two months at the County Prison in Hackensack for possession of smack further distinguished him as the only student in the school's history who could claim seasoned rapists and thieves as his teachers. Mike Dumbrowski was a triple threat.

Unlike Jerry and English, who'd been sentenced as juveniles for drug use and had just returned from two-month stays at Bergen Pines Correctional Center in Paramus, Mike was home, but not yet free. He was originally sentenced to one month and a year's probation, but his time was doubled after he broke the jaw, three ribs, and a kneecap (small hands and all) of an older, bigger inmate who insisted on calling Mike's only friend at the prison "Gimp" because of the way the man walked. For two years Mike Dumbrowski would have to report weekly to a parole officer named Asshole.

Silence.

"Okay, maybe it's no one now, but someone comes in on us, English, get this, if he comes up these stairs 'cause he wants to hear about baseball, I'm gonna off him is what, then I'm gonna take a bat and flatten it out against your skull so your head looks like one of them run-over pennies we used to put on the railroad tracks."

My body tightened.

A beetle, smaller than English's dead one, crawled toward Mike, who squashed the bug with his thumb, then rubbed the lit end of his Chesterfield across its back. After the orange sparks died off, he kept

rubbing, like he was erasing a word, until all the paper from the cigarette was shredded.

12 ◈

GUMPTIONED-OUT

"**N**o shit, anyone comes in we don't know who, we off 'em. I ain't getting busted for using so they can send me back to prison. Prison's not
like juvie, you know. It's way worse. I'm not goin' back. Someone
comes in and surprises us, it's gonna turn out to be *his* surprise. Anyone
got problems with that?" The question was stated, not asked.

Each of us looked at Mike. Then we looked away.

The smell of burnt bug shell and loose tobacco filled the room.
"Someone comes in and sees us with horse, we. . ."

"You know, Mike, it's not just 'H', you know," Jerry added, flicking
his flashlight on and off. "Someone comes in and they got us for breaking and entry. It's not just the drugs."

"But no one's even living here," I offered, "so you can't really call
it breaking and entering."

Mike told Jerry to cut the on-and-off shit with the flashlight. Then
to me: "Yeah, it is too breaking and entering. You stand up in front of
a judge and he's gonna say B&E. It's still B&E even if you don't break
nothing to get in or cop nothing once you're there. What're we gonna
say? We got a friend named Felix who lives in these here apartments so
he knows who moves out, and when, so it's okay? That Felix told us we
could stop by at midnight to shoot up, just so's we don't break or cop
nothing?"

"Yeah, *right*. Or step on nothin' too. Like a pet bug that didn't never
do noth. . ." English stopped himself.

"Yeah," said Jerry. "And maybe Felix gets hired as a realtor and sits
at a desk next to the other ties and dresses and shit in the rental office
here. We're potential customers, right? No way, man. We get caught
here, it's breaking and entering."

"What's a railtor?" asked English.

"Some little fucker comes up here, we go away for possession too.
It ain't just B&E. That's how it is. I gotta spell it out for you?" Mike
complained. A slap of the streetlamp light caught the side of his jaw,
and blackness chopped off the top of his head, as the silhouette of a

monstrous moth blundered across the wall behind him. "And I'm the one who got this here stuff for you, so they bust me this time for dealing. Besides, I'm the one who got history. Scum-sucking Asshole's just waiting to send me back. Just waiting. Someone comes in, I don't care if he falls 'Please Godding' to his knees. It's over. Could be security checkin' on empty apartments or a pharmacist comin' home from work. . . whoever it is, if his head's in the stars he can't see nothing but shine."

"What's a railtor?" English repeated his question as he sat down on a ladder-back chair, the one piece of furniture in the otherwise barren room. "A guy who makes chairs like this here one with backs on 'em that look like railroad tracks that go straight up?"

Mike jumped in: "A lot of good *straight up* is ever gonna do you. Try spitting *straight up* in the air and watch how it comes right back down in your face, English. Maybe we oughta start calling you the 'Straight Up Kid', 'cept the highest up you're ever gonna get is your own spit in your face. You want up, take another hit of what's in this here needle. That's the only way you're ever gonna get anywheres higher than you are right now."

English didn't respond. Mike was too tired, or high, to continue. Jerry looked like he was back in Van Gogh's sky. I welcomed the break.

My mind was clear. Just as clear as several hours before when I chose not to shoot up with the rest of the guys in the apartment. I wanted to be there with them; I didn't want to be high.

Ripping the momentary silence as if it were edged in bright yellow, something scraped across one of the brick steps leading to the entrance door downstairs. My hand jabbed into Jerry's flabby stomach. "Hear that? Someone's downstairs. Outside." I unconsciously slipped a sliver of tobacco out of the end of the unfiltered cigarette I was smoking and kneaded it between the orange parts of my fingers into a tiny ball.

Mike's back was no longer buried into the hollow of sweaters and jackets on the floor. His head spun toward the stairwell. His eyes, glazed and reddened, stared straight ahead. I could see him working at standing up and trying to focus his vision. Shaded into sharp relief by the slanted light of the streetlamp, a white scar running like a tightly stretched wire across the back of his right hand hung just a few inches from my mouth.

"There it is again!" My body stiffened. "Mike!"

Heightened street sounds below confirmed that the building door had been opened.

I thought about how I would wrap up a nickel bag and put a bow on it for Felix if it was he downstairs. But I knew Felix Ybañez was away, staying with his grandparents in Newark.

Felix lived at Forstops Village, and he regularly informed us which apartments were vacant. But not this time. It was *me* this time. I had heard Mr. Lefkowitz telling my grandfather about his next-door neighbors who had just moved, and I told my friends. This time it was me.

Mike looked accusingly at English, who avoided his eyes. Mike distinctly remembered telling English to lock the door behind him. English was the last one in. It never surprised me when English fucked up.

I wasn't sure if Mike would actually go through with this. As far as I was concerned, he was less dangerous than he made himself out to be; after all, he lived in a house with a metal deer in front. Besides, these days I couldn't see Mike bothering to be violent—executing physical pain took gumption, and since drugs, the first friend I made in Garrison City appeared to be gumptioned-out. At least that's what I was counting on.

Hidden by the wall at the top of the stairwell, we unintentionally secured our places according to age, English at seventeen years old following Mike, with Jerry and me, both sixteen, just behind. Whoever was unfortunate enough to be walking up this stairwell at 5:30 A.M. had no idea just how bad a night he was about to have. I was at the end of the line. Overhead, at the front of the line was a rough, splintered board clutched in a wiry, white-scarred hand.

13

BLOOD AND CHEERS

Waiting at the top of the stairwell at 5:30 A.M., the DiMaeoli fear that'd immobilized me two years before at Take Five infiltrated my body once again. Mike saved my ass that day; I was still indebted to him for that. Frankie Valli's falsetto refrain rubbed its tongue against the window. *Big girls don't cry. Big girls don't cry.* The refrain became the wail of a bully and the whimper of a boy. In the background there was another refrain, this one more obscure, like smoke: *Only you can prevent forest fires. Only you. . .*

I looked to my left into the distorted shape of light cast across the wall, a warped diagonal streetlamp streak—shriek—breaking the geometry of the room, and I saw and heard what I saw and heard all too often when I needed to see or hear nothing at all. What I saw was leaves budding on trees, children surrounded by family and friends,

Howie running toward me followed by my father making like a poor imitation of Gil MacDougal at the plate—home movies that didn't allow for even one second to be edited out. Especially one second.

I couldn't get the scene to disappear as I stood there watching my father's short-sleeved, heavy-biceped arms uncoil awkwardly toward their target—he looked like a lefty swinging a bat righty for the very first time—his youthful target just waiting to be stunned before collapsing, a deadly explosion surrounded by laughter, shouts, and cheers. Then the cheers would go silent. But the big gestures and teams of little, wide-open mouths stayed.

And Jacob Schaech with a bat in his hands.

Trickling blood.

Howie, broken.

Part III

PICTURES AND POEMS II

14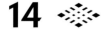

WHO WERE YOU IN THE PAINTING, STEPHEN?

I bet you've got a great looking tutu. Pink. That's what I thought when I saw Diane Adamsohn the day she told me how impressed she was with the assignment I had handed in. "The Sidney Goodman poem and the notes you wrote about the other two paintings: best in the class. By far. I mentioned it to Mrs. Bilheimer."

"Really? Hey, thanks. It was a terrific assignment. That's what got me going!"

I had said the right thing, so right it made her blush. And I said, "sure" when she asked if she could read my poem to the class.

As far as I was concerned, she could do anything she wanted. Anything. I liked her. I liked the blackness of her long, straight hair, the way her calves quivered slightly with each step as she walked across the front of the classroom, how her nostrils widened and then pinched when she laughed, her look of concentration, like a child about to place her top block way up high. And I loved that my poetry impressed her.

In Marchwood, only one of my teachers took my poems seriously. No matter how busy he was, Mr. Engsberg always responded the next day to the "extra credit" verses I left in his school mailbox. Mr. Engsberg struck me as more of a "col*lage*" man than the Ivy League "*col*lege man" my mother saw. He was pieces glued together: He screamed unmercifully at unmotivated students, and he looked lop-sided because the length of his trouser legs on all his pants never matched—one leg ending above his sock, the other hung at the heel of his shoe, as if the tailor who fitted him had a thing against tape mea-sures. But he was kind, and he was Marchwood's most sophisticated teacher, just like Diane Adamsohn was Garrison City's best looking one.

Mr. Engsberg once dismissed my apology for taking up so much of his time, claiming he found it difficult to unwind at the end of his day without reading at least two or three poems, so I was actually doing him a favor by providing him a much needed "literary fix." "You keep writing them, Stephen, and I'll keep reading them." He not only read them, he talked to me about them, at length.

Like almost everyone and everything else important to me, Mr. Engsberg remained behind when we had to move away from Marchwood.

This was the first time in Garrison City anyone besides my grandfather had said anything good about my poetry. Grandpa Oscar had been reading and critiquing my writing for years, introducing me to the works of poets like Walt Whitman and Wallace Stevens. When I was six years old, he read me Lord Byron's *The Destruction of Sennacherib*. It made such a deep impact on me that ten years later I never knew when wondrous warriors might charge from the sleep of my childhood into the dreams of my teens:

> *The Assyrian came down like the wolf on the fold,*
> *And his cohorts were gleaming in purple and gold;*
> *And the sheen of their spears was like stars on the sea, When the blue*
> *   wave rolls nightly on deep Galilee.*

My grandfather gave me poetry, but he could hardly be considered objective where the writing of his "grandson the poet" was concerned. Ask him, and everything I write is brilliant, so, for me, his literary appraisals don't count. Miss Adamsohn was "truly impressed." That's what she said. That counted.

When class began, she placed the reproduction of *Tryout* back on the ledge of the blackboard where it had rested during last week's class, made a few introductory remarks about my paper as she walked in front of her desk, sat on the edge of it, and arranged her skirt to cover the knees of her dangling legs, and began reading:

"'Is that you?' the naked ballplayer bays, in his barely hearable way. . ."

Although I was seated near the back of the classroom, it was as if she were whispering the words directly into my ear. I could feel her warm breath against my skin. I never realized how sexy air could be.

"*But seats are for sissies, for cowards who can't stand to stand any longer. . .*" What the teacher read was no longer mine. She had taken my words and made them better; she made them hers.

My mind wandered as I gazed at the two points toward which the center of her upper lip rose. My body stiffened. "*. . . his reflecting skin sweating dreams along the veins of his shivering crotch. . .*" I wandered as I gazed at my teacher's ankle, which was encircled by a thin, gold chain, my fingers slowly moving from the shiny metal links to her ankle just beyond, her skin causing the delicate piece of jewelry to glow, my teacher's skin soft, so unbearably soft beneath my undeserving, suddenly tingling, fingers. Thank you, Miss Adamsohn, for letting me touch. . . "*An 'Aha!' hits the hitless hitter. . .*" My hand wandered across her calf and up the inside of her thigh. . . *Other "Aha's!"* and unspoken thank you's "*. . . now more high pitched, as if from a wizened bird's babbling beak. . .* " I wandered. None. Not even one. There certainly was not even one teacher like Miss Adamsohn in Marchwood. The move to Garrison City had its plusses.

Alone with Miss Adamsohn, my hand wandered, working its way up her leg. Her skin seemed to redden, but she barely moved. I placed my lips against her knee, but I didn't kiss her, I just slid my face up her legs, slowly, until I felt her hand stroking the top of my head and her thighs sandwiching my cheeks as I. . .

"Stephen, have you ever done this before?" The student teacher asked. "Stephen?"

Would she ask me to stop if I told her I hadn't? I didn't answer.

"Stephen?" she repeated. I didn't want to stop. I couldn't. We could talk later. She said my name several more times, but I remained silent.

"Schaech!" someone seated near me whispered.

"Yo, Shakespeare!" Felix called out. A few students laughed. "Where were you, Shakes?" Felix asked. "She's talking to you."

"Who?"

"Bawlamer, that's who."

"*'Aha!. . . Aha! Aha! Aha!*" shouted someone seated in the back of the class.

"Have you ever done this before?" Miss Adamsohn repeated.

Did I do it wrong?

"That was wonderful, Stephen. I hope you appreciate what you did."

Great! I must've done it right. I didn't know what to say. Of course I appreciated it. But I liked it a lot better when we were alone. I could feel everyone looking at me. Where had they all gone, and why did they have to reappear so abruptly?

"I really would like to know," she repeated. "Have you done this before?"

I made a point of not looking at her legs. "Done this. . .? I'm sorry, I. . ."

"You must have. I'd be very surprised if you said this was the first time you ever tried anything like this. I found it so exciting, Stephen. Honestly. So direct. For someone so young, you express yourself in a very sophisticated way."

A couple of students laughed, but I didn't, as I suddenly realized what had happened. The rest of the class hadn't gone anywhere, only I had.

Don't look at her legs, I told myself. *It'll only get you in more trouble.* In front of Felix, in front of the whole class, she was exposing me in front of everyone, reading my mind. Out loud.

"Stephen?"

How did she know what I was thinking, and if she knew, why was she being so complimentary? Was she that cruel? Was she just setting me up for an incredible, public humiliation? A blue-faced clock drooped across Diane Adamsohn's skirt and legs. I tried not to look. The hands of the clock remained perfectly still.

"I'm sorry," she said, as she finally, mercifully, recognized the depth of my embarrassment. "It's just that I was so impressed. Truly. It doesn't diminish your poem if this isn't the first one you ever wrote that was inspired by a picture. I'm just curious is all."

Oh. My poem.

The hands of the blue-faced watch moved, and I heard ticking. Then the watch disappeared.

It was my poem that she was so impressed with.

"Stephen?"

I didn't answer.

"Shakes. You okay, Shakes?" Felix asked.

"Did any of your other teachers ever have you write about a painting before?" Miss Adamsohn asked. "Mrs. Bilheimer told me you used to write poetry at home sometimes. Do you still?"

My poem. That's all anyone in the class knew. That's all she was talking about.

"No, not really," I offered.

"Well, you should think about it. If what I just read is any indication, you owe it to yourself to take your writing seriously," she said, as she toyed with her bracelet. Her finger movements were awkward, as if she were having trouble opening a jar of peanut butter. "You have a gift, Stephen. A gift."

I smiled, but remained silent. I knew all too well about gifts.

Of course, my answer to Miss Adamsohn's question was only half true. The "No, not really" referred to my never having written about a painting before. That, I never did. But I did write. Religiously. I began writing poetry (if you could call it that) when I was nine or ten years old–poems about farting and burping and penises and vaginas—for the entertainment of friends, and I have since filled hundreds of pages with words. My brother liked the ones that made him laugh or contained phrases I'd get in trouble over if my mother read them, but Howie made fun of my more serious attempts—especially the ones that "don't even rhyme"—so I stopped showing them to him.

I started writing with even greater seriousness shortly after he died.

❖

Having finished reading my poem, Miss Adamsohn began talking about a short story she wanted us to look at. "Page 44 in your textbook," she said. I was looking, but not at the story. I was looking at her legs dangling over her desk. Great legs. Then my attention focused on her ankle, the one encircled by the thin gold chain. "Careful," I told myself, as I looked away. I wasn't about to get lost looking at Diane Adamsohn again here, now, in the middle of class, in front of everyone. The classroom clock moved in slow, classroom time. While my fingers wrapped tightly around the thin stem of a yellow pencil capped at the end by a pink eraser, my eyes examined the scratches on my desktop. The scratches formed a chair, not unlike the one positioned next to the naked batter in my poem based on Goodman's painting. Batter and spectator. . . two people, one chair: a regular musical chairs—without the frantic pace. I left my seat in class and allowed myself to enter Goodman's painting—or was it my poem? I took the bat from the batter's hands and replaced him at the plate. The sole spectator, who had been standing in the distance, walked slowly toward the chair positioned next to me and sat down. It was Diane Adamsohn. "You owe it to yourself to take your writing seriously, Stephen," she said. Then she disappeared. Startled, I looked around and saw a continuous line of familiar figures—Mike Dumbrowski, English, Jerry, Mrs. Gustin. . . emerge from the body of the distant man, walk across the ball field, and sit down in the nearby chair. One figure dissolved into the other. Each wore an oversized, drooping, blue-faced wristwatch showing 1:30, and each one said the same thing: "You have a gift, Stephen."

15

FANTASY

If a gift is lethal, is it still considered a gift?

I often fantasized about being a batter and my father's head being a ball. I knew I could make it happen. If you know you can make a fantasy happen, is it still considered a fantasy?

The closest I ever came to revealing my batter dream was during a talk with Mr. Engsberg. "Too bad things didn't happen the other way around that day at Memorial Field," I confided. "Too bad it wasn't Howie (or me) who accidentally creamed my father, instead it going the other way around. If I could have the day over again," I said, "that's how things would play out. Maybe they still will some day. With me pinch-hitting."

Initially, Mr. Engsberg left what I said alone, but shortly before I moved from Marchwood he told me he was disturbed by the "numinous serenity" (his words) he saw in my face when I had described my fantasy to him several weeks before. It was an intense discussion until, right in the middle of it, his wife dropped off their fourteen-month-old daughter at his classroom. After that, we kept getting interrupted by the little girl tripping over chairs and desks and Mr. Engsberg tripping over the cuff of his long pant legs while he tried to protect her. I don't know what his daughter liked best: the desks, what was inside them, falling, or being caught by her father, but she obviously found life thrilling.

While we followed his daughter, Mr. Engsberg told me that he couldn't imagine a young man of my discipline and intelligence ever acting on such a violent impulse as that I had revealed to him. Such detached, tranquil anger, he said, made him feel like he had just been kicked in the chest. And he'd seen it before in me, his "favorite student."

It was a long conversation, but I don't remember too much more about it because I stopped listening halfway through. He meant well, but I didn't think he could understand my feelings toward my father any better than his daughter could've.

From then on I kept my father fantasies—and how to make them real—to myself. They may make some people feel like they had just been kicked in the chest, but for me they produce the opposite effect. I bring them up to myself whenever I need to settle down.

I guess we all have our ways of maintaining our equilibrium. My grandfather silently ticks off the Hebrew months of the year when he wants to calm himself: *Tammuz, Av, Elul, Cheshvan, Kislev, Tevet. . . .* Me, I picture my father and think: smothering, drowning, electrocuting, poisoning, bee-stinging, beating, stabbing, hit-and-running. . . . It works every time. It's a gift.

 **16**

BIBLICAL ART

"**A**nyone want to see Stephen's batter or his outfield owl in person?" Diane Adamsohn asked. The painting was in a gallery on 57th Street, she said, where she had bought the reproduction she showed us. She got no response to her question, nor did she get any when she asked how many of us ever went into the city to visit art galleries.

I considered raising my hand, but I didn't want to be the only one. Besides, while I had, in fact, sometimes visited museums with my grandfather, we never went to galleries.

"But you live only 20 minutes away. It's just over the bridge," she pointed out. "Since I've been living in New Jersey, I bet I've gone into the city just about every single Saturday. I love to go gallery-hopping. Most of the ones I visit are in one area. Half of them on one street."

"We go to the city. Only we don't go to no galleries," Ryan Sugar informed her.

"Try going in a little earlier so you have time for something new. You might surprise yourself. You might even learn something."

That Saturday, I took a bus into Manhattan to see Sidney Goodman's painting. Jerry was busy. I didn't ask anyone else to come along.

Goodman's painting was in the Dintenfass Gallery, on the tenth floor of a midtown office building in what I later learned was the heart of the New York art world. Walking into the elevator, I mistakenly pushed the button for floor nine, which brought me up to a gallery exhibiting the paintings of 15th- and 16th-century artists. A sign outside the door read BIBLICAL ART. I had all day. Why not start there?

Most of the paintings were dark and somber. And boring. But one of them made me want to duck. . . then it whacked me in the gut.

The moment I saw the picture I knew how I was going to give my father the gift that he deserved!

My shahning skills kicked in immediately. I strode barefoot across rocky terrain as if it were a grassy field. Blue sky, not a breeze for miles, but my hair and warrior robes whirled in triumph. My weapon swung at my side. Its stony partner in crime—no, not crime, retribution, liberation—lay embedded in the hairline of my target, who lay at my feet where blood flowed in pretty lines from the severed head of the evil Goliath.

Not that I would kill my father with a slingshot or a sword. That's not it. Not exactly.

Better than that! More subtle. More me.

Perfect solution. Perfect crime.

I'll shahn him to death!

 **17**

FOR HOWIE

How could I not have thought of this before? "What troubles you worst about yourself," my grandfather once told me, "can sometimes solve your worst troubles. What do we really know from weaknesses and strengths?" Looking down at the vanquished giant and then up at the boy who conquered him, I imagined a shahn.

There I was, my skills honed to the point where rabbits and giants and fathers—no, just *my* father—fell at my feet with slingshot stones in their heads, the collapsing Jacob Schaeching the earth with greater force than a thousand collapsing Goliaths.

At the sight of my fallen foe, I found myself running in place, my arms raised like a triumphant boxer, like Howie after hearing me finally agree to be his campaign manager, his owl. *"C'mon, Stevie. I'd do it for you,"* he'd pleaded. *"Besides, hardly anyone'll know who you are, you'll be all covered up by the costume. Invisible."*

I'd done it then, and I did it now, and I would do it one more time—for real.

For Howie.

 **18**

THE YOUTHFUL DAVID

Sure, there were details to work out, but I finally had a plan, one that I had absolute faith in. After all, it was the bible that was going to show me the way to kill, so it had to be what I was looking for: The Way. *The True Way.*

I would enter this picture and make what happened inside it come true. I would leave no evidence behind, nothing, yet the killing would hang boldly on a gallery wall for all to admire. It was flawless.

The Youthful David
by
Andrea del Castagno

Castagno, Andrea del (Florentine, 1417/1419–1457) *The Youthful David,* c. 1450, tempera on leather mounted on wood, height: 1.156 (45 1/2); width at top: .769 (30 1/4); width at bottom: .410 (16 1/8); Widener Collection, Image © 2006 Board of Trustees, National Gallery of Art, Washington, D.C.; Photo by Richard Carafelli.

Again, I raised my hand in triumph, this time to direct the drift of clouds. Then I de-shahned and read the label on the wall.

The Youthful David
(Sometimes referred to as *David with the Head of Goliath*)
Andrea del Casatagno, ca.1403-1457
Painted Shield, leather on wood panel
On loan from the National Gallery, Washington, D.C.
  (Widener Collection)

Dave. Sookie DiMaeoli had it right after all. Sort of. From now on, he can call me Dave all he wants. And the National Gallery, a great public museum in the heart of our nation's capital—perfect! Me (sort of), committing a murder in broad daylight, before countless witnesses—more every day—yet no one will see. Like my painted counterpart, I'll be a hero, my brother's keeper. Or at least his redeemer. I will feel no remorse because it won't be *my* hand that slings the stone. I'll leave that to David. The biblical one. His crowning achievement. And mine.

Just before walking to the desk to buy a small color reproduction of the painting to practice with at home, I spotted David and Goliath in another, sunnier setting. The label beneath this painting, *David and Jonathan*, identified the third face in the picture. I knew that Jonathan referred to the son of King Saul, to whom, I also knew, David had just presented the head of the giant Philistine. In this picture, by an artist with a great-sounding name, Cima da Conegliano, the boys looked like brothers rubbing shoulders amidst blue skies and mountains, bushy clouds and cloudy bushes, castles, streams, and winding pathways of golden sand. Strolling through summer, shouldering swords and sling-shots, two happy campers accompanied by a decapitated head. David was a hero. I wanted to be him.

Inside the gallery in New York City the sun was shining. Inside my grandfather's apartment back in Jersey, a young circus girl stood with perfect balance upon a great big ball. For the moment, the world gleamed and teetered.

I bought the reproduction, which I folded into my wallet, sandwiching it between two dollar bills—David and Goliath and two Georges—stepped back inside the elevator, and pushed ten.

19

TRYOUT

The slick, parqueted floor of the Dintenfass Gallery was empty, except for a cherry wood desk, where a good-looking, neatly dressed woman with careful hair sat. There was a simple elegance about her dress and jewelry, and a refined manner to the way she unfastened the gold clasp of her pocketbook, which matched the initials on her bag. The off-white walls looked like they'd just been painted, as clean as the blotter on the receptionist's desk, which looked nothing like the one in my father's Marchwood office—all ink and sandwich-stained and covered with notes like "Stinchcomb Brothers Dry-Cleaning" scribbled across words like "lettuce" and "prostate."

Without me, the gallery would've been silent. When I became conscious of the sucking sound my rubber-soled shoes made as they rubbed against the floorboards of the room, I tried walking in different ways to get them to shut up. The way that worked best was walking on just the balls of my feet, putting most of the pressure near the big toes, but even that only helped a little. The gallery receptionist graciously ignored my squishing. Class act. Besides worrying about my shoes, I kept unconsciously checking the tiny metal rectangle that dangled from the top of my zipper, and consciously tapping my back pants pocket to be sure my wallet was there, housing its new tenant, David.

It turned out that *Tryout* was the only Goodman painting included in this group exhibit. I never heard of the other artists, and wasn't particularly impressed by their paintings, but, then, I hadn't come to New York to see *their* work. Nonetheless, I purposely postponed looking at *Tryout*. My grandfather had taught me to view exhibits the way we both ate cupcakes: Icing last.

In my imagination, *Tryout* filled a city block, but it turned out to be only about the size of the receptionist's blotter. In effect, the batter in *Tryout* had assumed Herculean proportions. But in fact, he and his bat could've fit inside a box of Band-Aids. So, at first, the painting disappointed me.

But who cared? This couldn't be anything but a great day after my experience downstairs. Life had provided me a plan. For death.

 **20**

FAMILIAR FACE

The sun streaking off the grass just outside my shadow made me squint. "What're we watching?" I asked the solitary spectator or judge or umpire—or whoever it was painted into Goodman's outfield shadows beside me. "And what're we doing on the field? If the ball comes toward us and we get called for interference, we're gonna feel like jerks." I could hear the jingling car keys and loose change in the man's pocket. I inched away from him because his body odor threatened to spoil the moment. The two dark rings around his armpits, the only visible flaws undermining the watcher's shiny-shoed presence, reminded me of the huge, split-second eye spots I once saw on the underside of a butterfly's wings, two black circles nature must've put there to give the beautiful insect the time it needed to startle its predator and fly safely away. (Who says "beautiful," or even "pretty" can't be scary?) Except I couldn't imagine this eyeless watcher bolting away from anything to spend the rest of his afternoon gliding through summer breezes.

I tried to see what the watcher looked like, but no matter where I positioned myself, the man's face stayed dark. If he's going to treat me like I'm invisible, the hell with him. I walked over to the sideline and then toward the batter.

Despite the empty stadium seats, I heard cheers when I got between first base and home plate—then jeers, instructions, and screams. "It's up to you now, Stevie." "Make him pitch to you! A walk's as good as a hit!" I smelled the green of spring leaves, tasted the stale pink of seven-inning bubblegum, and felt the black tape wound around the handle of a wooden bat. "Good eye, Stevie! Make it happen!"

Then I felt a slight touch on my arm and a barely audible question. "Stephen?" It took me longer than I wanted it to before I could work my way out of the batter's box.

It took me even longer to place the voice and face with a name. She was pretty—very pretty—and she looked familiar, but I didn't recognize her. "I didn't expect to see you here." The way she said it gave me the impression that maybe she did expect to see me.

"Before the exhibit ended I wanted to see this painting," I said. "I wrote about it in school."

"I know. I was. . ."

"Oh jeez," I interrupted. "I didn't realize it was you. Hi, Miss Adamsohn," I said as I extended my hand. "I'm not used to seeing you, uh, outside of class."

She brushed her bangs with her fingertips. Her hair was blacker than the deepest shadow in any of the paintings I had just viewed. The navy blue, short-sleeve blouse and dark jeans she wore were not as dark as her hair or the eyeliner that intensified her eyes. Besides the eyeliner, she wore no make-up. Despite all the darks, she looked brightly colored. And young. No different from the girls in my classes. And small. I'm only about five-feet-seven, but I was easily half a foot taller than her.

"I think it's great that you came to see the painting."

"I wanted to see it before it. . ."

"That's great, Stephen, great!" At first, everything she said had an uncomfortable, yet genuinely enthusiastic, "Great!" to it. I liked it every time. "And I feel great that I might have had something to do with your coming into the city to see. . ."

"You had a lot to do with it, Miss Adamsohn. You're a good teacher." I hadn't meant to compliment her. My unpremeditated words didn't so much express my thoughts as create them. At least I restrained myself from saying "great," which would've been too much.

Her face reddened. We talked a little longer and then she said she didn't want to interfere with me while I was trying to see the exhibit. "I know what it's like when you want to look at art, alone, but people keep bothering you."

"Oh no, Miss Adamsohn, you're not bothering me. I wouldn't've come here if it weren't for you. Anyway, I've been looking around in this show a long time already. I'm going to be leaving soon. I wanted to go to a whole mess of places before going home. What time is it now, do you know?"

It was 1:30.

"What other shows are you going to see?" she asked.

"I don't know. I just thought I'd walk around. Any suggestions?"

21 ❖

LEARNING TO SEE

Miss Adamsohn seemed to know everything about the New York art scene. She suggested that we walk around together, if I didn't have any plans. It'd give her a chance to talk to someone from Garrison High closer to her own age, someone who wasn't a teacher or administrator. She smiled. "I might learn something."

We visited many galleries. Sometimes we walked slowly, stopping before each and every work. From sheer excitement, we virtually ran through other exhibits. She was brilliant and naive, and certain exhibitions brought a lot of "Greats!" out of her.

Through Miss Adamsohn, I was able to connect the colorful, textured dots giving shape to what, without her, would've remained frustratingly formless. She loosened up the geometry of Mondrian, and gave order to the accidents of Pollock.

But she also asked and listened. Surprisingly, our roles sometimes reversed, and I found myself teaching the teacher. My favorite moments were when we both talked at once, each of us urgently wanting to let the other in on our personal revelations. Occasionally, we didn't get past the entrance. "Unh uh," she'd say, shaking her head upon catching a quick glimpse of the work inside. "Let's go next door." "Good idea," I'd readily agree, although I couldn't really understand how she was able to size up a show so quickly. No matter. Her confidence and impulsiveness excited me. Hell, I wouldn't've cared if the gallery walls were bare; it was thrilling just to be walking around New York City with a woman like Diane Adamsohn.

She told me she was taking a few art history courses at college. "No contemporary art, though, which is what I really like the most. But I paint all the time." From the time she was in junior high school, she had been taking classes in downtown Baltimore at Maryland Institute College of Art. The name sounded imposing, but it was really a friendly place, she said. "I've always loved looking at art," she said. "Entering other worlds. But even better than the history courses were the painting classes. They weren't just about learning how to paint. They were more about learning how to see."

"You sound like my grandfather," I blurted.

I could see that she was taken aback by my comment, but, kindly, she tried not to show it.

"Not just how to see what's going on inside a painting or sculpture, but learning to see what's going on all around you. How sunlight bounces off metal, or is absorbed by flesh, or washes across the wall of a building. And how to see the connections with things just waiting to be seen, things we overlook because we never really learn how to use our eyes. That's what they teach you at the Institute. That's what makes the classes so great."

Things just waiting to be seen. The enthusiasm in her voice colored her cheeks and made the satiny blackness of her hair blacker and more satiny.

"That's what I like about the way you write, Stephen. You see connections; you look hard at things."

Recognizing she had unintentionally embarrassed me, she changed the subject.

"I paint all the time. Even up here while I'm in New Jersey. When I walk around the galleries in New York, I think about things I learned at art school back home." Brushing her hair gently away from her face, she added, "I don't know. I've just always loved looking at pictures." And then, "Hey, please, why don't you call me Diane? I'm not that much older than you, you know. Three, four years at most. In school you can still call me Miss Adamsohn. Okay?"

"Okay. Great. . . Diane." I had never called any of my teachers— even substitutes or student teachers—by their first name before. She was right. Calling her Miss Adamsohn was like calling Mike "Mister Dumbrowski."

After a few hours Diane said, "Enough gallery-hopping. How about hitting a museum? I'll show you my absolute favorite painting ever! I saved the best for last."

"Just the way I eat a cupcake."

Diane smiled broadly. "I know just what you mean. Icing last."

22 ❖

DREAMS IN YELLOWS AND BLUES

The painting was smaller than *Tryout,* yet the image filled the room. "This Vermeer never fails to open itself up to me whenever I stand in front of it." Diane spoke in a whisper, as if she were standing before a sacred object. "It's bigger than every single one of those ten-footers by de Kooning, Kline, and Pollock we saw today. Except for maybe that Rothko. That was big like this one. Don't you think?"

"Yeah, that Rothko looked so simple at first, but then it didn't turn out to be. That painting really got me going," I said.

"Sure did. You walked right inside it. I liked when you talked about the small paintings sometimes looking a lot larger than the big ones. Some pictures just suck you in deeper and deeper," she added. "You end up so far in, it makes it hard to see anything else. Funny how we held onto that Rothko. It had such a strong effect on both of us. It doesn't always work like that when you go around looking at art with someone. Half the time you wind up arguing over what you're looking at."

Young Woman with a Water Pitcher
by
Johannes Vermeer

Vermeer, Johannes (1632–1675), Dutch, 17th Century, ca. 1662. *Young Woman with a Water Pitcher.* Oil on canvas. H. 18 in., W. 16 in. (45.7 x 40.6 cm.). The Metropolitan Museum of Art, Marquand Collection, Gift of Henry G. Marquand, 1889 (89.15.21). Photograph © 1993, The Metropolitan Museum of Art.

We talked and talked. Then we both got quiet.

An elderly couple walked out of the gallery, leaving us alone with the Dutch Masters. I stepped away from Diane and her favorite painting. We had developed an unspoken understanding, each sensing when the other needed room.

As Diane gazed at the painting, I walked around the rest of the gallery, looking first at the other Vermeers. A solitary female inhabited each image. In one, a young woman dozed; in another, a lute player (who perhaps lulled the woman to sleep in the painting nearby) sat tuning her stringed instrument before a huge parchment map hanging on a wall, the single note of her lute providing the only sound in the two paintings.

I went inside the sleeping woman's picture. I wanted to wake her and tell her all about my perfect afternoon with Diane Adamsohn. . . Diane. . . maybe ask her about the dream she was lost within, or at least point out that she was going to have one sore wrist when she awoke, but she looked so content that it seemed cruel to awaken her. I thought about whispering in the sleeping woman's available ear, telling her how lucky she was to enjoy such sonorous lute playing and such pleasant dreams. After all, when reason sleeps, dreams can be full of bats, owls, and other hideous monsters—others' dreams, that is, can be full of such things, but surely, I would be quick to concede, not hers. The dreams of Spanish artists (Goya, for instance) are often dark, haunted scenarios infested with inky bats flying blindly out of control; no bats for Vermeer—as my grandfather once pointed out to me, Vermeer dreams in yellows and blues, the colors of parakeets.

"Sweet dreams," I whispered under my breath as I tiptoed away, my rubber-soled shoes harmonizing comfortably with the lullaby of the lute.

The harmony of the moment was short lived, as my footsteps were abruptly overwhelmed by a riot of voices pouring out the open door of a tavern located several paintings away. I approached the canvas and read the accompanying label: *The Smokers*, by Adriaen Brouwer. I didn't recognize the artist's name.

Again, I shahned. As I entered Brouwer's tavern, a long-haired man seated in the middle of the canvas slammed down his drink and, with a wide-open mouth, burped a loud "Hey! You're new around here, ain't'cha?" directly into my face. Several brown, antenna-like nostril hairs descended into the arc of a tobacco-stained mustache that curled up at each end like smoke swirls. The man's breath stank, and his voice made the same scraping sound his stool made when he pushed himself out of the center of the painting to make room for me at his table. Reflections of the man's watery eyes shot back my image, causing me to turn away.

The grimy tavern overflowed with people who sucked in all the air and blocked out all the light—an old-time Dutch version of Take Five, bulging with belches, laughter, and screams. I was momentarily stunned by the voice of the painting. Hesitantly, I joined the revelers at their table. From inside the tavern I couldn't hear the lute player, I forgot all about the sleeping woman, and I could no longer see the hooded maiden who had invited Diane into her home. They lived on the same wall, within the same quiet gallery, inside the same busy museum, yet, surely, Brouwer's tavern revelers and Vermeer's reflective Dutch maidens would never share a table or even exchange glances.

Soon after the hairy-nosed drinker asked me, "Hey! What'll you have?" Vermeer's dozing woman suddenly reappeared. I glimpsed an image projected across her sleeping mind, but the picture dissolved before I could bring it into focus. The sleeper was still seated at a tapestry-covered table. Her eyes remained closed, her ear still leaned on her bent right hand, but she was no longer asleep. Beneath closed eyelids, her eyes darted back and forth like fish rippling the surface of a lake. She was reflecting on what she'd just seen in the patterns of the tapestry before her.

The shouts of cheering spectators quickened the tapestry's colors. Patterns romped. With closed eyes, she was watching children playing in a field. As I struggled to distinguish faces, I heard a young ambulance driver say, *"We'll take good care of him, ma'am. I promise."* There was blood all around. The cheering within the dozing woman's dream abruptly stopped, which woke her up until a long, single lute note pulled the woman back into her sleep.

Returning my attention back to the table of revelers, I ordered a beer, listened to the stories of my fellow drinkers, and then, less settled than when I had entered, I left the tavern. "Come back anytime, Stringbean. We're always here!" a voice called out above the sound of a stool scraping wooden floorboards.

Repositioning myself into the middle of the gallery, I stood, alternately looking through the open door of the tavern and the open window of Diane's quiet interior. Only after I could once again hear the plucked string of a lute did I rejoin Diane, who was right where I had left her, her eyes full of shimmering gold and brilliant blues.

Diane remarked that although we'd been together all afternoon, when she felt the need to be alone, I sensed it and silently walked away. My return was just as well timed, she said.

She told me about the Towson State education major whose ring she had worn for almost a year. She thought about him every day for months after he had taken his ring back. A museum filled with pictures was the last place she could ever imagine having spent an afternoon with him. Even if she could've talked him into a day of looking at paintings, he'd never have been so in sync with her needs as to know just when to come and go. And he would've been the one to do all the talking, even though he didn't know or care anything about art.

When I asked Diane why the Vermeer she'd been gazing at was her favorite, she said that standing in front of it was not like standing in front of it at all, but more like being *in* it. The painting itself was like a window, as far as she was concerned, not just to look through, but to be inside of. "Strangely enough," she added, "when I'm inside it I feel like I'm looking outside, as if I'm looking through the window to somewhere meant just for me. It's hard to explain, maybe because the subject is so much about privacy."

Privacy. I apologized. "I didn't mean to be pushy," I said. I suddenly saw the painting the way Diane did. I felt like an eavesdropper, a voyeur, with my nose in a place it didn't belong. Of course I understood perfectly well what she meant about being inside the painting, but I didn't say so.

"No, no. I wish I could explain it better." Her eyes were soft. "I guess I always feel sort of peaceful and isolated when I'm with this painting. It's more calming standing here, even with the chaos of the city, than when I'm home in my apartment, alone."

"You like being alone?" I asked.

"Sure, don't you?"

I didn't answer. I looked toward the tavern painting that I had just left, and then at the sleeping woman.

"Oh, that's right. You do have very particular feelings about being alone, don't you?" She paused. "Your 'isolation' is very different from mine, I think." When I looked away she added, "Your poem, based on the Goodman painting. I wanted to ask you, Stephen, who were you in the painting, the batter or the spectator?"

"What makes you think I was either?"

"Am I wrong?"

"Read a lot of Nancy Drew, do ya?"

"If you're not comfortable talking about your poem with me, I understand."

"No, no, no. That's okay. I don't mind talking about it. Especially with you," I added, lowering my eyes. "Which one? I don't know, I guess I mostly see myself as the batter."

The spectator stood far apart from the batter. Barely noticeable. Nothing like one of those loud-mouthed, hostile fans who carries on a one-way conversation with a slumping ballplayer throughout a game, and then goes home and takes a nap because his scratchy throat hurts from all his screaming. I didn't say that, like a memory that closes its eyes but never completely shuts out the past, I believed that the spectator was part of the batter—distant perhaps, but always there, one lop-sided without the other, like only one Smith Brother pictured on a box of cough drops. Like me without Howie.

I said none of this to Diane. I said: "You know, I just moved here last year and I don't have too many friends, at least none that go back too far, and I guess I was feeling a little bad about that when I wrote the paper for your assignment. Even before I moved here I was feeling kind of isolated, I guess."

"So we're both new," Diane said. She looked like she wanted to say more, but she didn't. "Are you sorry you moved, Stephen?"

"I don't know. Marchwood was nicer than Garrison City. I was happy there. I felt important."

"You don't feel important here?"

"Nah. Not especially. Not at all, actually. But that's not really it." I heard my voice crack. No more talking, I told myself. No more feeling sorry for myself, out loud, in front of a kind, older girl, a teacher—a teacher who I couldn't stop looking at.

Diane stroked my cheek. My whole body reacted. I raised my eyes and saw genuine care in her face. I liked the way my own face looked reflected in her eyes. I liked it enough to confide, as my hand touched my wallet tucked safely in my back pocket, "I didn't want to move. We had to."

November 2, 1965

English Class: Mrs. Bilheimer/Miss Adamsohn
"What do you see when you look at this painting?"

UNMEASURED MARKINGS
(based on *Songstress with Lute* by Johannes Vermeer)

"Rare and timeless maps
lead to unknown, nameless places."
    "If I find one should I read it?"
"Few can. Quivering marks trace the songs
of white-tailed faun,
and strum the barbs of birds. They shiver
through thickets of sea-blue trees and lull
the pressure of boulders buried deep."
    "I'd get lost trying to follow such markings."
"Lost, yes. In time.
Sheets of parchment may get you there,
but discard them once you arrive,

as everything pictured will have faded
or fled on the backs of chameleons."
    "But places don't fade or change their colors.
    Boulders buried deep stay put."
"Oh?"
    "Then what would I do, lost in such an unsettled site?"
"Wait for the lute player, the cartographer's daughter,
whose ballet of fingers unlock leaded glass,
blue and green and shades of kingly purple shapes
fickled by the sun. If she finds you,
she just might lead you home."
    "A tutu-ed tutor? Fingering a lute?
    How would she do that?"
"She would draw you a map."
    "A jigsaw type with Oklahoma silver
    and Jersey orange cut-outs?"
"For your little brother, perhaps, but yours
would be special, outdated and ahead of its time.
A fine and fragile drawing
leading to unexplored places,
it would trace the songs of white-tailed faun
that quiver for you alone.
    "When can I go? And where will I be when I get there?"
"In time, in time. That's when you can go
and where you will be when you get there."

—*Stephen Schaech*—

Part IV

WITH OR WITHOUT A CAUSE

23 ❖

ANOTHER TRYOUT

I excelled at childhood. I wasn't as good at adolescence.

Somehow, though, the Little League home runs I hit as a ten-year-old were still going to bat for me five years later. Ridiculous, but true.

Just weeks after I moved to Garrison City High School, I began to appreciate the importance of history. The way people first know you is remarkably lasting; images change with great reluctance. In Marchwood, my reputation as a strong athlete colored the way my friends and coaches viewed my ability on the field, despite the fact that I no longer stood out. History can be a great hiding place.

There were no "befores" for me at Garrison City High. I had moved just in time to be considered for the school's basketball team. Perfect timing, I thought, since this was the only sport I had left. I gave up baseball after Howie's death. The only other sport I liked and was any good at was basketball. But I didn't make it through the final cut, so now everything was up for grabs. In Marchwood, my friends were the guys on my teams. I had counted on making new friends in Garrison City the same way, but it turned out that I had no teammates.

The friends I made at Take Five cared little for sports. They cared about how many times they'd gotten laid (or, at least, how many times their friends *believed* they'd gotten laid), how much liquor they could down without puking, and who could take who in a fight.

The sport that mattered most to my new friends was shooting pool. In this regard, English Otis was the Willie Mosconi of North Jersey.

With English, pool was more than a game and his ability more than skill. To see English bank shots, shoot combinations, open up a cluster, or play position on his way towards running out a table was to see Leonardo da Vinci modulating the smooth skin tones of the Madonna.

In a game of straight pool, he could run two or three racks easily, his lanky body smooth and stately as he circled the table. He'd pocket eight, ten, fourteen balls at a time, making sure to leave himself a break ball to open up the next rack so he could keep his run going. It wasn't lining up a shot and sinking it that made it so hard for him to lose, he claimed. In fact, he said he didn't know how anyone could miss if a shot was halfway sinkable. "It's all in the positioning of the cue ball," he insisted. "Any fuckwad can sink two or three shots in a row. But you gotta know what you're doing if you're gonna run a whole rack. You wanna really shoot pool, you gotta know how to play position, how to use English."

English Otis's position was that cue balls were made to spin, not just roll. The paths of balls curved, hopped, stopped dead, and reversed their direction at the will of the kid with the same-sized fingers. The simplest shots got complicated, although he certainly didn't see it that way. "After a while," he claimed, "you don't even have to think of compensating for the English. You don't think nothin'." He had heard someone say that once, and he liked the sound of it. He even looked up *compensate,* in case anyone called him on it, and he used the word whenever he could, whether it belonged where he put it or not.

The fingers of English's right hand formed a solid bridge for his cue, and he had a sure eye. When English's object ball rolled toward a pocket, the ball shrank and the pocket swelled. His understanding of the geometry of the table, his ability to bank shots, the precision of his position play, and his unfailing composure (even when large sums of money were involved)—all this was exceptional.

All that deprived him of billiard greatness was shame and time. Time: he didn't take it. When he missed, it was usually a simple shot. That was his style, he said. He couldn't help it. "If I think too much, take too long setting up, I'm fucked." Planning, he claimed, "was just what you do when you don't know what you're doing. Brains are in the gut, not the head."

What he didn't say was he didn't want his hand resting on the green felt any longer than it had to. Why did his greatest skill have to involve the display—for all to see—of his hands? I'm convinced that what ruled his rhythm was zipping past the shame of his same-sized fingers, which is also what made his game so gracefully compelling to watch.

Everyone admired his speed. It was his signature, like the way his head bobbed up and down when he was on a roll. Although his quickness was occasionally his undoing, it usually worked for him. But it was not the substance of his game. What truly marked English's pool shooting was his unfailing intelligence.

Yes, that's what it was: intelligence. The intelligence that seldom accompanied English into a classroom pulsed, like blood, through every vein and artery of his body when he held a pool cue. "I don't know," English once confided to me, "my pool game's just smarter'n me, seems like. Makes me not me anymore. Makes me way more better." English—bending over the table, his right arm outstretched, his left arm pumping back and forth in soft and steady swings, mind focused on calculating the next five or six shots—was a chemist stirring his test tube, a mathematician puzzling over an equation, a chess master studying the board. English Otis: Billiardus Emeritus.

English was a junior, a year ahead of me, so I never saw his academic blunderings firsthand. Clearly, his scholastic shortcomings didn't stem from a simple lack of interest. I knew English read and studied more than anyone suspected, but calculation helped him earn a reputation as vigorously dumb. Calculated Stupidity. I had the feeling English worked harder at this than he did at letting people know what he knew. But who knows? At Garrison High, it was cool to be dumb. It was all right to shine occasionally, suggesting brains were there if necessary, like a concealed weapon. But in the case of English Otis, where stupidity was concerned, I never knew what was feigned and what wasn't. Was he a big little kid playing dumb by strumming his bottom lip while humming? Was his preciously protected intelligence his private hiding place? Or was his hideout the perfectly visible ignorance he flaunted daily?

Like that time at the nurse's office: ignorance or wit, or what? It occurred a few days before Mike fractured DiMaeoli's leg. My math teacher, Mr. Laociano, who also served as basketball coach, had just taken the twenty-six students trying out for the team for their physical examination. Upon entering the office, Ryan Sugar, dressed in gunmetal-gray gym shorts and a black t-shirt like his friends, stuck his fingers in his nostrils and made a face. "Lotions and disinfectants," Miss Schirmer, the school nurse, explained. "Then it reeks of cleanness, like bleach," Ryan complained. "Worse," he added. "Smells like cat pee."

"Which brings us to our first order of business," Nurse Schirmer interjected. "I want each one of you to leave a urine specimen on the counter by the filing cabinet. Next to the Ace bandages. And make sure you put your name under your plastic cup. I'm not a mind reader."

"She's not a nurse either," I overheard English tell Jerry. "If you was sick, Schirmer'd be worthless 'cause she never wears one of them white hats or nothin'. She don't even have a nametag on her chest."

"And what the flyin' fuck is a urine specimen, Sal?" Sal was English's nickname for Jerry ever since he saw *Rebel Without a Cause*. "I swear, if Sal Mineo had red hair, he'd be you. I mean, he'd still be Sal Mineo, hair-wise and all, but he could be you if you didn't hear him talk." No one else saw the resemblance, but that didn't bother English.

"Go into that stall over there, take one of them cups, and fill it up with spit."

English's face lit up. "Really? No shit. I never had to do that before. I had to put a cup under a table once when I knocked over this yellow sauce my mother made to put on top of this meatloaf one time when my aunt and her kids came over. There was a whole hard-boiled egg inside the meatloaf that my mother did on purpose 'cause that's how my old man likes it, and the sauce kept on drippin' off the table, so how I took care of it was I kept on running into the kitchen and emptying the cup and then I'd run back to catch the sauce 'cause it kept drippin' and gettin' the floor all yellow and shit no matter how fast I ran. Fifty, sixty times I must've filled it up, or maybe forty, and then my mother got this big sponge from under the sink and got the rest of it, and one time at this doctor's office I had to pee in a cup once, but that's the only way I had to fill it up. It didn't feel like the normalest thing I could be doing at the time, but this is even weirder."

The idea of filling up a cup with spit sounded great to English. "The lady who told me to pee was a nurse. *Supposably*; I wasn't sure at first. Looked sorta like my aunt except older. Younger than Schirmer, though. She was wearing white shoes and one of them little hats and a nametag and everything, so I did what she told me to."

"Yeah spit, everybody's supposed to. I think they use it to check your blood pressure or something."

"Thanks, man. I wouldn'tve knowed what to do. Where'd ya learn all this shit from? I wouldn't want no one thinkin' about how I didn't know what a urine specimen is." He complained about how small the cup was, but he was confident he could do it. Then, after positioning himself behind a curtain that walled off one of the stalls, English placed what Nurse Schirmer had provided him on the floor, bent over while keeping his knees straight, and let his saliva dribble down. His aim wasn't too accurate at first, but he eventually got the hang of it. It took him about five minutes to fill the cup.

When he came out from behind the curtain, there was no one left in the office except the teacher and the nurse, who were impatiently complaining about "waiting for Godotis." The stench of urine, fattened by the smells of rubbing alcohol, iodine, and Mercurochrome, filled the room.

"What were you doing in there all that time, pulling your pud?" Coach Laociano taunted English. "How long's it take to piss in a cup?"

"Sorry, Coach."

"Put it on that table, and get your butt down the hall. And make sure you don't stop and take a leak on the way. I want to go home tonight."

In big block letters, English neatly printed "Sal Mineo" on a piece of paper and placed it beneath his cup. Then he sprinted back to the gym.

He didn't make the team.

24 ❖

BETTY CROCKER
AND JAMES DEAN

Several weeks after English and Jerry had befriended me, the three of us were walking in the halls on our way to our last class. We stopped as Mike Dumbrowski approached.

"Shit, man, don't go upstairs," Mike informed us with a smile. "Ybañez is puking his guts out. It's disgusting,"

"Where is he?" Jerry screamed twice. "I gotta get up there fast. I wanna hear it hit the ground! That's the best part!"

As he ran upstairs, everyone within earshot laughing, English told us how much he hated to see Jerry run. "Sal don't look like Sal to me when he runs. It used to be he was really fast. Fastest in the grade, growing up. But look at him now. When he runs his fuckin' hip jerks out so far with each step his hair pounds against his head. D'ja ever look at his hair when he runs? I betcha it hurts."

Mike disagreed. "He never bitches about his hip. I don't think he feels it no more. His mother told me he was lucky, Jerry was. It healed real good, she told me."

"Not his hip. His head. I betcha he gets headaches when he runs from all that hair bouncing on his head. And it probably weighs more'n other guys' hair 'cause it's red. I bet it's a lot more heavier. Waddya think? Think red hair weighs more'n other color hairs?"

Mike and I glanced at one another.

"I'm just saying, you know, like water drippin' on your hand for a coupla hours or somethin'. After a while your hand hurts. I tried it once. In the bathroom. Not once. A million times. Maybe not a million. Five, six hundred thousand. Probably more, even. Somewheres around that. All at one time. You know, like over and over and over, the water keeps on dripping 'til you can't stand it no more, and you gotta compensate by not thinkin' about it or nothin'. You don't think it's gonna hurt 'cause it's just these stupid-ass drips from a faucet, you know, five, ten drips you don't feel diddly squat, but. . . and it'd be even tougher even if the water was colored 'cause then it'd be more heavier. I was gonna do a science project on it when I was in sixth grade—you know, figuring out how come water'd weigh. . ."

"What happened to his leg, anyway?" I asked. "I know it has to do with a car accident around Englewood Cliffs, but I never heard just what happened."

"Wasn't just his leg," Mike said. "His arm too. It was paralyzed for a while, but that got better so now you can't tell nothing was ever wrong with it. I didn't know him then."

"I did," English said. "We grew up next door of each other, almost next door, Batman and Robin, right on Washington Avenue."

"So what happened in the accident?" I asked again.

"Even though we lived right next door we didn't used to be close 'cause my mother hated his. Still does. Other way round too, I guess. That don't matter no more, but it did then, when me and Sal were little. First time I remember liking him was eating at school. First or second grade, something like that. Me and Sal, we swapped lunches. My old lady'd slop twenty pounds of ham or bologna on a sandwich so's if I pigged out on it I couldn't think about nothin' else for the rest of the day besides taking a crap. Sal, his mother'd just give him one piece of meat in his sandwich. He said she was a cheap bastard where it came to sandwiches, and that mine ought to give her lessons in Betty Crockering, which I told him was a hangin' crock 'cause his mother's cooking was more smarter'n mine, at least sandwich-wise."

"English, what the fuck's any of this got to do with Jerry's accident?" Mike complained.

"I don't know. Nothin', I guess. Only I just thought about how we started swapping lunches with each other and kept on 'til high school. You know, how come we first got to be good friends, and all, me and Sal."

"So what happened?" I repeated.

"We started buying our lunches at school when. . . "

"He's fuckin' certifiable," Mike complained.

"I mean about the car accident."

"Oh, it was just bad luck, man. Bad fucking luck. You know. He shouldn't even've been there. He was only about eleven or twelve. His brother, Warren, brung him. He was taking him somewhere in Teaneck. Somewheres off The Avenue up near Liberty Road. *Supposably* to drop him off, but it never happened. I guess they wouldn't even've been on that hill if Sal wasn't with them."

"You never met Warren. Shit, he was a bad-ass. Bright red hair like Jerry's and a red goatee, and arms so big your both hands couldn't fit half way round. Ask Dumbrowski here if he wasn't bad. Go on, ask him. Was Warren bad or what, Mike? Was he bad?"

No answer.

"Anyhow, what happened was Warren and a friend of his, this guy Kenny Giaquinto, who just got his license a few days before, and a guy named Mishy Finch, the three of them, they're in the car with Sal, and they're on Palisades Avenue. That's back when everyone was into haulin' down streets at night with their headlights off. Hundred miles an hour. More. Palisades was perfect for it. Sal told me it was Mishy's idea to turn off the headlights. Mishy was a real Dean freak. Dean's *Rebel Without a Cause* just came to Garrison City for the first time and with Dean getting killed in that car wreck only about seven or eight years before and all. . . when was that? '55, '56. . .?"

"Fifty-six, I think," Mike said, his attention shifting to a group of girls coming down the hall. "Hey Gloria, your skirt gets any shorter you're gonna hafta start wearing panties." The girl made a face but remained quiet. "Laini, how's it going?" Mike called to the pony-tailed girl in the center of the group. She waved to him. Then, with more enthusiasm, she smiled at me, pointed toward my shirt, and said: "It's nice. Is it new?" and her friend, Gloria, added, "It's just the right color for you, Stephen."

Before I had a chance to respond, English affirmed: "Ybañez is right. Check it out. Laini, Heather, Mandy. . . they're all into him. Shakes here's got the moves."

"Yeah, even Gloria," Mike joined in. "Her nipples get all hard and shit over the color of a word-rhymer's shirt. Maybe I should learn to write some poems some." Then, as the girls continued down the hall, Mike grabbed his crotch and called out, "Hey Gloria, you like color so much, c'mere and I'll put some in your cheeks."

"Yeah," English continued, "Mishy thought he was James Fuckin' Dean or something. I bet he liked having Jerry in the car with him 'cause he looks so much like Sal Mineo. He does you know. Bust my chops all you want, but you gotta admit it. I wouldn't call him Sal if he didn't look just like him. Anyways, Mishy starts combing his hair like Dean and talking like Dean and walking around looking like he was always pissed off and depressed, just like Dean. I heard Mishy seen *Rebel Without a Cause* every night it played there at the Palace Theatre. They're probably up there right now. . ."

"Where? At the Palace?" Mike interrupted.

"No, you know what I mean." English pointed his head toward the ceiling of the hallway. "Up there."

"Where? On the second floor watching Felix puke?"

"You know what I mean and you know it. I bet they're in heaven right now, Mishy and James Dean, talking about their car crashes with Mishy doing his Dean imitation for Dean, who's probably sick as shit of the James Dean look 'cause every other dead guy he meets probably looks more like him than he does and. . ."

"English, what the fuck." English had gotten on his friend's nerves even before the sandwich story; now he was sawing with a dull blade. At least he wasn't going on about sputniks and lunar modules, which Mike especially hated hearing about.

"You know, 'cause lots of guys are totaling their cars and I'm not saying it's Dean's fault or nothing, but. . ."

"*Jasna Cholera*!" With a sharp motion, Mike Dumbrowski pushed himself away from the locker he was leaning against. "Shakes asked you about Jerry! How did Jerry get hurt? That's what he asked you. If you're gonna tell him about Jerry, then tell him about Jerry! We don't give a tit or a testicle about no goddamn James Dean!"

"What's wrong with James Dean?"

"We was talking about Jerry! That's what's wrong with James Fuckin' Dean."

"Okay. . . okay. . . okay. So what was I saying?"

Mike helped him out. He slowed down a little. "You was saying how everyone was into tear-assing down Palisades Avenue at night with their headlights off, and. . ."

"Oh yeah, that's right. And you know how it can get blacker than one of them black holes in outer space on Palisades Avenue and all, and how once you've passed through its event horizon the gravitational pull of the black hole dooms you and you can't. . ."

"English!" English had passed through Mike's event horizon.

"So all's I'm saying is the center of those guys' black hole was this cement bus stop, and Giaquinto's whipping down Palisades in this mint-wicked machine doing about fifty, maybe sixty, maybe more, and he forgets where he's at. He thinks he's at the bottom of the hill, you know, a ways away, where the Palisades goes like this, so Kenny steers into the curve like he's at Palisades Amusement Park or some shit where rides can get boring 'cause it don't matter which way you spin or how sharp the turn is—you're on a track, you're safe—but there's no track and no curve where Giaquinto is now and. . . BADOOM! Giaquinto plays chicken with this concrete bus stop. Swerved too late."

With the word *badoom*, English slammed his open hand hard against a textbook he had been holding. The pop of his hand echoed down the cinderblock hallway, causing the group of girls who had just passed to spin around. Returning his attention to them, Mike commented with surprising sincerity, "I wouldn't mind any coppin' a feel from that Gloria."

English continued, "Giaquinto, he thinks he's at the bottom of the hill, but he wasn't even close hardly. Fuckin' car wiped out half the bus stop, but the bus stop wiped out the whole fuckin' car. Sal's brother Warren shot right through the front windshield. They found him about thirty feet away. Sal told me they found Warren's left leg about a half hour after they found Warren. I don't know how Warren missed the bus stop. But it don't matter none. He was dead soon as he hit the ground. All over the place and cut up, you know, flesh-wise, and puffy-like. Sal said his mother didn't even know who Warren was. With all the blood, you couldn't even tell if he had red hair or what. Warren was riding shotgun. That's why I don't like to sit in front if the guy drivin' is even a little high or anything. No way, man. Not after hearing about how Warren ended up in all these small pieces. Shit.

"Anyways, Mishy gets killed too, but Giaquinto and Sal made it. The only thing Sal has to show for it is his leg, you know, when he walks, and the way his hip jerks out all kind of funny-like when he tries to run. He's lucky though. He could've ended up a lot worse. Like his brother."

"It gives me the creeps, that friggin' story," Mike said. "Warren was something else, Warren was."

"I didn't know he had a brother," I said. "Never heard him talk about it. Damn, how do you get past a thing like that? Jerry's always so up and all."

"He *is* up," Mike countered.

"You'd think. . ."

Mike stopped me. "You'd think what, man? Palisades Avenue's not what Jerry's about. Not for a long time it ain't. Jerry's about Jerry. Warren's dead six years already."

"Yeah, but you don't get over something like that."

English remembered Jerry's mother coming to his house a few weeks after the accident, "without any sandwiches or lettuce or stuff," to tell him to try and get Jerry to go out, or at least to get him to talk about his brother, but Jerry wasn't having any of it. "He just hung out in his room all day doin' nothing," English said. "That's when he started painting pictures. All day long, seemed like."

I said I didn't think people could get over something like that, not for a long time. "Especially if it was on account of him that his brother and the rest of them were on that road in the first place. I mean, I know it's not like he was driving or anything, but. . ." I didn't get to finish my sentence.

"What's that got to do with it, that they were driving him some-wheres? Eleven years old. You want him to take credit for steering that jam jar into a concrete post? Jerry's not still slipping in the skid marks of the car he was in that night when he runs funny now."

"But that *is* why he runs like he does," I objected. I knew this was the wrong thing to say, but I couldn't help myself.

"How long you think those skid tracks are gonna stay soft?" Mike cursed.

"I don't know. A long time though, I bet. I'm just saying. . ."

"Yeah, you're just sayin'. At first that's what it was like, sure. But that was a long time ago. Now it's just the way his bones healed from a car accident. You're seeing it all fucked up. You're seeing it like you want him to be a dead kid's brother all the time. And like he was the guy that killed him."

"You're a Jew, right?" Mike asked, staring at me.

"Yeah, what about it?"

"It's only that my old man works for this Jewish guy who's always feeling guilty for stuff. He got out of Germany before Hitler got too far with all his killing, only I don't think he ever really got all the way out of Germany in his head, the Jew. Most of his family came with him, but a lot of the guy's friends stayed behind, and he never saw them again. My old man always says, if the guy can blame himself for something or blame someone else, he always ends up blaming himself. It don't really bother my old man or nothing. I think sometimes it makes it easier on the rest of them in the office even. Only he can't figure out why the guy always wants to whip himself about shit that's none of his business to feel bad about in the first place, and why he's always harping about Germany, and how he never suffered like the way his friends did. I mean, he's not in Germany no more. Right? Only he sort of still is. Too bad, 'cause he's doing good here in the States, the Jew guy—he's got a house and all in Dumont—only I don't think he sees how good he's doing."

"So what's that got to do with being Jewish?" I asked.

"My old man says that's the way Jews are, is what—always ready to feel guilty about shit they don't have no business feeling guilty for."

"And you believe that?"

"I don't know. He just says it, is all. He says plenty of other stuff too about Jews, only you don't want to hear it."

November 21, 1965

English class: Mrs. Bilheimer/Miss Adamsohn
"What do you see when you look at this painting?"

SHOTGUN SHOES
(based on *The Red Model* by René Magritte)

Laces untied, little brother left behind,
he raced to the dented door, screaming
firsties and dibs, staking claim to sit with Dad.

In charge of the radio's bright blue dial,
and lavished in a big-armed embrace
(prizes for the fastest runner),
he read road maps with names like Piscataway.

The Red Model
by
René Magritte

After a Bic's flick and a manly spit,
"Front seat" tied his shoes.
"Shotgun" now reigns on the vinyl throne
of a souped-up '56 Merc burning rubber.

Raised-collar car rewards:
the right of a right-hand man to sag
cigarette-tipped fingers in the wind,
and shout out at short skirts.
In the slumped solitude of back seats, Friday night freedom
becomes belts wrapped around arms marked with crooked tracks.

"I Spy," is now a lightless, midnight game
played at shattered windshield speed.
Vinyl throne is overthrown
by thrown-off doors and tires screaming,
laying claim to lives left behind.

—Stephen Schaech—

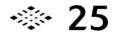 **25**

DECOMPOSING

"My old man never goes "uh" or "um" when he's spoutin' his opinions," Mike said. "He always knows just what he's thinking. That's what I hate about him: no second thoughts. So maybe he's got it wrong about the Jew guy, I don't know. Says he kind of likes him, but to tell you the truth, he. . ."

A woman's voice suddenly scratched through the conversation like a rip in a scrapbook photograph. It was Mary Gustin, my chemistry teacher.

"It looks like one of your friends has gotten himself into something serious this time, boys."

English stepped back and smiled when he saw who it was. Then he leaned toward me. "My father says Cigar Legs Gustin was already a dinosaur when she was *his* tenth-grade teacher," he whispered. She was wearing a blue and red floral dress that came to her ankles. The designer who figured out this dress never counted on the likes of Mary Gustin framing his idea. I recognized the design from the pictures filling one of my favorite books in my grandfather's house, the flowers springing originally from the watercolors of Georgia O'Keefe. Perched upon a garden of satin poppies and roses, Mary Gustin's deteriorating face and beaky nose brought to mind another painting from the same book—a bone-dry, toothpaste-white cow's skull floating before a red and blue background, a painting that once caused my grandfather to proclaim: "A *nifter-pifter* cow and some colored stripes. That's all. Yet every time I see it, *eppes,* the Pledge of Allegiance salutes the gray matter that dusts my brain. Go know."

I looked back at the teacher's dress, and wondered if it was the same one she wore when, twenty-odd years ago, she explained to English's father how mercuric oxide decomposes into mercury and oxygen when it is heated. For thirty-two years Mary Gustin had been explaining chemical principles such as this to disinterested high-schoolers, and for thirty-two years those principles remained true and steadfast. The decomposition of mercuric oxide was a process destined to endlessly repeat itself. Some things didn't change. I liked that.

But most things did. I wondered if thirty years ago Mrs. Gustin's legs looked as much like wrinkly cigars to English's father as they did now to English. Decomposition may exist outside of time in the world of chemistry, but how about chemistry teachers? To look at Mary Gustin, you'd have to figure that decomposition did what it wanted, wherever it wanted, to whoever it wanted.

Apparently, right now it wanted one of my friends. It remained for Mary Gustin to explain: "It appears Felix Ybañez has gotten himself into a peck of trouble."

"Nah, he's just sick," English corrected. "Mike just told us about it. Upstairs puking, right, Mrs. Gustin? Right, Mike?"

"Your friend Felix is sicker than you know, Edward. And his stomach troubles are the least of his problems."

The serious look in English's eyes kept the teacher talking.

"You know he. . . well pardon me, but I'm afraid he vomited all over the second floor." As she said the word *vomited,* her fingers fussed with a strip of clear plastic that wrinkled out of her pocketbook. Avoiding our eyes, she unfastened the lock on her bag and hastily tucked away the plastic wrapping, which smelled like celery.

"Yeah, Mike just told us," English repeated.

"And do you know what caused his intestinal disturbance, young man?"

"I don't know. A flu or something? Mike didn't say nothing about that part."

"Guess again, Edward," Mrs. Gustin said flatly.

"Why don't you just tell us what you think you know and we don't," Mike demanded, "instead of jerking us around."

Mike's comment earned him a gelid stare from the teacher, who straightened her back and paused before saying, with the pace and intonation of a telephone operator, "You may delude yourself into believing your way of communicating hastens getting to the heart of a matter, young man. But believe you me, it gets you nowhere. I like neither the tone of your voice nor your choice of expressions."

Her head and shoulders stiffened more, then she twitched her fingers as if brushing away his words as she might brush away an annoying cobweb stuck to her eyebrows and ears. "It is high time you boys learned that there is a way of expressing yourself that will bring forth the desired results, and that there is a way of communicating that will result in nothing of the sort. Nothing whatsoever!" And then she was gone, the discordant rip across the scrapbook photo of friendship, quickly mending.

November 30, 1965

English Class: Mrs. Bilheimer/Miss Adamsohn
"What do you see when you look at this painting?"

HIGH SCHOOL RAINBOW
(based on *Bauhaus Stairway* by Oscar Schlemmer)

Dreaming in black and white
on a stairy slope of colorful choices,
a black and blue boy toe-balances a secret
behind an unseen, unsound wall.
He prays: God bless my ups and downs
and my hiding place,
where I'm invisible. Invincible.

"Jerk!" mutters a girl who spies him.
She thinks about her parakeet, Miss Diz,
who flies into walls and falls.
Damaged green and gold feathers.
She thinks: "Everyone knows the capital of Maine,
even Miss Diz. Yet I blew it on my quiz."

He thinks: "What a hiding place."
She: "Goddamn Maine."
He: "Goddamn blackheads." But, "God bless white powder."
Then the boy's balance breaks.

Bauhaustreppe (Bauhaus Stairway)
by
Oskar Schlemmer

Oskar Schlemmer (1888–1943), *Bauhaus Stairway*, 1932, Ól auf grober Leinwand, 161 x 113 cm, The Museum of Modern Art, New York, Courtesy of U. Jaïna Schlemmer, © 2007 The Oscar Schlemmer Estate, and Archive, Secretariat: IT – 28824 Oggebbio (VB), Italy

Black and white dreams and unanswered prayers
stain the unmoved metal stairs.
X, Y, Z. Everyone gathers to see.

—*Stephen Schaech*—

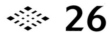 **26**

AN EGG SALAD SANDWICH AND A BAG OF SCAG

In fifth period, Felix felt sick. When he asked his math instructor, Daniel Laociano, if he could go to the bathroom, Laociano said no, which turned out to be a bad call because Felix left the classroom anyway, and when the guy tried to stop him, Felix threw up on both sleeves of his teacher's sport coat.

After attending to Felix the best he could, and then cleaning up in the bathroom alongside him, Mr. Laociano returned alone to his classroom and met with little success in reestablishing order. While Felix remained in the john, an office employee was sent with the combination to Felix's locker to get his books and anything else he'd need to take home from school. Stuffed into a corner of the locker behind a wool sweater, thirty-seven cents in loose change, and a two-month-old sandwich (possibly egg salad, hard to tell), were a bag of marijuana, a hypodermic needle, and a small frosted envelope of white powder. The powder was heroin.

The office employee notified the principal, who contacted Mr. Laociano. As the teacher returned to the boys' room to confront Felix, they met in the hallway. Laociano ignored the lack of color and lifeless expression on Felix's face.

"Do you have any idea what drugs can do to you, young man? Are you out of your mind?" An angry, red oval suddenly blotched the left side of the teacher's neck. "And bringing them into school—what are you, nuts?" Daniel Laociano's tour of duty with the Marine Corps in Korea ten years before, and his present role as basketball coach, laid the foundation for his well-conditioned body. Bigger around than my thighs, his arms and neck looked like sun-bleached telephone poles. Today, his military discipline, which ordinarily served him well, was absent from duty.

"You must be out of your mind!" He screamed it in Italian first but then, composing himself somewhat, went back to English. Teachers and students from several nearby classrooms had begun to look on.

Laociano's Italian momentarily calmed Felix, who loved the sound of foreign speech. He thought of himself as multilingual, partly because his parents spoke both Spanish and English at home, but mainly because he could swear in about a dozen languages. His multilingualism consisted of a mere two or three words or phrases in Japanese, Norwegian, and about ten other tongues. But, not surprisingly, he spoke Spanish quite well. And Polish—with the help of Mietek Dumbrowski, Mike's father, Felix's vocabulary was steadily growing.

"*Lo siento*," he apologized, "but I don't feel so hot."

"Of course you don't feel well! Do you realize what you are putting into your body? How this can ruin your life? You're not going to kill yourself. Not in this school you're not." Laociano ran his fingers across his closely cropped hair with such force that he must have bruised his scalp. "You want to throw your life away, go and do it off school grounds, goddammit, you pathetic little punk!" His eyes underlined "pathetic." It made an impression with the on-looking students, and the hallway grew quiet. Yanking Felix's arm, Mr. Laociano ordered him to move.

"I don't feel so good," Ybañez repeated, pulling his arm away.

"Don't you countermand my orders! I said come with me!" Then, more calmly, and with an awkward attempt at kindness, he said he was trying to help.

Felix gave him the finger.

"You son of. . ." Laociano stopped himself, even as his fingers dug through the flesh of Felix's arm.

Again Ybañez attempted to pull free, but he had little strength. He looked faint, green. "You got an X, Y, and Z in your name?"

The pressure of the teacher's fingers lessened. "What?"

"'Til you got an X, Y, and Z in your name, you don't talk to me with nothing but respect. Hear what I'm saying, man?" Mucus glazed the coarse black hairs that rimmed his upper lip.

Again, Felix stuck his middle finger straight up in front of Laociano's nose, this time adding a German subtitle to his gesture: "*Du bisch der hingerletscht Füdischläker!*" which Mr. Laociano ignored as simply the delusional, ranting jibberish of a drug addict. "This isn't just a school matter," he warned. "You're probably selling this filthy stuff. A pusher. You come with me. I'm calling the police."

"You do what you want, bro, but you don't get outta my face I'm gonna heave all over you again," Felix warned. Cheers from on-looking students stimulated the teacher's anger more than they strengthened Felix's resolve. He was doing his best to simply remain standing.

"I'm not your 'bro,' young man, I'm your teacher," is all Laociano said at first, but the rest of Ybañez's words were not wasted on him. He could probably still smell undigested lunch on Felix's shirt. Everyone could. The teacher looked down at the rust-colored spots splattered across his wing-tipped shoes and swung his body around, forcefully bending Felix's arm behind his back. Felix screamed.

"Leave him the fuck alone!" Mike shouted. "You're breaking his fuckin' arm. Can't you see he's sick?"

"You just keep your big mouth shut, Michael. This is none of your concern."

"You don't tell me what's my concern. He ain't done nothing to you. Let go of his arm or you and me're gonna dance."

"Don't you threaten me! I've had enough lip from you and your delinquent friends. Losers, every one of you. Bunch of goddamn suburban hoods." With those words, Laociano bent Felix Ybañez's arm further. Turning his attention back to Felix, Laociano declared: "I'll give you X, Y, Z."

Because by this time the hallway was filled with more and more students jockeying to see what was going on, I missed what happened next. What I did see was Mr. Laociano, clearly not yet realizing he was no longer on his feet. His legs were splayed out wishbone style, his right arm fanned the air in halfhearted jabs, and his nose was bent toward his ear like a Picasso portrait. A slowly widening circle of blood and saliva muddied the collar of his shirt, while a dark line of blood stretched from his eye down alongside his mouth, filling his left hand like coffee dripping into a cup.

All the shouting stopped. Despite the blood, the teacher looked more embarrassed than hurt.

A strip of skin dangled from the middle knuckle of Mike's right hand, exposing a pink gash. "Fuckin' A," Felix was saying, more to himself than to anyone else. "Fuckin' A."

"Here, Mr. Laociano. Take this," Ryan Sugar whispered, hesitantly extending a folded white handkerchief, as if sneaking someone an answer during an exam. Laociano's olive-brown skin, in its loamy way, had cooled toward a feeble gray. His clammy flesh seemed to startle Ryan as their fingers momentarily touched, or maybe it was the color of the man's hand, which was whiter than the handkerchief, half a dozen shades lighter than the potato color of his unexpectedly spindly ankles and shins that showed beneath the cuffs of his hiked-up trouser cuffs. The handkerchief quickly turned red and wet. Laociano threw several more punches into the air before mumbling for his glasses. Like the browns of his clothes, his voice took on the sound of a hum.

"What's Booger doing with the snotrag?" English asked no one in particular.

"Here're your glasses, but I don't think they'll do you much good." Ryan needed both hands for the glasses, which the fallen man, who seemed to have forgotten what they were for, put under his nose and smelled. "I love the scent of freshly cut grass," he said, heading south with his singular map of twists and turns.

"Guess that *pendejo* won't be so fast to mess with Felix Ybañez next time," Felix said weakly, but with pride.

"Damn straight, bro," Mike agreed, examining the gash on the back of his hand, which now extended from his knuckle to his wrist in a straight red line.

Mike licked his cut. His face remained expressionless as he looked down at the fallen teacher, but the deliberation with which he tongued the blood on his hand displayed an obvious, unconscious pleasure, like a cat preening in the sun.

"Shakes, look at how small his eyes are, Shakes," English whispered. "Like them little pink erasers on the ass-end of pencils." I hadn't seen English come up beside me. "I don't believe Laociano's eyes, size-wise I mean. Look at 'em."

"English, what're you talking about?" I asked.

"I always thought his eyes was a lot bigger'n everybody else's, but without his glasses on, they're no bigger'n mine. That was always the one thing I kind of liked about Laociano—besides him looking like such a fuckin' potato head, all brown and everything—him having them bad-ass manhole-cover eyes. But it was just his glasses. I guess that's what glasses do, compensate for bad seeing by making your eyes bigger. I never thought of that before now."

"D'ja see Dumbrowski take him out?" English continued. "Spang in the nose. D'ja see it, Shakes? One punch. BADAAM!" As he said this, Mr. Compensation pounded Ryan Sugar in the neck. Ryan, who'd been standing next to me, quickly moved away. "Mike shrunk Laociano's eyes. Far out!" There was respect in English's voice. "C'mon man, I'm getting you outta here," Mike said as he placed his arm around his friend.

"*Arrivederci,* suckers!" Felix mumbled, as he shaped his hand like a gun and clicked his thumb. Then he spotted me and added, *"Zei gezunt,"* just before he vomited down the front of his shirt.

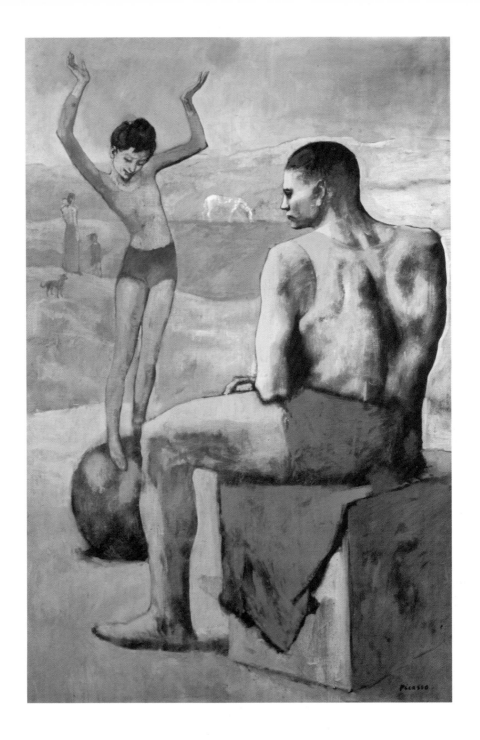

Young Acrobat Balancing on a Ball
by
Pablo Picasso

December 14, 1965

English Class: Mrs. Bilheimer/Miss Adamsohn
"What do you see when you look at this painting?"

IMBALANCE
(based on *Young Acrobat Balancing on a Ball* by Pablo Picasso)

Enthroned in chiseled silence, the circus pharaoh,
shadowed in boulder-backed calm, watches
acrobatic innocence roll glistening hieroglyphics
into chilly sunburned sand.
What story will the child inscribe
before breezes (or sneezes) erase it?
And what drained, dreamy eyes, he thinks,
as she twists, a windless windlass Alice,
to anchor and keep aloft the sphere
of a weightless wonderland between her hands.

Between performances he sits, stone still, questioning:
How long 'til she hops or falls off
that Humpty-Dumpty-belly of a ball?
Would a fall break her into pieces,
      or just make more of her,
      or be what wrongs her,
      or make her stronger? Or just make her cry?
Is it true big girls don't?

The dawn she buoys between her hands—
the weight is too great for her to bear. After all,
everyday a dawn becomes a dusk—
warm, worn, and washed clean—
like the naked path of a tear.

Balancing acts and strongman stunts
used to be so easy,
all the circus man wanted to see or do, forever.
Meanwhile, he sits like an Egyptian king,
treasuring a chest
of experience, a box dressed
in the liquid echo of sky
cleansing the bottom of a dusty well.
Keeping her balance
keeps her busy. So does the task

of keeping the unmapped globe she cups
(a dot too big for the stem of its "I")
from crashing down like a bubble,
killing mockingbirds and memories,
razing mushrooms so big that pretty girls in party dresses
must sway on the backs of kings' horses
to touch their umbrella tops.

With light and limber limbs, the scribe
plucks from heaven a bead of rain from a broken cloud.
Global in its pearly roundness, the raindrop
is her offering to her off-season king,
who performs his most strenuous stunt:
allowing his child to fall.

—Stephen Schaech—

Part V

FAMILY AND FRIEND

27 ◈

SAD EYES

"*Vas troiedica oigen zee hut.*"

"Grandpa?" I often understood my grandfather's Yiddish from what surrounded it in the conversation, or because I'd heard the expression before. Not this time.

"What sad eyes she has. Such a little thing, with such sad eyes. Don't you think, Stephen?"

When I look at the reproduction of circus performers in its peeling, gold-leaf frame hanging in front of me on my grandfather's living room wall, I don't see the girl in the painting the way my grandfather does. Preoccupied, sure, but sad? The young acrobat looks okay to me. Picasso painted it, Grandpa Oscar told me five minutes ago. And five minutes before that. Five minutes from now he'll tell me again.

It's often the same pattern when I visit. Great conversations punctuated with my grandfather's repetitions. Before we moved to Garrison City, not far from where my grandparents live, every Sunday my mother used to drive forty-five minutes to reach her parents' apartment from our home in Marchwood. My father seldom accompanied her; most of the time, Howie and I did. After we moved, my mother and I continued our weekly visits together, but for the past year, I prefer visiting on my own. Now, door-to-door, not ten minutes by foot separates the Bialintzes from the Schaechs. The proximity allows me to visit more, and the more often I visit, the more I notice how often my grandfather repeats himself. Not that I mind. I enjoy his repetitions; I find them relaxing. They provide time for me to lose myself, to dream. To Shahn. Like right now.

No longer just sitting in the living room of my grandfather's New Jersey apartment, I'm presently standing on a ball, outdoors, not a tree or building or road in sight. Just sand: sunny, undisturbed, in-between-sold-out-circus-shows sand. Miles of it.

I've become a younger, darker, more agile, and even skinnier version of my sixteen-year-old self. I'm a girl with outstretched arms, long legs, and a pretty red bow in my hair. There's a man sitting close by. He's not old, but he's older than me. Twice as much, I bet. Even more. Yes, definitely more, he has to be, because I have a feeling he's my father. As long as he's there I'm safe. My eyes work their way up and around the seated circus performer, who's content to do nothing but watch his young daughterly acrobat balance on a ball. As if some of him was chiseled off by time, the picture-perfect man only has one leg and half an arm. All that's left but, apparently, all he needs. His sharply shaded body, right-angled like a straight-backed chair, is nothing like me: a softly lit, all-arms-and-legs girl whose feet never touch the ground. The man loves me, loves watching me chip away my challenges. His watchfulness keeps me from falling.

Normally, I'd stay in the painting until my toes tired from gripping the ball, but that won't work now with my grandfather sitting so close by.

As if seeking to penetrate the starlet's thoughts through the touch of his fingertips, my grandfather strokes the glossy, magazine-cover face of a child, the words *LADIES HOME JOURNAL* crowning her hair, *HOME* emphatic, like a misplaced underline, directly above the girl's eyes. "What could possibly make someone so young be so sad?" he asks me.

When I don't answer, my grandfather asks, "You don't see the sadness?"

Easing myself out of Picasso's sand-filled world of father and daughter strongmen and ball balancers, I sit down on the couch next to him and regard the magazine lying across his lap. Is home a place of sad eyes? Is that what the old man's talking about? The girl looks to me like she just stepped on a dead bird, her eyes more sorry than sad. He repeats his question. "I don't know, Grandpa. I just hadn't thought about it. I thought you were talking about the girl on the wall behind us."

The old man turns toward the picture. "Picasso," he says. Then, shifting his attention to the young girl in the painting, he notes how sad she too looks. "Much too young for such sorrow," he adds slowly, "like this one."

I follow my grandfather's gaze back to the magazine. The young cover girl can't be more than eight years old, but since when do low numbers yield only playground happiness? During one of my grandfather's more lucid periods, which could last all day, or, occasionally, even several days running, I could imagine the old man answering his own question: *"Eight years old or eighty, what does sadness or pain know from age?"*

We had taken our usual positions on the living room couch. As always, my body slumps into the deep cushions, while Grandpa Oscar, as is his custom, sits up straight. For my grandfather, every piece of furniture designed for sitting is a hard-backed chair. A sharp *Bergen Record* crease, connecting the crumpled bodies of Secretary of Defense Robert McNamara and President Johnson, edges its way beneath our thighs like an umbilicus, giving birth to ever-more mangled world events every time we shift our weight.

"So, *nu*?" Grandpa Oscar asks. "Do you see it? Do you see what I mean about her eyes?"

My attention remains on my grandfather, whose attention remains fixed on the magazine. Her eyes don't look so sad to me. What's sad are *your* eyes, Grandpa. What's sad is that there's just one crummy magazine alone on this table with no books keeping it company. That wouldn't have been the case three years ago, B.C., before cataracts. Before cataracts, my grandfather was ageless. Howie and I both thought so.

No one in the family knows how old Grandpa Oscar is, his records having been lost when he immigrated as a child to the United States from Russia. He was born sometime around the late 1880s, I figure. Grandpa Oscar's age remained up for grabs forever after, which always struck me as fitting. Oscar Bialintz can remember the day President McKinley was assassinated. For my grandfather, Willie Mays is that marvelous youngster in centerfield, the one who once said that all he ever wanted to do was play baseball—forever. *Forever*: As far as I'm concerned, that's what my grandfather has always been and always will be, like Picasso's seated strongman.

My grandfather's enthusiasm for life is childlike; his wisdom, the wisdom of the ancients. My grandfather's, my *zayde's*, eighty-plus cataract-free years have to do with atmosphere, not age. For him, the only member of the family who observes the sanctity of the Sabbath, time reaches beyond the mundane and artificial confines of what we try to stuff within the edges of a "second" or an "hour" or even a "day."

His aging is inconsistent. Sometimes, entire days'll go by with his mind remaining sharp. Before cataracts, every day was like that. He never lost track, slipping unaccountably into a private re-experiencing of the same moment of time, forgetting whose turn it is when he plays checkers, forgetting if he's eaten or which books he's already read, forgetting the names of my friends, even forgetting my name. Since my grandfather's eye troubles began, I never know which Oscar I'm going to get.

"Cataracts. They make it hard to see," my mother once explained, "like if you had a film of dirt smeared across your eyeglasses or across the windshield of a car. So we had it taken care of. Listen to your grandfather and you'd think he was blind. But the doctor took care of his eyes, pretty much. It's not like he can't see, he just can't read anymore. Believe me, it could be a lot worse."

"So sad."

"Grandpa?"

"Don't you think so?"

I looked back down at the magazine and examined the face on the cover of the *Ladies Home Journal*. "Yeah, I guess so. Sort of."

Before cataracts, books were everywhere in the Bialintz household. There were books sprawled across the floor like picnicking families. Other books stacked themselves into piles and laid themselves out in rows. Some sets displayed Roman numerals lining their spines. Inevitably, a single book lay atop a sheet or clean white pillowcase on the bed, the leathery, old but undusty smell of the book's cover blending comfortably with the lingering fragrance of laundry detergent and fresh air from the clothesline.

And there was always a book in Grandpa Oscar's hand, or inside his head. Sometimes I think that my grandfather has lived too long inside his beloved novels, where he has left behind little pieces of himself. I have a feeling that many of his present-day words and sentences are hiding within the pages of his most convincing books. After all, I know what it's like to get lost—completely, exhilaratingly lost—inside the creation of someone else's imagination. The thought terrifies me every time I shahn, even though I would never give up any of those transporting, transformative experiences. Even the scariest ones.

My grandfather has often boasted that he read bravely, completely open to the possibilities offered by each author. Fittingly, the majority of his books came into the world and faced it boldly, bound in nothing more than solid colors punctuated by a few embossed letters.

Most of the book jackets became torn and faded. Having rested upon the kitchen counter for several weeks straight, *The Ancient Mariner* endured so many puddles and sprays that many of its pages stuck together, its stained binding buckling like an ocean wave. A few of the books slipped into handmade cardboard cases, where their wisdom remained well protected. Some of the books were tall and thin, like the sinewy, six-foot-one-and-a-half-inch man of letters whose name and address was handwritten across the blank page just inside each front cover. Other books were short and squat, like Leah, the lettered man's wife.

Grandpa Oscar's eye problems resulted in a tidier apartment. To make room for more practical considerations, Grandma Leah sold or gave away any books the shelves couldn't hold. A flat surface like the tabletop, once peopled with distinguished voices, now provided a spacious home for the actress with the eyes. Before cataracts, if the young actress had lain there at all, she would have opened herself to the eternal voices of Maimonides, Spinoza, Goethe, Dostoevsky, Gogol, Dickens, Twain, the Brontës, Lewis Carroll, Jane Austen, and a chorus of others who would have congregated long before she was ever purchased at the supermarket check-out. Perhaps she would hear the responsive reading issuing from the pages of the well-worn prayer book, the *siddur*, that Oscar carried with him every Saturday morning to synagogue and never put down, except to take the Torah from the ark and carry it against his chest around the aisles so the congregants could kiss it with the fringes of their *tallit* or the tips of their fingers.

Grandpa Oscar was slated for commerce, not schooling, but that didn't deter him from fulfilling his dreams, as he himself never tired of explaining to me. "My people," he would say, "could afford to send but one of their children to college, so who did they choose?" I always played dumb. "Who do you think they chose? Naturally, they sent their eldest son, Stanley. Tradition. But what did Stanley know from education? Or care about it? I was the studier. *Oy Gotenyu*, how I studied. I carried so many books home, my arms would cramp. Every day. I was the one who helped Stanley with his schooling. So what if he was my senior by a full three years?"

I had heard this story many times while growing up, but lately my grandfather had focused on it more and more often. For emphasis, he tapped his long bony finger forcefully into the palm of my hand.

Grandpa Oscar always referred to Uncle Stanley as a kind boy. "But where is it written that kindness and scholarship must hold hands?" My grandfather described how his brother's mind was always elsewhere, how Stanley liked fiddling with things, how he'd take apart the radio and *potchke* with the wires, always starting these *meshugene* projects he'd never finish. "But do you think he cared for books?"

I shook my head.

"That's right. Not even this much," Grandpa Oscar would contend, positioning his thumb and index finger a hair's width apart, like a child conveying how much spinach his mother should put on his dinner plate. "*I* was the reader. What did Stanley care for books? So who do you think was sent off to college? I want for you to guess. Go ahead. Who do you think?"

I guessed.

"Yes sir. Stanley, may he enjoy the blessings of Paradise, he was the one who was sent to college. Me? What did I do?"

"You cut school and took the subway to The Polo Grounds so you could sit in the bleachers and wolf down hot dogs and watch Willie Mays, the 'Say Hey Kid,' run down fly balls in centerfield." Lately, this had become my response, inevitably provoking my grandfather to release my hand and ask me with a smile, Why did I enjoy twisting an old man's head so much?

"Only kidding, Grandpa," I would say before giving the correct reply: "You didn't *kvetch* about it."

"Nosiree. I never complained." Grandpa Oscar would state as his fingers regained their squeezing intensity. "But wasted money is what it was. My parents threw away their savings on him, the whole *schmeer*, and that is what he let them do. Pure waste."

"So what did I do?" Oscar posed the question proudly.

I knew my lines by heart. He read and studied on his own, and became a lawyer ("a darn good one, I dare say!" he always added proudly) through the sheer will of his motivation. Oscar Bialintz was never so alive as when he relived his youth.

Recounting further details of his past tired the old man, who grew silent and still, until, out loud, he wondered why.

"Why what, Grandpa?"

"Why do you suppose a *yinga maidel* like this should look so sad?" he asked, directing his gaze down toward the magazine before him.

"*Yinga maidel*, Grandpa?"

"A pretty young thing like her. Why do you think?"

I had no idea, but I offered to read the article to him so we could find out together, the old man accepting the offer with the proviso, "But only if you feel like it."

Before I began, I asked my grandfather if he knew who the *yinga maidel* with the sad eyes was.

He smiled. It pleased him to hear me incorporate Yiddish words in my conversations. "Where do you pick up these expressions? What a *bonditt* you are! *A leben ahf dein kepele,*" he said, which was his way of telling me how smart I was. "Yes, she has such sad eyes, doesn't she? Why don't you read for me the story inside the magazine, Big Boy, and we can find out already together from all this sadness."

So I read. It was an article about a young actress who, two years before, had starred in a movie about a Negro man falsely accused of raping a white woman. The movie was filmed from the point of view of the girl pictured on the magazine cover. Neither of us had seen the film.

My grandfather said it sounded like a book he read a few years before. "*To Kill a Bird.* A hummingbird, or something like that."

"You're right, Grandpa. Mockingbird. It says here in the article the movie was based on a book."

When I finished reading the article, I placed the magazine, face up, back onto the table. The cover immediately caught my grandfather's attention. "What sad eyes she has," he said.

"How's that, Grandpa?"

"She has such sad eyes."

"The girl on the cover?"

"Yes. Do you see? I wonder why such a pretty young thing should look so sad."

My grandfather gazed at the magazine cover, then with his finger he caressed the child's forehead, tracing over the letter J that overlapped the girl's hair, which was thick and curly like mine.

"Would you like me to read you about her so we can find out why she's so sad, *Zayde*?"

Grandpa looked at me without answering. His finger remained gently pressed against the girl's hair. "That would be nice. I would read it myself but I've been having trouble with my eyes."

So I read the article aloud, again.

Before cataracts, Grandpa Oscar seldom showed any interest in popular entertainers such as the mockingbird girl. Show business was my grandmother's area. Grandma Leah did not read much: just a magazine article to scan while she sipped her coffee and rested her bunioned feet upon the living room couch. She kept *Moby Dick* on the linoleum floor beneath her kitchen cabinets so she could stand on the back of the great white whale to reach her porcelain bowls on the top shelf.

Although my grandmother might leaf through one of the few books in the apartment containing photographs, Grandpa Oscar believed much of life's magic and mystery was contained in the word. "Words are holy," he would explain to me. "God created the world through the word. 'God *said*: Let there be. . .' and the world came into being—through the power and sanctity of God's word. Christians, they talk about the moment of Christ's conception when the *word* was made flesh, like in that Annunciation painting we looked at, in the book on the hall table—the picture where the archangel Gabriel tells Mary she is carrying the Christ child within her." I winced beneath the sting of my grandfather's rounded fingernail driving home its point as he declared, "Believe you me, there is nothing more powerful than the word. Nothing."

And then came the quote, the oft-repeated quotation that was as much a part of my grandfather as my grandfather's bald head and bony finger:

"When a good man dies, his soul becomes a word and lives in God's book."

The quote came from the pen of a rabbi, Abraham Joshua Heschel, whose writings inspired my grandfather, but I couldn't imagine anyone—not even Heschel himself—believing that statement more deeply, or been more deserving of its message, than Oscar Bialintz. I was convinced of it, as surely as I was convinced that my own soul would never grace a book that could exist as part of God's sacred treasure.

What word would my grandfather someday become? I wondered. And would it be a word I could even recognize? Not likely, since I knew only the language of the living, and surely God's book would consist of configurations buried deep within a sense of awe and mystery that only the dead could fathom.

And how about my father? What had God already inscribed invisibly across his forehead? And Howie, how about him? Was he now, already, one of God's words? I turned to steady myself by looking at the picture hanging on the wall behind me, but the girl just kept falling off her ball.

Aloud, I read the article about the young starlet several more times until I finally laid it face down and slouched into the welcome of the sofa's cushions. Grandpa Oscar's back and neck were straight. His inability to see the photograph of the actress relieved his concern for her. Thereafter we sat and talked until we were called for dinner, my fingers resting securely within the protective embrace of my grandfather's hand, like a book slipped into its case.

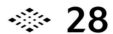 # 28

TO MAKE THE WORLD STRANGE

Lines linked them. Smudges and erasures did too. It wasn't the first time my grandfather posed for Jerry, who had recently surprised his model with a gift. "You want to make him happy, Jerry?" I asked. "Here's what you do: Paint him a portrait of JFK. There's no need to pay him for posing. He likes doing it; he always says so. But if you're set on giving him something. . ."

When Kennedy was assassinated, my grandfather cried, "*A feier zol im trefen!*" and then he further inflamed the fire by adding that, for what he did, Oswald should be like a lamp and hang during the day (for a thousand years), then burn in hell during the night (for even longer)—three firsts: my grandfather cried, wished someone ill, and said "hell" in front of me.

My grandfather was so moved by Jerry's portrait of Kennedy that he immediately found a home for it on his living room wall near his Picasso reproduction of the girl balancing on the ball.

Whenever Jerry needed a subject to draw, Oscar Bialintz was always available. And although my grandfather often repeated himself and sometimes fell asleep in the middle of a conversation, there were periods when his deteriorating mind functioned with precision. And, strangely, even when he lost all recollection of the past few moments, his sixty-, seventy-, even eighty-year-old moments remained fit and trim. This day with Jerry and me was one of Grandpa Oscar's best days in months, although it clearly drained him because shortly after he finished posing, my grandfather fell asleep in his chair and kept right on sleeping through dinnertime and his favorite TV programs. Then he got up and went to bed for the night.

It's your country. Our country. We must unite. We must band together and fight to keep what's ours.

"Make the radio louder, *boychik*. That young man talking about fighting for our country is making an important point."

The speaker's voice was hot and brittle. *"It starts out slow. A law here, a bill there. . . all in the name of equality and education. . . and you don't even realize you are losing your freedoms, freedoms our forefathers fought so hard to win. This is our country. We must protect our rights. . . preserve our values. . ."*

"This fellow knows from what he's talking. Yesiree! And just listen to his passion!"

Freedom, my grandfather was convinced, was the most precious gift a democracy had to offer, not just government freedom, but the personal freedoms individuals allowed themselves. The ability, when necessary, to sweep into the future and leave the past behind, "Like when the Jews said 'Enough already!' to Pharaoh and escaped out of Egypt." My grandfather looked hard at me and added, "We've all got our personal Egypts to throw off." I didn't return his gaze.

"I hate to ask you again, Mr. Bialintz, but could you move your head over a little this way some? Yeah, just like that. Great." The point of Jerry's pencil became a shadow cast by the protruding form of a nose. What was flat was getting rounder by the minute.

"Of course, Jeremy. I'm. . ."

"It's Jerry, Grandpa. Jerry."

He promised to sit still, adding: "You think I want to get fired?"

The shrishing of Jerry's pencil momentarily overlapped the radio's background murmur before disappearing beneath the speaker's impassioned voice.

". . . our way of life. They are robbing our families in New York City, in Newark, robbing us by taking our jobs. We must. . ."

"Too often we take away our own freedoms," Grandpa Oscar continued. "We accept what we are given and assume what we know is all there is."

"How so, Mr. Bialintz?" With the side of his pencil point, Jerry roughed in an ear with a large lobe. Above this area, he worked Oscar's head as if he were drawing a cue ball, rounding the form with shades of gray.

"I'll give you a f'rinstance, Josh."

I didn't correct him.

"Take this portrait. You draw my face in a certain way because that is how you have learned to *see* my face. The trick is to allow yourself the freedom to see it in a way no one ever saw a face before. In *your* way. Adam looking into the face of Eve. Even before that—Adam looking into the face of God!"

"Yes, that is what it is, looking back to that one point everything else is pulled out of. I call it God; you can call it whatever you want. But believe you me, that is where all our looking goes back to. Everything is there. Like Rabbi Rosen liked to say: 'It is all inside God, and God is inside it all.'" Looking at me, he talked about God being not only in the good, but in the bad and the painful too. "Everything part of us, part of life, is part of God," he said. The light in the room glistened off the windows of his glasses. "I am saying this for myself as much as for you, Big Boy. It is easier to say it than to see it."

Returning to Jerry, my grandfather continued, "Like with your pictures. You want to draw a face as you see it *now,* right now, which is different from how you have ever seen or drawn a face before. *Nu?* So how do you do such a thing?"

Jerry remained silent.

"Not an easy one, is it? No sir. How do you get yourself to see the world around you as strangely as possible?"

"Strangely?"

"Sure. Strangely. You want to make the world strange, no? That's one of the things artists do—open up new possibilities, for themselves and all the rest of us."

"What was once yours becomes theirs. Don't wait 'til it's too late! This is our country, not. . ."

My grandfather went on to tell Jerry about the time he was taking his three-year-old grandson for a walk and the child fell in love with a line. The child insisted on taking it home, but the line wasn't going anywhere.

"You want for me to tell you why the line was so stubborn, Jonathan?"

"It's Jerry, Grandpa."

"No, it wasn't Jerry, and it wasn't even a sundial. It was a shadow cast by the trunk of a tree. For seventy years I hadn't looked at a shadow like that. Brand new eyes made it strange for a tired-eyed old man. No better way to see than with the wide-eyed wonder of a child," my grandfather professed. "*Oysh,* how I had to work to explain what a shadow was."

Unwittingly, Jerry looked at the shaded side of Grandpa Oscar's nose. I did too. A cool, reflected tone glazed the area, adding color, dimension. I hadn't noticed the subtle modulations before my grandfather's story.

Jerry assumed I was the one trying to pull the line off the grass, since he didn't know Oscar Bialintz had ever had any other grandsons. But I had heard this story before and knew that my grandfather was remembering Howie, whose name remained unspoken. For me, that was the best part of the story.

Soft, wrinkled fingertips stroked my cheek. "Without strangeness the world would wither and die. Take it from someone who knows from withering." He paused. Then he declared, "I in your years have already been. But you in mine. . . ."

A familiar expression. My grandfather always says it without a hint of condescension. It always fits the moment—well, almost always. *Yich in dina yahren hab shoyn gavein. Ober de in mein.* . . I know it by heart. I know it better in Yiddish than English. My grandfather had said it in English today for Jerry's sake.

With polite fingers placed just below the prominent cheekbones of my grandfather's face, Jerry repositioned him.

My grandfather continued, talking about how the world was chock-full of whisperings that people ignore every minute of every day—himself included. "Little hints from God," is how he put it, "that ought to sound large in our heads—but are seldom heard from."

As if to hear better, Jerry unconsciously leaned forward and got his left earlobe gently pinched by wrinkled fingers. I smiled, grateful for the accepting expression on my friend's face.

"I think I understand, Mr. Bialintz, but does that mean I'll just end up being a copycat if I keep looking at other artists' pictures?"

"No, no, no. What you are doing by looking at other artists is important. Healthy. Enjoy yourself. Look, look all around, especially now, at this point in your life. I like to hear you talk about the artists you favor. You remind me of myself as a young man when I was trying cases in Brooklyn, or even before, when I was studying to be an attorney."

Jerry spread his fingers against his jaw and cracked his knuckles.

"Art and the law are very much alike, you see."

"Art and law? I wouldn't've thought they had a whole lot in common."

"On the contrary," my grandfather countered. "Both the lawyer and the artist," he said, "must make the past live all over again in the present." The "Old Masters" gave Jerry ideas about his own paintings, did they not? And something to strive toward. "That's why ladders were invented," my grandfather quipped. "To remind us to reach."

He was an *alter kocker* now, but that's how it was for him also when he was a young man, Grandpa Oscar explained. If he had a legal brief to prepare, he'd research related cases and take from them precedents that'd help him support the case on which he was working. In that way he would construct something brand new from what had come before. My grandfather wagered it would be the same for Jerry, that Jerry would take what he needed or liked most from each of the artists he studied, and from all of them together fashion something fresh, where "the whole kit and caboodle" would be his. His alone.

Sounded good to Jerry.

"*. . . their children will be stealing the seats in the colleges where your children should be sitting. This is our. . .*"

My grandfather's eyes focused tightly on the doorknob of a closet, all his concentration centered on maintaining the position of his head.

"You can relax your shoulders if you want, Mr. Bialintz."

"Okeydoke."

Jerry's pencil became the gaze of his eyes, which burrowed into the crease formed by the pressing together of Grandpa Oscar's closed lips. The pencil point started on the left side of the crease and proceeded slowly across, carefully describing the bottom of the top lip, then the top of the bottom lip, the edge of the crease being first a result of pressure being applied downward from the upper lip, then upward from the lower part. "That way you really 'feel' the line," Jerry once explained to me. A year ago, the time it took Jerry to draw this line would've been measured in fractions of seconds. Today it took him several long minutes. A good part of what he was learning in his art class involved time, he told me. "How to slow down and look—really look— and really feel what you look at—and it has to do with learning more and more about what to look *for.*"

The voice on the radio grew louder: "*We must establish control. . .*"

"This speaker is more upset than the other one," my grandfather observed, "but he, too, makes a good point."

"It's the same guy, Grandpa. I've just been too lazy to get up and change the station. But go on," I coaxed. "Finish what you were saying about law and order. I mean, law and painting."

"Yes. We were talking about law and painting, weren't we? They are not so very different, are they?"

"*. . . Because if you don't, they will be going scot-free while the victims of their crimes will be left to suffer.*"

"Yes," my grandfather agreed, turning his attention back to the radio. "We must protect ourselves from injustice, just like this man is saying."

"*If you don't, coloreds will be taking over your jobs. Martin Luther Coon talks about freedom, but it's your freedom he wants! Are you going to give*" *that away? We must replace with law and order the anarchy beginning to take over our streets. Rise up against the niggers! We must. . ."*

"Now what is this about 'Martin Luther Coon' and, you should excuse the expression, 'niggers'? Why do they allow people like this to talk such rubbish on the radio? Talk like that. . . hate talk!"

Grandpa Oscar wanted the other man, the four-square one who had something of merit to say, to get back on the radio. "If my grandmother had testicles she would be my grandfather," is what he said in reply when I tried to explain that there was only one man, that the one on the radio now was the exact same one as the other guy. My grandfather wouldn't buy it. At least not the way I meant it. "We're all interrelated," he would insist. "Sure, we all touch; but that doesn't mean the exact same glove fits everyone's hand. God forbid."

Nonetheless, Oscar Bialintz certainly did not think in straight, narrow lines, so all his lines had a way of crossing, like disciplines such as art and law, which, he believed, moved in graceful, coordinated arcs like the vaulted ribs of a Romanesque ceiling. Even parallel lines didn't only *appear* to meet far away at an imagined vanishing point, like the iron rails of train tracks. For him, they actually did meet, eventually. He had a name for it, a name for that place where all lines (everything, really) came together yet were somehow capable of maintaining their distinctions. He called it God.

My grandfather took the past and wove it elegantly into his future. An intricate, hopeful tapestry made of shimmering, holy threads. As for me, weaving a pattern of hope or holiness out of my past was an impossibility. The past had too many frayed threads, and God's fingernail had gotten caught on one of them.

29

JERRY

"**W**here were you the last coupla nights, man, making pictures?"

"Yeah. I been working on a portrait of Stephen's granddad."

"Jesus, Jerry, sometimes I think that car crash fucked up more'n your leg."

Why anyone would choose to stay home on a weekend night—or any night—to paint a picture, was beyond Mike, English, or Felix. Ripping off art supplies for Jerry was their idea of sophistication, their five-finger-discount take on culture.

My mother complained about my new friends having nothing in common with the guys I used to hang out with in Marchwood. "What's-his-name. . . Jerry, your artist friend, yes. That was very nice, that picture he made for Grandma and Grandpa. But those others. . . they're aimless, the lot of them. Train wrecks just waiting to happen. Aren't there other. . ."

When I complained that she hardly even knew them, she said she didn't have to. "They don't have anything going for them," she claimed. "Aren't there any other boys for you at school, any nice Jewish ones for you to pal around with?"

"These are the guys I like. They make me feel. . ."

"Associating with dwarves, Stephen, does not make you a giant."

Although I'd never admit it to her, I understood my mother's concern. My friends in Garrison City weren't scholars, to say the least, nor were they what my parents liked to refer to as "clean cut," or what my grandfather would describe as *haimisch,* which further cleansed the notion of clean cut. But they had gone out of their way to befriend me when I was alone, and I owed them for that. And, mainly, I liked them.

The girls liked them too. Not the smartest girls, but a lot of the best-looking ones.

The outstanding exception to my mother's disapproval was Jerry. Him, she liked.

Jerry was hard to figure. He had more brains and talent than my other friends yet, just like Mike, English, and Felix, lately his conversation included little more than the highs and lows of shooting dope. Why? Was it just his close friendship with English, who was clearly falling in love with the drug? They'd grown up next door to one another. Always friends. What one did, the other did, like feet in a hurry, both dead-set on finding a ditch to fall into just so they could see how deep it was.

And Mike and Felix, they'd all been friends for years. The closeness and loyalty between them was visible. Did heroin just give them something to do? Something dangerous? Did the accident that hospitalized Jerry and killed his brother steer him in his present direction? Was that too easy an explanation? Was there an explanation at all?

I never brought up to my parents anything about Jerry's accident or his brother. They didn't know he ever *had* a brother. I hate to admit it—especially to myself—but for me, on the other hand, Warren's death was probably a good part of what drew me to Jerry.

I heard Mike and English's take on Jerry's car accident, but Jerry had never spoken to me about it. I wanted to hear his version. And I wanted to hear about his brother.

30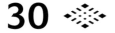

NOAH'S CARARAMA

"**W**hy'd he have to tell me over and over again to make sure his windows were rolled up tight, and to keep the headlights on?" Jerry bitched. "Ten times he must've said it. Twenty! What's he take me for, anyway?" We were driving to Paterson, the two of us, about twenty-five minutes west of Garrison City, on our way to get his father's Studebaker washed and waxed at Noah's Cararama. Bergen County's first car wash. "There'll be a lot more popping up over the next few years," Jerry's father predicted. "Take my word for it. In no time sponges and pails'll be a thing of the past." Again he told us to take his word for it. And not to forget to keep the lights on. "It can get good and dark inside the car wash. Don't worry about draining the battery; you won't be in there long enough."

"After you drive onto the conveyer belt-type thingamajig," he instructed, "turn off your engine, double-check the windows, and then just sit back and relax." He told us we'd feel like we were bone dry inside a washing machine.

Shortly after we left Garrison City, Jerry started telling me about Warren and the accident, and he continued his story pretty much non-stop for the remainder of the drive until, pulling onto the property of the car wash, he jammed on his brakes to avoid a horde of peacocks, zebras, donkeys, camels, and buffalo, all stacked two at a time on top of each other so high I had to stick my head out the window to see the kings of the mountain. Near the bottom of the heap, just above two giant sea turtles, was a pair of pumpkin-colored squirrels with tails longer than our car.

"Noah," Jerry blurted out. "My old man skipped this part."

The ceramic animals were a surprise, but an even bigger one was what Jerry told me upon getting back into the car after pre-paying. He said that it was he, Jerry, who caused the car crash! "I told everybody it was Mishy's idea to turn off the headlights, but I was the one who talked the kid who was driving into doing it." As he detailed what happened, Jerry kept looking around, as if to make sure he couldn't be overheard, even though we were alone, behind closed car doors and windows, half an hour from Garrison City, and almost ten years down the road from his brother's fatal accident. Jerry recounted how he baited Kenny Giaquinto, the driver, and his brother, who was sitting shotgun. "For the whole ride, I don't think I called Giaquinto or Warren by their names even once; it kept being Pussy this and Chickenshit that. Mishy, I left his name alone, cause it was already fucked up on its own." Jerry had heard Warren talking about other kids he knew peeling down Palisades Avenue in the dark, blind, which sounded like fun to Jerry. "My brother kept telling me to shut the fuck up, but then, all of a sudden, it's lights out, and that was it."

"What a waste," Jerry said, as he guided the wheels of his father's car into the grooves of a metal conveyor belt and turned off the engine. "I mean, the fuckin' crash didn't have to happen. But no one there steered it any different. Usually, my brother'd be the one to straighten all the crooked places waiting for me and him. Only not this time."

The calm afternoon was dry, hot, and sunny. Winter was in full unbloom inside the windowless car wash, and animals were all over the place, some painted on two nearby cinder-block walls, others—of the brightly colored, blow-up variety—pouring down and swaying mid-air from the ceiling like El Greco saints and sinners, only fatter. Full of dark clouds, the mural portrayed a fairly realistic rain forest. A tornado of monkey tails, ram and deer horns, camel humps, and donkey backsides streamed across the painting. Behind our rolled-up windows, we were mercifully protected from flying herds of hippos, horses, and lavender elephants propelled by a cyclone of machined weather.

In great detail, Jerry described the physical pain he experienced and his recuperation after his surgeries. "Warren dies," Jerry said. "Doctors tell me I'm never gonna move my left arm again, and I might lose control of my left leg too, which was getting numb. I can still remember thinking that I was never getting outta that bed. . . that I didn't want to, even if I could've."

"Then, while I'm still in the hospital, my old man buys me a rubber ball and tells me to squeeze. He goes, 'All day long, just keep squeezing.'"

As Jerry got to the word "squeeze," it stopped raining inside the cinderblock building, then it started drizzling, then, once again, there was an onslaught of aimed rain. I remember thinking that this must be what fish caught in a hurricane feel like. A lathery roller wider than our car submerged us beneath a pancake of blue-green slime which seemed to magically spin through a color wheel of slurpy surprises before settling on white, as the roller climbed up and over our car. The path it left was so thick the white foam turned the day black. Jerry, oblivious to the surrounding squeals of the machines, kept on with his story. "'Just concentrate on squeezing the ball,' my old man kept saying, 'and we'll beat this paralysis business. We'll get your fingers working first, then your whole hand, then your arm.' I believed him," Jerry told me, adding that he wanted to get better as much for his father as for himself, because Warren couldn't. "Warren was always my old man's favorite. You know, he was the first and all, but now my brother was gone, and I was the only one left. I thought if I recovered, somehow that meant my brother did too. It gave me something to go for. At first I didn't mind—at least I didn't say anything—when my father called me by the wrong name, like when he'd say, 'Don't worry about your leg, Warren. It'll take care of itself once you get your hand moving.' But he's still doing it."

As our Studebaker inched forward, cloth straps hanging from the ceiling whacked our car, washing away most of the lather. Water seeped through the top of the car windows. Then it began leaking through the front windshield. The water was brown, making the inside of the car dirtier than when we first picked it up. Jerry didn't notice.

"Eleven years old, lying in this hospital bed, my arm dead, I'm doing nothing but concentrating all day long on getting it back to life, and half the time my old man can't remember my fuckin' name. At first the ball'd just drop outta my left hand while the fingernails of my other hand would drill into whatever I happened to be holding, or into my palm. Then, after only six days, one of my fingers moved, and then pretty much my whole hand."

I looked down at my fingers, grateful I never had to worry about getting them to do what they should. They knew where to go without me having to draw them a map or even pointing them in the right direction. Then I looked down at my soaking feet and decided to lift them up onto the front seat, as Jerry explained that he was never without the squeeze ball his father had bought him. Even after he regained full control of his left side (it took almost two years), he continued to exercise and strengthen his hand by squeezing that ball—until Felix started calling him "Cojone."

The water coming into the car didn't seem to be bothering Jerry any. Riveted by my friend's account of his recovery, I ignored it too. Jerry went on to explain how, just before his thirteenth birthday, he lost his faith in his powers of concentration and control. He was at a bowling alley where a man competing in an "Over Thirties League" occupied a nearby lane. The man's left arm hung limply at his side while he rolled the ball down the alley with his good arm, his right.

"He was this Oriental guy, my old man's age," Jerry said. "I was only eleven when I took care of the problem with *my* arm, so I couldn't figure out why this guy never bothered to fix *his*. I was convinced it was just a matter of concentration, so I decided to take care of it for him myself. I spent the whole rest of the afternoon aiming all my energy into the guy's bad arm." Jerry jerked his wrist so his hand, palm down, sliced the air. A card dealer out of cards. "Nothing happened. Not Jack shit."

Jerry went back to the bowling alley every week for almost seven months, never saying a word to the partially paralyzed bowler, just watching him, and concentrating. "Big waste of time," Jerry said, shaking his head, "like thinking that me getting unparalyzed would help my father with Warren."

"After the league ends, I never lay eyes on the guy again." Then he added, "Total waste. . . except I learned you can't make some things happen. . . or unhappen. Some things are just some things."

Jerry finally noticed that something was happening inside his father's car, kind of a slow-motion easing into the situation that, with no in-between, abruptly shifted into high gear. "My old man's gonna kill me!" he screamed. "He's gonna fuckin' kill me!"

That's when we both noticed how dark it had gotten again, only this time it had nothing to do with thick suds covering our windows. The darkness was accompanied by silence. Sudden silence. Or maybe not so sudden; I hadn't noticed when it first got quiet.

When the water machines started running again, we soon realized that the guide rails we were on weren't moving. Brushes, rollers, straps, and sprays whirred, then, even behind the closed car windows, the whirring became thunderous. The water stopped coming in, but the machines got even louder. For about five minutes we sat shouting to each other, waiting for our car to move. While we waited, Jerry lit a cigarette, which provided a puny light, and finally, with no coaxing from me, decided to resume his story.

To keep him occupied while at home, recuperating, his mother bought him a box of art supplies. It turned out that the woman who was so good with lettuce and all things green, was just as good with pigments and sketchbooks. Almost immediately, brushes and colored pencils replaced baseballs and his brother Warren's hot rods as the primary objects of his attention. Despite his shouting so I could hear him, I noted the lack of emotion in Jerry's voice when he referred to his brother's hot rods and their diminishing influence.

"I hope you don't mind my asking, Jerry, but how long did it take you to be able to talk about him? I mean. . ."

He cut me off. "I still have dreams about him sometimes. Lousy ones. And the car crash, that too; not as much as I used to, but more than I want. I've had a long time to live with it," he reflected, "and I guess it's gotten easier over the years. I mean, what'd'ya want me to say? I wish it didn't happen, but it did. I wish Giaquinto knew better than to listen to a dumb-ass eleven-year-old, but he didn't. He was stupid. Stupider than me, even."

"I could do all the wishing in the world, and I'm still not going to paint the Sistine Chapel. It's too high a reach." Then, softly, "Only why did it have to be me who made this particular thing happen?"

I didn't know what to say, and Jerry had chosen to remain silent under the roar of the moaning machines. Ten, fifteen minutes passed. As a distraction from the awkwardness that filled the inside of our car, I checked my back pocket; David and Goliath were dry and undamaged.

We still hadn't moved. Water started seeping in again. We'd waited long enough. There was no choice but to leave the car behind and make our pitch-black, soaked, soapy, eye-and-tongue-burning, ear-splitting, waxed way out.

We got shampooed all over. And worse. The water jets waiting for us like a firing squad, left marks underneath our clothes. The crappy taste of detergent stung our throats, Carnauba Car Wax burned our noses and clogged our ears, as both of us felt our legs fly over our heads. We slithered and stumbled across sudsy manta rays and octopuses, staggered into rollers, metal nozzles, spinning disks, hanging straps, walls, orange, blue, black, purple blow-up animals, and each other until we spotted overhead a deflating, ass-trumpeting donkey propelling its plastic way backwards out Noah Cararama's primeval animal preserve. The donkey died before reaching the afternoon light, but Jerry and I made it. As we stepped onto the dry, quiet parking lot of the car wash, Jerry pulled a plastic peacock feather from his hair. Where was the owner? Jerry wanted to know.

Noah was on vacation, we learned, sailing. Jerry told the cashier, the only person we could find who seemed to be in charge of anything, to go fuck himself when the guy offered nothing more than, "I guess we've still got a few kinks to work out." Beyond that, he was too busy to hear our complaints.

Jerry wanted a towel.

And his money back. And for anything he could blow his nose into.

But mainly, he wanted someone—*anyone!*—to tell him who came up with this lame-brain wet dream of a way to clean a car. "I mean, what the hell's wrong with a simple sponge and pail, anyway?"

Noah, the fuck, could fuckin' go fuck himself and every fuckin' thing that fuckin' crawled, for all Jerry cared. So could the cashier.

"My old man's gonna kill me!" he kept ranting. "Take my word for it. He's gonna wring me out to dry!"

He was right. I mean, what the fuck, his father told him ten times to roll up the windows. And twenty times: "Keep your headlights on, Warren."

Part VI

PICTURES AND POEMS III

31 ◆

WITHIN THE IMAGE

"**W**hy not?"

"Because I have chores to take care of, that's why," the hooded lady answered. "And you're going to get all wet and muddy if you don't take your hand away from the flowers in this window box. Be careful! Please! And watch where you're stepping! The tulips look bad enough right now without you trampling them to death. I'm sorry, I simply have too many things to do here in the house than to take a stroll with the likes of you, you wanting to stop and guzzle at every tavern we pass, leaving me waiting outside like a cocker spaniel 'til your stomach's so ale-bloated you have no other choice but to urinate against the bricks of some building, all the while thinking you're doing your honey-pie spaniel a great big favor by promenading alongside her through the streets of Delft."

"Jeesh. A simple 'no' would have been just fine. You don't have to be so snippy about it. I was just asking. And when was the last time you saw me guzzle, or urinate against a brick wall?" I asked, trying to ignore her reference to urination as I cleaned off my tulip-muddied hand by wiping it against my trousers. "Can I at least come in for a few minutes so we can talk? We hardly ever talk anymore."

"Cute, Stephen."

"Thanks. So, can I come in? For a minute? What's a couple a minutes?"

"Well. . . all right. I guess it'd be okay. But remember, just to talk."

"Why, my dear hooded lady, please! You are my teacher. What did you think I had in mind?"

She smiled and invited me into the corner of the room where her Dutch master had painted her into place three centuries ago.

"Not such an alone painting any more, is it?" I asked, slipping further out of character.

For the past three Saturdays, Diane and I met in New York City in front of Vermeer's painting and improvised. Diane assumed the voice of the youthful, three hundred-year-old Dutch maiden whose left hand was forever destined to clench the silver water jug, and whose right hand fingered a slightly opened, lead-glass window. What the Dutch maiden saw outside the window changed each week. I assumed many roles. Several each week. I was an offstage student, truant officer, confidant, villain, lover. Next Saturday I was going to be a document repairman who had to come to mend a tear in the parchment map.

Diane and I never rehearsed. We savored the surprises.

"There, now let me remove this mantle so I can see your shiny black hair," I said, climbing in through a lead-glass window. "Ah, so smooth, and just look how it shimmers in the light. Did you just wash it? It's so beauti. . ."

"What do you mean, did I wash it?" Diane said. "Of course I washed it! I wash my hair every day!"

"I just meant. . ."

"And anyway, you know, you could have come in through the door." She was annoyed she had to move her arm to make way for the formerly unseen man. She had not moved her arm for. . . ever, and had understandably grown attached to the position.

"That's why they make doorknobs."

"Yes, well, do you mind if I ask you something?"

She didn't mind.

"Your hair is beautiful, yet. . ."

"Probably because I just washed it."

"It is beautiful, yet you hardly ever let anyone see it. How come? The way that mantle covers your head, you look bald."

Composing herself, Diane's right hand lightly touched the imaginary mantle that I was now holding. She placed her other hand against her forehead and slowly ran it back over her head. "It's the style. I don't know. No one ever asked me that before. My mother and grandmother believe it's unseemly to be seen with an uncovered head."

"So you always do what others do? What if they shaved their heads, would you shave yours too?"

The woman's fingers moved from her mantle to the silver belly of the pitcher sitting on the table before her. She rubbed the basin beneath, then she gripped the pitcher handle. The fingers of her other hand smoothed the pleats of her billowing, blue skirt. After centuries of touching nothing but wood, the texture of cloth must've felt good against her fingertips.

"Never." She paused, then added, "Because I know how much you like my hair." Her eyes fixed on the red and blue patterned cloth covering the table. "I like the way you look at my hair." Then she paused again and added, "And I like that you want to touch it."

32 ◈

KISS

"I want to touch you right now, Diane."

Diane looked outside our painting to see if anyone else heard what I'd said. The dozing woman in the painted room hanging nearby was fast asleep. A lute player, distracted, strummed the strings of her lute. Brouwer's tavern was closed for repairs and renovations.

For four weeks Diane and I had not touched; we hadn't even held hands when we ran across the busy streets of New York City. We were together every day, all day on the weekends, which never lasted long enough. We laughed and held our noses as we tried futilely to wipe up Diane's Shalimar perfume that opened inside the glove compartment of her car. Sometimes we excited each other by the lively seriousness of our conversations, an experience new for both of us with someone so close in age. We met only seven months ago, yet neither of us had ever enjoyed such a complete friendship.

"I want to touch you."

"Stay in character, Stephen."

"I'm trying."

Diane placed my fingers against her hair. A sable-brushed hand, just learning to appreciate silver vessels and the comforting texture of cloth, stroked the back of my hand and then my wrist. Flesh. Warm, youthful, soft flesh.

My fingers buried themselves in the blackness of Diane's hair. I could smell the lingering residue of shampoo and the scent of the lipstick that barely coated her lips. I stroked the back of her head. The solidity of her skull against my fingertips surprised me. Before, it was all so unreal. Her hair weighed less than pollen. We looked at each other intensely—or maybe it was just about time, our eye contact lingering the slightest bit longer than either of us expected—and I leaned toward her.

Diane's eyes darted away from mine, as the quarrel of a middle-aged couple standing about twenty feet away threatened to smear the moment as if it were a wet painting. So often we would avoid letting our eyes lock, something always making one of us look away at that very moment when what I was hoping for between us seemed like it was just about to happen. When her eyes returned to me, she said softly, "Wait a minute. I thought you were going to come in just to talk. I thought we were just going to talk."

Talk. Yeah, talk, we were great at that; that was easy for us. The tough part, for me at least, was keeping my hands, my lips, and every other big and small part of me off her. For seven months, every time I looked at Diane my eyes were my fingers. I looked at her from further inside myself, my whole self, than I had ever looked at anyone before in my life, not only taking in as much as I could and hoping that if I looked at her hard enough when we were together I would remember the details of her when we were apart, but imagining more, much more, imagining touching and holding her—what I craved more than anything—the trickiest part having to do with trying to look cool while I was burning up. I wanted to caress every inch—*any inch*—of Diane's body, but I didn't. I was afraid.

"No yeah, I was. I mean, we were. I don't know. . . I got distracted—and you did too, I think. Anyhow, we talk a lot. Don't. . . don't you think?" I asked, flip-flopping between man and boy, and there and here, and real and not, and confident and scared—scared that I might screw us up. I mean, she was my teacher, sort of. Smart. Great looking. Everything. Who was I, compared to her? Sure, I wanted more, but I loved what we had, and I didn't want to lose any of it.

"Yes. We do," she said, tugging on one of the buttons of my shirt to guide me toward her. I guess I should've gotten lost inside the moment, but I suddenly became self-conscious, or more to the point, I became conscious of the pressure bulging inside me that was furiously jamming its head against my zipper.

I would've liked to relax and enjoy the kiss—smell her cheek and hair, savor the peculiar taste of lipstick and the softness of her mouth. But, inevitably, whenever I kiss a girl for the first time, I'm too busy. Too busy thinking. Once again I found myself yielding to the inevitable. I had developed my own technique, taken mostly from what I had seen on the big screen at the Oritani Theater in Hackensack, or the Palace in Garrison City. I wondered whether Diane had seen any of the same films I had, whether there was much difference between a high-school and a college kiss, whether Baltimore girls did it the same as Jersey ones, whether my breath smelled, whether I should use my tongue; I wondered if Diane knew what was happening down by my zipper. There wasn't a moment's break in the "whethers", the "wonders", the "*ifs*".

And then, of course, there were the pictures. El Greco, Vermeer, Goya. . . sacred, serene, and sexy paintings hanging cock-eyed in empty spaces, banged against my thoughts. I thought for a moment about trying to take advantage of my shahning skill to make the kiss more special, but I decided to hold off. Who knew where that might lead?

About halfway through our kiss I added a mental notch on a tally that, before this very moment, would have lined up last against my friends. Before this very moment, that is. Diane could put me at the head of the line and win me bragging rights, if I wanted. She was a great kisser. She was gorgeous. She'd been driving for three full years, for chrissakes! But I knew I could never mention any of this to anyone. I wouldn't want to—Diane was too special.

Too bad. Mike would've loved it.

The Youthful David placed his slingshot on the ground and looked away. A strongman sitting on a box turned his head toward me, winked, and then disappeared, as a girl balancing on a great big ball slowly closed her eyes and thrust her hips in my direction before she drifted sensually out of sight. The tired tulips in the boxes hanging outside the window of Vermeer's maiden lifted their petals toward the sun.

Then everything disappeared except Diane's lips against mine.

"Finally," I thought to myself, or maybe I said it out loud.

"It's about time," she whispered.

February 28, 1966

WHISPERINGS

Head cocked, the marionette waits, anxious
to make proud she who brings him to life.
Then, beneath a rain of lines, staged high above the ground, the dummy
    dances.

As rhythms of a sawdust song
seep through the wooden veins of dangling arms and legs, music takes the
    string puller prisoner.

Intoxicated by her date's sway,
her body shakes with the strains of her ten-fingered ballet.
Swans and lakes and nutcracker suites
redden the palms of her hands.

Of course every symphony has a final note, sometimes before
it is ever played. Marionette strings must untangle
for tomorrow's show. But first, one last tongue
and fingertip exchange; as their heads draw near,
they whisper to each other in chorus:
    "I love the way you pull my strings."

—Stephen Schaech—

❖ 33

DEADEYE, THE WEATHERMAN

Over the next three months, while we were secretly seeing each other, I said very little to Diane about my father and my Garrison City friends. I felt that even their names threatened the fragile bond she and I had formed. She felt right to me; my friends didn't anymore.

Right. What an understatement. Perfect was more like it! Nothing ever felt so right to me before: the way she spoke to me and inspired me to speak to her, the way she understood and accepted me, the way she taught me (inside and outside the classroom) about the world, the way we were together.

Yes, she felt right in every way, so smooth and perfectly right. Diane's breasts, at first cool beneath my palms, would instantly warm to my touch the few chances we got to be alone together. Her arms and back, too; it made me feel powerful having such control over her body heat. She called me her weatherman. And her nipples, at first soft and bendable beneath my fingertips and tongue, would stand at attention the minute I started stroking them. I had to keep myself from laughing the first time I noticed this, which I'm really glad I did, since laughing would've given away how stupid and inexperienced I was and certainly would've destroyed the mood. Sure enough, it did turn out to be a major mood killer the one time I let myself kid her about it, after I had grown more confident with her. I know I should've waited 'til we were finished before I brought it up, but it got the better of me. "That's just what happens when a girl gets excited," she informed me.

"Oh."

I thought it was magic or a special talent of hers (or mine). There was so much I didn't know that she did. Although we didn't go all the way, Diane brought out skills in me within weeks that would've taken me years to develop without her guidance, although I always got the feeling that she was learning along with me.

She never kidded about the part of *me* that saluted *her* advances, and how quickly it did, or how often, and how hard it was for me to get it to resume its at-ease position. Talk about power and control. The smell of her hair was enough to make things happen. Hell, all she had to do was say my name in her special way, and it was a done deal. "Stee-phen-Schaech." Diane was the sexiest drill sergeant in the history of the unarmed forces. Stee-phen-Schaech. A-TTen-Tion! Front-and-

Center! Three was quickly becoming my lucky number. Thankfully, Diane was too classy to ever bring any of that up out loud.

NO, no question about it, Diane felt right to me in every way.

Meanwhile, my friends were beginning to feel more and more wrong.

And then there was David.

The Youthful David, my accomplice in executing my father's demise, he was another story yet. I wasn't sure about him. I never brought his name up with Diane, but I saw him regularly.

He also brought out skills in me within weeks that should've taken years to develop, although altogether different ones than Diane exposed. One time, for example, shortly after we started working together, David and I were walking in the desert when a rabbit bolted from behind a rock like a fugitive. Without hesitation, I swooped up a stone and launched it from my slingshot with such force that it ripped through the animal's chest cavity and embedded itself in the trunk of a nearby tree, splattering blood, bits of bone, and fur across a cluster of shiny green leaves. David looked at me. "Excuse me for taking the Lord's name in vain," he said, "but Goddamn, you're getting good!" Having a master slayer on my side was paying off.

Despite our museum improvisations, with Diane there was always one constant: I remained physically inside myself and outside the pictures, only allowing my imagination to enter them. On the other hand, with *The Youthful David*, I was always outside myself and inside the painting.

He was my teacher, and I was developing a special bond with him. Most people, if you ask them not to do something, they do it twice as much, thinking it's funny. Like Felix calling Ryan Sugar "Booger." "Booger Sugar." David once called me Shawn because of my ability to shahn. I asked him not to call me that, so he never did it again, which impressed me. Everything about him impressed me—except his refusal to leave the land of his ancestors and face my father in Garrison City. To be *there* for me. David was resolute: "Find a way to lure your father into my world, and bury him here, Stephen, or find another partner." Period.

Over the past few weeks my entrances and exits in and out of David's world were becoming surprisingly fluid. At home in my bedroom, I made a slingshot and practiced with it in the woods near my grandparents' apartment. There, I couldn't always count on hitting my target. But standing beside David, Goliath's head at our feet, I was deadly.

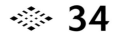 # 34

PARKS

Diane and I spent one spring afternoon walking amidst trees at Van Saun Park in Paramus. We considered going to Palisades Amusement Park—she had never been before—to see the new fun house that replaced the one destroyed by fire two summers before. "Even if it's closed, we ought to go there. It's got this moby saltwater pool. I bet it's the biggest one in the world," I bragged. "You can't live up here in Jersey, ten minutes from Fort Lee and Cliffside Park, Diane, and never go." But she was afraid of running into people we might know. She was afraid they'd have something to say if they saw us together outside of school.

We went to Van Saun Park instead. Our first conversation there focused on Diane's family. Her parents weren't religious, she told me ("observant" was the word she used), but they had insisted that Diane get bat mitzvahed when she was thirteen. She didn't get much out of it at the time, but she was glad they made her go through with it. "I'm pretty sure I'll do the same if I ever have a daughter," she said.

I never dated a Jewish girl before. Not many to choose from in Marchwood or Garrison City. Likewise, I was a first for Diane, who told me how her parents and rabbi pushed back the date of her bat mitzvah and accelerated her sister Avril's Hebrew studies so that, even though she and Avril were born fourteen months apart, they could celebrate the occasion on the same day.

"In my family, we never let time get in the way— *supposed-to* time, anyway. You know, like this is *supposed to* happen now, and that's *supposed to* happen then." Her parents never bought into things like that. Their marriage itself went against the grain of time. "My mother is six years older than my dad," she said. "He teases her about it all the time. Calls her 'Grandma.'"

"Imagine that," I taunted. "A young stud, and somehow he gets hooked up with an old lady. Wonder what he saw in her."

Diane's response was a playful punch. I told her she hit pretty good for an old bag.

"'Old bag', huh?" she laughed. Then a trace of doubt coated her smile, and she unexpectedly stopped laughing. I knew what she was thinking about, but I had no intention of encouraging a conversation that might cloud our sunlit afternoon. "At least no one's going to call me a Lolita," she said. "I guess that's something."

"Me maybe," I said, "not you. I guess I'm the Lolita, or Lolito, in this duo—sort of."

"Thanks a lot, Stephen. That makes me feel much better. If you're the Lolita, what does that make me?"

"An old bag?"

Ignoring my sarcasm, slowly, curling her lips with great care around each syllable, she caressed the name that'd stuck in her head: Lo-Li-Ta. *My sin, my soul*, she said, reciting (she later explained to me) one of her favorite parts of the book, the very opening, where Humbert Humbert talks about the lyrical, seductive nature of his young lover's name and how its sound steps down in three tongue beats from the roof of the mouth to the back of the teeth. "Stee-phen-Schaech," Diane said, tantalizingly. My name never sounded so good. On her lips I made my mouth water, or at least my name did. "It starts behind the teeth, moves to the lips, and goes down the throat," she said.

Sexy syllables. No one could make the letters and words in a book come alive like Diane. Most people *read* written words. She *tasted* them.

Diane called my attention to several broken headstones poking through a patch of tall weeds near where we were walking. I had been to this park half a dozen times before without ever noticing them. "I learned to read when I was four," she said. "In a cemetery."

Diane described the graveyard, which was located near her home in Maryland. Her mother's parents and an aunt were buried there. It was one of her mom's favorite places, and it became one of Diane's favorites too. Her park. There were all different types of birds there, she told me, and every kind of tree. When the wind blew, she said, it was like a choir singing—from all the different kinds of leaves rustling.

"Yeah, trees," I said. "But what about the death part? When the wind blew against all those slabs of stone, I bet there wasn't any music."

Diane said she never thought of it as a sad place. Or morbid. Just peaceful and full of stories. She used to walk through the paths there with her mother and sister, and Diane would sound out the names on the headstones. She said she could literally feel every letter through her fingertips.

"But what if it snowed," I said. That stopped Diane. "Then all the letters'd get covered up. Everything'd be gone. Even the words. It'd be like death twice."

"Sure, sometimes the letters would get snowed over. But after the snow melted it'd be like the letters had been reborn. I'd just have to go back a different day to see them, to feel them against my flesh."

"My mother made it all real," Diane continued. "Even the people buried there. My mother would tell me about the ones she knew or had heard of, and she made up stories about the others. Each name had a history. Real husbands and wives, and parents, and grandparents."

"And children," I added.

"Yeah, children too, sure."

"And you didn't find that sad?"

Diane shook her head. "My mother just made it all seem like a natural, peaceful part of life. That's where I learned to read."

"A happy cemetery. That's one for the books," I said. "Think I'll stay out of *that* library."

"My mother flipped pillows," Diane said as she hopped off the rock we'd been sitting on and brushed off her skirt. "Growing up, if I was sick in bed, she'd come into my room just to turn my pillow at the exact right moment to cool off the back of my neck." Turning to walk down one of the park's stone paths, Diane added, "Kind of like the way you all the time seem to know what I need, even before I do."

Diane straddled a tree that'd fallen near our path. Her feet didn't reach the ground. I sat facing her on a branch projecting from the trunk, my mind savoring Diane's last comment until my gaze distracted me by following a long, sharp hill visible behind her shoulder. I unexpectedly saw myself sliding down the incline. Snow or no snow, for me, slopes always arouse the icy thrill of laying face down on Howie's back, sledding. I always rate every significant slope I see based on its sleighride potential—and my inner rater is always five years old. Until now. Suddenly I was sixteen years old, whipping down a snow-covered hill, Diane on her back with me on top of her, neither of us worried where we were headed.

"I don't care who you could think of, no one's mother could possibly know her daughter better than my mother knows me." Then she added, "except maybe about shaving my legs."

Her comment let me openly look at Diane's stockinged legs. Besides her face, it was my favorite part of her body. Although I looked at them a lot, I usually sneaked my looks. Around Diane I was almost always horny, but I didn't like to show it. She didn't move away when my fingers grazed her ankle, nor when the palm of my hand settled upon her calf.

"My mother's legs were naturally hairless. She thought they stayed smooth because she never shaved them, so in junior high, when I became super self-conscious about the hair on my legs, she insisted I ignore it, claiming once I started shaving my legs my hair would get thicker and grow faster, and then I wouldn't have any choice. She didn't say 'no' to me all that much; so when she did say it, I felt like I had to go along with her. 'Whenever you can say yes, say yes' was one of her main principles for childrearing."

Not a bad thing to believe in out of all the choices available, I thought to myself. A soft, cool pillow of a mother.

"Anyway," Diane continued, "even though it'll probably sound dumb to you to hear how uptight I was about it, I can remember a whole year of dreading school just because of my legs. I used to wear knee socks even though I knew they were way out of style. I wore them up to here," she said, motioning just above my hand. "I had dark hair, so I felt like a gorilla."

I couldn't take my eyes off Diane's legs. How could they ever be anything but a cause for pride? She had a tiny beauty mark on her calf no bigger than the dot of a pencil point. I wanted like hell to kiss it, but I just touched it instead. She didn't move my hand away when I slid it up to her thigh.

35

TRAINS

Diane must've talked for an hour or more about her family. She told me about her father's objections to her enrolling full time at the Maryland Institute, the art school in Baltimore where she'd taken summer classes for years. She said he didn't mind her going there for occasional courses when she was in junior high, or even high school, but he'd be damned if he was going to spend his savings so she could hang out with a bunch of social misfits and learn what wouldn't amount to anything useful for her later in life. He was convinced she wouldn't have any way of making money later on if, as a college student, she majored in art. Whatever Diane said made no difference.

Diane's face reshaped itself in anger. "He always thinks he knows what's best for everyone. My mother couldn't do anything about art school for me. She tried, but he was just too set against it. Besides, she went to Goucher College when she was my age. She didn't get a degree, but she took courses there off and on for a couple of years. My father brags about how he barely finished high school. He thinks my mother is Madame Curie—not that he'd know who Madame Curie was. He figures if Goucher was good enough for my mother. . ." Diane fidgeted with her earlobe, then she added, "The oddest thing is that I know my father loves looking at my paintings. As much as anyone. More, even."

"And it's not as if he doesn't put stock in creating things himself. He can work for hours in our basement on this huge train set he keeps up all year round. Always adding to it. Working on his trains is the one thing Avril and I like to do with him. At least we used to when we were little."

"He was great with the electrical parts. I loved designing the scenery. I'd help him with the tunnels and roads and things we'd set up on the board around the tracks. It fills almost our whole basement. Hundreds of trees, some bridges, fields, a playground with a swing set; we even made a fake baseball field. And then there's this little gatehouse with a man in a blue uniform who slides out from behind a red door every time the train goes by. . ."

"And shines his lantern," I interrupted. "I know the house! Well, it's not a house really, it's more like a plastic shed with white walls and a red roof, right?"

"On a green metal base."

"With a railroad crossing sign," I added, "and the guy inside the shed's got a lantern in his hand. My brother and I had one just like yours! It was my favorite part of our trains."

"Your brother? I thought you were an only child. You never mentioned having a brother. How about sisters? Any of them hanging around the house?" She laughed.

I didn't.

Why'd I have to go and bring up Howie to Diane? Besides my family, no one in Garrison City knew I'd ever had a brother. Not even Jerry.

"Older or younger," Diane asked.

I pulled a craggy piece of bark from the branch beneath me. "Three years older. He was the same age as you."

"Was?"

My face or the "was" must've told her to leave it alone. Anyway, she didn't ask any more questions.

A passengerless park train with kiddie railroad cars chugged past us. The locomotive had moose ears and steam whistling out its dozen antler openings. The train looked lonesome, but at least it was keeping itself busy.

I ripped another sliver off a piece of bark, rolled it between my fingers, and pressed it beneath my thumbnail. "What other kinds of buildings does your father have set up around his trains?" I asked. Change doesn't come easy for me except where subjects in the middle of conversations are concerned.

"Gas stations, banks, churches, all different kinds," Diane replied, accepting my sudden redirection, but just like for me, apparently, the gatehouse was always her favorite, and her dad's too. "He even made a life-sized model of the front of it, with the red door and all. It leans against one of the walls in their basement. Everything else he made is train-set scale," she pointed out. "He carved these little deer and placed them near rocks that he called boulders and he made *thousands* of fake trees. Oh yeah, and *millions* of colored leaves. They're fake, but I swear, when you walk downstairs the room glows, and you can smell autumn, my father's favorite season. He'll sit upstairs watching *Jack Parr* on TV, and all the time his hands are busy shaping these eensy leaves to cover the ground around his train tracks."

Every Van Saun Park leaf suddenly looked huge. It was a warm day for February, so why were the paths we were following covered with leaves of such intense autumn-yellow that it looked like the sun had exploded beneath our feet?

Diane started telling me that her father also created a small cemetery sprawled out between two of his railroad crossing posts, but she stopped herself, perhaps remembering my past-tense reference to Howie. Instead, she said something about toy trains usually winding around Christmas and snow, which had nothing to do with her dad's setup.

"He's not the easiest guy to get along with, but if I was downstairs with him it was different. Even if I'd break something, it wouldn't matter. Downstairs he's a pussycat. It's the only time he'll listen to what you have to say. Like one time when my sister had gotten into some trouble, I remember my mother didn't tell him about it 'til he was working on his trains, even though it meant waiting for hours after he got home from work and making believe she had just found out what had happened."

"Not that you could be in the basement with him any time you wanted. I mean, like if he was alone watching his trains run, or fixing one of his transformers, and he happened to be mad about something, he'd call me over to the stairwell and I'd have to stay at the top, and he'd yell at me from down there, and that'd be it for the day. There'd be no way he'd let me work with him after that. Even now when I'm home, if I know he's in a bad mood because I see he's eating his crackers—he eats crackers when he gets mad—I try to sneak down into the basement while he's busy adding ballast or spreading leaves around the baseball field or something, 'cause I know I'm okay once I've bridged the stairwell between us. If I ever have anything important to talk to him about, I do it around the trains."

"Ever try talking to him about art school while he's in the basement?"

"Sure. Plenty. But it's always the same with him, no matter where the subject comes up. I've always hated him for that. Me in art school is the only topic that consistently trips on the stairs."

"I love painting more than anything, more even than teaching. But that doesn't make any difference with my dad. I tried explaining that if I want to be a good art teacher, first I have to be an artist. You can't teach what you don't know or what you don't do yourself. I've tried to tell him how I know I'll always make paintings, but how even if I couldn't make money that way when I got out of school, or if I didn't teach, I could do lots of other things with a good art training that I could make a living out of. . . you know, like painting murals, or being an illustrator for magazines, or designing clothes or store-front windows, or working in a gallery or museum—I could do a million things to make money if he would just let me go to art school and study what I love."

"And?"

"And he'd say, 'Yeah, like you could be a waitress, for example, so you could support your habit,' as if waitressing would be the worst thing in the world. To him, my art's just a hobby, or a habit. He's never heard a thing I've said about any of it."

Diane paused and then added, "If my grandfather was still alive I bet he could've gotten my father to listen to me. My father never heard a thing his own father had to say, but he was all ears with my mother's dad."

"It's not like that with my father at all," I told her. "His dad died before I was born, so I don't know about him, but he doesn't get along with my mom's father too well."

"I can't imagine anyone not getting along with your grandfather, Stephen. Not the way you talk about him."

"It's not like they argue or anything, they just don't have much to say to each other. I don't think my grandfather ever felt like my father was good enough for my mother, you know, his only daughter and all. And my grandfather probably always knew he was a lot smarter than my dad, and I could tell that he thought my mother was too. My father was always the type of guy intimidated by books and talking, you know, serious kinds of talking—the type of stuff my granddad lives for. And on top of all that, my father doesn't have any patience for religion. I don't think he even believes in God. I mean, I've never heard him talk about it or anything, but you know how deeply my grandfather believes. I've told you how much it bothers him if he ever misses going to *shul* even one Saturday morning, right?"

Diane nodded.

"Well, my father's just the opposite. I can remember how it bothered him when he had to attend my cousin Minda's bat mitzvah service years ago. He made a huge deal about it–huge for him, anyway, since he never gets excited about anything, good or bad."

"Funny thing is, even though they don't seem to have anything in common, something happened a couple of years ago, and ever since then my father and grandfather have had a lot more to say to each other than they used to. Given what happened, I'd've thought they'd be talking less, although given how kind and forgiving my grandfather can be and all, I guess I shouldn't be so surprised. I could never be as big as him about certain things. I don't think I'd ever really want to be either, to tell you the truth. I think sometimes compassion can get in the way of how you really feel."

Diane waited for me to continue, but she soon realized that I had said as much as I was going to. I liked that she didn't ask me what I was talking about. Maybe patience and respecting other peoples' privacy comes with extra years, or at least being older than the person you're talking to. All I know is most girls would've pressed me right then and there to find out what had happened. Not Diane.

So far, I couldn't find a single thing I didn't like about her.

We started walking again, hand in hand. Following a path bordered by a dense grove of pine trees, we came upon the kiddie train, stationary this time. Although the seats were designed for five-year-old passengers, Diane and I squeezed in, almost. Immediately, the wheels started rolling. From inside the train, the park looked out-of-whack.

"It used to be my father hardly ever spoke and I hardly ever saw him," I said, ignoring the antler steam. "This last year he's talking. I don't really like to talk to him all that much, but if I wanted to I could now. Before, I couldn't."

"What do you think made him change, Stephen?"

"I don't much care. After being one way all his life, I don't want to hear what he's got to say now that he's finally decided he wants to be some way else. I wish I could get him back for how he used to be with me and my brother, and for other things too. Some day I will."

36 ❖

TARRED AND FEATHERED

I don't think Diane appreciated how serious I was about paying my father back for what he did to Howie. Or what degree of payback I had in mind. I'm glad she didn't.

"I got *my* father back once," she said. "Right after we had a scream-ing match one time about me going to art school. After he went to bed I went downstairs and tarred all his train trees onto this big windowsill we have in the basement. Not just the sill, all around the window too, and then out onto the wall 'til I ran out of trees. And I took this tun-nel he liked, one we built together when I was about eight or nine, and I tarred it to a ceiling tile above the train set."

"Tarred, you mean like roofing tar?"

"There was a big can of it in the basement. Thick, gooey stuff. Black. I hated the smell, but it worked." She made a face, as if distracted by the stench of memory. "So you know what happened when he saw what I did? Nothing. He threw out the ceiling tile and the tunnel, and just went upstairs with a box of crackers, turned on *The Jack Parr Show*, and started making more trees. Never said a word about it to me. Not a word. We still have an empty square where the ceiling tile used to be."

"What about the windowsill? When the wind blew, were there all different voices—like a choir singing—from all the different kinds of leaves?"

"Very funny, Stephen. No, it wasn't like the cemetery. At least I never thought about it that way. But it's odd you bring that up. The trees are still there. He never touched them. He calls it the Adamsohn Garden. Claims it's full of dead trees that are going to live on forever." Diane straightened her back, trying in vain to get comfortable. My knees hurt from being jammed against the back of the seat in front of me. The undersized kiddie train taking us around the park seemed to be shrinking by the minute.

Diane's story brought to mind a recent conversation I'd had with my grandfather about something he'd read by Rabbi Abraham Joshua Heschel. One line in particular impressed me, and I quoted it to Diane.

"'The deeds people do,' Heschel says, 'are used by God as seeds for the planting of trees in the Garden of Eden.' Something like that. I don't remember it exactly."

"This deed," Diane corrected, "wasn't so much planted as glued. Tarred."

"Heschel was writing about how people end up creating their own gardens through the things they do."

"And your point is?"

I didn't realize how judgmental I sounded until I heard the annoy-ance in her voice.

"Never mind," I said, getting up from my cramped quarters to perch on the top of the wooden seat back and let my legs rest on the arms of the chair. "It was just a stupid train of thought." I had intended the pun, thinking it might get me off the hook, but it didn't work.

"Don't give me that," she complained. "What's your point, Stephen?"

I wasn't sure. Probably I had wanted to impress Diane with something that sounded smart. At least that was part of it, but it came out wrong. When I told her I didn't know what my point was, she insisted that I give it a shot.

"I don't know, it's just that your dad got a kind of hellish version of paradise because of something he did to you, something crummy. But now it's your garden too. And the way you describe it it's a permanent fixture underlying everything else in your house. Your whole family's living with this pissed-off, dead. . . petrified forest. . . of Eden in the basement. Something about it doesn't feel right."

"The thing is," Diane interrupted, "it was a sore spot for pretty long, but it's not anymore. It's strange. It had all this charge at first, and then it was just a reminder of a fight we'd had. Gradually it changed on us, like it went through different seasons. The trees are still all glued down, but now they mean something different. Now when my father looks at the windowsill, he'll look over at me and say kind of kidding to whoever's around, 'Don't mess with that one.'"

"Besides, it's not like you're Mr. Turn-the-Other-Cheek. I was mad, and I took it out on my father. Believe me, I wanted to do a lot worse. I'm not saying it was a smart thing to do or anything. But he got over it. He wouldn't talk to me for two weeks, but then it was over."

"It was my mom who reacted; what I did to my father really shook her up. She took this painting I made of flying hummingbirds—one I had hanging over my bed because it was my favorite—took me and it to our backyard, and made me watch while she emptied a gallon of tar over the painting, frame and all. Then she went back inside without saying another word, leaving me staring down at this mound of black that looked like a dead bat with broken wings."

I thought what a good fit the expression "tarred and feathered" was in this case, but I kept it to myself. Instead, I asked her what she did after her mother killed her favorite painting.

"Nothing! No way I was going to give her the satisfaction of seeing me react. No tears. Nothing. She wasn't getting anything from me she could bring back to my father."

"So when he saw what your mother did, did it take some of the sting out of your tarring his train stuff?" I asked.

"She didn't tell him until he started talking to me again."

"What'd he do when he finally found out?"

"He went right down to his train set, sat on the floor, and cried."

❖ 37

"HOW DID HE DIE, STEPHEN?"

Later, during our train ride in Van Saun Park, I told Diane about Howie. It was his death, I told her, that caused me and my family to move away to Garrison City. My mother was four months pregnant with my brother when my parents first moved to Marchwood; Marchwood without Howie wasn't Marchwood any more—it was hell. People looked at me and my family funny after Howie died, but we stuck it out there for two more years before we finally took off.

I must've talked nonstop for more than an hour, enough time for us to get in and out of the tight confines of the train twice. I recounted story after story to Diane about my brother. Now that he'd come into the open, he had no desire to leave, and for the moment, I was incapable of putting him away.

The kiddie train drove up to us once again, and despite what my knees had to say about it, we boarded. "If you could shake heaven like a blanket," I concluded, "half the people up there'd fall out, like lint. But not Howie. He'd stick. He could be a bastard sometimes, sure, but he was a great brother. Hell, I realized one day that before he died I'd never lived a day of my life without him being in it. We spent so much time together, especially when we were little."

"I wish my memories went back like yours do, to when I was really young," Diane said, "like when I was three or four years old."

Childhood memories are great, sure. But who knows how first-hand, or true, they really are? The retold tales of countless friends and relatives are probably all over them. Accurate or not, after a while it doesn't matter anymore.

"Howie was my best friend," I told Diane as I strummed the button of my trousers just below my belt buckle, "only I didn't know it 'til he was gone." Then I added, "You know, it's funny. You like cemeteries so much, and I never even saw my brother's grave. I never went. I couldn't."

"How did he die?" I think Diane regretted the question as soon as she asked it. Especially when she saw my chin quiver.

The train slowed down long enough for me to reach out the window of my rail car, pick up a rock, and throw it at a tree. The rock ripped through a cluster of dead leaves, which fell like brown snow.

"He got hit in the head with a baseball bat during a Little League game," I said.

Diane tightened her hand around my forearm. The thought of someone dying like that. Her cold, red cheeks grew pale.

My voice was inexplicably mechanical. "There was this guy over by the backstop, wasn't even in the game or anything, just screwing around, and Howie ran by to get a ball. Howie wasn't watching. . . neither was the guy with the bat."

38 ◈

SILENT TREATMENT

Neither of us spoke when I finished telling Diane about Howie's death. I couldn't bring myself to tell her about my father's role in it.

Shortly after we climbed out of the train, a rustling of leaves caught my eye. About fifty feet away, a browsing, white-tailed deer looked up from the fallen twigs and branches on which it'd been feeding, and fixed me in its gaze. Mirrored along both sides of the deer's backbone was a faint ribbon of white spots. I didn't call Diane's attention to the animal, but I think she knew it was there.

"I'm sorry, Stephen, if what I asked led you to think and talk about things you didn't want to."

"No."

I followed finger-like bands of shadow cast from branches as they wrapped around the tall trunk of a pine tree. Behind the pine, other shadows laced the gray, dappled coat of the deer, which was almost invisible in its graceful grazing. It disappeared behind one slender tree trunk after another like a silk thread woven through a carpet. I directed my attention back to Diane only after a cloud eliminated the shadowed patterns and the deer vanished altogether.

"Say your life was a painting and one day, all of a sudden, a jar of dirty turpentine fell and spilled all over it, wiping out what you liked best. That's what it's like, him not being here anymore."

"He showed me how to do things. And he didn't even know he was doing it. It was cool having a brother like Howie. He was even treasurer of the whole student council when he was in junior high. His being so popular made *me* more popular in Marchwood. I could mess with kids bigger than me if I wanted—kids I knew I couldn't take—I didn't have to worry about it. I always knew no one would ever mess with me 'cause then they'd have to deal with Howie. It was like having Mike Dumbrowski for an older brother whenever you needed a Mike Dumbrowski, only Howie wasn't as crazy or mean as Mike can be."

"Who's Mike Dumbrowski?"

"Howie didn't die right away," I said. My abrupt return to Howie's passing coincided with a pair of steam-whistling antlers making themselves heard.

"It took a week before Howie died," I said. "Eight days, to be exact. I never got to see him after he got hit, but from what my mother told me, I don't think he was in any pain, really, you know, with all the medication he got in the hospital and all. Only that he was mad."

"Sad?"

"Mad. He was mad at my mother for making him miss his baseball game. Here he was dying and he ends up lying there stewing about a game. With Howie you never knew how he'd react to anything. It was one of the things I liked most about him."

Seeing the confusion in Diane's face, I explained further that after they got him in the ambulance, Howie made my mother promise she wouldn't let him miss this baseball game he was supposed to play in the next day. That's what he was worried about on his way to the hospital—a stupid game.

I sat down on a tree stump, picked up a fallen branch that looked like a cane, and leaned my chin upon it. The kiddie train, which had chugged on, reversed its direction, pulled up next to us, and stopped. We stayed where we were.

When I resumed speaking, Diane had to lean in close to hear me.

I explained that the team they were playing had made a big deal about beating Howie's team the last time they competed. Howie and his friends kept talking about how the next game wasn't even going to be close, how Howie's team was going to kill them. He was really pissed when he found out he missed the game. He had no idea how hurt he was. With the word "hurt," my voice cracked. Diane hugged my arm.

"So your mom promised he wouldn't have to stay at the hospital?" Diane asked.

The pace of my sentences slowed. I explained to Diane how Howie underwent brain surgery shortly after his arrival at the hospital. He wasn't angry. Not yet. He didn't know what was happening. "All he cared about," I told her, "was singing,"

"Singing?"

"Some dumbass song—'Furry Murray Got a Yul Brynner Haircut.'" I sang a few bars for Diane. "Howie kept going over and over it. Probably the doctors shot him up with something just to shut him up."

I explained how, the whole next day, Howie slept off the operation. When he finally woke up, he asked a nurse, who'd been sitting in his room, how long he'd been asleep. She told him, and then she ran down the hall to get my parents, but when they got to my brother's room he decided he'd be damned if he was going to give them the satisfaction of conversation.

It was Sunday. He'd missed his game.

Of course my parents didn't know he was mad. They just knew what the doctors had told them, which was that if he did recover from the procedure he might not be able to talk because a bone from his skull had been pressing down on the part of the brain that controlled speech. So when he didn't talk to them they thought he couldn't. "For a whole day, the last day he was still 'with it,' he could've talked if he wasn't so damned pig-headed—if he wasn't so pissed about missing his stupid game."

"How do you know he could talk?" Diane asked.

"We found out later he'd talked to the nurse. He did say a few words to my parents the next day before he fell into a coma, but they couldn't understand him. He died that Friday."

39

ALL ABOARD

We shared a bedroom, my brother, the night watcher, and me. There were train rails, and a locomotive made its rounds, circling, like clockwork, the beds of would-be passengers too big to climb aboard. But we could dream.

The locomotive was empty, but not the white plastic booth. With each passing of the train, out came the night watcher, dressed in blue, a faded hour painted across his wrist. Hanging from his outstretched arm was a lantern with a light bulb smaller than a pearl. A toy marking time in the dark.

One night the light bulb dimmed. Nobody saw it, not even the watcher, who normally spotted such things. The train derailed, and has run crooked ever since.

I am now too small to board the locomotive; the night watcher is bigger than life. I guess we were always fated to grow apart. Only my brother remains the same. And the dream.

—Stephen Schaech—

 **40**

LETTER

April 4, 1966

Dear Diane,

This is the first time I'm writing to you without Vermeer or Picasso looking over my shoulder. It feels good. I just wrote a poem about my brother. I guess between your telling me about your dad and his train set with the Lionel gatehouse, and me telling you about Howie (which I can't believe I did), I got inspired.

The poem, and our conversation yesterday, reminded me of something that happened about ten years ago (I was just starting first grade), and I thought you might like it. This is what I remember.

Since I was about two years old, I wanted a haircut like my father's and my grandfather's—the kind with a hole in the middle. I never thought of it as a bald spot, just as a style that older, stronger, smarter guys got to wear. Every time I went to the barber's I'd explain what I wanted, as if I had never brought it up before, and every time he'd say, "You've got plenty of time for that, Stringbean." Sometimes he'd look at my mother, thinking maybe this one time she'd tell him to go ahead, so I could get it out of my system, but she never did.

I guess I thought of myself as a trendsetter, so the day before school started I had my friend Stuart cut my hair. I wasn't in kindergarten anymore. First grade was real school, and I needed a grown-up haircut.

I couldn't figure out why my mother got so upset when she saw me in my new, older style haircut. As a two-part punishment, she cooked me liver for dinner, and shook her finger saying: "You wanted a haircut with a hole, you got a haircut with a hole. I don't want to hear another word about it." Then she shook her finger even harder. "And don't expect to miss school tomorrow, mister, because you're going." She made her point with the liver part. But I didn't get what she meant about missing school. Why would I want to do that? I couldn't wait to get there and show off the top of my head.

I got up extra early the next morning so I could stop and say hello to my rabbi. He was one of the first people I'd tell whenever something big happened for me. He'd always make a fuss about it. I imagined, after seeing my haircut, Rabbi Rosen would let me hold the Torah when my grandfather took my brother and me to services the following Saturday. I knew you had to be thirteen before you were supposed to get that honor, but I figured since the rabbi always talked about the importance of ancestry and tradition, the Torah rule wouldn't apply to someone who had a haircut like a father and a grandfather.

It turned out that Rabbi Rosen wasn't at the temple. What was there—it was always there—was the big black sign with its white plastic letters, each letter the size of my arm. The sign rose about halfway up the height of this huge umbrella pine tree that protected everything beneath it from the sun and rain. That morning the sign informed all of Marchwood about Rabbi Rosen leaving for a two-week trip to Israel. The synagogue would be closed until he returned.

Since there were only a few Jewish families in our town, a couple of phone calls would have gotten the message around just as well. But this sign was the rabbi's microphone to Marchwood. The day after the last election, you might not know who was the new president, Eisenhower or Stevenson. But by the time you digested your breakfast, all of Marchwood knew the rabbi was away, that in two weeks his sermon would address the story of Cain and Abel, and that at the following Sunday's Hadassah meeting, he was going to show color slides of Jerusalem.

But I'm straying. Because the rabbi was out of town, I got to the school-yard early. Right away I figured out what my mother meant about me not missing school. While this second-grader bent me over in a headlock, kids targeted dirt bomb shots at my bald spot. By the time we put our right hands over our hearts and pledge allegianced, if someone had given me a choice between eating nothing but liver all week or going to school, I'd have picked liver every time.

Tears did no good; the next morning there I was again, lunchbox in hand, bald spot in my throat. As I passed the rabbi's sign I almost didn't look up, since I had just read it the day before. But I did look. And I saw a new message:

IN HONOR OF RABBI ROSEN'S GOING TO ISRAEL
ALL MALE CONGREGATION MEMBERS SHOULD
WEAR YARMULKES UNTIL HE GETS BACK. AMEN.

As I read the bold white letters, my hand stroked my smooth, veiny, bull's-eye-scalp, and I felt my mouth forming a smile. A yarmulke—a beanie—that'd do it! It would cover my nakedness! What luck. Two weeks was all I needed!

Then Howie scooted from behind the umbrella pine. At the base of the tree was our ladder lying on its side, and a pile of large white, plastic letters. My brother was holding a blue and gold yarmulke matching the one he was wearing. He placed the yarmulke over the hairless circle on my head and kissed one of my eyes. We marched to school hand in hand, our arms and legs synchronized like soldiers.

"Where're you running?" I called to Ari Gleich, one of the other Jewish kids who attended my school. "Home to get a skullcap. I didn't know about it."

Gil MacDougal would never have thought of changing the letters on the sign, even for his most loyal fan. Only Howie would've thought of something like that. For doing what he did, my mother didn't make him eat liver or miss any of his baseball games, or stay home when his friends went to the movies, but Howie said he wouldn't've cared even if she had.

People shouldn't die in the middle of baseball games, especially heroes.

Sincerely,
Stephen

Part VII

NOT DIAMONDS

41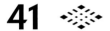

TRIAL AND ERROR

What Diane started, heroin came close to finishing: my withdrawal from Jerry, Mike, English, and Felix. My friends increasingly extolled the virtues of shooting up and minimized its drawbacks. I didn't.

"But you never even tried it, Shakes. How can you knock what you don't know nothing about?" Each of my friends offered the same argument. Maybe they had a point. I figured they'd be more likely to listen to me about trying to quit shooting up if I was able to speak from experience. At least that's what I told myself at the time. Really, I think that the truth was, I just wanted to try it out to see what all the fuss was about. Or more simply, I wanted to get high, and my friends convinced me that a heroin high was about the best one out there.

The first few times I shot dope, I skin-popped a small amount and felt nothing—certainly nothing compared to the buzz I felt when I stuck my nose into handkerchiefs soaked in Carbona Cleaning Fluid. And I felt nothing compared to everyone else who was nodding out around me. The only thing more uncomfortable than being straight while everyone around you is bent out of his mind is being alone while everyone around you is coupled up, fucking their brains out. There were no girls at Mike's house to make me feel alone the first time I mainlined.

Mike said my problem the last few times I shot up was that I didn't take a big enough hit, and that I only skin-popped, which Felix said was all right, but made sure to add, "Don't get no kind of rush that way."

"Make sure you take in every pearl Ybañez here fishes outta his personal pool of smarts, Shakes," Mike said. "I mean, anyone who drives to Newark to buy green shoes has to know what the fuck he's talkin' about, right?"

"Still breakin' 'em in," Felix said, rubbing the front of his right shoe against the back of his left pants leg. "And they're olive, not green."

"Anyhow, I'm just sayin', gotta go right into a vein with horse if you wanna get the whole high," Felix insisted. "What's the point of shooting up, man, if you're not gonna go for a rush?" Felix considered himself the authority where shooting up was concerned, since he'd been at it the longest.

"So what'd'ya think, Mike?" I asked.

Mike told me to take off my belt and tighten it around my arm to pop out a vein.

About ten minutes after he emptied a syringe into my arm, I still didn't feel much, so he gave me some more. The extra hit did it. Not in a good way.

"You're okay," Felix said. "You didn't take that much."

"I'll be right back," I said.

"On your way back from the can, Shakes," Mike directed, "get me a smoke from Olive-Not-Green over there, willya? I'm all out."

Not much bigger than my school locker, the basement bathroom must've been a room of the Dumbrowski house that got no attention because no one used it—or maybe it was the other way around. It was an armpit. Mike had said when his mother was home she was always cleaning. Clearly, Mrs. Clean had missed a spot.

But what an extravagance, nonetheless, a house with an extra bathroom. Where I lived, there wasn't anyone who at least twice a day didn't *hurry-up* someone else in the family because they "hadda go." So many five minutes' worth of waiting seeming like so many hours. An extra bathroom was what my mother once told me she always wished for when she blew out her birthday cake candles.

What I was wishing for now was for the sweat to stop sliding down my chest and back. When I ran up and down a basketball court, I didn't perspire, yet here I was, sitting still in the middle of winter, dripping like an icicle in July. I hated sweat. I saw it as life's way of crying across my body just before I threw a punch, or got one thrown at me; the owly humiliation of a clammy costume.

I sat there for about ten minutes doing nothing but sweating, when Mike knocked on the door. I didn't answer.

Although the fear of ODing was tempered by a certain degree of romanticism, a heroin overdose was a real and present threat. Since it was cut in the Bronx, where we got it from guys we didn't really know, you could never be sure how strong the stuff was that you were putting in your veins. Felix had ODed twice (not counting the Laociano experience at school, which was far less frightening and repulsive than the other two times), but both times he got away with it. I was there one of the two times; the sight of my friend looking so helpless and gray and vomit-soaked just before he lost consciousness contributed to my initial resolve to pass on repeated invitations to cut school and share syringes at Mike's empty house. Two other guys from Garrison High weren't as lucky as Felix. And then there were always reports, as well, about others—now dead—from nearby towns.

Nothing like that, I told myself, could ever happen to me. But if it did, I decided, it would only be fair. Lately, such trains of thought steered me in directions I would never have imagined before the word "payback" entered my thoughts. After all, it could just as easily have been Howie who was my mother's "only child" as me. Howie hadn't even wanted to go to the ballgame that day, but my mother insisted. *Don't you know how much Stevie would like his big brother to watch him play in a big game, Howie? You can spare one afternoon. Even your father's going. We spend too little time together as a family these days.*

But payback or not, for months I resisted my friends' entreaties to see for myself how cheap and easy it was to find a piece of paradise. "Nickel bag is all it takes," was how Felix put it. Five bucks. Who couldn't afford that? So, finally, I went along for the ride, and after a while, no matter how dark it was outside, I didn't care if the headlights were on or off.

42 ❖

THE BIRDS AND THE BEETLES

"You all right, Shakes? You want a smoke or something?"

I told Mike I never felt "this kind of fucked up before". All sweaty and everything. Something's wrong. Each word felt like sandpaper rubbing the inside of my mouth and around my bowels.

Across the crumpled cover of a magazine crammed on the floor between the sink and toilet, the wings of a bird—a raven, crow, bat, I couldn't tell—overlapped Alfred Hitchcock's pudgy, silhouetted nose. Hitchcock didn't seem bothered; maybe he even liked the breeze from the wings when they flapped. Hoping the distraction would settle me, I opened the magazine to a five-page-spread about the director's most recent film. The first page of the article was discolored from sink splashes or piss. I preferred to think "sink," but the truth was, I didn't really care all that much.

Sweat continued to pour down my back. To settle myself down, I thought about killing my father. The old standards came to mind first—smothering, drowning, poisoning, beating, stabbing. . . but then I remembered the Youthful David, who I'd been carrying around in my wallet, and I thought that this could be a good time to further plot my father's demise, which I was determined to pull off if I ever made it out of this bathroom.

The future King of the Jews survived Noah's car flood with just a few wrinkles. He still looked strong, vigorous, and, I speculated, smart enough to execute my plan—if I could just figure out how to bring my hero and foe together.

"What'd'ya say, Shakes? You all right?"

Mike's well-intended interruptions made it impossible for me to further script my plan. Besides, what was going on inside my body offered even greater distractions. Unable to focus my thinking, I placed David alongside the magazine lying on the floor.

"Shakes?"

A beetle crawled out from the base of the toilet into Goliath's beard, where it vanished before reappearing beneath David's left foot, leaving a wiggly trail of giant blood in its wake. I thought about flicking the bug off my reproduction but, remembering English's comment about his beetle's poisonous bite, I hesitated. Lucky for me, unlucky for the bare-footed David, who dropped to his knees, clutched his big toe, and collapsed alongside the head of his defeated enemy.

The bug's bite was lethal!

Transfixed, I stared at the crumpled body of Goliath's conqueror. Defeat at a bug's feet.

Casually, the insect crept out from under the foot of a paper hero and made its way across the outstretched wings of a bird, two birds, a whole flock. Then it crawled back onto the bathroom floor and rubbed its shell against my shoe, as if taunting me, or offering its services.

"You either have to find a way to lure your father into my world and bury him here," David had told me, "or find someone else to help you."

Mimicking a gesture I once saw Felix make, I formed my hand into the shape of a gun, aimed it at Goliath's head, and clicked my thumb. *Arrivederci*, Jacob.

 **43**

AMOK

Spotting an empty box of Smith Brothers cough drops lying in the corner of the room, I pierced it for ventilation, delicately shepherded the dangerous beetle inside, and put away my reproduction. Considering the care I took with the insect and my excitement over the prospect of bringing it home with me, I felt like I was two-timing English. And David. Even David's best friend, Jonathan.

"Stephen?"

Normally, plotting my father's demise calmed me down. Not today. My sweat glands kicked back into gear. I tried my Grandfather's Hebrew-months technique, but all I could remember was *Av, Elul,* and *Tishrei,* a frustratingly incomplete chant.

Sweat.

Back to the magazine:

Amok.

Back to Mike:

"Stephen."

My grandfather:

Av,

Elul,

Tishrei.

Sweat.

The magazine:

Amok. Amok. Amok.

PTAKI.

PTAKI.

PTAKI.

Av,

Elul,

Tishrei.

Smith Brothers.

Back to Mike.

He was talking to me, but the bathroom door muffled what he said, which didn't matter since I wasn't paying attention anyway.

The magazine article was filled with "amoks" and "PTAKI's". As I scanned the pages, the two words kept catching my eye. This movie in the article was about birds, too many of them, all of them out of control.

It was a new movie, still showing at the Palace. I had made a point not to see it. I liked the thought of a bird nibbling my fingertips and earlobes, bathing beneath the drips of a kitchen faucet, talking to its mirrored self inside its cage, or all puffed up sleeping peacefully upon its wooden swing. No way I wanted to chance such thoughts getting "amoked" to death.

For as long ago as I could remember—until our parakeet, Miss Diz, flew away just before our move to Garrison City—Howie and I had a pet bird. Howie wanted a dog; my parents didn't. "You don't have to walk parakeets," my mother said, "and they don't shed much," to which my father added, "Parakeets don't fart, and their turds are small." Birds four, dogs nothing. Aside from a turtle that lasted less than a week before my mother clogged up the toilet trying to flush the poor bastard away, birds were the only pets welcome in our small Marchwood apartment. Howie named our first parakeet Fido. Fido didn't bark, but I loved him. Almost as much as I loved Miss Diz.

Sitting on the toilet in the one part of the house the Dumbrowski's dog, Vujo, refused to set paw in because it inflamed his snout, I was surprised to see myself suddenly sitting uncomfortably on a ladder-back chair in a living room I did not yet understand. I was having great difficulty keeping myself seated.

I returned to the magazine. On the second page of the article there was a large black-and-white reproduction of a movie poster. The designer's name was printed below: Bronislav Zelek. Another name was printed bigger and into the poster itself: *Alfreedo Hitchcooka.*

PTAKI made up most of the poster. *PTAKI.* The word was repeated, over and over and over, little and well ordered near the top (as if far in the distance, the letters so small and faint they were hard to read), growing progressively bolder, darker, and more reckless as *PTAKI* swooped down the image, the power of the repeated word flocking with so many more of its kind that, together, they appeared ready to attack whoever had the balls, misfortune, or just plain stupidity to pick up the article. Centered near the very bottom of this tumultuous design, wings erupted out of the ear sockets of a human skull, the thick, black, spiky fringes of the feathers overturning the increasingly aggravated letters.

"Stephen, you're frightening me. What are you doing, sitting and staring at that wall, just sitting and staring?" It was Grandpa Oscar's voice. What was *he* doing here? Beads of sweat shivered across my forehead. I couldn't imagine what my grandfather was talking about. I wasn't staring at a wall; I was looking at a Polish movie poster in a magazine.

Mike told me to open the door.

My stomach wouldn't quit. I flushed the toilet.

"Hey, Mike," I called. "What's *Ptaki?*"

"Pappi? What the fuck're you talking about, Shakes?"

"*Ptaki.* What's it mean? D'ya know?"

Mike didn't know, so I asked him to see if Felix did. "I think it's Polish," I said.

"What the fuck you talking about, Shakes? And what'd'ya want from Felix; he's a spic, not a Polack."

"He's always talking to your father, right? Always getting new words from him. C'mon, just ask him. Ask him if it means 'birds.'"

Mike came back empty. "I look Polish to you? Ask your old man. Mietek'd know," was all Felix had to offer, other than asking Mike if he had something against green or something.

"C'mon, Shakes. Open the door," Mike demanded. "You're starting to piss me off."

The bathroom turned white in a blizzard of bird crap. Birds collided, breaking their magazine wings, before bleeding into the wet floor where I unconsciously dropped them. Alfred Hitchcock's glossy profile remained intact until the film director turned his head fatly toward me and winked. Then he tightly closed both his eyes and pulled up his nose and top lip in a grimace of pain as his dampened paper face reddened before beginning a series of cranial breaking-aparts and merging-back-together-agains. My stomach twisted as I witnessed the man's toilety cheeks stretch to reveal the skull bones beneath, and his eyes and mouth open into a chasm of anger, fear, and pain like a screaming, black-and-white, bald-headed, Edward Munch version of Sookie DiMaeoli.

I placed my hands over my ears, but it didn't help. "OOOOHHHH OOOOOWWWWWIIIEEEEEEEEEEEEEEEEE!" The shriek nauseated me and made my head throb. I tasted my own puke, but swallowed it back down.

"Shakes, c'mon, open up," Mike repeated, more aggravated this time. "I'm growing a fuckin' beard out here waitin' for you."

Mike's comment brought back to my attention the box of Smith Brothers I'd placed on the sink beside me. It was making noise. I focused my attention just above a strip of red letters printed across the bottom of the front cover where a trademark illustrated the head and shoulders of two black-suited, black-bearded brothers.

"Not yet. We just want to sit here a few minutes."

"You okay?" Jerry joined Mike. Then Felix offered a "Yo, what's up, yo?"

"We'll be okay," I said. "We're just reading and waiting for a train."

"We? Train? What's going on, man?"

I didn't know. The air was full of feathers. Aspidistra Avenue had disappeared, taking the Dumbrowski house along with it. I couldn't locate myself and I was no longer seated on a high-backed chair looking into the changing images painted across my living room wall. *I was above the chair, my head tipped back, mouth open wide, feet wedged between the bottom two rungs of the chair back. . . floating, floating in a sky that was suddenly, mercifully, featherless.*

"Give me a minute. I just want to see if I can catch one of these stars in my mouth when it falls. Me and my brother used to do that all the time when we were little. . . only it was with raindrops and snow." Black cough drops dripped from the sky into the waiting mouths of the two men crumpled across the bathroom sink.

Later, Mike told me he felt like he was getting the ass-end of something. Probably didn't have any front to it either. What did I mean, brother? I had never said anything to him before about having a brother. Mike waited until the sound of water refilling the toilet tank stopped, and then he asked if I thought maybe he'd given me too much horse.

"I don't know. I don't know what too much feels like. I just know I feel all shitty. All inside-out. And upside-down."

Mike told me to just sit there for a few more minutes and I'd be all right.

"Mike, it's not your fault if you did give me too much. It wasn't you. I know it's not your fault," I kept saying, straining to keep my fear locked behind the bathroom door. It was just payback, I thought to myself. Or my half of a Schaech brothers' curse.

I floated off the wall and out of sight. The ladder-back chair first remained where it had been, then it disappeared. Dreaming of flying bodies and birds and high-floating baseballs, I heard a train whistling its song alongside the frightened, pleading voice of my grandfather: "Please, Stephen, enough with the wall. Look at me. Tell me what's wrong. You're scaring me."

"Shit man," Mike said. "Quit wiggin' out on me. You're okay. I didn't give you that much. What're you getting so all bent outta shape for?" The other guys in the house gathered near the door.

"My insides are moving all kind've funny," I repeated. "Too fast. I mean like around my head and chest. Everything feels off."

"Wait a minute," Mike said. He paused, then he cursed. "I didn't give you too much. I know I didn't." He paused again. "Sheeiiit, man. Don't you know what's happening? You had me going, but I just figured it. You're not sick. I don't think you're even sick at all."

"Far out. That's right, man," added Felix, who was now in on the conversation with the bathroom door. "He's not sick. He's great. Fucking *estupendo*! It's poetry, Shakespeare, roses-are-red poetry. Take it from Felix Ybañez. Holy Mother of Jesus, stop crybabying and dig it, you fuckin' candyass. You're doing great and you don't even know it."

My mood changed. Everyone's did. Everyone started to laugh. Except me.

Felix was beside himself, a knotted balloon that just came apart. I couldn't remember hearing him or any of my other friends laugh like that for. . . I don't know how long—since they started shooting up. "Fuckin' A, man," Felix kept saying. "Fuckin' A. Shakes, give'm a book of poems and he's all over it. Every word. Get him high and the *ptaki-brain* right away starts bitchin' and moanin'." Felix's words, racing a minute ago, were slow and slurred.

"What're you guys laughing at? My blood feels like it's flowing on the outside of my veins, and you think it's funny."

"You're not sick," Mike said. "You're having a rush is what! A great fuckin' rush, Shakes. That's what it's all about. Get off the can and get into what's happening for you."

"Fuckin' A, man," Felix kept repeating. "Fuckin' A."

"Kee-rist almighty, Schaech. You scared the shit outta me. You got me standing here outside the can like an idiot talking to a goddamn door, and you're in there floatin' and you don't even know it. You're lucky I don't strap a belt around your arm and pump a couple more spoonfuls in you."

"A rush? This is what a rush feels like?"

"*Oui, monsieur,*" Felix confirmed. "You hit the jackpot, dipshit. You're the one who's supposed to be so smart—the one all the teachers want to rub your dick; the only one who knows things like how rare my name is. . . ."

"Your name?" Jerry said.

"Shakespeare here knows the whole thing what I'm talking about. Don't know diddly squat about what's a rush, but he knows I'm the only one around here what's got letters in his name that really count. None of you jerk-offs even knows that, I bet. Go on, Shakes, tell 'em about feliXXXX YYYbaañññññeeZZZZZZZZZZ!"

Alphabet man had to sit down on the floor. "Gonna blow my high if I don't get outta here." Felix's body was closing down. His neck appeared unable to support his head. Contrasted with his olive shoes, his unfocused eyes, peeking out through weighty eyelids, looked even redder than they were.

"His name?" Jerry repeated.

"How should I know this is what a rush feels like?" I complained. "I never had one before."

I was sure as hell having one now.

"You don't want it, *kemo sabe,*" Felix mumbled, "give it to me. Just hold on and ride it into one of them black holes English likes so much all the time."

In less than a minute, my stomach settled, and my terror—a profound, scummy terror—turned to ecstasy.

As I exited the bathroom, I told Mike I was starting to feel better. "No shit, Sherlock," he taunted.

Felix overheard us. "Fuckin' A, man. Fuckin' A."

 **44**

BENT SPOONS

Seated on the floor below the syringes and other equipment used for shooting up, I thought this was the way life ought to be, but hardly ever was. Just when things look like shit, there ought to always be someone around to come along and say: "Lookit, asshole. It's not like that at all. You thought it was shit, but it's diamonds. Fuckin' diamonds. You just weren't looking hard enough. Or maybe you just didn't know what to look for."

Mike sat down and put his hand on my shoulder. It was a surprisingly tender touch. Mike was like that. You could never figure what he had in him.

I looked back to the sun shining on my living room wall. Near the middle of the sunshine hung, freely suspended, a small silhouette shaped like the state of Idaho. Then Idaho grew thinner and more graceful. Then it turned into a spoon. Then the spoon bent.

I surveyed the tabletop and then commented that there was probably a better spoon, meaning a straighter one, upstairs in one of the kitchen drawers by the sink. I told Mike I'd go up and get one.

"What for? This here one's plenty good. Wha'd'ja think was wrong?"

"The handle? It's all bent."

"It's supposed to be. I bent it. Look. You put the snow in the bowl of the spoon, drop in a little water, and cook it." Mike lifted the spoon above the flame of his Zippo lighter. "Here, lookit, watch how quick it boils. Then alls we gotta do is set it down on the table here, let it cool a minute, let the syringe suck up the tasty juice, like so, and, if the spoon ain't bent, the horse'd spill out when we put the spoon down on the table." Mike enjoyed demonstrating his expertise. He had mastered the art of scag—buying it, shooting it, getting into its high, hiding the wares, hiding its effects—the way English had mastered the game of pool. Mike Dumbrowski: *Opiatis Emeritus.*

Mike handed the syringe he had just filled to English, who had come to the house late, and then he bummed a cigarette from him but didn't light it. His eyes drooped and then his head.

A passing cloud erased the sunshine from my living room wall, taking the spoon with it.

"That's how it ought to be." I reflected. Say you got something bent outta shape; someone comes along and explains to you how it's supposed to be that way—that it wouldn't work right otherwise.

Yeah, that's how it ought to be, but that's not how it is.

Except lately, with Diane. That's what I was thinking about when I nodded out along with everyone else.

Ten minutes passed before Mike broke the quiet. As he picked up the bent spoon that English left behind, he said softly, so that just I could hear him, "I been thinking, Shakes, I gotta tell you, you don't need this bullshit. You know, horse and shit." He put his arm around me like before. "Me, I sort of do, same as I sometimes need to beat the crap outta someone. Don't matter if it's some dude gettin' in your face or a fuckin' pharmacist minding his own fuckin' business. Sometimes you just gotta do it. Juices me up. And I'm good at it. Yeah, it's one of the things I do best." He was straining. "Me," he continued, "I don't think enough people appreciate kicking someone's ass; you gotta enjoy it on its own, you don't always got to wait around for moods like revenge to get it going."

I thought how revenge isn't a mood, and I almost blurted that out, but I caught myself. Good thing; Mike's fist in my mouth for giving him attitude or, at best, a dirty look, is all my comment would likely have gotten me. But mostly, I didn't want to interrupt him because his voice was sincere, and I wanted to see where this out-of-character sincerity was headed.

"Kickin' ass is like this great rush," Mike offered, "just as good as dope or sex. But fighting's not your bag, and I don't think getting into dope's a smart way for you to go either." He left out the sex part. "Me, I'm probably pretty close to who I'm gonna be for the rest of my life. You, who knows? You got other things. . . school shit and stuff. . . putting words on paper. . . pictures." Mike lit a cigarette and took a long drag. *"Mon-a-fuck-in-Li-sa."* Each syllable of the mysterious woman's name came out wrapped in its own private, pulsing bubble of smoke. Then he repeated her name, this time spitting it out and twisting his mouth into a mock smile. "Or the guy who painted her, Michael-fuckin'-angelo. You and Eppers both," he continued, "you like looking at pictures, don't ask me why—especially ones where me and I bet half the clowns walking around in museums lookin' at 'em slow and serious and all quiet and shit can't even tell what the hell the thing's supposed to be about, or even *of.* And then there's the marble statue people with their carved white eyes and white lips and their bodies stuck in all these weird poses with half the time their arms and noses broke off and their dicks, too." He took another drag from his cigarette. "I don't get it. 'Course that don't mean I'm so thick that I'm sayin' there's nothin' there, just that me, myself?. . . besides the naked women?—and I don't give a rat's ass how fat the broads were back in the old days, I could look at *them,* even with their white marble nipples and tits that'd break your teeth off. . . but besides the naked chicks—I don't get none of the whole art thing. But who knows?'"

He moved his arm off my shoulder and let his head drop. His voice was slowing down, making its way back to its familiar Mike Dumbrowski snarl after having taken a quick, rambling, English Otis detour. "Horse'll fuck you up. I don't want to see that happen to you. You hear what I'm saying, Shakes?"

I found myself suddenly distracted by the flare-up of tiny red veins fracturing the whites of my friend's eyes. "And don't ask me to tighten the belt for you no more neither," Mike added, his demented-looking eyeballs staring hard at me. "I'll put my fist in your face 'fore I shoot any more junk in your arm." As I instinctively looked toward his fist, I thought about what a good move it was keeping my mouth shut on the revenge/mood thing and likewise, not pointing out that Michelangelo didn't paint the Mona Lisa.

For the past month, Mike had been saying he was through with dope. He was usually high when he said it. But I was surprised to hear him counsel *me* against shooting up. I had never before heard him try to talk anyone out of doing anything, especially something stupid or dangerous.

"You hear me, Shakes? And I ain't supplying you with no more scag either, so don't ask. Gonna have to get it somewhere else."

I thought about Diane. What I felt when I was with her was a different kind of high. Better.

"You're right, Mike. I'll get it somewhere else."

"Shakespeare, you ain't listenin'."

As I sat staring at the once-again sunless wall of my living room, I heard water refilling a tank behind a closed door. The inside of the once-white toilet bowl was almost black. My stomach turned, and I felt like I did earlier. Jerry, English, and Felix were nowhere in sight. Then, as an empty rectangle of light reappeared on the wall, the cloud that had spirited away Idaho and the spoon swallowed up all the stars in the sky and moved on. Trailing just behind was a flock of birds—ravens, crows, bats. . . I couldn't quite tell. All that remained was a shadowed image of two boys sitting side by side. And frantically scratching away inside a box stuffed in the pocket of one of them was a beetle who I was going to name David or Jonathan or Fido.

45

FLIPPING, TICKING, AND SPRING-CLEANING

"Lucy, I'm home!"

Home. . . bird. . . home again; home. . . bird. . . home again.

I had arrived home to find my mother lying on the couch, watching television. *In this house by the railroad tracks, where I now found myself remembering my return from Aspidistra Avenue, I was alone. My solitary walks along the tracks were always followed by more solitude yet, so it was reassuring to recollect a time when there was someone waiting for me.*

Home. . . bird. . . home again; home. . . bird. . . home again.

Streaks undulating across Lucille Ball's TV-screen face. Tony Randall's magazine eyes and forehead glossing my mother's stomach. The actor's warm, *Ladies Home Journal* skin tones lay in stark contrast to the black-and-white print of my mother's housewifely dress.

My mother seldom read anymore. An occasional magazine. As a child she would sit enthralled, listening to her father's story voice, handing Grandpa Oscar book after book until he finally taught her to read. Two years ago she lost her prize inheritance: Oscar's love for books.

With her left hand, my mother bent the corners of the magazine cover. In her right hand was a strip of cellophane rolled into a thin cylinder that she kept in constant motion.

Home. . . bird. . . home again; home. . . bird. . . home again.

In my imagination, I walked the train tracks until I reached the dead bird. Then I'd return to the house. It was a house by a railroad, a house which, as yet, remained strangely ill-defined except for the constancy of the daily passing of a mysterious trainman in his shadowy locomotive, and my grandfather's plea for me to "snap out of it."

"Please, Tatella, snap out of it. Enough with the wall already. You're scaring me."

I couldn't get my grandfather's refrain out of my head. The words were clear. Unclear was where I was and what I was supposed to "snap out of."

My mother and I remained silent as our attention was drawn to the TV. Lucille Ball was sitting still in her television living room, but the image on the screen kept rolling up like a winding window shade. Likewise, I stood still, but inside the cough box hidden in my pants pocket, a busy beetle practiced gymnastics in the dark.

"See if you can play with the horizontal hold knob, Stephen. It keeps doing that. It stays still for a little while, but then it somersaults. It's making me dizzy."

"I can never get this thing to stop flipping once it starts."

"Try the antenna."

I adjusted the knobs beneath the television screen and the antenna set on the radiator just behind it. A nail clipper lay on the floor near the couch, right next to my mother's slippers. I noticed a long, chipped nail on one of my mother's bare toes.

"Your back hurting, Ma?"

"The past two weeks more than usual."

"Want me to cut your toenail?"

She looked down at the nail clipper. "How'd you know?" Her voice was tired. "I got the others, but this one darn toe has it in for me. I can never reach it."

When I sat down and placed my mother's foot in my lap, a reflection from the wall hanging suspended just above her glazed the TV screen with bands of red, brown, peacock blue, and mustard yellow obscuring Fred and Ethel Mertz, who had just entered Lucy's apartment. The normally bland black-and-white Fred and Ethel never looked so good.

My mother had just read about Tony Randall speaking out against the U.S. troops sent over to Southeast Asia. "Imagine, the very best 'second banana' on either stage or screen criticizing the United States in public."

"If the public thing bothers you, Ma, close the magazine and he'll be undercover."

Her silent stare shut me up. Turning my attention back to the TV, I noticed that Fred and Ethel had been replaced by John Cameron Swayze, who was going on about a Timex watch—*It takes a licking and keeps on ticking*—that had just survived a fifty-foot plunge into icy waters. Invincible.

Suddenly a scratching sound inside my pants caught my attention. The TV static and watch ticking, combined with the scratching going on inside my pocket, triggered a harmony of hatred in my head that was so clear I could whistle to its beat. If the kids on *American Bandstand* could creep inside my head they'd rate my song right up there because, as they'd say: *"You can dance to it."*

John Cameron Swayze. So much music in a single name—well, not exactly a single name, three names. Three, Howie's magic number. Perfect!

Okay, I thought. *Jonathan Swayze it is.* I hereby name thee—my venomous, unquiet, conspiratorial, eight-legged secret weapon who crawled into my life to exact justice—Jonathan David Swayze. In time,

JD, in time, we will pay my father back. He'll take a licking. The clock is ticking.

My mother's voice. "Speaking about Southeast Asia," she said, "is there much talk in school these days about Vietnam?"

"No."

My mother waited, but got nothing more. My concentration shifted from names to nails. As quickly as he filled my thoughts, Jonathan David Swayze disappeared and was replaced by the act of evening out the curve of a toenail without catching the tender flesh underneath.

"And while we're on the subject of school, Stephen, where were you today?"

"Uptown. Hey, how come you're home so early, Ma? You stay home from work? What was it, your back?" I placed the nail clipper on a table at the foot of the couch.

"I mean before you went uptown." Although she spoke to me, my mother's eyes remained fixed on the rolling of the image on the TV screen. "I'm talking to you. I said where were you?"

"At school. Why?" I had the feeling I was being tested and had gotten ten points deducted, maybe twenty. I wondered if the toenail'd be worth any extra credit.

"Because they called, is why. Someone from school." Again she asked where I was. We went back and forth a few more times. "So how come they said you weren't there?"

"I don't know, Ma. Oh, wait. I know what it must've been. I wasn't feeling good this morning, so I went down to Nurse Schirmer's office. I must've been down there when Mrs. Gustin took attendance. This stupid TV, I can never get it to work."

The Mertzes rolled up and down the TV screen. Fred looked shorter and fatter than usual. Ethel looked the same, only busier.

"Fine. I'd better call them back then and let them know what happened." When she started to rise, her body jerked, as if responding to a needle of heat bursting down her leg into her toes. She stretched back into the couch.

I was momentarily grateful for her pain. "Stupid TV," I complained.

"Stephen. Look at me. Where were you today?"

I didn't look.

"Stephen, take your head out of the television set, and look at me!" With her newly trimmed toenail, my mother scratched an itch on the heel of her other foot.

Get a life, Fred and Ethel. My mother can go stuff her damn questions. Tony Randall, screw you. "Okay, Ma. Okay. I cut school. I wasn't down at the nurse's office during attendance. I lied. But I really don't feel well. I swear. I'm sorry I lied to you, Ma, but. . ."

"Stephen, I need this like a hole in the head." It wasn't just my lying, she said, or even that I had cut school. "There's a lot of things that I want to talk to you about. Your roughneck friends for example. . ."

"Ma. We've been over that. You. . ."

"Don't get smart with me, young man. Besides, maybe we need to go over it some more." Which is what we did. I could tell there was something else on her mind, but we never got to that.

Home. . . bird. . . home again; home. . . bird. . . home again.

Lately, my mother and I were talking less and less, but more and more, what we were talking about was the same thing: my friends. She directed her gaze toward the still-flickering television. She looked tired, beaten. I looked at her and thought how full of fun and surprise she used to be. I never knew what to expect. Even the notes she'd leave on the kitchen counter for Howie and me every day when we came home from school gave me something to look forward to:

If I'm not here, it's because I ran off with the circus. I'm going to water the elephants. I left snacks for you in the fridge. Leave one of the Milky Ways for me in case I come back.

Love,
Mom

Her notes to me were shorter now:
Make yourself dinner.

"I just know you can do a lot better, Stephen," my mother complained, referring to my friends. Again.

"Could we maybe talk about this a little later, Ma? My stomach feels really lousy. I just want to lie down for a little while."

She didn't care how I felt. The answer was no, I couldn't go into my room. What I could do was switch the clothes.

"Ma. . ."

"You heard me. Get started. Bring the winter clothes from your closet downstairs and bring your spring and summer clothes up. Then you can start on my closets."

"But it's still winter. Why do we have to. . ."

"Winter's almost over. We'll get a head start on spring."

"Aw, Ma. Can't I just. . .?"

"Don't make a federal case out of it. And don't you 'aw Ma' me, mister. Just do what I said. Now! You can be sick later." She dropped the strip of cellophane on the back of Tony Randall's head lying across her stomach. The delicate touch of the cellophane stirred the actor so he slid off my mother's body and disappeared within the closed pages of the magazine, the strip of cellophane marking his place. "And don't you dare let me find out you ever cut school again. Now just do as I said. And I do not want to see any faces."

When my mother's "do nots" replaced her "don'ts", it was her way of saying, "Case closed."

So cleaning out my closets was the way I spent the end of the second day I shot heroin. Each trip downstairs was punctuated with my vomiting; each dry-heaving trip upstairs concluded the same way. Mike had given me too much after all.

Jonathan David Swayze remained in my pocket until I finished with the closets. My mother remained on the couch. Like a single star in the sky, a speck of light glanced off the edge of the metal nail clipper onto the blackened television screen where her eyes were fixed. She seemed unaware that there was no picture. Or maybe she was struggling to adapt her vision to the darkness, not unlike what JD was probably doing since he crawled across the wings of high-flying birds into an empty box protected by two brothers.

46 ❖

SPACE TRAVEL

The back and forth of my arguments with my mother about my friends, the back and forth image on the TV screen, and my trips up and down the stairs brought to mind one of English Otis's theories of outer space exploration. English's stories often wound up in outer space. "The sun's on one side and the moon's on the other," English had explained one night in the darkness of a recently abandoned Forstops Village apartment. To demonstrate his point, he had curled his hands as if skimming the surface of a beach ball.

"Oh yeah? Then how you gonna explain astronauts landing on the moon side and their cocks not turning into icicles?" argued Felix Ybañez.

"What're you kidding? They aim for the line, dipshit. That's how. It's all in how close to the line they get."

"Oh, the line. I should've knowed. Why didn't I think of that? The line."

"Yeah, the *safe* line. The one between the sun and the moon," English explained. No one interrupted him.

"Let's say the space ship lands on the moon side of the line. If the guys in the ship stay inside their eyeballs'll freeze. Right? 'Specially if it's night. I mean, forget it from hell to breakfast if it's night. You got any clue what it's like, cold-wise, on the moon after the sun goes down? Especially at night. Okay, I'm not saying you're wrong, Ybañez, you know, about freezing and all. If a mess of astronauts end up hanging out the whole time on the moon side of the moon and sun at night 'cause they can't find the line—if that's what it is—they're good as dead."

"Especially if it's nighttime, I bet," Jerry added. He wasn't sure if English was serious or not. He never was sure. None of us was. "Nighttime on Planet English is the worst."

"Damn straight," he agreed. "Nighttime'd wreck you the worst with the freezing and all. But what they do is they get out straight off and head for the safe line so's they can hop across it from the moon to the sun to the moon and like that. Back and forth like crazy. Ping-pong, you know? I betcha it really gets their hearts compensating 'cause besides all the back-and-forths, the weight of all the stuff they got on their backs. . . you know, like oxygen pressure actuators, and hoses and shit. . . alla that equipment's gotta knock them out real good."

"I hate to be the one to break the news, Mr. Ping-Pong," Jerry taunted, "but I got a feeling the mother ship's left without you, bro."

"I'm just saying, Sal, I mean maybe some kind of chemicals they got inside their bodies or in their space suits gets them used to the temperature changes and after a while they can stay longer and longer on each side. But mostly they just pop back and forth 'til they get back in their spacecraft and fly home."

"I musta been out the day we went over this stuff in science," Felix offered, gently dropping his argument with English. No one picked it up.

English was tough to figure, forever spilling over the lines. More the off-target space ship than the dead-on spaceman, English was always taking you places you'd never figure. One time in particular, I was taken completely off guard. "Shakes," English had whispered, "I got a secret for you if you promise not to tell no one."

"Go ahead, English, shoot. Whatever you tell me stays between us."

English placed his left hand inside his pants pocket. His head bobbed up and down. "I've been walking around the last couple days with this thing, but I want someone else to know it. It's nothing bad or nothing. Fact, it's pretty good, I guess. Only I don't think no one around here'll get it 'cept maybe you, and I didn't want to tell it to the wrong one 'cause I didn't want it to get spoiled or nothing. I don't know. I guess Jerry'd be okay to tell it to, but. . ."

"What is it, English?"

English moved his left hand as if to grab a better hold onto something I couldn't see. As English remained silent, his hand continued to move. I looked toward my friend's pocket. "You got crotch rot or something, English?" English didn't laugh.

Beginning to question how much I wanted to hear the secret, I took a small step backward. Did he have a beetle in his pocket? JD Swayze's brother? With what he thought were his same-sized fingers, was he stroking a weapon? Or unconsciously playing with himself out of nervousness. . . his own thicker version of my mother's cellophane roll? English looked around before speaking. His face was dead serious, and pale. There was no one near, but he whispered.

"I can't hear you, man. You gotta say it louder."

Placing his mouth close to my ear, he whispered again. His breath smelled of Lucky Strikes and salami. I still couldn't hear him.

Slightly louder than before, "I got into Pratt."

"What's a Pratt?"

"Pratt Institute. It's a school. In Brooklyn."

Before I could stop myself, I laughed. "You what?"

"I got in."

Pratt Institute? It'd never occurred to me that the flight path English's future followed might ever loop over a college campus, much less land there.

I hoped I might get to go to college some day, but not right off. First I'd have to figure out what I'd do there. I wasn't good at anything related to school besides writing poetry, and I had never heard of anyone going to school for that. Anyway, first things first. First I needed to take care of business with my father. How that turned out would lead to what came next. Hiding out? Prison? A job? Travel? Poetry? Who could say? If all went well, I planned on working for a few years after graduating from Garrison High, helping to support my mother in case my father never bothered to take out life insurance, then I'd take it from there. English was the first one of my friends who had ever brought up the subject of college. For my own sake, I was glad he had.

"How do you know, English? It's too early. No one knows about getting into college yet."

"I found out eleven days ago, goin' on twelve. I got a letter from the engineering department." He moved his hand again. "I got it in my here pocket."

"Eleven days ago?"

"They call it early admission. They want me to go there. You believe it? They want me to go to their school!"

"No shit, Eddie?"

"No shit." Then he added, "Maybe I'm not so thick as everyone thinks." He laughed. "I'm not, you know. Knowin' things–wise. A real college mook, that's what I am. I always knew I wasn't dumb like everyone thinks, just no one else knew it. Guess maybe I didn't want nobody to know. To be honest with you, maybe I'm not so sure 'bout it myself still." His cheeks flushed.

If English could get accepted into college, I thought to myself, maybe I could too. "That's absolutely great, man!" I screamed at my friend. "Absolutely great! What do you mean, 'You guess it's good.' It's *fan-fuckin-tastic*, that's how good it is!"

English allowed the trace of a smile to coat his lips. "You think so, Shakes? You really think it's a good thing? I mean. . ."

"You tell your parents, English?"

"Nah. I didn't tell no one about it yet. 'Cept you, now."

For eleven days Edward Otis had been holding on tightly to the most important achievement of his life. He had been keeping it hidden away, folding and crumpling it up out of fear, afraid to bring it into public view. I thought about my own folded paper hidden away in the wallet I kept in my back pocket. The Young David. . . what would he think of English's news? English Otis: certainly no King David, but heroic in his own right.

English hadn't told anyone, not wanting to hear: "Big deal," or "Probably a mistake," or "You really think you're going to fit in with a bunch of college kids?" or "I'll give you a year, tops, before you flunk out," or "Where do you expect us to get the money to pay for this?" or "So what? So fuckin' what?"

It wasn't his grades. Eddie Otis participated in no extracurricular school activities. His combined English and math SAT scores were only slightly above average. Nonetheless, his application for college admission could not be ignored; he had scored 740—within sight of a perfect 800—on the math part of the SATs. Apparently, the mind that was capable of understanding the geometry of orbiting balls atop a pool table was just as capable of understanding the geometry that was presented on a piece of paper.

"But there's another part, Shakes. About going to college." He paused.

"What's that, Einstein? That they're giving you a free ride 'cause they saw you shoot eight ball?"

"That I don't know if I should go or not. I mean, what if I don't make it? What if it turns out I don't really got what it takes after all, you know, like everyone already thinks?" Then he added, "I don't want to find that out." I could hear paper crumpling inside my friend's fingers, as English's eyes pleaded with me to tell him what to do. English's fingernail pulled at a corner of his acceptance letter like it was an out-of-tune guitar string.

It was a movie going on inside a pocket. One part of the script was clearly written out for the main character to review at his leisure: *We are pleased to inform you that. . .* but the rest was up for grabs. I looked toward the trousered commotion created by the anxious imprint of my friend's hand. I envisioned English's hidden fingers clinking keys and coins in a silent film muted by a paper soundtrack, the mash of tissue and a letter from an admissions officer named Bedoya.

Buried at the base of a trouser pocket, the film was lit by doubt and darkness. I remembered a poem I wrote based on a Daumier painting Diane brought to class back in November. The artist portrayed a barker trying to drum up business for the carnival act of a strongman. One of the lines I wrote was: *Thrill to the darkness behind the curtain.* At the time I was thinking of the darkness as hell—an unlit unknown. It struck me now that the dark unknown didn't have to be without light. Fear and anxiety need not be painted in ink-black brushstrokes like a flat cartoon, like the dark road that ended the life of Jerry's older brother. Like everything else, fear could be exhilarating, and in this case it presented itself to English in typewritten letters that took four paragraphs, a whole page, to spell one word: *future.* Why had English so quickly stuffed the word away in an attempt to bury it?

I thought about how, every time I first walked into a darkened movie theater, a jet-black wall blocked my path before my eyes adjusted. Blackness was seldom without light; sometimes it was just a matter of taking a breath and waiting.

"English," I said, "you're afraid to find out whether or not you've got what it takes for college, but that's just what you've got to do. You're the one who likes black holes. Well, you just got one in the mail—or at least a map pointing you towards one—and you stuffed it away, and now you've got a chance to look into it and see if there's anything there for you. Could be dicey, sure, but college could also be like a map to guide you through one of those black holes."

"I get what you're saying, but I don't know, man. You know how sometimes the thought of something's a lot better than the thing itself? Even like some people, even. Don't ever tell him I said this, but take Mike, f'rinstance. Did'ja ever think about how sometimes the thought of Dumbrowski's more better than Dumbrowski himself, you know, like when he's all pissed off and shit at you about something?" English paused and then added, "Or how other times Mike's a lot better than what everything you think about him oughta make you think? It's like that, Shakes. Most things just don't match up, even when they're supposed to be the same thing." The inside of his pocket made noise again. "I know what you're saying about black holes and all, but what if it turns out I'm stupider than this here letter thinks I am, or even, what if college turns out to be not so good as I'm thinking right now that it is? What if me and college both fall flat on our fuckin' heads? What then?"

"I guess you won't know 'til you sign up. Hell, you know how Mike likes to say you're 'certifiable,' English? Now you can tell him 'a certificate's a certificate—especially when it's a diploma.'"

"Yeah, I like that, Shakes. Whatever the fuck you just said."

April 12, 1966

English Class: Mrs. Bilheimer/Miss Adamsohn
"What do you see when you look at this painting?"

CRUTCHES OF CONFORMITY
(based on The Blind Leading the Blind *by Pieter Bruegel)*

Sustained by a tangled train of wooden stakes,
their unsure steps shift
at the whim of a sightless leader.
Leaning upon crutches of conformity,
seeking from windowless skulls, they wander,
wondering "Are we there yet?"

On track to derail
the pull of a puppeted line,
they glory in the thrill of stumble and pain
and the ignorance of ignoring
a parable's refrain:

"Shall we move forward?"
"Yes, right away!"
"And the others, what of them?"
"If we fall, they will fall too.
If we move on, they will follow."
"They will always follow?"
"Until they fall."

—Stephen Schaech—

 **47**

CLEANING UP

I wasn't the only one spring cleaning came early for that winter. The next few days saw a marked increase in the cleaning activity of Felix,

English, Jerry, and a number of other Garrison City high-school students I was less friendly with. Under the watchful eye of Lieutenant Brannick, Felix was ordered to clean out his school locker on Tuesday. It was English's turn on Wednesday. Jerry and I were the end of the week.

Brannick was just following school policy. If, for a serious offense, a student was to be taken out of school by a police officer, the student was summoned from the cafeteria during lunch period, told to empty his locker, and then brought down to the principal's office.

My friends and I ate together every day during lunch period at school. Throughout the past week our table seemed to seep out further and further beyond its boundaries like a spreading stain. Each day there was more room, as each day Lieutenant Brannick led someone else away. Early Friday he came for Jerry. By lunchtime, Friday afternoon, my sandwich was all alone. With each bite, I shrank a little more and the table swelled.

English, Jerry, and Felix had all streamed into Hilton Hoffmeister's office and listened to one half of a phone conversation while the school principal contacted their parents. By the time my mother received her phone call, my friends had all been sent to Bergen Pines to, as Hoffmeister put it, "clean up their acts."

"No, you must be mistaken," she insisted. "Not Stephen."

"Apparently they've been keeping an eye on your son and a bunch of his friends for several months now, Mrs. Schaech. I'm afraid Stephen got involved with the wrong group of boys. No, there's been no mistake, ma'am, I'm very sorry."

Then, "Mrs. Schaech? Lieutenant Ray Brannick here. Garrison City Police Department. I need you to meet me at the Hackensack Courthouse, Division of Narcotics."

48

SCITOCRAN EVER SINCE

Fingering a hangnail on the side of my thumb, I sat alone on a wooden bench in the outer office of room 124. Stationed behind a nearby counter was a sullen, gray-haired man, smoking a mentholated cigarette. The smell of menthol always made me queasy. Especially today. The clerk shook his head once or twice in response to something I asked, but he never spoke to me. Beside the man's ashtray stood a wooden statue of a naked male figure. The figure was encrusted with nails driven into its torso and limbs. I recognized it as a commercial replica of the kind of African sculptures my grandfather and I were drawn to every time we visited the Metropolitan Museum. My grandfather was unable to explain to me why all the nails. Not knowing made the statue more exotic, frightening, tortured, bizarre. Why would anyone drive nails into his body, or let anyone else do it, for that matter? I thought of the needles that my friends and I put into our bodies. Eyeing the standing figure, I was determined to remain seated. Anything to differentiate myself from the hammered statue.

Behind and just above the clerk's head hung a color portrait of Lyndon Baines Johnson, looking serenely presidential. No one could tell me that the Commander in Chief of the United States of America didn't have some kind of major problem chewing at his gut. But there he sat, relaxed, secure in his well-pressed suit, his hair combed, hands washed and folded before all those unwrinkled rows of stars and stripes. Only when his eyes met mine did the president's face reflect any degree of tension, his expression subtly shifting from confident to condemning, his condemnation projecting outward toward the mess I was making of *my* life, not inward toward any of his own potential presidential or personal problems. Apparently, it made him feel better about himself to see me under the gun.

The clerk paid no more attention to the Johnson portrait than he did to the nearby African statue or to me. For him, the face hanging overhead could've been Jerry's black-velvet version of John F. Kennedy or a picture of Mary Gustin's great-grandmother; it made no difference. He looked comfortable in his disinterest. I envied the man his boredom. I didn't bother with him any more than he did with me, but boredom had nothing to do with it. In my case it was self-preservation: I couldn't fit anything about him inside my head right now.

SCITOCRAN.

Each of the transparent, blocky letters outlined in blue across the outside of the glass door before me was reversed, but that's what they spelled when I turned them around in my head: SCITOCRAN. The word made no sense to me. Since Brannick had walked over to my table in the school cafeteria, nothing made any sense. Everything was SCITOCRAN. All day long. Except Diane. Hell, it was SCITOCRAN ever since I left Marchwood. Even before.

Then two vertical rows of shiny silver buttons sliced through the word. The letters still made no sense, but they looked better with the silver circles bobbing up and down, left and right through their stenciled transparency, as if the word was supposed to be sung, Guy Lombardo style, with silver circles directing the voice along an invisible set of musical scales. Or perhaps there was a secret waiting to be discovered in the third line, the convoluted one that would form when I connected the two lines of circles with. . . with what?

As a kid, I loved to "connect the dots" when I found those puzzles on the backs of cereal boxes and in magazines or comic books. The secret of the numbered dots excited my imagination as my crayon followed a crooked path. The creation of the path was always tinged with enchantment and endless possibilities. The completed koala bear or rhinoceros was always a letdown.

Suddenly, the thought of English's concern that college might turn out to be a letdown struck me as absurdly and sadly beside the point. Had he blown his chance to ever find out what kind of college mook he might turn out to be? The pattern of dots that led from Batman and Robin trading the sandwiches their mothers made for them as kids to English and Jerry having their food slopped onto their plates by unfriendly inmates at Bergen Pines had fallen hideously out of order, English's koala bear recklessly hodgepodging into a rhinoceros (a koalanoceros?) to form a rather pathetic-looking hybrid. I wished my friend well.

Since moving from Marchwood, my own life was more about *dis*connecting the dots than connecting them. Before, there were patterns. This point led into that, which led inevitably to a logical configuration. No more. In Garrison City everything was in between and untogether. Important pieces along the way were always missing or out of order. Forty-six, forty-seven, thirty-eight, fifty-one, seventy-nine. I felt like a helpless spectator watching my own lifeline disentangle as it aimlessly slipped off tracks designed to give it direction. Soon there'd be no discernible line at all, just a constellation of dislocated moments littered with deflated zebras.

The two rows of circles bobbing and mingling with SCITOCRAN kept getting bigger. Then Van Saun Park came into focus. "Someone moved Paramus to Hackensack," I thought to myself, "and brought the woods indoors. And replaced February with May." I heard Howie. Three times. Woods and parks and playing fields always made him sneeze. Something about the grass. Then, as suddenly as the woods and Howie had appeared, they vanished; time and place mercifully, if only momentarily, wriggled back into their calendars and maps, the months climbed back into their gridded positions, and Bergen County realigned itself, as I recognized the trees and fields for what they really were: a fabric designer's view of spring blossoming across my mother's new jacket.

The color in my mother's cheeks had been sucked into the dull red drains of her eyes. The rest of her face was white. Here and there, a purple vein.

She'd been crying, something I'd never seen her do before, not even during those last two years in Marchwood when she had every reason to. As she reached to push open the door, the man behind the counter saw an exposed, paste-colored wrist barely thick enough to support the hand coming out of it. The clerk looked toward me. "Get the door for this lady coming in, will ya? She looks like she could use some help; door's kind of heavy and it gets stuck." I didn't think he was capable of putting so many words together in a row.

My mother looked out of place, which gave me comfort, a feeling based on being somewhere first. I had been at the narcotics office for almost an hour already, so I belonged here more than she did. Even if punctuality wasn't anything to write home about in this case, it gave me a fleeting sense of superiority—even strength.

 **49**

WEAKNESS

She looked old. I never gave my mother's age much thought before. She was old enough to be my mother, to buy me matching shirts and pants, to stay home from work to be with me when I was sick. But that didn't make her old. Just older than me. Until this moment, Sarah Schaech was who she was and did what she did in relation to me. To her family. But seeing her outside this glass door, allowed me for one objective click, to see her. . . new.

She looked so different from the serrated, white-bordered snapshots of her stuck starkly against the black pages of our family photo album. The pictures dated mostly from the 1930s, '40s, and '50s, with only one or two from the last couple of years. The album aged with every handling, as yellow flakes of glue splintered from the backs of recently dead or just out-of-focus family members, and whole pages tore from their binding. *In my mind an image appeared of my mother and a diapered Howie, my mother's Kodak face happy, happy and timeless, Howie, held high above the glossy, black-and-white water of White Meadow Lake, his arms and legs wriggling a life of their own—all image, no sound—impossible to know if the dripping infant was squealing with joy or pain, impossible to know if my mother beamed from Howie's thrill or from her just-past memory of serenely dead-man-floating until her chin-strapped, vinyl bathing-capped head was yanked out of the water by Morris Lefkowitz's flubbering grand-daughter, Joyce, the girl's screams recoiling from my mom's not-dead startle.*

"I thought you were a beach ball!" the child had cried, her arms still wrapped around my mother's half-submerged head. My mother told me the "Joyce-story" every time we looked at the photograph. Judging from Sarah Schaech's toothy, Kodak face, Howie was happy. 1947. It would be two more years before I would swim into the picture.

"Stephen, do you have any idea what you are putting me through?" My mother wiped her nose, and then told me to sit up straight.

She pulled a pink Kleenex from her pocketbook, wet it with her saliva, and rubbed it across my chin. I flinched slightly but kept my mouth shut. She stopped when she realized what was on my chin was a dried-out pimple that wouldn't rub off.

"Talk to me," she ordered.

I admitted to some of the ways my friends and I had gotten high. Mainly pills and pot, I said. I didn't mention cough medicine, cleaning fluid, or scag.

She wasn't surprised about the other boys, she said, "but Jerry? And you, Stephen, I just don't understand. For a smart boy, sometimes you can do awfully stupid things." Then she looked at me intensely, and whispered, "Listen to me. Are you listening?" She paused. "I said are you listening?" I listened. "When they ask you about your part in all this with the drugs . . ."

"Yeah, Mom?"

"When they ask you about it. . ." she grabbed my chin between the fingers of her right hand so I faced her squarely, "you don't have to be George Washington."

"Ma?" She was hurting my chin.

"Lie. Do you understand me, Stephen? You lie!"

50 ◈

BAZZAZ

After almost three hours of questioning, waiting, and being moved from one room to another, I was taken back down the corridor to room 126, right next to the outer office where I was sitting when I first arrived. My view of my mother was blocked by a tall, heavyset Negro, his dark, thinning hair cut short and intent on making its way toward silver. Later, she told me that when they spoke he stood close enough for her to hear the sound of him winding his wristwatch, and she could smell his breath. Above his shirt pocket, the man wore a black and gold embossed nametag: MALCOLM BAZZAZ. I only got parts of their conversation. Every once in a while I'd lean my head out of the room to try to see and hear better.

Pacing, the man said that my friends had not been a good influence. I got that, but I missed what came next.

Then, "You're looking to see where the noise is coming from."

"Excuse me?" my mother asked.

"I saw you looking at my shoes. It's not the shoes; it's my ankles."

What the hell was he talking about? I leaned my head out from the room where I was seated and saw Officer Bazzaz lifting his pants legs, exposing a pair of yellow, green, and black diamond-patterned socks with a bright blue hot rod embroidered where the sock bulged from the bone that protruded like a speed bump on the side of his ankle. I noticed that his green socks matched his tiepin, which blended into the constellation of green dots decorating his tie. Big man, big waist, knobby little ankles. Little-kid socks. The kind I wore ten years ago.

"Ankles make this cracking noise whenever I pace," Bazzaz informed my mother. "Nothing I can do about it. From all the ligaments I tore during my school days in the Bronx, and after too. Football. Running back for Fordham University." He pronounced the name of the sport, position, and school as if the letters of each word were capitalized. "Fordham, we were a real force back then. Kings of the mountain."

My mother apologized if she was staring. "I'm afraid my mind was somewhere else," she said.

"That's quite all right. Everyone does it. Wife says I'm a regular Captain Hook's crocodile. Claims she can always hear me coming. Almost thirty years now she's saying the same thing. Lately, she sings a new tune: 'Your body took a licking, but it keeps on ticking'—that's what the wife says." Demonstrating, he walked in a circle, all the while playing with the stem of his watch. His steps snapped like bubblegum air pockets popping. He smiled. My mother smiled back.

"About my son, Mr. Bazzaz."

His ankles quieted, as if out of respect for the obvious worry in my mother's voice. "Not a good influence at all, those friends of your son. But, believe me, it could have been a whole lot worse. A whole lot."

As my mother searched her pocketbook for a tissue, my eyes momentarily hit on the shine of a golden "B," an over-sized centerpiece on the narcotic agent's belt buckle. "B" for Bazzaz I guessed. Or "behemoth," or maybe "bees," as in the sound of a winding watch? Bubble gummy ankles—starts with a "B" too, I thought. The guy had huge hands, yet until now I hadn't noticed them. What I did notice, even from more than twenty feet away, were the cluster of wrinkles around his happy forty-maybe fifty-year-old eyes, which contrasted sharply with his little-kid ankles. Bazzaz: It didn't fit him. Maybe in his younger footballing or hot-rodding days, but not now. Bubble gum: That fit him better.

"However, rest assured, Mrs. Schaech, those boys will not be the cause of any more problems for your son—not for anyone. . . for a bit anyways, three, four months, thereabouts." The long ash of a cigarette dangling from his lips bounced off Bazzaz's belly, bursting silently against the floor.

Another narcotics officer entered the room where I was sitting and led me out. The ash from Bazzaz's cigarette was still smoldering when I reached him.

"While your old friends are away, you might want to take the opportunity to make new ones, son," Officer Bazzaz suggested.

"Yes, sir. I'll try." That's what I said. What I thought was: "You pick your friends, I'll pick mine. They don't need for me to turn my back on them. Especially not now." My friends, whatever their faults, had been there for me when I needed them; now it was my turn. I'd just have to work something out between them and Diane. It was time my two worlds came together. The time my friends were going to spend away at Bergen Pines—and Mike at prison—would help straighten them out. I was sure of it. Things'll be different when they get back, I thought to myself. I know it will.

"I'd pick more wisely next time, son," the man suggested.

"Yes, sir."

"He's okay, Mrs. Schaech. I don't see him getting into more trouble. Especially with his friends out of the picture."

For the next ten minutes he described to her where they were. "Bergen Pines is for juvies, juvenile offenders," he explained. "Right here in Bergen County." My mother also learned that, besides my best friends, five other kids from the high school, whom she knew only by name, had all taken up residency there as well. He left out the part about Mike going to prison. It turned out that I was being sent home because no one thought I had anything to do with heroin, which meant, no matter what other illegal substances I might be experimenting with or illegal acts I might've committed, I was okay in the hearts and minds of my interrogators.

They had it right about heroin; there wasn't much I liked about it, whereas there didn't seem to be anything about it, on the other hand, that my friends *didn't* like. The drug had changed the dynamics of hanging out. The world had become slower, more dangerous, and ultimately—for me, at least—more boring.

Everything was smack. Where to get it, where to shoot it, who to shoot it up with. I had wanted a way out. Diane offered me that and more. Much more. Then came Lieutenant Brannick and Malcolm Bazzaz.

Bazzaz and four or five other narcotics officers had come and gone throughout the afternoon. They questioned me about several luncheonette and pharmacy break-ins around the area. Apparently, one of the robberies resulted in the severe beating of a pharmacist, a guy in his sixties. They brought up Mike's name and someone I'd never heard of. I swore I knew nothing about any pharmacist. Satisfied I was telling the truth, the agents didn't dwell long on this line of questioning.

Figuring I ought to admit to some kind of wrongdoing, I said I drank cough medicine.

"You gave your own name when you signed for the bottle of Robitussin DM? Why'd you do that?"

"The lady behind the counter asked me for my name, so I told her. Was that wrong?"

"Most of you kids give false identification when you sign for that stuff, so there's no record of your purchasing a nonprescription narcotic."

I said I never thought of that.

Without moving his head, Bazzaz's eyes pitched toward his colleague standing on the other side of my chair. His expression said this kid was too stupid or naïve or, more astonishing yet, honest to be shooting up and hiding it from anyone.

Nonetheless, shortly thereafter, I was made to stand naked while I was searched for needle marks in hiding places like the crook of my arm, behind my knees, between my toes. The guys examining me seemed disappointed that I hadn't used my body for a hammering post like that African statue on the counter across from where my mother sat waiting.

I was an insect pinned to a board, existing solely for display and analysis. I looked around the room for a picture to disappear within, but the walls were bare. The tile floor was cold beneath my bare feet. It shivered through my goose-bumped body, making it impossible for me to stand still for my examiners. Twitching limbs bore witness to my humiliation.

"He's clean," Bazzaz finally decided. Case closed.

From Bazzaz: "You got away with something this time, boy. Keep hanging out with the wrong people, maybe next time you're not so lucky." Then he added, "I see you in here again, you're mine."

Part VIII

BIRDS, BOOKS, AND BOULDERS

51

VIEW FROM A BRIDGE

From Bazzaz to beetle. Jonathan David Swayze was waiting for me to feed him when I returned from the narcotics agency. JD wasn't moving around as much as he did when I first introduced him to the dry, fishless aquarium that served as his new living quarters, but I wasn't worried; I knew that his recent sluggishness was due to his extra ounces. Weight was great. It meant that my beetle was packing more poison.

JD had new living quarters, just like my friends did. I was relieved that I didn't, although I felt a little guilty about being able to come home.

After feeding JD, I immediately telephoned Diane. I should've told her long ago about my friends and drugs, but I'd never said a word about either. Tomorrow was Saturday, which meant Diane and the museums, the best part of each week. Although I hated doing it, I called her to cancel our date.

"It wouldn't look good for you to be with me tomorrow," I said. "In case anyone saw us, I mean."

"It wouldn't look good any day, Stephen. I could get in a lot of trouble if people knew we were seeing each other outside of school. I mean, we're not just *seeing* each other, after all. It's not what anyone had in mind—especially me—when I came here to student teach."

"It'd look worse tomorrow."

"Let me worry about tomorrow. Why don't we meet somewhere now and talk. Maybe I can help you sort things out." Sounded good to me.

Not to my mother. "After what you just put me through today, you expect to go right out and fraternize with God knows who? You're not going anywhere I can't monitor what you're doing and who you're doing it with," she exhorted. Her voice was granite, but it softened when I explained that one of my teachers wanted to talk about what'd been going on with me lately. "Miss Adamsohn thought I might need a friend," I said.

Diane borrowed her aunt's car, and we drove to Fort Lee, leaving the car in the parking lot of a Chinese restaurant within walking distance of the George Washington Bridge. Following the narrow footpath that spanned the bridge's length, we stopped at a point that over-looked the trivializing 400-foot sign topping the cliffs on the Jersey side of the Hudson River. Ancient billboard rocks. I'd never seen the cliffs unlettered, so I never questioned the advertisement being there, until today.

Gazing down from my bird-like vantage point would ordinarily have caused my senses to sharpen. Ordinarily, I'd've heard the cars passing loudly behind me, each one honking, humming, stuttering, coughing, farting, pinging, or braking with its distinct voice, like the leaves in Diane's cemetery, only louder and more polluted. My eyes would've lingered over the bouldered cliffs, bright orange in spots from the glistening sunset, cliffs that stood like a wrinkled page for the eighteen-foot-high letters that spelled out PALISADES AMUSEMENT PARK. I'd've smelled the heaviness of the car exhaust fumes beneath the breezy fragrance of wind and water. Ordinarily, I'd've been unnerved by the thrilling emptiness filling the space between me, the weathered metal railing, and the faraway river below.

Not today.

"But you weren't sent away, Stephen," Diane said. "You'll be back at school Monday. There's nothing on your record to interfere with anything you might want to do in the future. You weren't hurt. You were fortunate."

"I know that. But, still, I, I don't know. Everything just feels so screwed up, disconnected. It's like us sitting up here, suspended, look-ing down into nothing, separate from all the cars whizzing by behind us." I flicked my cigarette over the railing in front of me and followed its silent fall until distance completely inhaled it.

"My brother's dead. Since his death, my father, Mr. Rigor Mortis, suddenly he's got blood pumping in his veins." I examined the yel-lowed skin on the fingers I used for gripping my cigarettes. "Yesterday did a real number on my mother. She looked more together at Howie's funeral than at the narcotics place. And when I finally make friends here in Garrison City, everyone tells me to lose them and find new ones, which is besides the point anyhow since they're all gone. And even if. . ."

Diane let me rant without interruption. When I finally stopped, she talked a little, and then I ranted some more. We went back and forth until I was talked out. And relieved. What a difference. Diane was right when she said I needed a friend.

Sensing that I was through talking for a while, Diane described her own experience since coming to Garrison City, how she had to wrestle with some of the same feelings of isolation troubling me now. "Besides you, Stephen," she said, "I have no friends here." Diane claimed the need to distance herself from the students in her classes, yet her age excluded her from the after-school plans of the instructors who spent their time with their spouses or children.

"How about teaching?" I asked her. "Was the move up here so you could student teach worth it?"

"I love teaching! From my first day in kindergarten, I wanted to be a teacher." But besides that, she said, what made her move to New Jersey really worth it was *me*.

Suddenly, the first half of my day shrunk.

Later, in response to another one of my questions, Diane remarked that student teaching had turned out to be even more rewarding than she'd anticipated. When she stood in front of a classroom, her natural shyness allowed her to empathize with the most reserved students. Before coming to New Jersey, she was one of them, she said. "If my high-school boyfriends ever voted on someone to win an 'Inhibition Award', I would have won by a landslide. 'Most Inhibited', that would be me. I'm telling you, if any of the guys I hung around with or dated ever overheard my conversations with you, Stephen, they'd be shocked by how many words in a row I could put together. Being quiet was one of the main things I was ever good at. My ex-boyfriend used to tell me so all the time. Sometimes he'd replace 'quiet' with 'invisible.' He meant it as a compliment."

"Trust me, Diane, there's nothing invisible about you," I quickly objected. "The guy sounds like an idiot."

I asked her to tell me about him.

"Bruce, he was a year older than me, which impressed my friends but intimidated me. Then again, even with guys my own age I was always unsure of myself."

Hard for me to imagine.

Then, instead of offering any more information about the jerk who didn't seem to know anything about the person sitting next to me, the look in Diane's eyes intensified, and she said, "With Bruce I always felt inferior, for no good reason—if there ever is one. He never made me feel *jangly*, or important, like you do, Stephen. Always do. And he's nowhere near as smart as you are."

I kissed her, but I didn't know what to say, and I think the candor of her own comment embarrassed her as much as me. So she changed the subject back to teaching, one of her favorite topics. I was glad she steered it that way and not back to drugs. She had a way of knowing the right thing to do and when to do it.

Calling the shots at the front of the room, Diane told me, enabled her to see herself, and be seen by even the most disruptive students, as an in-charge member of the class. This was new for her, and she liked it. "Teaching is amazing," Diane said. "Like guiding students through the Salinas Valley of John Steinbeck's short story, *The Chrysanthemums*.

It was one of my first days of teaching, and it was just amazing. I don't know what the kids in the class thought about our discussion, but I loved it. The separate lines of dream and reality came together for me during that class. *The high, gray-flannel fog of winter closed off the Salinas Valley from the sky and from all the rest of the world. On every side it sat like a lid on the mountains and made of the valley a closed pot.*"

"I remember every word spoken in class that day," Diane said. "'How does Steinbeck set up the mood of his story?' That's how I started. 'How does he evoke the state of mind of the main character?'" Diane laughed. "It was probably the first time I ever used the word 'evoke,'" she said. "Anyway, no one answered at first, which scared me—I was afraid I was about to bomb—but then you raised your hand and created for me a perfect moment. I wanted to hug you." "I would've hugged you right back," I said. Diane kept going. "You talked about the image being claustrophobic, like life in the valley where the story was set, and how the lady in the story felt trapped, which went along with the feeling of smothering you got from the image of a lid fitted on top of a pot."

"Then I think Laini Adin said something, right?" I asked.

"That's right!" she said. "I can't believe you remembered that. Laini talked about pots playing a part in the story also because the man who came into the lady's life was a fix-it man, repairing mainly pots and pans. 'So it's cool,' Laini said, 'how the author brings in pots right away, in the very first sentence.' I could've hugged her, too. You and Laini did most of the talking, but by the time the bell rang, half the kids in the class had joined in!"

Diane's joyous remembrance of her "perfect moment" was rubbing off on me. We had both temporarily forgotten all about needles and narcotic agents. Well, neither of us "forgot." It was more like we'd come to an unspoken agreement to shelve that subject for the time being. I guess we both needed a break from it. Stepping back can be a great way to go forward.

Diane talked about having no one to share any of her teaching experiences with until she met me by accident at the Dintenfass Gallery in the city. "Then we walked around the city together all day, and I got to know someone I didn't want to say goodnight to."

Diane let her fingertips graze the back of my hand. "You know, Stephen, having no friends and no history can be good in some ways. There's a kind of freedom in it," she observed, "if you choose to see it that way."

"You sound like my grandfather," I said.

"I don't think I like the sound of that."

"No, no. I mean it as a compliment, and I'm not talking about the 'quiet' or 'invisible' kind. What you said is the type of thing my grandfather might say to me right now, and my grandfather has always been one of my favorite people in the world." (I was presently adding a new "favorite" to the list, I thought to myself.)

Suddenly my train of thought changed. "Shit!" I blurted out. "I hope my mother doesn't tell him anything about today." She had promised me she wasn't going to say too much about it to my father—no more than necessary—which probably wouldn't be too hard, I reasoned, because he's not the type to ask too many questions. And I didn't care what he'd have to say anyway. But what about my grandfather?

"And if she does?" Diane asked.

"If she does? If she told him Jerry and my other friends, and me. . . we've been shooting dope? Diane. I'd never look the same to him. As far as he's concerned, only degenerates fool around with drugs. I'm his only grandson. I think it'd kill him to find. . ."

"I have a feeling he's a lot stronger than you think, Stephen. I've never met your grandfather, but if he loves you anywhere near as much as you love him, I know he'd deal with anything you might ever shove his way. Anyway, it's not as if you're addicted to any of the drugs you've been fooling around with or anything. Right?"

I jerked my hand away from Diane's and smacked my fist against the bridge railing. Why'd she have to ask me something like that? I shot dope a couple of times. That doesn't make someone a drug addict!

Neither of us spoke for a few moments. I placed my hand on her stockinged knee, gently, and we talked.

Later, she said, "So you did something stupid. Okay, you did it and you were lucky. You got away with something. Now you just have to take advantage of the break you got. Nothing so very bad happened."

Nothing bad? She didn't have to stand naked in front of a bunch of goddamn cops, or whoever they were, looking for needle marks. When she talked about how much worse it could've been, I didn't stop her. "You could be dead," she said. "You know how easy it is to kill yourself by shooting poison into your body? Or you could've developed a habit, or gotten sent to that shelter where they sent your friends." I didn't say anything when she said all that. But when she said I was probably lucky that all of this happened—that was too much.

"Lucky?" I spit the word out.

A Conway Twitty song rode by on its way to Manhattan, a Midwestern voice filled with New Jersey fumes, followed several car-lengths behind with Little Anthony and the Imperials.

"Yeah, lucky," she repeated. I just didn't see it yet, she claimed. I didn't see yet what it was about today that I could learn from. She said more, but that's what it all amounted to, until she added, "What was going on for you with your friends is over, Stephen." She put her face against my neck. Her cheek felt warmer than I expected. "It *is* over, isn't it?" I don't think I had ever before heard a question stated so earnestly. I looked at her before I answered. Unlike what I heard in her voice, her face was expressionless.

"What do you mean?" I whispered. "What's over?"

"The drugs thing. Your fooling around with drugs."

"Of course it's over! You think I'm crazy?"

"Don't be mad at me." She moved my hand up to her thigh and covered my fingers with hers.

"Since we've been seeing each other, I started backing away from my friends," I confided. "Yeah, I tried drugs before. . . pot mostly; I like to have a joint once in a while, pills. . . hard stuff only a couple of times."

We didn't speak, and the surrounding traffic momentarily disappeared. I shouldn't've kept this from her until now. I looked at her. I had no idea what she was thinking.

Until she told me.

She told me about her sister, who had a drinking problem and had been involved with drugs since junior high school. Last year, Avril and her boyfriend stole a car and drove it through the window of a pet shop. Killed dozens of salamanders, lizards, and two dogs. The car also knocked over a couple of trash cans filled with about five thousand crickets waiting to be fed to the hundreds of reptiles for which the pet shop was best known. Most of the crickets survived and escaped through the broken shop window after scavenging beneath Avril and her boyfriend's bloodied hair and clothes. Avril was sentenced to eighteen months at a Bergen Pines-type facility in southern Maryland.

"So what you've told me about you and your friends, Stephen, doesn't shock me. At all. But it turns me off, and it scares me. For you. And for us—if there's going to be an 'us.' You and your friends are just getting started with something that my sister is working hard to get over. I'm praying she will, but I don't know. To be honest with you, I don't think she ever will. She just keeps making the same stupid choices."

"I know where heroin can lead, Stephen, and I'd hate to see it take you there." Diane looked down at the water. "And I'm sure as hell not going along with you. I've already been, with my sister and her friends, and nothing about it interests me. Believe me, absolutely nothing."

I asked her more about her sister, and she told me. "Avril is one of the reasons I left home to do my student teaching up here," she added. "My parents wanted me to get away. Maybe they were right. Anyway, if I didn't come here I'd've never met you. I'm hoping that's a good thing."

Of course it was a good thing. I thought often about what a *great* thing it was. But for the moment, my thoughts kept cringing over the kind of reaction her sister must've gotten from her parents when they found out about the stolen car, the drinking and drugs, and the dead lizards and dogs. If Diane got the silent treatment for two weeks from her father just for planting trees, and her hummingbirds got tarred and feathered by her mother, what must their reaction to Avril have been? After all the crickets, I couldn't help thinking that she might've welcomed the kind of silent response her father favored.

Lifting my hand from her leg to kiss my fingers, Diane told me that she loved me. Behind us, an oil truck steamed by. "I'm glad I was able to tell you about Avril. I want you to know everything about me."

"I love you," she repeated. "And I don't want anything bad to ever happen to you. Promise me it never will."

I didn't promise anything. What I said—loudly, because of the passing truck—was, *"I love you too!!"* I screamed it with such conviction that Diane laughed.

Then the breathtaking bridge and everyone—Conway Twitty, Little Anthony and the Imperials, everyone—passing across it simultaneously exhaled.

52 ⬥

HALLELUJAH, SPLASH

"I love you too!" Was that *my* voice? Where these words were concerned—as in many other areas of our relationship, including those having nothing to do with words—both Diane and I were virgins. The closest I ever got was "love always" at the end of each of the letters I wrote to Maura Laganella when she went to Camp Chicopee the summer after sixth grade. I didn't mean to blurt it out now, so resoundingly, here. Important, virgin words such as these were meant for quieter, less polluted places, like mountaintops.

Or even loftier sites.

Let them dance in praise of the Lord,
Let them celebrate with drum and harp,
Let His faithful sing in triumph. . .
(and while they're at it),
Let them rejoice as they hear me (first time ever) Proclaim:
I LOVE YOU, DIANE!
Hallelujah and Praise Be and Holy Shit! I love you.

I can still remember the first time I uttered certain words or phrases. The first time I said "pungent," I was at the house of one of my fourth-grade friends, finishing off a slice of lemon meringue pie that kept making my left eye close. "Mea culpa" was sixth grade. In the tenth grade I spit out the word "douche bag" and almost instantly DiMaeoli screamed. Ever since, I've associated "douche bag" with wailing and relief.

Sitting then along the edge of the G. W. Bridge, I could swear I saw the Fort Lee and Cliffside Park boulders rock giddily back and forth. My declaration to Diane had just escaped without pausing to check with me first. "I love you, too, Diane. I love you, too," I declared again and again.

I looked to the sign adorning the cliffs.

IN HONOR OF STEPHEN SCHAECH'S
DECLARATION OF LOVE
ALL MALE CONGREGATION MEMBERS SHOULD
WEAR YARMULKES NEXT TUESDAY. AMEN.

Then the letters changed back to PALISADES AMUSEMENT PARK, and underneath, smaller, another message: SURF BATHING.

I moved my hand up Diane's bare thigh just above the edge of her stocking. She pulled her skirt down over my hand, but didn't stop me from exploring. I moved slowly, gently. My tongue touched hers and danced behind her lips. I slipped my fingers beneath the elastic strip bordering her panties. The feel of her skin beneath my palm excited me, as did the thick, coarse hair and moisture against my fingertips. Diane understood my excitement and responded by stroking a part of my body that no one but me had ever touched before.

Under the bridge, a cigarette that a young, jubilant man flicked over the railing somersaulted into the sky and glided back and forth within Hudson River breezes before penetrating the surface of the water like a diver with his back arched and his toes pointed. The cigarette barely caused a splash, and even if you listened carefully you couldn't hear the tiny hiss it made, but its fiery, yet enchantingly slow, gracefully awkward freefall was downright exhilarating.

April 17, 1966

BRIDGE
(based on *The Resurrection* by El Greco)

While I sat, he rose, a tornado in repose,
jolting earth and Eden. With eyes closed,

192

The Resurrection
by
El Greco

El Greco (Domenikos Theotokopulos). *The Resurrection.* Oil on canvas, 275 x 127 cm. Inv.
825. Muso del Prado, Madrid, Spain. Eric Lessing/Art Resource, New York

I read tomes of carved and stone-cold pages. Now I know
the child who would later stroke
kindred letters and bio notes, as tales were told
of fathers, sons, and holy ghosts.

Naked within wintry tombs,
warmed only by the pomp of a soldier's plume,
I dozed, missing what went down—or up. No excuse.
Me alone. I blew it.

By a well, connecting earth and a frozen hell,
a noble maiden, dressed in humble robes
warmly exposed, and then consoled, my sorrow.
She said, "Moments of freedom are blessings."
But the most surprising words were mine.
Her eyes and my virgin replies sure did revive time.

When I awoke, my friends said, "Holy Moses,
you missed what God composed!"
What do they know?

—Stephen Schaech—

 **53**

KILL HIM AND GIVE HIM BIRTH

The night I returned from the bridge, I had two dreams, one for me, one for my brother. In my dream I was at home, working on a writing assignment that Diane had presented earlier in the week, this one inspired by an image of Siva, a many-armed Indian deity. "Not exactly Venus de Milo, is it?" Diane had kidded as she placed it upon the ledge of the blackboard.

My poem may have read something like this:

Kill Him Already or You'll Always Be Dead

Dead Fred's at the top of the stairs,
agile, sly, and crazy.
Running in place, smiling face,

Dancing Siva
Anonymous Artist

Dancing Siva, Early 8th c., anonymous; Vanni/Art Resource, New York; Temple of Kailasanatha, Kanchipuram, Tamil Nadu, India

the man-child, Jonathan David Swayze,
takes a lickin' but keeps on tickin',
kickin' all the while.

The late bug-man is lethal, scheming his way
into the shoes of Fred Astaire, beware.
A tornado in repose:
bare feet, bent legs, snapping fingers, flailing toes.

Why die? Tick tock, clickety clack, tick tock.
Tapping tunes with flapping arms, he tries to fly.
Time for Resurrection. . .

That's as far as I got—I think—but it wouldn't've mattered if I'd completed what I'd started because, just before my dream ended, I tore up what I had written, which I soon regretted because once awake I could barely remember any of it. I had a feeling my poem had something to do with licking a clock rather than what I've rewritten for myself, but I couldn't reason through that line of thought, so I stuck with what I rewrote.

"One of your best yet," Diane insisted after hearing about the lost poem from my dream. "Every word in its perfect place. I'd bet on it."

"But you never even read it, so how can you be so sure it was good?" I challenged. "Maybe all the words were *wrong*."

"In dreams, Stephen, everything is always just so, just as it was meant to be."

"There you go again, Diane. I'm telling you, you'll get along great with my grandfather."

"I can't wait to meet him."

"But I don't know about the dreaming stuff," I said, not wanting to change the subject. "What I wrote in my head was probably nothing special. Just *seems* like it was 'cause I can't remember it now. If you can't remember something you can't criticize yourself for it."

"Criticize? How can you criticize a dream, Stephen? How can you criticize a dream?"

"What if it's a nightmare?"

"Nightmares are only dreams, and dreams are just what we need them to be, whether they make us happy or sad. They're there for some reason. It's up to us to figure out what we're going to make of them. Don't you think?"

That's not how I saw it, I said. What I believed was that sometimes nightmares could work on a person so bad that that person wouldn't ever want to go to sleep again.

Yes, that's how she might have expected me to see it, she said, adding, "And as far as 'criticizing yourself' goes, Stephen, with you, I'd change that to 'punishing' yourself. I think that's more like it. I don't know why 'punishing', but that's what it feels like to me."

My second dream centered on a letter from my grandfather to Howie. It captures the lawyerly voice Grandfather Oscar always assumes when he writes anything, even birthday cards, which this is, sort of. There was no danger I would lose these words upon awakening because they didn't exist only in the drowsy rhythm of my dreams, to be lost once the dust fell from my eyes. In her treasured scrapbook, my mother had saved the letter for Howie, who always made sure his hands were clean when he held it.

New York, August 21, 1949

Dearest Howard,

This will indeed be a labor of love, for it is being written to my cherished grandchild, who I know reciprocates my feelings. This letter is special, as it is written just for you. Normally I write to mommy, and in the body of the letter, Howard is the subject of interest. But this one will be different, for it will speak directly to you—and in instances where others will be mentioned at all, it will be entirely coincidental.

You see, boychik, you will be four years old your next birthday; you are becoming a big boy already. Therefore we must begin to think of you as an individual who merits a letter for your very own. Particularly so, in view of the fact that you so enjoy going with mother to the post office every day to post and receive the incoming mail.

So here goes your zayde's first personal letter to his sweet little man, Howard.

If it were not for the fact that I wouldn't think of depriving you of even one second from the many years of happiness you are entitled to as a child, I would earnestly wish you were a few years older already so you could actually read and understand and also appreciate this letter, how I feel about you, dear child, and what you mean to me and all those who know and love you as I do.

In time you will realize just what such a bundle of sweetness bearing the name Howard has meant to each of us since your birth; what rejoicing your smiling self has brought into our lives. Riding home from Marchwood on the bus, my heart is filled with your joyous squeals as you float back and forth upon that blue metal swing of yours in the park. My love for you is bound-less, and the more I give you, the more I seem to have inside me and the richer it makes me feel.

I think of you, dear boychik, and I am reminded of the saying, "God could not be everywhere—so He made big brothers." Of course you know you will always be my eldest grandchild. Now that your daddy and mommy are on the eve of a new "Blessed Event" and your anxiously awaited "Little Sister" or "Little Brother" will be here in about two months, kaynahora, and that everyone, including you, will love this child dearly, please be assured of one thing—no one can ever take your place with me. You are my one and only Howie.

With tons of love to you and your family,
Grandpa Oscar

Part IX

WITH A VASTLY OPENED EYE

54 ◈

SUPERMAN

"**S**tephen?"

"What's wrong, Grandma?" With just two or three syllables of Leah Bialintz's telephone voice, I could always intuit my grandmother's mood. Put a microphone in the hands of Perry Como, Julius La Rosa, or any other of my grandmother's favorite performers, and out comes a story told with lyrical emotion. Put a telephone in the hands of Leah Bialintz and a less tuneful but no less emotional story swells through the lines.

"Stephen? Is that you, sweetheart?"

"What's the matter?"

"Please come over, Stephen. Maybe *you* can talk some sense into your idiotic grandfather. I know *I* can't."

"Grandma, Grandpa isn't. . ."

"*Oysh*! You always defend him. Before you even know. Stephen. He listens to you. So do you think just once he should maybe listen to me? Even once? Is that asking so much? *Red tsu der vant*!"

Red tsu der vant! I wasn't sure of that one—'go talk to the wall,' something like that. The few times I could remember hearing this Yiddish phrase it was belched in exasperated response to inflexibility.

"What's the matter, Grandma?"

"Aaach. You know how your grandfather can be when he gets something into that head of his."

As I waited for her to continue, I looked down at the curled, fat Yellow Pages, a permanent fixture on the counter just below the kitchen telephone. The book was opened to REAL, page 854. I leafed through the section—851 to 865—fourteen pages devoted to REAL. I wondered if IMAGINED was in the Yellow Pages too, and if so, how much coverage it'd get. REAL stood alone. Strange. I had always conferred equal time and importance to reality and imagination. I even thought the two were inseparable. But there it was, in the top left corner of the page, divorced from its mate, and accompanied instead by a three-digit number and an underlined "R": REAL. My eyes scanned one line down and read: REAL ESTATE—RESIDENTIAL. Filling one third of the page below this heading was an advertisement printed over a blueprint-type diagram of the interior of a house. The advertisement read:

LET BEN HAYES
HELP YOU THRU THE REAL ESTATE MAZE

Apparently, the intricacy and confusion of reality was not lost on Ben Hayes. As my grandmother spoke, I thumbed through the pages. I wondered what Mr. Hayes might have to say about IMAGINATION. N—NURSES. . . M—MOVING AND STORAGE. . . L—LOCKS & LOCK-SMITHS. . . I—that's it, I. Under the listing I, I found ICE. . . ICE CREAM & FROZEN DESSERTS DEALERS. . . IDENTIFICATION CARD SERVICE, IMMIGRATION & NATURALIZATION CONSULTANTS. . . I scanned the pages. Back and forth through the "I's". It wasn't there. There was no IMAGINATION in the Yellow Pages.

"So, does anybody think I could convince him to get such an idea out of his head? I should live so long, with my high blood pressure no less!" my grandmother complained.

"He should listen to me? Who am I? Chopped liver, that's who I am! Or a *kvetch*. That's right! When he gets something like this into that head of his, I become a *kvetch*. God forbid he should. . ."

One thing about Grandma Leah's phone conversations, there was always time to leaf through a book.

Why should he listen to her? she kept repeating. Why? Because what he'd gotten into his head this time could kill him, she kept answering herself. He could break his neck, God forbid, or his leg.

"Grandma."

"Mr. Feinstein next door broke his leg two years ago and he's never been the same. Ida is still tying his shoes for him. She's a saint. My heart goes out to her."

I looked up "HAYES". I found "Hard Body Health Spa", "Hats by Lazarus", "Hauling Services, Inc.", but no "Hayes." I pictured an out-of-shape, middle-aged realtor puffing his way up the stairs of a high-rise to show a client a recently vacated apartment.

"But does he listen to me?" my grandmother continued.

"Who, Ben Hayes?"

"Who?"

I didn't answer.

"Why should he listen to me?" my grandmother complained. "What could I know? I don't read the books your grandfather reads. He's the knower. Whenever he gets something in his head and I should try to reason with him, I'm all of a sudden thin air. I don't know why I. . ."

"Calm down, Grandma, please, and tell me what's the matter."

"What's the matter? You want I should tell you? They were talking, that's what's the matter. No, bragging—not talking—bragging. Like babies, both of them, two *shtarkers* bragging about how strong they are and how fast they run, and 'I can run faster than that,' says one, and then the other can run even faster, and 'in my day I could. . .' and then your grandfather comes up with: 'Why don't we just put it to a test,

Yankel? We can meet tomorrow at sunup in the field behind your apartment at Forstops Village, and we'll see just who is the faster, me or you.'"

"A race? Is that what this is about?" I closed the Yellow Pages. On the face of the book, just below the dates November, 1964-October, 1965 was a painting of a dramatically sunlit house, starkly cut out from the sky. A fussy-looking house in a very *un*fussy-looking painting. Printed in the painting's lower right-hand corner, paralleling a stretch of train tracks running across the base of the picture, was the name Edward Hopper.

"A race. That's right. In the morning when the milk is delivered. Do you have any idea how cold it is in April when the sun is just starting up? Where does he think we are? Palm Springs?"

"But what's so bad about a race?"

"So bad? *Gotenyu*! You want I should tell you what's so bad?" There was, of course, no way to stop her from telling. "He could have a heart attack, or drop dead," she railed, "or worse" (which included at least twenty other grim possibilities). "And Morris Lefkowitz—don't ask! One of their oldest friends, he and Irma were the reason my grandparents moved to these apartments in the first place. "Morris," my grandmother screamed, "is already on medication for his. . . "

I moved the phone further away from my ear. My grandmother's voice sizzled like a gnat. I looked down at the painting on the cover of the phone book. The painting was quiet—no people, no cars, no pets, no birds in the sky, not even a train in sight. The house was vacant, desolate. But no FOR SALE sign either; Ben Hayes hadn't heard about this one.

Or maybe there was one inhabitant. No more; one at the most. All alone. Staring. Sitting in a chair staring straight ahead at the sun shining in through the second-story window, the one window with its shade pulled up. What kind of person would live in such a nowhere place? Inside the house I imagined the unimaginative, out-of-shape Ben Hayes sitting all alone, a red, black, and yellow patch-square afghan (the kind Grandma Leah made as a gift for any occasion—wedding, graduation, new baby) draped across his lap. Having just arrived home from work, where he had spent the past eight hours winding his way through the real estate maze, the exhausted realtor sat there all weekend, mindlessly staring at a chunk of sunlight cast upon an upstairs bedroom wall. Vivid imaginings would fill the blank, impermanent squares of sun trapped inside the house. Ben Hayes, all alone. His phone number unlisted.

"We're not talking about two teenagers here—even if your grandfather and his pals still see themselves that way." "Grandma, Grandpa will probably forget all about the race in half an hour. You know how he forgets."

"All of a sudden you're a mind-reader? He'll *forget*. He won't forget, Stephen. Take my word. He's been talking about racing for the past two days. That's all he talks about. Over and over with his *faccocta* race. He forgets he just told me. That's the only thing he forgets. It's coming out my ears already. About this he wouldn't forget. Believe me."

Streaking across the bottom of Hopper's painting of the isolated house, I imagined an exhilarated Oscar Bialintz and a dispirited Morris Lefkowitz, their rundown feet, gray like railroad track gravel, sending sooty dust into the air and making it difficult to see not only the columns of the porch down below, but the rooflines of the house way up at the top of the picture, as well. By the time Morris passed the heavily shadowed front door, Grandpa Oscar had run off the side of the painting. "You cheat-ed," Morris screamed in short, out-of-wind bursts. "You star-ted be-fore an-y-one said READ-Y. . . GET SET. . . GO! A race doesn't count un-less some-one shouts REA-DY. . . GET SET. . . GO!"

"Stop blubbering and run!" my grandfather shouted. "Let's see what you've got, *Yankel*!"

As Morris ran off the edge of the painting, my attention wandered back to the phone. "What do you want me to do, Grandma? You want me to talk to Grandpa, I'll talk to Grandpa."

"He'll listen if you talk to him. I know he will." These words were accompanied by the sound of metal chair legs scraping across linoleum. I visualized my grandmother settling into one of the wide-cushioned chairs surrounding her kitchen table. She sat with her legs apart, each foot firmly planted on the floor, her stockings rolled down to her ankles. "Pick it up!" she would reprimand anyone who scraped one of the chairs across her floor. "Pick it up or I'll hear about it tomorrow from Mr. I'm-Trying–To-Live-Out-My–Life-In-Peace-And-Quiet downstairs. To hear him talk you'd think a locomotive drives through his front door every time our fannies wrinkle the kitchen cushions."

Again she asked me to talk to her husband. "For me, sweetheart" she implored. "Talk to him before he does himself damage. What would I do without your grandfather? He could fall and break his neck. Mr. Superman. Next he'll be wearing a red and blue cape."

The image conjured by my grandmother's comment was irre-sistible. Suddenly, the telephone I was holding was on its hook inside a telephone booth, my Clark Kently grandfather about to leap out in a single bound.

"Don't laugh. The older he gets, the younger he thinks he is. Lately, every meal I fix has to be something his mother used to make for him when he still had to have his mittens pinned to his jacket. His Majesty's cravings—pot cheese with noodles, herring and boiled potatoes. . . who ever heard of such combinations?"

"I'll call him tonight."

"No. Come over now. Please, Stephen. For me."

Charity: That's what I appealed to, my grandfather's sense of charity. I pointed out that if Oscar won the race, as we both knew he would, how did he think Mr. Lefkowitz would feel? Why put him through that? A man who doesn't accept defeat easily or with grace. And don't forget Irma. Then Morris would have to face Irma, who would know for sure her husband wasn't the fastest runner of Forstops Village. My argument worked. I knew it would. I knew my grandfather.

But the discussion wasn't over. "Just between you and me, Big Boy," Grandpa Oscar whispered before I left, "how about if we meet early in the morning sometime this week so you can time me? I'll just race the clock. Lefkowitz says he can circle the track behind his apartment in less than five minutes. We'll just see how long it takes *me*. Only don't mention it to Grandma Leah what we're doing. You know womenfolk. She's gotten it into her head I'm just an *alter kocker*, too old to do anything besides watch *Guiding Light* with her on the machine. Your grandma is a good woman. Her heart is stronger than you even know. She loves me and takes good care of me, but sometimes she can out-*kvetch* an entire mahjong group of mother hens."

It took me longer to talk my grandfather out of racing the clock than it did to talk him out of racing his friend.

55

MORRIS? ARE YOU THERE, MORRIS?

And then the panting stopped. Grandpa Oscar crossed the finish line.

He lay on the ground, concentrating all his energy on breathing. One breath. Then another. Then nothing. No movement of the lungs or stomach. A long time without a breath. Too long. And then a faint breath, just one. Then, again, nothing. Finally he inhaled, but he couldn't exhale. "Breathe, Grandpa, breathe!" I pleaded. Complying one last time with my wishes, Grandpa Oscar breathed out the air.

His lips were white. These same warm lips that had so many times kissed away my hurt, praised, consoled, counseled, and kidded me on so many occasions, now they were silent and cold and white. And his teeth were brown. Decayed. I never noticed that before. The fingers on my grandfather's left hand twitched gently, gracefully, like a choreographed drowning, and then they stopped. His chest rose and fell a few last times. Then that stopped too, as a vastly opened eye penetrated deeply into my horrified gaze. I prayed for "once more," but he had no more to give. "What sad eyes you have, Big Boy," Grandpa Oscar's stare seemed to say. "And I know why such sad eyes. Sad and full of shame."

A thin line of black blood beaded the floor just to the side of my grandfather's head. The blood didn't come from the battered part that I could see; it came from inside his ear. A splintered three-and-one-half-foot-long 2x4 2-by-4 lay beside him. Embedded in the wooden fibers of the board were strands of white hair. White. Everything. White, like a shroud, bleached the walls, the windows, the ladder-back chair, my friends, the drugs, my grandfather's sneakers, his lips, the blood beading his ear—everything, everything was drained of the warmth and pulse of color. Everything was white, except his teeth, which were still brown, and the blood on the floor, which was suddenly turning lighter and lighter gray. White, pure white—once it meant possibilities, goodness, innocence, gaiety, radiance. . . especially radiance—now it meant death, colorless and appalling death.

I was alone in the room, as alone as I ever was before, shut off from my grandfather and from my friends standing above me, watching. I closed my eyes because the whiteness stung, but that bright vibration was trapped beneath my closed eyes as well, and it stung even more in there.

"Breathe, *Zayde*, breathe!"

My grandfather looked like he was swimming when he fell, his arms flailing as if the air were water, as if his arms thought if they flailed fast enough they would keep his body afloat. But the air offered no resistance, and Oscar Bialintz sank into the floor.

When I heard the sound of board meeting brittle bone, and as I saw my grandfather about to sink, I felt a throbbing in my own head. Everything was unreal. The bruised baseball, suspended just outside the window of apartment 11B like the light bulb of a streetlamp, was not real, but the raised red seams curled across the ball's white leather hide cast stitched shadows just like the seams a real ball would cast. Unreal stars suspended high above the roof of apartment 11B sparkled across my grandfather's sunken cheeks. A locomotive bellowed inside the living room wall, accompanying the *tu-tu-whoo, tu-tu-whoo* of an owl. There was no owl, no locomotive, no ball. But I saw and heard them.

I had wanted to catch my grandfather in my arms, but I couldn't move.

"Shit, man," Mike had cried. "I didn't mean to get *you*. I thought there was two of 'em. You jumped in front. Wha'dja go and jump in front of him for, Shakes?" No one but me had yet recognized the shadowed, six-foot figure who had made his way up the stairs.

In that moment of stillness just before the board in Mike's hands came crushing down, I recognized just how wrong this all was. It was not an intruder, I realized too late. And even if it was. . . "But it's my. . ." I couldn't even scream to make things stop. I saw the splintered board. I saw the light from the streetlamp smacking against my grandfather's smooth, bare skull. "Mike, no!" Jerry screamed. "It's Mr. Bialintz!"

". . . Anyone comes in we don't know, we off 'em," Mike had said. "Someone comes in and surprises us, it's gonna turn out to be *his* surprise. Anyone got any problems with that?" I had remained silent then and I was silent now. We were all silent.

"Morris? You there, Morris?" Oscar had called. Afraid he might awaken Morris's wife, Oscar's call to Morris was hushed. Upstairs, my friends and I had heard a man's voice on the stairwell. There must be more than one on the steps. Gotta get 'em both!

The man carried a glove in his right hand as he climbed the brick stairs leading up to the door marked 11B. His gloves had protected his hands from the morning cold. They had protected his knuckles while he tapped on the door and then opened it. "Morris? You there, Morris?"

Morris was not there, he was fast asleep in the apartment next door. Grandpa Oscar was in the wrong apartment.

"Morris? Morris? You ready?"

"Breathe, Grandpa, breathe!"

"You ready to run with me, Morris? To show me what you got?"

Mike watched two ever-widening lines of blood stretching down from my forehead to my chin. "Why'dja go and jump in front of me?" As Mike spoke these words he swung his arm outward, releasing my grandfather's glove. He didn't even know he was holding it. When board and head collided, my grandfather's hand had jerked upward. Reflexively, perhaps to protect himself from what he thought was a punch, Mike reached for the intruder's hand. He grabbed his glove instead. Mike was holding the glove when he swung the board the second time.

"Breathe, Grandpa. Breathe!" After my grandfather stopped breathing, I stood up, and for an instant I faced Mike. "Why'dja jump in fronta me?" my friend screamed, as he threw the glove down the stairs.

My head throbbed. Where was I? I heard nothing. Saw nothing—except the sting of my grandfather's ancient, accusing eyes staring deeply into mine. And I saw his hand, his woolen-gloved hand falling down the stairs.

Or was the glove coming up the steps, reaching toward me? I couldn't tell, since everything about what had just happened with my grandfather seemed to happen in reverse time—outside of time.

Nothing in the Forstops Village apartment remained focused or still, except a high-backed chair and a glove, the glove which suddenly was not flying down the stairs, or up the stairs, but hanging motionless, waiting, waiting for me.

So many times Grandpa Oscar had reached out his hand to me. So many times we had sat hand in hand on his couch in Garrison City.

The blood from my forehead stained my shirt. Where was I? I didn't know. I needed the protection of my grandfather's touch. And my grandfather needed me. "Here I am, *Zayde*," I called, as I reached out with my whole body, flinging myself into the black hole of the stairwell for one final embrace.

The stars are not wanted now: put out every one.
Pack up the moon and dismantle the sun;
Pour away the ocean and sweep up the wood;
For nothing now can ever come to any good.

(excerpt from W. H. Auden's *Funeral Blues*)

Part X

LINES

56 ❖

HIS CHAIR

Stunned, upon the ladder-back chair in apartment 11B, I had lost my place. Withdrawing through a devastating stare, I sat alone, waiting, in a house by a railroad, a weightless house despite the nearby train tracks that wanted to anchor it to the earth, a house that ran nonstop in and out of time through a familiar place that I could not, for the life of me, identify. This is where I sat, waiting, waiting for. . . what? 11B had disappeared, but the chair remained; it kept the house grounded, and it kept me from wobbling out of control, from drifting away, forever.

The aged chair—with its thick oak legs tapered toward tarnished metal feet, here and there past-life traces of blue-gray, black, green, turquoise, and ochre paint peeking out through fading grains of wood, the chair's slatted back climbing, climbing, well past the height any head would ever look back to for support, its no-nonsense "L" shape making basic accommodations for bends, like at the knees, but none at all for curves; like the sway of a spine, is highly nuanced in color, yet simple in form. Comfortable enough. No, not comfortable, tolerable says it better. Merely tolerable.

But safe.

My mother, with her uncompromising joints, would've groaned out loud every time she rose after conforming to the right angles of such a stiff throne. But she would discover, as I would soon learn, that as long as she sat there time would take a deep breath, inhaling not only as much sorrow, but as much distance as it could absorb, and she would feel no pain as she sat upon its painted, chipped-away, scratched, cigarette-burned, butt-polished seat (the only curves apparent being the water rings that scarred the grainy surface like wooden acne), lost within the chair's timeless spell.

Two weeks ago, when the former tenants, the Ippolitos, vacated apartment 11B, they took everything with them except the ladder-back chair, the one piece of furniture left behind by the previous tenants as well. The chair lent a sense of ordered stability to the Ippolitos' otherwise nondescript home. Everyone knew the story: Two summers before, when Merisi, senior member of the family, learned that his shoe store, Newark Bootery (in Ippolito hands for three generations), had been set ablaze by rioters, he found staring solace in the chair's firm discomfort. "Suburban Sun Undone by Urban Burn," read the headlines. Almost a lifetime before, Merisi spent a gleeful afternoon on that same upright piece of furniture frolicking upon his uncle's knee, playing "ah bom bootz," their foreheads slowly touching on "bootz," baby Merisi giggling with each bounce. In between the "bootzing" and the Bootery's fiery demise, myriad joys and miseries settled upon the throne wrinkled by fading grains of wood. More than once, Merisi had sat there with his wife on his lap facing him, the two of them looking to add to the number of Ippolitos living in apartment 11B. Everyone knew the story; their gossipy neighbors downstairs could hear them above the joyful groaning of ladder-back feet rubbing enthusiastically against the floorboards.

Joys, sure, the chair had seen its fair share, but there had been sorrows, too. After the loss of his business, Mr. Ippolito never again sat on what his family had always referred to as "His Chair."

Now it was *my* chair.

 # 57

SHIVA

Sitting on my chair, I remembered the Marchwood living room gatherings immediately after Howie's funeral three years ago. I had just become, after fourteen years, my parents' only son. For a week, my family and I would sit *shiva* to honor and grieve Howie's death. Seven warm, sunny days; the weather had gotten it all wrong.

Aunts and uncles I hardly knew, neighbors and friends, Mr. Engsberg and a few of my other teachers, along with people I'd never met from both inside and outside the Marchwood community, came to pay their condolences. Initially, I stood to shake hands or hug and say "Thank you for coming," despite my grandfather's explanation that, traditionally, during *shiva*, mourners are not only excused from such courtesies, but are discouraged from using them. "People will understand," he said. "The bereaved heart, Stevelah, has no room for such formalities."

I eventually followed my grandfather's advice because, despite all the visitors, I discovered that the room expanded, and a protective, chasm-like space opened up between me and them when I was sitting. Lost on my ladder-back chair in an isolated house by an inaccessible railroad, I could remember how comforting it was back then to lose myself in my own home, seated in the center of a crowd.

The chair was out of place in this memory, but I took it with me nonetheless. Most of it, anyway; the chair legs seemed to be cut short in the image I was retrieving from the past. Was I altering details to conform to my recollection that during *shiva* my parents and I sat on low stools and seats? My grandfather had explained that the mourning family should sit lower than those who came to pay their respects so that we'd be closer to the earth, which would reflect the low state of our feelings.

But there were only two stools in the house, and because my parents claimed them, I was given a special chair, one with Toulouse-Lautrec legs and a ladder-like back. Besides the legs, I remembered the chair looking an awful lot like my ladder-back. Who knows? Maybe it was the same chair. After all, time can play tricks with memory, just like memory can play tricks with time.

Despite Rabbi Rosen's careful planning, he didn't bring enough prayer books or yarmulkes from the synagogue to accommodate all the mourners during the service part of the afternoon. No one expected such a turnout.

I enjoyed sitting and reading my parts aloud from the *Siddur* during the responsive reading in English led by the rabbi. But standing to *daven*, chanting the prayers written from right to left, I found myself leaving the protection of isolation that I craved. When I sat, I repeatedly stuck my finger in between my neck and the tie with the tight-fitting starched collar of the white dress shirt my mother made me wear. Standing, the cuffs of my suit jacket, which I hadn't worn since my Bar Mitzvah almost a year ago, hung at an embarrassing midpoint between my wrists and elbows. Earlier in the day, my mother had commented that I needed a new suit. The thought of shopping ever again while Howie was lying inside a box in the last clothes he'd ever wear, made me queasy. The next time the congregation was directed to stand, I remained seated.

Of course, I stood to recite the Mourner's Kaddish, the Hebrew prayer for the dead. Having had my Bar Mitzvah less than a year ago, and never having lost a close relative before, this was the first time I was ever called upon to recite Kaddish. It punctuated the service, so I had several chances to get it right, but the pace was way too fast for me. To fit in, I faked the words, content to be whisked along by the abstract rhythm of the sounds, my mumbles doing their best to get lost in the crowd of worshipers, *Yisgadal v'yiskadash schmai raba. . .* Thinking about it now, what comes to mind is being swept along a high-speed version of the conveyor belt at Noah's Cararama—only this time, dry, no Jerry, and zebraless.

Late in the service, when Rabbi Rosen directed the mourners to rise, I rose, but deciding that this would be the last time I was going to be bothered by my starched collar and short jacket sleeves, I took off my sport coat and tie. I could feel my mother's eyes on me, but I focused on my grandfather's words: *The bereaved heart has no room for such formalities.* I opened my top button, and then, while the congregation remained standing, I sat down, unbuttoned the rest of my dress shirt, and took it off. Somehow, sitting there in my undershirt made me feel more alive, more free. It also made me feel less angry at what was going on around me: less angry at the vegetables, eggs, and cookies on the dining room table, less angry at my clothes, less angry at the well-meaning prayers that were infuriatingly late, and less angry at Howie for having gotten his head bashed in. But nothing could make me less angry at my father. Nothing could do that, ever.

The visitors annoyed me. I knew I ought to appreciate their kindnesses, but I didn't; they were well-meaning people who'd come to console the inconsolable Schaech family. But when they spoke with me, their eyes shifted uncomfortably between my T-shirt and face, and then, with see-through plastic utensils and paper plates in hand, as they waited with quiet sobriety for the "okay" to dig into the funeral food laid out before them, they stood around the dining room table condemning my father. They thought I couldn't hear them, but I could, and I didn't like what they were saying. That was for me to say, not them. All their condemning did was to give me something else to be angry about. I mean, it was an accident; Jacob Schaech didn't kill his son on purpose! It was our family, friends, and neighbors' job to cut him some slack, because if they did that, then I didn't have to.

A group of neighbors who had pitched in to help arranged bagels and round, seeded rolls; little crustless sandwiches; hard-boiled eggs; lox; cooked vegetables; rugelach; cubed pieces of fruit; and chocolate cookies into neat and orderly rows. I hated all these circle and square snacks lined up so strictly. I resented them almost as much as I resented the prayer books Rabbi Rosen had stacked in neat piles beneath the living room window. Bagels and cookies, like prayer books and prayers, could no more paint an orderly, pleasant, no less righteous, expression across the face of disaster than could Hitler hide behind the fake smile of a clown. The well-meaning rabbi and neighbors, like the well-meaning weather, had it all wrong.

After prayers, the food was devoured. Mrs. Murray, in charge of paper cups, had forgotten to bring them, so the bottles of juice and soda that were opened went un-poured, which was fine with me, and the pink punch remained untried inside its huge see-through bowl, squares of ice floating around the rim like a broken necklace. The food didn't work out either. Like the prayer books, yarmulkes, and the ice in the see-through bowl, there wasn't enough to go around.

I was grateful my parents had decided to keep the casket closed for the funeral. I wanted to remember Howie how he was; to hold onto the memory of Howie's vital, chubby features; his wide forehead; ballish nose; large, dark eyes; and that mole underneath his cheekbone in the very fleshiest part of his face. I never gave the mole much thought before, but now I couldn't get it out of my head.

The length of Howie's casket surprised me. It was small. Big enough for me, sure—but Howie? Had I caught up to him in height when neither of us was looking?

But what surprised me even more than Howie's un-heroic dimension was how much my father dominated my thoughts during the silent readings. I was supposed to be thinking about my brother, but my father wouldn't get out of the way. Mainly, I kept making up schemes to pay him back for stepping out of his invisibility just long enough to screw up so many lives. If this is what forsaking invisibility did for you, I wanted no part of it.

And then there was that other surprise. All afternoon I'd purposely avoided looking my father's way. For all I knew, he had skipped services. He never liked going anyway, and today must've been the worst ever. So when I did see him standing alone, his hands filled with hard-boiled eggs and chocolate chip cookies, his chest hairs sticking out of his T-shirt —because, just like me, he had taken off his jacket, tie, and dress-shirt!—I had to sit down one last time. Had he taken his shirt off for my sake? Highly unlikely!

Seeing him shirtless almost made me put mine back on, but I didn't, and he didn't, and I have to admit that seeing him like that—as ridiculous, rude, and inappropriate as it must've looked in the present circumstances to those around him—made it easier for me. What "it" was I couldn't say. Maybe it had to do with me feeling ridiculous, rude, inappropriate, and less alone. I don't know.

My father probably could've helped me understand what I was feeling if I ever asked him. But I'd be damned if I'd do that.

58 ❖

REMEMBERING

There I sat, in my ladder-back chair, in a strange house, remembering one of the shittiest days of my life. I couldn't leave this secluded house, nor this uncomfortable, yet comforting, chair; not yet—although I knew I ought to be home with my parents to sit with them once again, this time for my grandfather who could no longer answer his grandson's questions.

Other questions tormented me, too. Could I have prevented what happened to my grandfather? Did I cause it? Where am I? How am I going to get out of here and go home?

I remembered the many times I sat asking my grandfather questions in my parents' Marchwood apartment. Whenever I thought of those times, I thought of them with great fondness.

I thought back to a particular afternoon when it was my grandfather who was full of questions. Grandpa Oscar had stroked the glossy hair of the girl whose sad eyes graced the cover of a *Ladies Home Journal*. "What could possibly make someone so young so sad?" he had asked. What he wouldn't have done to ease the young girl's pain, whose sadness transported him back in time to a youthful sorrow of his own.

He spoke to me that day about how his parents could only afford to send one of their two sons to college, so they chose his brother, Stanley, their firstborn—Stanley, who didn't care about school or learning.

I'd heard this story many times before, but this time was different because this time I asked what exactly he did when he worked to help pay for Stanley's tuition. "How did you earn money before you became a lawyer, Grandpa?"

My question struck him. I can still remember how silent and rigid he remained before his hands finally began to move, how he picked up a newspaper lying on the table before him, tore out a page, slowly, and folded it in half. "Like this," Grandpa Oscar said, as he folded the right hand half of the folded page in half again. "And then this way," he continued, as he divided the other half of the folded page. He folded and folded, and then, dissatisfied, he discarded the paper. The tearing, folding, and crumpling of pages were the only sounds in the room. "I worked in a paper factory, folding paper into boxes for gloves." Grandpa Oscar said, more to himself than to me.

He was remembering.

"For gloves?"

"Gloves. Yes, gloves. Not like the gloves the baseball players wear, mind you. Mitts—not baseball mitts, like the one Grandma and I bought you when you played Little League. *Oy Got*, how I loved to watch you run around those bases; a regular Willie Mays you were. And not mittens like children wear, but gloves like the kind we wear when it gets cold out. Winter gloves. Woolen gloves, knit gloves." Grandpa Oscar's face took on a warm tone as the fingers of his right hand pushed down through the spaces between the fingers and across the palm of his left hand. "Yes, I made boxes for gloves, the boxes the gloves went in."

My grandfather's voice and hands grew more and more animated, his hands folding page after page into incomplete, ill-shaped boxes. "Like this," Grandpa Oscar explained, his body taking the lead in remembering what his mind had long ago forgotten. His hands grew more and more sure of themselves as they pulled out of a kind of darkness and dormancy an occupation tucked deep inside his body for almost three quarters of a century. "Then, dipping and schmearing, I would dip my brush into the glue and seal the box just like this," he said, gracefully twisting his wrist in slow motion, as if he were applying the finishing touches to a canvas. The anger and frustration that'd glazed his face when he spoke about Stanley and college had vanished. In its place was concentration, pleasure, purpose. . . youth.

For Oscar Bialintz, now there is no more youth and no more old age. Because of me.

TRAIN TRACKS TELL TIME BETTER THAN CLOCKS
(based on *House by the Railroad* by Edward Hopper)

Within a slanted square of sun,
a scene stains a living room wall.
Squinting gaze. Gaze fades. Stain remains.
Like a motion picture stuck, the seen scene persists. Projectionists can't
    change the reel.
Unreal thunder. Steel machine. Soot and steam.

From the porch, the boy waves. The trainman keeps going.
Everyday the same: sun, silence, a rumble, and a wave.
The stain remains.

Walking the tracks, the train stings and the porch shrinks.
    "Train tracks tell time better than clocks,"
    thinks the boy. "With train tracks, nows-and-thens
    get more minute, but not like minutes.
    Always, you can retrace your steps
    and bring the past back to size.
    Who knows? If you could rule time's dimensions,
    maybe you could sneak within and swap.
    Slightest bit too big or small and "'now"' becomes "'ago,"' like a ladder
        stepping into the stars,
    or down below."
Meanwhile, the stain remains.

—Stephen Schaech—

House by the Railroad
by
Edward Hopper

Hopper, Edward (1882–1967). *House by the Railroad*. 1925. Oil on canvas, 24 x 29 in. Given anonymously. (3.1930). Digital Image © The Museum of Modern Art/Licensed by SCALA/Art Resource, New York

59 ❖

HOUSE BY THE RAILROAD

My friendship with the trainman developed slowly. Outside, I'd lean against one of the porch posts and wait for the old man who I never met at less than thirty miles per hour, but who I could count on to be there the same time every day in his locomotive, a machine big and black as death, yet shimmering with the splendor of a starling, with the trainman waving to his young friend who lived in the grand white house.

I was lost inside a house plopped in the middle of an Edward Hopper painting that inspired a poem I once wrote. I didn't remember shahning, but there I was.

From the porch, the boy waves.

Was the old man real? Or the train or the house? Who knows, or cares? It felt right, and that was enough for me. Diane had said that in dreams everything was always "just so," that no matter how strangely they might wrinkle the surface, a little deeper down, in dreams, everything was always precisely as it was meant to be. I'm thinking now that she got that right, and that the difference between a shahn and a dream had to do with how things were "meant to be."

The more I saw the trainman, the more I liked and trusted him. Partly, this trust was based on distance. Although he and his steamy, steely voice reached out ever nearer as he passed, the iron line of the railroad track, raised like an exposed spine, neatly separated us— which was just how I wanted it. Paradise was a solid line separating me from. . . everything.

I thought: *What I love most dies—because of me.* Distance and separation is what I craved. And time.

I dreamed about the hills the old man passed and how someday he'd take me along with him. Each time I glimpsed the engineer, I saw mountains painted intense primary colors with rows upon rows of tall, violet tree trunks dotted silver by beetle-bitten leaves. The leaves sang and danced across densely woven webs of delicate blue branches intertwined like the twigs of a bird's nest. I tracked a butterfly toting the menace of see-through eyespots that circled the entire surface of its dreadfully beautiful wings. Keeping pace with the winged insect, I followed its reverse flight back to its caterpillared crawl in the sand, a crooked trek leading back to the moment just before it first tasted life.

Birds and branches. Snowfalls and turtles and the fragrance of tall, leafy grasses. I saw birds, like naked children running through a summer lawn sprinkler, flying in and out of ivory circles of smoke spurting from a locomotive, fat-bellied birds with long, reedy legs, "S"-shaped necks, and furry, green, first-basemen's-mitt beaks hanging from cheeky faces puffed out with all the right words to all the wrong stories.

I saw animals that looked like ponies sporting horns that stretched like branches in a forest, and I wondered how such little bodies on such little legs could bear such big, complicated thickets. I saw packs of animals blended together, and I saw a solitary turtle, older than Mesopotamia. Its head, buried within a patterned, leathery shell, reminded me of an aborigine's painted shield, the kind I saw with Grandpa Oscar at the Metropolitan Museum. As I watched the turtle inch from summer grass to smooth, fresh snow over hills of unnamed places, the harmless, stunted beast carrying its house wherever it crawled, I wondered what messages and dreams the turtle left behind as the snow chilled its bottom.

Dreams, that's where I preferred to live now, like an animal dreaming of butterflies, curled up tight within the warm protection of the earth, content to wave a wand across winter. So I dreamed myself upon a chair inside a house inside a painting. A demonless, solitary house haunted by a stare. And I invented a friend whose dieseled sleeves were streaked by turtle breezes and leaves bitten by beetles—beetles of a different breed than Jonathan David Swayze.

A BOY'S DREAM
(Written by Dr. Richard Kalter, a writer who was my grandfather's friend. It's as if he was thinking of me.)

In a boy's dream
a faraway whistle mixes with crooked tracks
alive with rot and repair. Time discarded him
in a by-the-way place bordered by straight lines
and gridded beds of gravel
to wait for another train.

On the yard's edge, feeling out there, away,
echoing simple trip, mantle to mountains and back,
guilty feet leave the closed doors of the heavy house.

Pacing, he can hear the faraway call of a clang and a chant:
    A whistling trainman,
    a hooting owl

rallied a moment
to come out and prowl.

The boy, older now, writes a single line
and reads it in silence (how many times?):
    Deep within our dreaming souls,
    images bathed in gleaming light
    stir our secrets and our shame, determining
    how we yearn and what we mourn.

His head nods.
In a flash the journey starts again.
His high step enveloped in whistling steam.

60

THE EARLY WORM
CATCHES THE BIRD

Watch for winged warblers where, upon swooning their last breaths, the sweetest-sounding, most vividly feathered ones—those who spent their flighted lives with nests and shared worms in mind—become notes and float forever after upon God's chorus of aviary breezes. Is there such a choir?

I hope so.

Home. . . bird . . . home again; home. . . bird. . . home again.

In my mind, I walked the train tracks until I reached the dead bird. Then I'd return to the house. I was always careful not to walk beyond the bird. "Death is plenty far," I figured. Anyway, for now I was incapable of going any farther. Or getting too close to it, either. I couldn't even bring myself to poke the tiny bird with a stick or nudge it with my shoe, as if the stick or shoe would disintegrate on contact and expose my bare finger or toe to something vicious that would instantly contaminate my whole body.

"Funny," I thought one day, as I gazed down at the delicate, blue heap. The bird looks asleep, not damaged. Not dead. The two lifeless rocks it rested upon appeared leveled by the impact of the bird's fallen body, a whim of fate killing two stones with one bird. And I also thought, "Funny, I figured by this time the bird'd be eaten or at the very least, a column of ants would've found him and be scrawling leggy lines across his body." But no such thing. The bird was the picture of dreamy health.

As if in response to my thoughts, a rust-colored caterpillar angled over the two stones, having made its way across the surrounding gravel, railroad tie, and rail, which cradled the dead bird, then it inched its way over the black bead of the bird's polished eye. I half expected to see the caterpillar complete its squirm, turn around, and retrace its momentarily humped path. "Why not? Feathers have got to feel a lot better than gravel, splinters, and steel," I reasoned.

I remembered a story Felix once told me about how, when he was about eleven years old, he happened to climb a metal pole near a corner of Forstops Village. "Wasn't the climbing up it," Felix had explained, "it was the sliding down. Wore out the crotch of my pants. Fuckin' A. Over and over again, you know?" He bobbed up and down enthusiastically as he looked toward his groin, the way English often did during one of his stories. "First time I ever felt anything like that down there," Felix explained, testing out some new Polish phrases he picked up from Mike's father. "*O Bozé!* I mean, if I didn't think there was a God when I woke up that morning, *Matko Boska*, that pole would've damn sure made me a believer."

I recalled a book Howie found on one of Grandpa Oscar's shelves. The book was all about the human body and how it worked. No nude pictures, but I found the part about masturbation fascinating. One line in particular came to mind now: *The manner in which an individual first accidentally discovers masturbation often becomes the manner in which that individual will continue the habit.* Felix'd be the last one on the truck every time, I thought to myself, picturing him bald, working for the Garrison City Fire Department, and using his body to make the pole inside the station the shiniest and smoothest one in the county. Fuckin' A.

Gazing at the dead bird relaxed me. The thin lines of the bird's legs looked like tiny twigs from a leafless tree, the kind of twigs I'd've casually snapped off and pressed gently into the space beneath my fingernails as I went for walks with my nine-year-old brother. As so often happened lately, the space and time between the walk on the tracks and those long ago walks in the woods collapsed.

"Here, Howie, here's another one."

Howie sneezed. I waited. Two more sneezes. Then Howie said he couldn't fit anymore rocks in his pockets. "Anyhow, what're you gonna do with them all?"

"But this one's even cooler than the others," I pleaded. *"Um-kay on-way, Owie-Hay."* Howie hated it when I spoke Pig Latin.

"Come on." Howie conceded, as he stuck the rock in his pocket, along with about eight or nine others, a half-dozen broken pine cones, an acorn, and a deflowered weed. "I don't see why I gotta lug this stuff home every time we go for a walk. Mommy's just gonna make you throw it all out anyways."

I wasn't satisfied. "Hey, lookit the color of this worm, Howie! Let's take him home."

"No, leave it where it is. This is probably right where it wants to be. And if it isn't, I bet it's on its way somewheres even better."

"Yeah, sure, liar. You just don't want to put him in your pocket."

"There's plenty of scurvy worms 'round the house already. 'Sides, what're we gonna do with it?"

"It's not a 'it'; it's a 'him'; and he's not scurvy. And we could play with him, is what we could do. We could put him in a shoe box and put dirt and grass in the box and feed him ants and teach him tricks and. . ."

"Stevie. . ."

"If we leave him here he's gonna get ate up. I know it."

"Yeah, well, Mommy's not gonna want you to have a pet ant."

"Worm," I corrected.

"That's what I meant." Howie sneezed. I waited for the next two, but they didn't come.

"Something's gonna eat him," I said. "I know it. It's a stray. If it was a dog you'd bring it home, 'cause you like dogs. You just don't like stray worms. I know it. How come you don't? *Ow-hay um-kay*?"

Howie said he wanted to go. Something in the woods was beginning to bother his throat, and I was getting on his nerves real bad. He called me "poodle ooze," but I didn't care because I didn't pay attention to him.

"He's gonna get ate up, Howie. I know it. How come you don't like stray worms like I do?"

So Howie stepped on the worm and twisted his foot back and forth into the dirt. "Now he won't get *ate up*. Or stray ever again."

"I hate you, Howie! I hate you!"

Throwing out some new curses he'd recently perfected, Howie told me to forget the stupid worm. Then he took my hand. He didn't want me to fall, he said, along with, "C'mon, Stevie. Mommy's waiting."

What killed the bird? I wondered. I ruled out the possibility of the bird's death resulting from an act of suicide, which was how English had once explained to me the hit-and-run death of a squirrel we'd seen dart under the wheels of a Buick. I'd seen birds kill themselves by crashing into a window. But they were not *kamikaze* birds; there was nothing suicidal about crashing into the invisible, just a case of poor vision, faulty planning, the assumption of safety and predictability, a misguided attack at their own reflections, a crummy sense of direction. . . or just plain bad luck.

Life is full of nasty surprises. A sudden storm comes along and knocks a bird right out of the sky, the kind of storm the British artist, Turner, liked to paint, where wind (every painting I could remember seeing by Turner was about wind) had its way with the weightless body of flying birds, while below, a locomotive steamed forward, unhampered by all the sky's huffing and puffing. A lifetime ago, those un*kamikaze* birds crashed head on, as Jerry's brother had, as my brother had, into the unseen, the unforeseen. Howie's and Warren's lives, and the lives of all those broken birds, just long, straight lines that got the surprise of their deaths.

How much better to be a train ruled by the power of speed, the awesome protection of steel, and the rigorous logic of machinery, than to be a bird.

I gathered a pile of dead leaves and laid them like a pillow against the edge of a train track. Eyes closed, I rested my head upon the leaves, pulled up my knees, and curled my body into the space between two railroad ties. Weeds softened the gravel underneath. Lying like this, I was back in Marchwood, walking in the woods, collecting rocks and worms and acorns with my brother. It-aye us-way uh-they est-bay art-pay of-aye uh-they aye-day.

 **61**

HANDHELD SHADOWS

If our friendship continued, I knew the trainman would eventually stop his train, which would spoil everything, so I retreated. I spent long periods gazing at sunless interior walls perforated by the cry of a train that I tried desperately to block out.

"Stephen, you're scaring me." I recognized the voice of my grandfather, but I didn't respond. *"What are you doing, sitting in this chair, sitting and staring at that wall? Look at me, Tatella! Talk to me," my grandfather* charged. His voice pained me, but I didn't move.

Then I did. I moved because of the trainman. I knew it was him by the sound. I'd grown so accustomed to the coming of the train that if

I'd been sleeping, the roar of steel against steel wouldn't've awakened me. The sound of the train was a sound like my own breathing, and like that, I'd've noticed it only if it changed.

This day the rumbling was different. Slower. And then there was no rumble. I looked out the living room window and saw the locomotive, at rest.

I closed my eyes and inhaled the house. The scent of yesterday's socks entered my nostrils, as did the odor from an open tube of Clearasil. I smelled Brillo pads rusting in the sink alongside dirty dishes caked with tomato sauce, and I smelled the blue ink of a ballpoint pen lying on a nearby shelf, considering how odd it was that blue ink should smell so different from red or black ink.

Diesely fumes filtered indoors from the panting train. The old man had come.

Inside the house, I watched the frightened flight of a blue-bellied bird as it banged into the walls and a mirror that contained my memories. Maybe I should cover the mirror, I thought, so the bird wouldn't break its neck, and I wouldn't have to see what I didn't want to see, or remember. I remembered how strange and disturbing my Marchwood apartment looked upon returning from Howie's funeral to see all the mirrors covered with towels and bed sheets. Grandpa Oscar had explained the custom of covering mirrors in the *shiva* home so the bereaved would not be inclined to dwell on such distractions as vanity. He gave me several other reasons, as well, for this custom, but that was the only one I could remember. I wondered if my parents would cover the mirrors before they returned from my grandfather's funeral service, since Grandpa Oscar wouldn't be there to remind them.

Over and over again the bird smacked into the walls and the mirror, fluttered in one spot, and then, defeated, slid to the floor where it remained until it caught its breath. I took a towel from the bathroom and covered up the mirror, but the bird kept banging into the walls.

Within the light-streaked wall before him, I saw a naked man with a bat holding hands with my old chemistry teacher, Mary Gustin. She looked refreshed, contented. Apparently, dating a ballplayer agreed with her.

Only partially visible, because they were positioned at the rear of a crooked line of visitors, stood Diane, Grandpa Oscar, and the train-man, his wide-open legs straddling the magnificently patterned shell of an ancient turtle. Slowly, they made their way forward to the porch steps. Then they vanished.

I stood before my ladder-back chair, looking out through the closed door at a single, standing figure. The figure was me. I looked into my own eyes. There were hours and days and years, as I stood motionless. And then the moment passed.

Somewhere, probably not so very far away, a young woman fastened the latch of a leaded glass window casement as she lowered a silver pitcher back down onto its basin. As the window closed and the woman's image disappeared forever from the glass, a little piece of eternity disappeared with it.

Part XI

UNHEARD WHISTLES

62 ◈

OLLIE OLLIE UMFREE

I used to love playing hide-and–seek with my friends. A tree was our home base. We had to place our feet in cupped hands to grab hold of even the lowest branch, but one pair of arms could reach around all the penknifed Marshas, Lindsays, Staceys, and Bobs, circling the trunk like a mother's hug. We hid while, behind closed eyelids, the seeker counted, ridges of bark pressing dark, broken lines into a youthful forehead unscored by cares. The trick was to beat the seeker back to the tree. Win the race and free the captured. *Ready or not, here I come. Anyone 'round my base is I-T it.*

I had a secret hiding place where I used to remain for hours after everyone else quit. Silent, safe, invisible. Overhead, gentle breezes stroked the veins of weeping, sickle-shaped leaves, turning ladybugs, kicking, onto their dots.

Today, silence turns tangled patterns of stillness into a furrowed forehead, as I long for "Home-free-all" but get "You're it" instead.

INVISIBLE
(based on *Sheet with Three Studies: A Tree, An Eye, and Partial Self-Portrait of the Artist* [inverted to show eye] by Rembrandt van Rijn)

Behind cascading summer leaves
blossoming down a boy's nostrils and off his chin,
like snot, or a windswept, waist-length, late-autumn beard,
a faceless eye is lost between seasons, and more.
Mud and weeds camouflage his hair. Below, blankness surrounds a black
*   hole with an eyelid.*

Standing on her head, an eyeless girl faces the boy.
Does she see him, or does she see the man beyond?
Or is she just counting clouds?
Centered between her and a cock-eyed old man,
whose dreams are squashed by the hilly midnight of his hat,
the off-centered boy floats between vision and time—
*   the old man's faraway stare over here,*
*   the eyeless girl there.*
At least the boy is right-side-up.
He can build on that.

***Sheet with Two Studies: A Tree and the Upper Part of a Head
of Rembrandt Wearing a Velvet Cap***
by
Rembrandt van Rijn

Rembrandt van Rijn, Dutch, Leiden 1606–1669 Amsterdam; *Sheet with Two Studies: A Tree and the Upper Part of a Head of Rembrandt Wearing a Velvet Cap*; Dutch, ca. 1642; Print; Etching; only state; sheet: 3 1/16 x 2 9/16 in. (7.8 x 6.5) (trimmed to plateline). The Metropolitan Museum of Art, Rogers Fund, 1970. (1970.705). Image © The Metropolitan Museum of Art

So, for now, the boy keeps his eye open
and hides, hoping to find, hoping to be found,
before his landscape blows away, the old man dies,
and the girl turns her back on him forever,
exposing the boy as, at most,
just a black dot on a white sheet of paper.

"Keep your eye open," the watcher tells himself,
for he knows if he so much as blinks,
he'll vanish.

—*Stephen Schaech*—

63

GOING HOME

The trainman may have thought he had come to free me, but I didn't want to be freed. Not yet. So I crept through the kitchen and out the side entrance. The old man and I were changing places. Soon, I'd be racing in a line towards red mountains overrun with exotic four-legged beasts and birds with "S"-shaped necks, while the trainman would be left standing all alone on the front porch of an isolated house.

Not long into my flight away from the trainman, I encountered a naked boy, cheerlessly perched upon a branch of a tall mulberry tree. He was crying. When he saw that he was being watched, he stared his stone-face at me.

"WWHHOOOOOOOOOOOOOOO ARE YYYOOOOOOOOOOUU?" the boy demanded? "AND WWHHOOOOOOOOOOOOO IS THE MOST REEEESPONSIIIBLE PERSON AT MAAARCHWWOOOOOOOOOOD PUBLIIIIC SCHOOOOOOOOOOOOOL?" Then he sank his chin into his chest and puffed up his cheeks. Showing off, he attempted to display the back of his head without moving his shoulders, but it didn't work. The boy began to flap his arms to balance himself. Harder and harder he flapped until he fell.

I didn't see the boy land because at the bottom of the tree there was a house that blocked my view. Inside the house, stood Diane. ". . . Because I have to, that's why," she wept into the telephone. "It's not as if I *want* to go back to Maryland, Stephen. You must know that. Not now. Not like this."

"Couldn't you talk to Mrs. Bilheimer or Gustin or someone? They love you at Garrison High. There's plenty of teachers who'd go to bat for you there. I know it. We didn't do anything wrong. You said we should wait and we did."

"Stephen, Mr. Hoffmeister himself called. He's the principal. He knows all about us. I just came back from his office. He wanted to see me. This way is the best. It stinks, but it's the best." Her voice shook.

"When will we see each other?"

"If he wanted to, he could kill my whole teaching career for good. He hasn't decided what he's going to do yet. I feel like someone took an arrow and shot it right through me."

I didn't know if she meant me or Mr. Hoffmeister.

"You know how much teaching means to me. He said maybe he wouldn't report anything to Goucher about what was going on between us. That maybe it won't be on my record."

"What do you mean 'going on between us'? You mean how you're the best thing that ever happened to me? That because of you for the first time in years I'm starting to feel good about who I am? What did we ever do that was so bad? Tell me. We never went all the way. You touched me, Diane, and it had nothing to do with hands. And I think I touched you too. Tell me we aren't good for each other. Go on and tell me if that's what you believe. We never let ourselves. . . you didn't let me. . ."

"Stephen, I didn't want things to end like this. I. . ."

"What do you mean, *end*?"

"I didn't deny you and I were seeing each other outside of school. I couldn't deny it. It's not just about intercourse. We did a lot more than kiss. We shouldn't have been together outside of school like we were. I was here in the role of a teacher, and I let myself fall for one of my students. I was the older one, I should have shown more restraint. You're not even twenty, and I am. Geez, Stephen," she said, as if grasping for the first time just how old (or young) I was, "you're not even eighteen. I should have known better. What was I think-ing?"

"What do you mean, 'what were you thinking?'" Her comment chilled my throat.

"Hoffmeister could get me in a lot of trouble if he wanted to. He really doesn't have any choice under the circumstances but to kick me out, and I don't have any say in the matter. It's almost the end of the term. I was going to have to return to Goucher soon anyway."

"When will we see each other?"

"You should have heard him. . . and seen the way he looked at me. He said I had seduced a student—he used the word 'seduced'—but it wasn't like that. It wasn't, Stephen, was it?"

She didn't let me answer. She just kept on, building more and more momentum as she described her meeting with Hilton Hoffmeister. I wondered if Hoffmeister referred to me as a "troubled" boy, the way he had when I was in his office with Lieutenant Brannick. Knowing Diane, I figured she'd censor what the principal had to say about me. But she did say he made her feel like an irresponsible child. And a tramp. She didn't censor that. She repeated several times that he'd accused her of seducing one of her students, one of *his* students. "Mr. Hoffmeister said I took advantage of you," she exclaimed, "and if I am capable of such behavior I have no business being in the teaching profession."

"That's ridiculous!" I objected. "He just doesn't understand. He's twisting it all around and making what happened between us into something it never was, placing blame where it doesn't have any business being placed. What's he talking about? He's taking something wonderful and turning it into something bad and making a big deal out of it!"

"It *is* a big deal, Stephen!"

"Yeah, but not the way he's making it out to be. Don't you see that? Let me come over, Diane. Let me be with you."

"Not now. Please."

"When, then?"

"I don't know. I don't know. But please, Stephen, not today. The last thing we should do is be seen alone together now. Besides, I promised Hoffmeister I wouldn't see you before I left. That I would just call you and explain what was going on."

"What'd you do that for?"

"I had to. He didn't even want me to call you at first, but he finally said 'okay'."

"If you leave I don't know what I'll do here without you. I need you, Diane."

"Stephen, this isn't just about you and what *you* need. To be perfectly honest, I just can't think that part through right now. I want to do what's right, I just don't know what that is anymore. Talk to Hoffmeister and he'll tell you that I never did know." Her voice broke as she pleaded with me not to make it any harder than it already was for her. "It's not as if I don't still love you," she added. "Things could never change just like that. But I need to be alone right now and try to sort things out. Please, Stephen."

I wanted so badly to come over, but she was right; this wasn't about what *I* wanted or needed right now. Except I wanted to be there for her this time, like she'd always been there for me. We went back and forth a few more times, but after finally accepting that nothing I could say was going to make any difference, I reluctantly agreed not to see her before she returned to Maryland. Then we hung up.

For several hours I remained at home. But I ended up ignoring her plea for me to stay away.

 # 64

WINDOWS

By the time I returned to my house, the trainman was gone. A pair of gloves lay at the foot of the front door. The gloves were caked with grease and dirt, so I didn't try them on, but I didn't throw them away either. I just held them for as long as it took to recall my visit to Diane's apartment.

In my imagination, I could see her clearly through the open kitchen window of her first-floor apartment. She was alone. Her aunt wasn't home. For a change.

I wanted to hold Diane. It had never before occurred to me that Diane would ever need me. She told me once how shy she was before moving to Garrison City. "Remember that deer we saw at Van Saun Park?" she asked. "Hiding, afraid to come out into the open? That was me," she said. I remembered the fragile, graceful, elegant quality of the animal. There I could see a connection with Diane. Shyness or fear; that was hard to picture. "Except with my closest friends," she said. "Around guys, I couldn't get myself to stop digging my elbows into my sides. It was you, Stephen, who brought me out of myself. You and teaching."

I had always seen Diane as the secure one, the one to teach and lead. She was good at it. Not like my friends. With them it was just like that Bruegel painting—following became a way of life; after a while you expected to fall, and then you did. Everywhere Diane took me, on the other hand, was full of goodness. And wonder. Now she needed me, and I wanted to be there for her.

By the time I reached Diane's apartment she had taken a shower and changed her clothes. She wore a bath towel wrapped around her head. I didn't tell her I was there; I just remained where I was, watching. I wanted to comfort her, but I knew Diane didn't want me to, and I was determined to honor what she wanted.

Basically.

There was another option though, one that might allow me to be with her right now and yet have no direct impact on her need to be alone. The option was, of course, to shahn. Okay, I needed a picture in order to do that, but maybe all I had to do now was loosen up what I thought of as a picture, and then hope for the best.

The present circumstances were tailor-made for me. Diane was standing nearby, separated only by a *window*. She used to talk about artists like Vermeer creating hauntingly believable three-dimensional worlds across the flat surfaces of their wood panels and canvases. Flat canvases opening onto the world like windows that looked into space, "became space," is the way she put it. "Magic." It was a good way of saying it, I thought at the time. Well, pretty good, but only as far as it went, and it didn't go far enough. I would've kept the "magic" part—I liked the word better than "illusion"—but I would've replaced "window" with "door," an open one, since, for me, pictures provided passageways through which the whole body—not just the eyes and mind—could travel.

But not this time.

The window turned out to be just that, a window, and what I needed, apparently, was a painting or a reproduction of one. No matter how hard I concentrated, I was unable to project myself into Diane's world. In fact, the more I concentrated, the more distant I felt from her.

For the first time, I truly understood Jerry's frustration regarding his inability to project, body and soul, his good intentions into the paralyzed arm of the guy at the bowling alley.

It wasn't the first time I understood that my precious gift was limited.

I looked back through the window and saw the sadness in her eyes. I couldn't bear the thought that I had anything to do with causing Diane unhappiness, any more than I could bear the thought of Garrison City without her.

As I thought this, Diane's left hand grasped the water pitcher sitting in a basin on a table that partially blocked her view, and her right hand brushed the wooden casement of the window. I stood watching. Her gesture with the pitcher reminded me first of our Vermeer painting, and then of something altogether different. . . of the customary washing of the hands performed by visitors before entering a *shiva* home.

After Howie's funeral service, my grandfather had placed a pitcher and basin outside the front door for this purification ritual. The

Marchwood pitcher was similar to the one Diane was holding now. "Judaism celebrates *life*," my grandfather had explained, "and this *shiva* custom symbolizes the washing away of the impurities associated with *death*."

But I also saw Diane's handling of her water pitcher as a washing away of Hoffmeister's name-calling. I sure hoped that's how Diane would have regarded her present actions, rather than as an attempt to wash away any part of her experiences with me.

As she opened the window and looked toward the flowers in the planter hanging just beyond, Diane saw me. Her slow, sad eyes implored: *Please allow me to be alone for now.* She looked injured, like the creature, the deer, in the painting we saw in one of the galleries in New York several weeks before.

The picture seemed real—not photographic real, but somehow truthful, or at least possible—but, of course, it couldn't be. A woman on her way out for the evening, head and neck, so calm and lovely, earrings, lipstick, every hair in place, attached to the body of a deer pierced by arrows. Antlers, fur, hooves. . . and earrings. If you stopped and broke it down, analyzed it part by part just in your head, it made no sense; but seeing it all together, somehow it did. I guess, ultimately, any painting can appear to "make sense" as long as the artist can make it "look right," no matter how crazy it might be at heart. The trick is, I figure, to see with the eyes and not with the brain.

The creature in the painting was wounded, fragile, but strong. The arrows confirmed her strength because they represented challenges overcome. At least that's what Diane said about the picture when we first saw it. I hoped she would soon see Hoffmeister's piercing accusations as challenges she, or better, we, would overcome.

Would she really stop seeing me because it might jeopardize her future teaching goals? I didn't think so. Everything I knew about her suggested she wouldn't. Surely she wouldn't stop seeing me because she thought it was wrong for us to continue seeing each other. She couldn't possibly think that.

The Little Deer
by
Frida Kahlo

Kahlo, Frida (July 6, 1907–July 13, 1954), Mexican; *The Little Deer,* 1946; Oil on Masonite; 8 7/8 x 11 7/8 in. From the collection of Carolyn Farb.

 **65**

RESTRAINT

Diane returned to Maryland the following morning. I spent the following night with my friends who had recently returned from their brief incarcerations. We gathered at the vacant Forstops Village apartment, the one located next door to my grandfather's friend, Morris Lefkowitz.

While my friends were away, my relationship with Diane had blossomed. Everything with her was fun and easy and had substance. We flowed. Except where sex was concerned.

Finding ways to be alone together was where the problems started. Diane wasn't comfortable with me at her aunt's house when her aunt was home—her aunt was always home—and she wouldn't come to mine unless it was to meet someone in my family, which never happened.

The few times we were alone, I grumbled when Diane stopped me from going as far with her as I wanted to, but the truth was, I was relieved that she did because I only knew what to do up to a certain point when I was making out with a girl, and I was sure my inexperience would shine across my youth, throwing our age difference into sorry relief. Sure, like me, Diane was a virgin, which I kind of liked, but a guy's virginity was nothing to brag about. I let her think I knew what I was doing, and that when I exerted restraint I was just putting her needs and wants ahead of my own. At the time I thought she bought it. I'm not so sure anymore.

I desperately wanted to know more about having sex, but I was too uptight to figure out how to go about learning. My friends, who may not have known too much about a lot of things, probably knew everything there was to know about this, but it wasn't like I could ask any of them for advice, especially where details were concerned. And what concerned me most were the details.

The best person to ask about things like sex was an older brother. I wished I could talk to mine.

Diane and I learned together, slowly. She marveled and giggled at my excitement when her tongue tickled my ear. I was emboldened by her request that I caress her backside "like last night." I loved how her thighs squeezed my cheeks when I kissed and licked her where she said she'd never been kissed and licked before.

I accepted the uncomfortably swollen feeling around my genitals and in my abdomen when we stopped ourselves. Patience, I told myself, or you'll risk losing the most important person to have come into your life since. . . ever. Patience. At least for now.

In other parts of my life I often "stopped short," as well, like what I did and said—or didn't do or say—around my friends and family. I liked distance and barriers more than most people did; they kept me safe, protected. But as my relationship with Diane grew ever more intimate, I was beginning to feel the gray shadows cast by closed doors within me being replaced by the colors of nature shining through open windows. For the past three years the air I breathed was dark. Diane had lit it up. Now she was gone.

66

FROM SCRATCH

Home. . . bird. . . home again.

I had anxiously wondered what part my friends were going to play in my life upon their return. I missed them. I knew Diane offered me more than they did, but since she left there was little to prevent me from returning to where I was before I met her.

Vermeer stilled a moment. Diane and I had set that moment in motion. A sense of order and harmony, even in the frowning face of a jaundiced and crooked turn in my life, reinforced my belief that, somewhere, an inaudible thrumming, like a heartbeat, played a profound role in determining the choices I had made. Those private beats played themselves out along paths not unlike the spiraling lines grooved into the records I listened to. No need for a nickel to start the jukebox; it was always playing.

Sure, there was a certain amount of luck involved—both good and bad—which inevitably tempered the direction of the line. Sure, the bad luck, and some of the bad choices I had made, resulted in scratches— even irreparable breakage—that blocked the steady spirals I might have followed. But then, who knows what the original, prerecorded rhythm underlying any individual's life is ever really like? Maybe some of the nastiest scratches shift the direction of that life for the better. More often than not, they probably just make things different—no better, no worse. Who can say?

But *what about Howie? What about my grandfather?*

That's where I was stuck, like a phonograph needle caught in a scratch. As I followed in my mind the path that led to my brother's death and the murder of my grandfather, I understood the expression "Start from scratch." Before, it had just been an expression, like so many others, born to be taken for granted. Now I knew what it meant.

Home. . . bird. . . home again. I walked back to the railroad tracks. When I reached the dead-bird point, I was not surprised the bird was gone. I placed a twig into the ground to mark the site of death. Then, for the first time, I walked beyond it.

I thought about Diane as I walked. She was a good person, a good teacher, and she was an artist. I regretted that I only got to see one picture she made: a self-portrait in pencil. Her paintings were back in Maryland, and she wouldn't let me see what she had been working on since she had come up to New Jersey. "When they're ready," she kept saying. "There's a whole series of them. They tell a story, but I'm not sure yet what the story is really about. I want you to see what I'm painting, but not until the whole series is done."

"You know," she had added, "I'd also like to show them to your granddad some time, if you think he'd be interested."

"Interested? You kidding? He'd love to see your work. He'll love it, and I know he'll love you! How could he not?"

How could I have been so stupid? How could I not have made sure that my grandfather got to see Diane's paintings, that the two of them got to meet?

Questions like these kept returning as I walked the train tracks.

Home. . . bird. . . home again.

Diane was gone. She left a pencil drawing for me, the self-portrait that I once told her was better than anything I had ever seen in any museum. Diane had said that she didn't know if it was really finished or not.

I told her it was great just the way it was, and that it looked just like her.

Attached to the drawing, she wrote:
Forgive me,
Love,
Diane

DREAM
(based on *The Sleep of Reason*
Produces Monsters by Francisco Goya)

"Go ahead. Fly," the boy pleads,
"with all those batters, beggars, and bugs you hold so dear.
Fly away and leave them where you land."

The Sleep of Reason Produces Monsters: Plate 43 of The Caprices
by
Francisco de Goya y Lucientes

The Sleep of Reason Produces Monsters: Plate 43 of The Caprices. First edition. Etching, aquatint, dryprint, and burin. Image 8 7/16 x 5 7/8 in. (21.5 x 15 cm). The Metropolitan Museum of Art, Gift of M. Knoedler & Co., 1918. (18.64). Photograph © 1994 The Metropolitan Museum of Art.

But for the owl there's no frontier,
except behind sad eyes, dreams, and a tear.

Vermeer's lute player lulled her friend to sleep.
Pleasant dreams, tunes,
and museum afternoons.
The dozing maiden dreamed
of sunshine and parakeets
painted in yellows, blues, and greens.
The unlulled, friendless owl spreads its sleepless wings.

Again, "Fly away. Go!"
But when the boy's owl's eyes close,
its feathers fade,
and the bird sinks
into a nightmare without reason,
of bats and balls
and invisible monsters
never out-of-season.

—Stephen Schaech—

 # 67

AND THEN THE MOMENT PASSED

I had no idea where I was or how long I had been walking. I kicked a stone and then I kicked it again. I missed Howie and the walks we used to take.

Then I saw what I had been walking toward ever since I marched past the dead bird. It was the train.

Hesitantly, I approached the old man. "I am glad you came," the man said. Then he added: *"Yich in dina yahren hab shoyn gavein. Ober de in mein. . ."*

I remained silent for a moment. Then, "I know that expression," I said. *"I in your years have already been. But you in mine. . .* But you want to know something?" I confided. "I'm not so sure I ever really understood what it meant. Not when I was a little boy, and not now, still."

"Perfect understanding, Stephen, is beyond time," the trainman responded as he climbed into the locomotive and turned on the engine. The pressure from the train rumbled across the tracks and up through the soles of my feet, making my shins feel like tuning forks. I remained where I was until the trainman reappeared and extended his arm. It was a gesture meant simultaneously to offer and receive. "Come with me," he coaxed, "and maybe you will understand."

I was surprised by our destination. "I just didn't expect to stop and watch a ball game, is all," I said.

The trainman urged me to keep watching.

What was so important about a Little League game? Although I didn't even know who was playing, I kept watching until suddenly, congregated around a wooden bench located along the third base side of the diamond, I saw my Marchwood Elementary School friends Stuart, Richie, Pat, and Kevin, as well as a group of boys who I knew from elsewhere. They were from two different towns, yet here they all were, about three years younger than they ought to have been, mixed together playing ball on a strange field, located somewhere along the trainman's route.

"Good eye, Jerry!" shouted Mr. Laociano, one of the coaches. "Make him pitch to you! Wait for a good one! We need base runners to tie it up!"

Even Mr. Laociano! And Howie! What's he doing here? I felt like I was doing forward rolls down a hill. I clutched the trainman's hand as I watched Howie running after a ball thrown by a friend of his, Mike Dumbrowski. "You did that on purpose," Howie complained. "Throw it to me, not to the kid playing first base!"

"Stay away from the field if you're not playing," Mary Gustin, the mother of the second baseman, shouted at Howie.

My mother, sitting on a wooden bench along the third base foul line, heard the reprimand. "Howard!" she called. "Howard!" But Howie didn't hear her, or he pretended not to. She turned her attention back to the game. Who was he hurting, anyway?

"The game's almost over," Mrs. Gustin continued her scolding. "If you boys have to play catch, do it over there." she directed, pointing toward the backstop. My eyes followed her finger.

"That's me!" I said aloud. "Over there, in the shadow by the backstop."

There was a familiarity to the scene I observed, but I didn't understand any of what was going on. I watched as my thirteen-year-old counterpart shouted words of encouragement to the batter: "Two and one, Jerry. Wait for your pitch." Then, I wasn't just *hearing* the words—my words—I was *saying* them. "A walk's as good as a hit!" I shouted from behind the backstop. "Make him pitch to you!"

"Just relax out there, Felix. Pitch it; don't aim it," instructed Malcolm Bazzaz, the coach of the opposing team. As he shouted his instructions to "just put it over the plate," the hem of Mr. Bazzaz's t-shirt heaved in and out, alternately exposing and concealing tufts of black hair surrounding a navel the size of an owl's eyeball. As I gazed at Bazzaz's navel, I could swear it stared right back at me.

Ball three. As Jerry Eppers settled himself in the batter's box, I prepared to take a few last warm-up swings. A long ash from a cigarette dangling from Coach Bazzaz's fleshy lips bounced off the man's bulging stomach, exploding silently onto the grass. "Come on, Felix. Get it over. You walk this kid and you're watching the rest of the game from the bench."

A ball came rolling toward me. Mike had intentionally thrown another one over Howie's head.

I didn't see the ball. My eyes were fixed on Jerry, who was kicking dirt around in the batter's box to get himself planted.

Howie caught up to the ball rolling toward the backstop. "Hey! Didn't you boys hear what the lady just told you?" Mr. Laociano shouted. "Get away from the field. Someone's gonna get hurt!"

"Where'd you learn how to throw, Dumbrowski?" Howie called to his friend.

"Shut up you fat faggot!" Dumbrowski hollered at Mr. Laociano. The coach heard Mike's outburst, but ignored it. "Wait for your pitch, Jerry," Laociano urged. "Wait for your pitch!"

One last swing and I'd be ready to take my turn at the plate. I felt strong, confident. I knew I could hit this pitcher. I'd been up twice before—I'd doubled, then homered. Howie had prepared me well, practicing with me day after day, month after month every spring and summer since I was big enough to swing a bat. We'd play together until Howie's arm would tire or 'til he'd grow bored, or my mother would call us in for pot roast and peas. Not much of an athlete, my father disliked sports. Besides, he never had the time nor energy after work to practice things like batting or fielding with me, so that had become Howie's job. No, not a job. Howie liked it, I know he did. And I loved it, our spring and summer ritual.

As I leaned into an imaginary pitch, I crouched slightly, brought my bat back, moved my lead foot forward, extended my arms, exploded my hips, and twisted my back foot into the dirt, as if I was squashing a bug. It was a perfect moment. My body turned with grace and ease, the power in my swing erupting from my legs just like Howie had taught me.

"Where'd you learn how to throw?" Running as he said this, Howie sneezed and tripped, his body bending at the waist, his head jerking forward with great force.

The sound of my Louisville slugger hitting into something solid and hard startled me. I was still behind the tree, away from everyone. On deck. There was no pitch to hit.

"Where'd you learn how to throw, Dumbrowski?"

Howie sneezed his taunting question to his friend before I swung my bat, but I didn't hear it until I had completed my swift, furious swing. Before I fully absorbed my brother's voice I heard something else. My eyes darted to meet the sound. Strangely, my eyes were already there, as time seemed to back up. I felt like a spectator gazing from afar at a piece of time.

"Where'd you learn how to throw, Dumbrowski?"

And then the moment passed. I was still watching it, but it was over. My bat had crashed into Howie's skull.

68

THEN THE CHEERING STOPPED

A thin line of blood trickled from inside Howie's ear onto the grass. In his right hand he held the misthrown baseball. Except for a reflexive tightening of his fingers around the seams of the ball, he didn't move. "Where'd you learn how to throw?" he mumbled. "Where'd you learn how to throw?"

I didn't move. At first, my eyes didn't follow my brother's fallen body. Then they did.

Then I collapsed.

I was still collapsed, but now I was once again on the sidelines next to the trainman. I saw that no one noticed what happened to Howie and me except my father, who ran to his two fallen sons. Everyone else's eyes were busy following the action on the playing field.

"Wait for your pitch, Jerry," Mr. Laociano shouted, "Wait for your pitch." My eyes opened. I looked in my father's direction, but I didn't see him. I didn't see him kneeling beside Howie. I didn't see anything.

"Ball four!"

Jerry ran down to first base. I walked toward the sounds of the ball-field and took my position at the plate.

"Where's your bat, Stevie? Go get your bat!" Mr. Laociano directed over sounds of laughter.

"Schaech's got the Shakes!" Sookie DiMaeoli taunted from the stands. Then to his next-door neighbor, the shortstop, Todd Kristy,

Sookie shouted, "Easy out! Easy out! Move in, Todd. Last time was just luck. Throw it underhand, Ybañez, this kid couldn't hit a dead horse if it was layin' on home plate!"

"C'mon, Stevie. Make it two. You can do it!" Eddie Otis cheered from the bench. "An extra base hit'll win it!" As he cheered for his friend, Eddie momentarily stopped twisting the ball he held in his left hand. "You get me a little lead here, I'll shut 'em down when I get out to the mound, Stevie. You can do it, man!"

Eddie had pitched a good game. He tired in the fifth and sixth innings, but the last two innings he had gotten back in form, and his curve was working as well as it had worked all season. "Keep throwing curves like that, Edward, and you're going to ruin your arm for pitching," Eddie's father continually advised. "You're too young for curves. Wait a year or two for your muscles to develop." It did no good. Eddie wasn't interested in pitching if he couldn't throw curveballs.

"Stevie! Go get your bat!" Laociano called. "C'mon Stevie. Just like last time! Make it two in a row!"

All my senses were heightened. To my surprise, not only could I hear conversations going on around me, but those in the stands, as well. "You can do it, Stevie. I know you can!" shouted a dark-haired girl from faraway. "Keep your eye on the ball!" She paused, then added, "And keep your hands soft!"

"Keep your hands soft? Where'd you hear that one, Diane?" her friend, Laini, asked, smiling. "At a make-out party?"

"I don't know," she shrugged. "My father always tells me and my sister that's what the good batters do. He says too many hitters tighten up and squeeze the bat too hard when they're waiting for a pitch." Laini was impressed. "If you think Stevie's good at baseball, you should read the poems he writes for Mrs. Bilheimer's lit. class," the dark-haired girl whispered to her friend as she folded down the top edge of her knee socks.

Someone handed me a bat. Everyone's eyes were on the batter, me.

Then the cheering stopped.

I got into my batter's stance and waited as I fixed my gaze on the pitcher's mound—the ball field's bald spot—where Felix Ybañez, moments ago, had stood facing Jerry. But Felix was no longer on the mound, he was running toward the boy who lay on the ground behind the backstop. Everyone was running toward the backstop. Everyone except me.

I looked over toward an empty chair on the sideline where my mother had been sitting. Where'd everyone go? Why'd it get so quiet? I wanted to sit down. I felt sick—sick and confused and alone and, despite the vastness of the space surrounding my isolation, claustrophobic.

I remained poised, listening to the sound of my fingers wrapped around the tape of the bat—my knees bent just a little, bat back, elbow up, my toes digging into the tips of my spiked shoes. I stood there waiting, waiting for my pitch.

I continued waiting, even after the trainman walked out to the pitcher's mound. I didn't see the trainman standing there; I saw only the pictures of my imagination.

Besides the trainman and me, the baseball diamond was empty. The young boy looked into the eyes of the old man, as the old man fingered the ball. When I finally saw him, I called to the trainman, "What's the matter? Gimme something to hit. Let's see whatcha got."

The trainman remained silent and still. Then: "No. I don't think you are ready yet."

"What're you waiting for? Pitch!" I squeezed the handle of the bat several times to prevent my hands from stiffening. The muscles in my shoulders tightened, and my thighs and calves began to tingle. Feeling myself growing dizzy, I spread my feet apart in order to better support my weight.

Without ever touching the ground, the ball that hung from the trainman's hand dropped and rose repeatedly, dipping and rising as if propelled by its own power, like a yo-yo without a string. Then the trainman's arm did the same thing. It stretched down almost to the ground, and the ball rolled out of his hand, where it swelled to the height of the trainman's waist, while his arm shrank back to its normal size. The trainman climbed onto the ball where he spent several moments wobbling. I stood and watched before I finally shouted to the trainman to throw the ball, but the man didn't throw. He just wobbled.

I lowered the bat from my shoulder and shifted my gaze from the pitcher's mound to the white-lined rectangle on the other side of the plate. A streak of sunlight filled the empty batter's box. I stared into the rectangle. My thoughts slipped sideways as if perched atop a record player's arm when its needle popped out of its groove. "*Look at me, Tatella! Talk to me,*" my grandfather's voice pleaded.

Only when my thoughts came to rest in the open, accepting hand of the trainman, did I begin to work my way back to the playing field, and then to my brother. "Excuse me," the trainman said as he led the way for us through the crowd. "The boy needs to get back there. To what just happened. Excuse us, please."

Behind the backstop, the trainman helped me return to where my father, with a bat in his hands, was standing alone. I knelt beside Howie. The trainman gently caressed the back of Howie's head, and then he left. It was 1:35 in the afternoon. I have not seen the trainman since.

❖ 69

TEARS OF FEAR

Two vertical rows of shiny silver buttons led down my mother's new spring jacket to her lap, where she cradled a bloody head. Expressionless, Howie looked into her eyes: "Where'd you learn how to throw, Dumbrowski?" My mother's lips moved as if to answer him, but she didn't speak.

I momentarily saw Sookie DiMaeoli's mouth form its Take Five wail. I remembered how his mournful scream had exploded through the congested high-school hangout like a derailed locomotive speeding out of control through the waiting room of a train station. The cry had started deep inside his body, maybe in his leg, and then burst out into the sunless room, scattering all over the place, landing nowhere. Now here it was again, DiMaeoli's wide-open mouth, positioned just inches above two vertical rows of shiny silver buttons. This time Sookie's wail was filling a sunny playing field. Then the sound diminished as his mouth dissolved into my mother's, which reappeared in its place. Her lips were barely parted. The most powerful part of her cry remained trapped inside her chest.

Looking into my mother's eyes, Howie repeated: "Where'd you learn how to throw, Dumbrowski?" Howie's face was gray. His hand, wet with blood, clenched the baseball he had retrieved. The ball had turned red like an apple.

I didn't move. I couldn't. Howie's body remained motionless, except for his lips, which kept chewing the same meal: Mike Dumbrowski and his lousy throw.

"I didn't see him," my father said haltingly. He said it as if he was trying out both the sound of his words and their meaning. "I didn't see him," he repeated, more loudly this time. No one was listening except my grandfather. Jacob's face was pale. "I didn't mean to hit him," he cried. "I didn't mean to hit him. He sneezed as he was running, and his head jerked forward right into my swing. I didn't mean to hit him." This time several people looked to see where these painful sounds were coming from.

"Come," my grandfather coaxed me. "Come over here with me, Big Boy. Howie will be just fine. You'll see. Let's give them some room."

What was wrong with Howie? *". . . Morris? You there, Morris? . . . You watching?"*

"Come," Grandpa Oscar gently repeated.

"Morris?"

"No, dear. It's me. Grandpa."

"Mike. You killed my grandfather! It was my grandfather!" I said from inside my house by the railroad, which was suddenly beginning to look an awful lot like apartment 11B.

"No, dear," my grandfather repeated. "I'm fine. I'm right here. You've had a shock. A terrible shock to your system. You passed out."

"*Zayde*. . .? But. . . I thought. . . are you okay, Grandpa? You okay? I thought you were. . ."

"You had a blow. Saying the strangest things. But you'll be okay, *kaynahorah*. Your color is returning already. Just stand still for a minute. That's it, Big Boy," Oscar said as he gently brushed away clumps of dirt from the back of my shirt and disentangled several more blades of grass from a curl of hair above my ear. A fat and fuzzy caterpillar floated to the ground.

"But you were dead. I saw it happen. We were in a dark apartment and you surprised us. You weren't supposed to be there. You. . ."

"*Tatella*, believe me, I'm just fine. Look at me. It's Howie. Not me. Your father accidentally knocked him over with a bat. My heart tells me that Howie will be just fine," he assured me, but he was quick to add, "God willing." He pointed out that the ambulance had already come, and that my mother would call from the hospital and let us know that everything was fine. I had the feeling that Grandpa Oscar's words were meant to reassure *himself* as much as me.

"I didn't see him," my father said again and again, drawing increasingly more attention to himself. "I, I must not have been watching closely enough to, to what was going on around me. My son sneezed. I'm sorry, I'm so sorry," he wept, the words drawn out painfully as if from a trance, over and over again, my father taking the blame for what I had done!

I saw this from afar; within my dream I saw and heard nothing. My eyes slowly examined the side of my grandfather's forehead. Grandpa Oscar was fine. My fingers caressed strands of white mixed into clusters of light brown aged hair growing just above my grandfather's ears, his earlobes dangling invitingly just as they always did. No bruises. Nothing. My relief found its expression in uncontrollable tears.

My grandfather explained, as best he could, what had happened behind the batting cage. After that, my joyful crying for my grandfather turned to tears of fear for my brother.

I returned to where my brother was lying, but three ambulance attendants hindered my path. "We'll take good care of him, Ma'am. I promise," the youngest of the attendants assured my mother. The name "Warren" was sewn with red thread across the attendant's shirt pocket. The color of his name matched the color of his hair. "We'll take good care of your boy," the young man promised, as he struggled in vain to pry loose my mother's fingers from Howie's, whose fingers of his other hand were resolutely clenched around the seams of his baseball.

My father stood motionless, hands at his side.

"Please Ma'am, you have to let go," the ambulance attendant said. "You can ride up front, but no one's allowed to ride in the back with the patients except us." When she refused to let go of her son's hand, the attendant tried again. "Please, Mrs. Schaech, we'll be at the hospital real, real soon. Then you can be with him all you want." He tried explaining that he could get in trouble if he let her ride in back, how their insurance didn't cover passengers back there. "Try to understand," he pleaded. "We're losing time."

Calmly my mother informed him that she was not going to ride in the front of the ambulance. She was staying with her son.

The attendant's attempted persuasions only strengthened my mother's resolve. Her words became screams. Her voice grew firmer. I didn't know my mother was capable of such anger. "Take your hand off my hand, I'm telling you! GET YOUR HAND AWAY! NOW! RIGHT NOW, GODDAMMIT!" Her free hand stiffened, echoing her grimacing face. She was screaming. I couldn't make out her words, but the language of her body and the color in her face made clear she was not going to be separated from her child. Her voice overwhelmed the siren of a police car just pulling up onto the grass. The ambulance attendant backed away as her body movements grew more awkward and extreme.

A pulsing sweep of red-orange light distorted the colors of blood and veins exposed beneath a wrinkled strip of skin torn from the side of Howie's head, which, even before the ambulance arrived, was showing color changes ranging from bruise purple to liver gray.

I followed the throbbing beam of light to a plastic bubble mounted atop the ambulance and watched as the stretcher holding my brother was lifted into the rear of the vehicle; my mother followed close behind, the movements of her body noticeably out-of-sync with the ambulance's steady, plastic pulse. "Thank you," she said softly to the attendant. "My son needs me." The suddenness with which she composed herself startled me more than the ferocity of her tirade.

"Where we going, Ma?" Howie asked. "Is Stevie's game over?"

"We're going to the hospital, honey. We'll be there in a few minutes."

My father stroked Howie's hand.

"I can't go to any hospital," Howie protested weakly. "I'll miss my game tomorrow. I know I'll end up missing it. Promise me you won't let me miss my game, Ma. Promise."

"I promise, honey. I promise. You'll be there for your game. We just have to let the doctors check you over. It'll just take them a few minutes. Then they'll send you right home. You'll see. Calm down. It'll just be a few minutes. I won't let you miss anything. I'm right here with you, *pumpkin*."

I remained kneeling even after the ambulance drove away with my father sitting up front and my mother and brother together in the back. "I didn't mean it," I said into the knees of my grandfather. "I didn't even know he was there! Oh, God, *Zayde*, I hurt Howie. It wasn't my father; it was me who did it. All this time it was me! What did I do? I thought I hurt you, but I hurt Howie! I never meant to hurt anyone!"

I was unable to compose myself until long after the crowd of onlookers withdrew. Rising from the ground, I picked up my brother's baseball mitt. The web between the thumb and forefinger of the glove had come loose. A thin, frayed strap from the web dangled like an untied string holding up a costume. My shaking hands jittered the strap, making it look like it was inscribing something into the air.

Far away, there was the faint whistle of a departing train and an owl's answering call. Then the sounds disappeared as I awoke from my delirium to find myself seated in a ladder-back chair.

In a dream we live seventy years
and discover on awakening,
that it was a quarter of an hour.
In our life, which passes as a dream,
we live seventy years,
and then we waken to a greater understanding
which shows us that it was a quarter of an hour.
Perfect understanding is beyond time.

—Chasidic maxim—

70

WHERE IS MORRIS?

"**Y**ou had me scared there for a while, young man," my grandfather complained softly. "Plenty scared. Do you have any idea how long you've been sitting in this chair, staring at that wall. . . just sitting and staring?"

I sat silent and motionless, my eyes fixed on the square of light tossed from a streetlamp onto the wall of a vacant apartment. The images I had been watching had disappeared, trailing after Mike, Jerry, and English, who fled the apartment earlier, just as my grandfather discovered me lying helplessly on the floor.

I was exhausted, despite the fact I had hardly moved a limb for. . . I had no idea how long I'd been sitting where I now found myself. What had I just witnessed? Often, when I awoke from a dream, it took a long time before I realized nothing had been real. And then I'd forget what the dream was about and be left with nothing but a feeling. Was this one of those times?

"So speak to me already, Stephen," Grandpa Oscar commanded. "Tell me what you have done. What shenanigans have been going on here?"

No matter how hard I tried, I couldn't remember what I had just seen. But I knew that whatever it was, the crux of it had truly happened. It was more than a dream.

"Those boys who ran away when I arrived, Jeremy and those other two, tell me what you were all doing here." My grandfather's eyes scanned the room, looking for his friend, looking for his friend's furniture. "And where is Morris?"

The lamplight on the wall softened and faded along with the remains of the night. As if still tied to its mothly memories, a butterfly flitted around the cold-blind eye of the streetlamp that had stared through the window of apartment 11B all last night.

Grandpa Oscar continued looking around the room, his eyes coming to rest on a cluster of debris strewn across the floor near the picture window: the cracked shell of a dead beetle sticking out from beneath a strip of cellophane; a half dozen crushed packs of cigarettes; and a single, bent spoon that glistened in the early morning sunlight. The dead bug looked like a sea turtle floating in the ocean. Specks of lamplight glittered across the cellophane, fallen stars cradled into cupped pieces of beetle shell.

"Answer me, Stephen. Where is Morris?"

 # 71

NOT THAT—THIS

"Nothing happened," I said. "It could have, but it didn't. Everything's okay." My words inflamed my grandfather's already heated state.

"'Everything's okay,' he says. Everything's okay. So this is your idea of okay? Look at you! Your neck. And your hand. Your thumb. You've been bleeding. And listen to what you sound like! *Du kannst nicht auf meinem rucken pishen unt mir sagen class es regen ist!"* Somehow he composed himself enough to translate what he was screaming at me (I think he wanted me to appreciate just how upset he was) *"You can't pee on my back, Stephen, and tell me it's rain!* I come to my friend's apartment and what do I find? My only grandson lying face down on the floor, I pick him up, put him in a chair, and then what? I'll tell you what. He sits there, and sits and sits, delirious with sitting. And what do I hear? 'Nothing happened,' that's what I hear, with a voice like someone gargling gravel no less. 'Nothing happened,' he says. You could have fooled me already with all your nothings!"

I had never seen my grandfather so disturbed. "Well, not *nothing*. I shouldn't've said 'nothing,'" I agreed. "Yeah, there was stuff going on, I'm not going to lie to you. But it could've been worse, Grandpa. A lot worse."

My grandfather talked right past my comments, focusing his attention on the whereabouts of his friend Morris. He wouldn't listen when I tried to tell him to forget about Morris for a minute.

"Grandpa, you don't understand. I stopped it. I meant to get in the way. I'm glad I did. It was worth it." I hesitated, and then I added, "Try to understand, Grandpa. I finally did something right."

I put my lips near the old man's ear and whispered, "It was Howie who helped me do what I did tonight, *Zayde*. It was Howie."

My words seemed to penetrate my grandfather's whole body. "You know," he said, "you have not called me *Zayde* for a long time, Big Boy. I have missed it. And I have not heard you speak your brother's name for just as long."

I explained that I saw what would've happened if Howie hadn't guided me tonight, if he hadn't been there to show me just how important it was to make things stop. Howie was there when I needed someone to be there to say, "Not that—this."

I was selective in what I told my grandfather. About certain details of the story I lied. I left out any reference to drugs. When I got to the part about my grandfather climbing the stairs, I said that my friends and I feared it was an intruder who would do us harm if we didn't protect ourselves and attack first. Still dazed by the feeling I was left with from my recent vision and disturbed by my inability to bring it back into focus, my words were slow and faltering.

I explained to my grandfather how English had stood behind Mike. Then came Jerry, and then me. Mike gripped the board in readiness. There was going to be blood.

I remembered trying to brush away something over my head. "I felt nothing besides hair," I acknowledged, "but I kept doing it 'cause I sensed something up there. I know this is going to sound weird, Grandpa, but all of a sudden I started thinking about when I was in first grade and had that stupid haircut, you know, with the bald spot. Like yours and dad's."

My grandfather laughed. "We couldn't talk you out of it."

"It was Howie who helped me back then. Remember?"

He didn't remember that part.

"Yeah, well he did," I said. "Big time. Howie made it okay. He put this blue and gold yarmulke on my head to cover my bare scalp. I can still feel the yarmulke against my skin if I think about it. I could hardly feel it, but I felt it. It was just like that tonight when I felt something above my head touching me, kind of guiding me."

"But there was nothing there?"

"I don't know. There was and there wasn't." I remembered how utterly clear-headed I felt at that moment, moving like dust in the darkness past Jerry, past English. "Anyway, Mike was holding a 2-by-4 over his head. We were all focused on the sound of these footsteps coming up the stairwell, I didn't know who was coming up. I didn't know it was you or anything, but I knew what was about to happen wasn't going to be good, so instead of just waiting for something bad to happen, I tried to do something about it."

Not since I started seeing Diane had I taken a hit of heroin. Each of the poems I had written had been a step in the direction away from drugs, toward Diane, toward Oscar, and now, simultaneously, both toward and away from Mike. The shame and humiliation I felt at the Hackensack narcotics office reinforced that path. What the hell, dope, joints, pills, none of it took me away from myself as I had hoped anyway.

I said none of this to my grandfather.

To him, I recounted the feeling of cool air brushing the skin at the top of my head as I tiptoed toward Mike. I told my grandfather how good it felt, and that it reminded me of Howie.

I had to tell the story twice. It was my grandfather's first memory lapse of the night. Grandpa Oscar had been particularly lucid and focused since he had come to the apartment, which was great for me since I needed someone to talk to. Maybe my grandfather could help me bring into focus the vision I had experienced earlier. Besides, I didn't mind repeating myself with my grandfather. It helped calm me down.

I left out most of what happened at this point in the story. He didn't need to hear about details like the mixture of fear and conviction that pulsed through my body as I crept up behind Mike. Why go into detail about seeing Mike's 2-by-4 begin to lower without understanding what that meant? Reliving these omitted details, I felt all over again how it took time for my mind to catch up to the pain in my body, how my rib twisted against the stab of Mike's hard, sharp elbow. As if it was happening all over again, I felt my knees hit the floor and then the palms of my hands, and I saw Mike raise the board again and turn his attention back to the stairwell.

"But what were you doing here in the first place?" my grandfather asked. I continued replaying in my mind my confrontation with Mike. For a little while longer, my grandfather's question would remain unanswered.

In my mind I replayed the scream that I let out as I crawled toward my friend, who turned once again, this time determined to put an end to my interference. I remembered how the footsteps on the stairwell ceased, and how Mike had raised his leg, as if to squash me, just as I had squashed English's bug shortly before. I remembered attempting a tackle, and how it had resulted in nothing more than a feeble fall.

"What the fuck're you doing, Shakes?" Mike had demanded. That look in his eye.

This was the first night the four of us were all together again. English and Jerry had just served a six-week term at Bergen Pines for possession of narcotics. For Dumbrowski, it was two months in the county jail. "Prison's a whole lot worse than The Pines," Mike had maintained earlier that night. "It's different than juvie. It's filled with all these old shits. Can't no one get along with them too much. Or you can, but only 'cause they've been there so long they're starved for new young 'tastes.'"

"I'm not getting sent away again! I told you that. I told all you that. None of you are getting me sent back there!"

I had reached up towards the wooden board while English and Jerry just watched. "Mike!" The name caromed off the walls and collided one by one into each of us like a billiard shot. As Mike grabbed my out-stretched arm and began twisting it, the footsteps on the stairwell resumed their climb.

That time at Take Five, my first time there, I was prepared to take whatever DiMaeoli thought he could give. Payback. I believed I deserved whatever pain I might ever receive; after all, it could just as easily have been *my* head ruined by my father's bat that day at Memorial Field. Howie wouldn't even have been there if it weren't for me. Indirectly, I was the cause of Howie's death; that's what I had always thought.

At Take Five I just stood there, waiting. This time I didn't wait.

Neither did Jerry, who saw how hard Mike was twisting my arm, and knew how determined Mike was to crush the skull of whoever was on the steps. . . at that moment, to crush anyone's skull—it didn't mat-ter whose it happened to be. Jerry's hand tightened around the flashlight he had been holding. He had only known me for the past two years, and for the whole first year we were little more than acquaintances, while he had grown up with Mike, who had always intimidated him, Jerry once told me. Why not? Mike intimidated everyone. I intimidated no one. Nonetheless, Jerry instinctively sided with me.

He flipped on his flashlight and shined it into Mike's eyes, momentarily blinding him. Mike immediately loosened his grip on my arm, which was all I needed. I tightened my free hand into a fist and slammed it into Mike's groin. The metal flap on Mike's zipper jammed behind my thumbnail, loosening the nail and tearing open the skin. Mike took the impact of my fist as if he were the post of a streetlamp.

"What're you doing!?" Mike had screamed through a spray of saliva, as he released his grip on my arm and unleashed his prison anger against my shoulder. The board cracked. The footsteps on the stairwell stopped. I moaned as my chin and cheek hit the floor. The heat in my shoulder climbed. Jerry and English remained frozen. Mike kicked me in the ribs, and I moaned again.

Mike raised his arms, but miscalculated this time and missed me with the board. He stumbled, regained his balance, and then attempted to attack me with his foot again. But he could not kick. He couldn't move, as a delayed, crippling reaction to my lunge tunneled from his groin to his chest. "You fuckin' punched me in the balls, you little kike!"

"Morris? Is that you, Morris?" a voice called from near the top of the stairs. "It's me, Oscar. Did you forget about our race? I hope I'm not intruding if you have company."

"It's Mr. Bialintz, Mike. It's just Stephen's granddad!" I heard Jerry call out, as a shoe smacked into the side of my neck.

 # 72

RETURN

While I was recounting what had happened in apartment 11B, flashes from my earlier vision returned: baseball gloves and bats, Howie on his back, blood, my father, me. Slowly, the details came together.

Since the very beginnings of my conversation with my grandfather, partial memories were inching their way, like worn-out worms, toward me. Suddenly, without warning, they bolted up and charged, piling into my face with such force I felt my teeth splinter. I gagged, and then started screaming, "Oh, my God! Oh no, oh my God!"

My screams startled my grandfather, who waited for more, for some kind of explanation, I guess, but all I could utter, over and over again, was, "Oh no! Oh, my God! Oh no!"

73 ✦

HESED

So long in coming, but when I remembered what really happened three years ago behind the backstop at the playing field, its impact was immediate and devastating. The most crucially important moments of my life and I had had it all wrong. All this time, wrong. Everyone was. "I saw it all, Grandpa! I was just sitting here, and it came back to me. I saw it all! I remember it now; it wasn't Dad after all. He was just protecting me. He must've picked up the bat I dropped. I hated him for killing Howie, and he didn't even do it. I did! He took the blame for what *I* did. I remember now. I can see it."

"Oh, my God. I killed my brother. It was *me*." I couldn't stop myself from repeating these dreadful words.

Nothing Oscar said could calm me down. He tried everything, but all he had to offer were words, clichés.

Until he confessed. That stopped me.

My grandfather knew it all along, he admitted.

He had to repeat his confession several times before I would believe him. He knew. He always knew.

I finally came to believe him, but then I could not look at him, nor could I hear more of what he had to say. I had heard all I needed to hear. But my grandfather continued to talk. When he finally stopped, I finally looked at him.

He averted his eyes.

Neither of us spoke.

When I broke the silence, I kept demanding to know how he could have kept this from me if all along he knew what really happened. How could he have let me think it was my father! "You let me hate him," I repeated over and over.

My grandfather didn't answer. For once he didn't have the words.

Never before had I used such an angry, exasperated tone with him. Never before had I cursed in front of him. Certainly never *at* him.

When he finally spoke, he pleaded for my forgiveness, offering little more explanation than that he just wasn't strong enough to tell me the truth. "You should only know, Stephen, I struggled over what would be for the best." He wanted to protect me, he kept repeating, he wanted to protect me, that I should only know how much he wanted for me to be spared the pain of knowing what really happened. He didn't allow his eyes to meet mine.

"The truth, Grandpa. The truth would have been 'for the best.' Isn't that what you've always taught me?"

"Who else knew? Mom, did she?"

"Ech. God forgive me," my grandfather pleaded. "I could not bring myself to talk to her or anyone else about what I saw. Not even Leah. Not even your father. For too long I remained silent. I told myself, if I don't tell someone today I will tomorrow, but then tomorrow came and tomorrow went, and still I remained silent. I was the only one who saw from what happened. Just me. And I told myself it was a secret I was supposed to keep. Believe me, Stephen, I did what I thought was best. Best for you."

The old man suddenly looked small, defeated. "There you have it," he murmered.

"You saw him take the blame, and never even said anything about it to mom? What do you mean, 'a secret?' How could you keep such a thing a secret? How could you, Grandpa?"

"I finally did tell her, Stephen. They were not doing well together, your mother and father, and I knew that my silence was part of the reason why. Jacob, God bless him, wouldn't tell your mother what really happened. It got to the point where I knew that I had to."

We spoke for what seemed like hours, with Oscar letting me do most of the talking. I repeated myself more than he ever did, even on any of his worst days. My voice shook. Sweat beaded my forehead.

My grandfather had little to say, or at least little that I wanted to hear, except when the subject of giving came up and what a gift Jacob had offered me through his actions. I knew this even without him telling me, but I liked hearing my grandfather describe what my father did at the playing field as a religious act, and how his keeping it from me was part of its holiness. "Giving without the recipient knowing about the gift or the giver is a true *mitzvah*," my grandfather said. "Giving with no 'thank you's' in mind. It is not only a religious duty, like all *mitzvot*; it is one of the very greatest deeds of kindness a person can ever perform." He used the Hebrew word, *hesed*, for kindness, when he said this. The word touched me deeply. My father and *hesed*, together—the pairing made me dizzy.

My grandfather took a handkerchief from his pocket and wiped the sweat from my face. "You have been through a great deal tonight. I am sorry I disappointed you. So sorry."

"You should've told me, Grandpa. You should've told me what you knew."

"I finally did tell your mother what I saw, and that changed things between your parents, Stephen. It changed things for the much better." I looked away when he said this and when he again asked me to forgive him.

Shortly thereafter he said, "Come, let me take you home, Big Boy."

I didn't move. I couldn't. I felt like I had been hammered to the chair. For the moment, all I could think about was what I had done—to my brother, to my whole family—and that I wanted my grandfather to hurt like I did for lying to me, or at least for keeping the truth a secret.

"Then I will just sit here with you," my grandfather said when I didn't respond to his suggestion that we go home. As he said this, my grandfather climbed like a child onto my lap and hugged me tightly. I remained motionless for several minutes before finally moving my arms and carefully cradling the fragile bones of the old man's torso.

That is how we sat, without speaking, grandfather and grandson, until I was ready, until I was able, to leave.

Standing outside on the brick steps, my grandfather eyed the door we had just closed, and observed: "You know what, Big Boy. I think we were in the wrong apartment. Morris lives in "C", not "B". Or "A", but not "B"."

With teary eyes, I smiled and shrugged my shoulders. "Oops."

"Come," the old man said. "Let's go home. Come already."

As we walked away, our bodies cast behind us a single, barely perceptible shadow that angled up, over, down, and across the cracks of the sidewalk. Behind us, apartment 11B was dark. The streetlamp outside the window no longer shot its gaze across the living room wall. Out of sight, the whistle of a locomotive inscribed its furtive message heavenward, as a graceful tangle of intertwining lives wove ever-new configurations, intricate and fragile, that only the dead could fathom.

74 ❖

DISTANCE

I lacked the words. What could I say to my father? How could I approach him? Who would have thought the cipher Jacob Schaech capable of such profound selflessness and generosity, this man who I thought I knew, a man whose main claim to fame, as far as I was concerned, was his nothingness. I had spent a lifetime resenting my father for playing such a minor role in my upbringing. Who would have thought he had within him such deep, deep, fatherly instincts?

I knew nothing about Jacob Schaech, after all. I didn't know anything about anything. Brooding, I kept my distance from everyone. I tried to write, but couldn't. I gazed at reproductions of paintings to try to find some balance, but there was none. Not for me. Not now.

Alone in my room, I stared at my bedroom wall. When I ate dinner with my family, I kept my eyes on my plate. If someone called for me, even if it was Jerry, who called often, I directed my mother to say I wasn't home. And I withdrew completely from my grandfather.

I had mourned for Howie when he died. The first year was the most difficult. Mercifully, the pain lessened with time. Only recently had I begun to feel somewhat at peace with my brother's death. Now I mourned all over again, starting from scratch.

Months after the accident, I overheard my grandfather tell my mother that it took ten years to bury a child, referring to how long the parental embers of love and loss took to cool. Ten years? I thought at the time that my grandfather was way off. How could you *ever* bury a child—or a brother? The pain of Howie's loss was too great for me to imagine ever coming to terms with it. And yet, I had begun to do just that.

Now I was starting all over.

I wrote to Diane. In my letter I enclosed a gift I made for her, but I revealed nothing of my recent revelation, nothing about my father or me in relation to Howie's death. A few days later Diane wrote a two-page letter back to me. I read one part over and over again:

. . . You asked me to hang the tree you just sent me onto my basement wall with all the others, but I couldn't. What you made for me—so many leaves so caringly glued to so many branches—doesn't belong with the rest. Its roots are kinder. You offered your gift as an apology for whatever you did to hurt me. But you did nothing wrong. It's me who should be asking forgiveness for the way I withdrew. I tried to deny how I felt for you because of how I was feeling about myself. Please forgive me, Stephen. I know I have been selfish, but being forced to leave the way I did really threw me. I returned home to Baltimore ashamed of myself for what I did. . . and for how much more I wanted to do—with you.

Stephen, I've never stopped loving you, but I need to be alone right now. Please be patient with me a little longer.

I understood Diane's need for time alone, but I also knew how much I needed to be with her, to talk to her. I wanted to at least telephone her, but I didn't. She had asked me for distance.

And she asked me for something else; in her letter she asked me for forgiveness. Forgiveness, what do I know about that? Me of all people, who didn't think for a minute about forgiving my father when I thought he was the one who swung the bat. Yet my father, yes, my father, the one person who I always thought knew nothing—knew nothing about anything—he forgave me instantly for hurting his son; he forgave me so completely that he let me and everyone else think he was the one who needed forgiveness. Forgiveness. I don't know anything about anything—especially that!

Alone in my room, I thought about the railroad tracks that ran behind our apartment in Marchwood. I remembered how Howie and I lived for the train and the trainman who always made it his business to slow down, wave, and blow the whistle of his locomotive whenever he passed. Everyday, Howie and I had to be there. No matter what we were doing, it was always less important than the train.

How many years did it envelop Howie and me in its steaming spell? I couldn't remember. I knew only that the train was gone.

75 ◈

CONVERSATIONS

After weeks of isolation, as was my custom when I was troubled, I finally sought out Oscar. Our exchange was awkward at first, but we soon found our familiar balance. We started talking in my parents' kitchen before making our way into my bedroom for more privacy. I avoided what plagued me most for a good part of our conversation: my feelings of guilt.

"Grandpa, sometimes I feel like. . . I don't know. . . I don't know how I feel. It makes no sense, but it's like what you used to say to me when I was younger, only this time I feel like I should be the one to say it."

"To say it? What is it you wish to say, Big Boy?"

"You know, '*Yich in dina yahren hab shoyn gavein. Ober de in mein. . .*' '*I in your years have already been. But you in mine. . .*' I don't know. . . sometimes I just feel like I can understand you better than I can understand me. And even though I know you were my age once, I just don't think you, or anyone else, will understand. *Ober de in mein. . .?*"

"Give me a chance, Stephen. Give anyone a chance. Who knows?"

I explained how I had tried not to think about Howie after he died, but that it was impossible. I compared it to holding my breath underwater. That's how it was for me with not thinking about Howie. Ultimately, I'd always have to give up, come up for air. With Howie, once I started thinking about him, we'd get into all these conversations where he would assume the role of not only a big brother, but almost a parent. "He'd put me down for lots of the things I'd do," I said, "that even I knew were wrong, but I'd do them anyway. I didn't like the conversations."

"Conversations with yourself," my grandfather offered.

"Yeah, sort of, but with Howie too, really. But now even that's getting all screwed up. . . getting worse."

"How worse?"

"Recently I started realizing that Howie's no longer older than me. I can't get him to age in my head. Remember, he had just turned sixteen when it happened, and now I'm almost seventeen. When I talk to him now I'm the older one."

I talked about how that changed things, how I felt that now I had to say and think things differently if I was going to keep on having conversations with him, because I wasn't the little kid anymore, and he was no longer the big brother. "That's changed," I said. "Lately I hear myself saying to Howie, *Yich in dina yahren hab shoyn gavein. Ober de in mein.* I hear myself sounding like you, Grandpa."

My grandfather smiled and stroked the back of my neck, his fingers unintentionally finding the same area Mike's foot had found only one month before. The bruise had not yet disappeared, but it no longer hurt the way it did before.

I said that I didn't think Howie could understand why I did some of the things I did now because Howie died before he got to be my age. And I didn't need anyone to point out to me that Howie was almost the same age when he died as I was now, and that it was me who prevented him from getting older.

My grandfather tried to intervene, but I wouldn't let him.

"I don't know, Grandpa. I'm not the way I used to be. And yet I'm not different at all. It stinks. It keeps coming back. It swells up and I have to live with it for a while, and then it disappears. But it never stays away for good. It keeps splashing back down on me. . . that I caused Howie's death, that every time mom looks at me she's thinking I'm the reason she's got an only child." I brushed the top of my head with the palm of my hand. "I feel like Cain sometimes."

My grandfather instinctively caressed my neck once again. This time he avoided the bruise.

"His death was an accident, Stephen. It was no more your fault than his."

"But he's dead, and I have to live with that!"

"Yes, live is what you have to do. I wish I could take away what happened. God only knows how I wish. But *nobody* can take it back. And if you are not careful, you are going to grow old inside yesterday. My father used to say 'you can't control your feelings, just your actions.' How I wish I could take away all the bad feelings you have about. . . about what happened in the past, but I can't. For the last three years you have been someone else, Stephen. And then this past month since you remembered what happened. . ." He didn't finish his sentence. "It hurts me to see it. Perhaps, God willing, new actions will lead you back to new feelings."

"Grandpa, I killed my brother!"

"*Shoyn genug*! Enough already with all your guilt! It happened, Stephen. It was an accident. A terrible, terrible accident. It happened to you and to me and to your parents and your grandmother and to. . . to *Howard*." The name broke on my grandfather's lips as the old man broke down. He wanted to say more but "Howard" was all he could get out.

For the past three years, Grandpa Oscar had not allowed himself to speak his dead grandson's name aloud whenever possible, as if that would make what happened less real. Neither of us had realized what the rule about Howie's name was until the rule was broken.

"It happened to everyone who loved your brother."

"Yeah, but it was because of *me*," I cried. I looked into the splash of lamplight slanting across the bedroom wall in front of me.

"Don't look there," my grandfather scolded. "Enough with the wall already! Look at me, Stephen. *Red tsu der vant*!" Oscar charged. "Your grandmother's favorite expression, 'Go talk to the wall.' But she only *says* it. She grows impatient because she thinks I don't listen, and right away she starts in with, *Red tsu der vant*! But you, you sit and *do* it. You sit and look and you talk and sit and talk to the wall like it was your best friend. I have seen how you sit and stare. Look at me!" he commanded. "Not the wall. If life is not the way you like, you have to work to change it."

"And if I can't? What then? I look back at that day at Memorial Field, and I can see everything just like it was, and I want like anything to get back inside it so I can change things back to how they were before I swung that damn bat. Everything was perfect until then. It was such a great day. Perfect!" *Perfect* nearly broke into pieces of glass under my tongue. "I can see it and hear it and smell it, but I can't get back inside it to make anything different. It's like Alice when she got stuck in that long, dark hall. Remember? She found a door that opened onto a beautiful garden, but the door was too tiny for her to get through. She could kneel down and see all the great colors of the flowers, even smell them, but she couldn't get through the darn door."

My grandfather seemed to be touched by my remembrance of *Alice in Wonderland*. He had read and reread it to Howie and me when we were kids. Often, we'd beg him to read it all over again the minute he finished turning the last page. With his grandchildren as audience, my grandfather never seemed to tire of reading the story.

We were talking about Howie, the hardest subject for both of us to talk about. We were talking, but I couldn't say out loud everything I was thinking. One thing I couldn't say was this: When my bat connected with my brother's skull, that moment pulsated with an exhilaration in its beat that I had never known before or since. *That moment.* Despite myself, I had fleetingly experienced a euphoric sense of strength, coordination. . . grace. Yes, I experienced a moment of grace just as I was killing my brother.

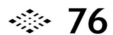 # 76

SECRET

All day long, I had been at the top of my game. Never before had I felt more in control. The fat part of my bat could not miss its target. A double and a home run. Both solid shots. It was like the felt tip of English's cue stick that could not miss striking the polished ivory of the cue ball at just the right point, with just the right force, in just the right game. It was like the flat of Mike's foot that split the leg of just the right person at just the right moment.

I couldn't deny it; a triumph of adrenaline had rushed through my on-deck body as a result of my bat meeting its unintended target with such impeccable accuracy. Unintended? God, I hoped so. Had I glimpsed my brother's presence at the last moment? Could I have stopped my swing? It all happened so fast. I swung at the air—just a warm-up swing—but there was contact. The sound was full and sweet—pitch perfect. Perfect feel—there was no sting in my hands as there was whenever the ball hit too close in on the handle, or at the tip of my bat. I was in perfect contact with life.

What happened next was fused with what happened just before, like two droplets of mercury touching. Since I remembered what happened that day, this next moment was so real and alive that at any time I could retrieve it and be pumped right into its heart. At any time, against my will, this hideous *beauty* mark could scar me, and it did.

So many moments in a life—gone, forgotten, hardly registering even as they're in the process of occurring; yet, this moment was forever present. I could paint a picture of it, and it would be more detailed than any picture I had ever seen hanging on the wall of any museum. This moment was a horizon line marked by a *vanishing point* that would not go away, and like the classic train track example illustrated in books on perspective, it sucked everything else straight toward it.

I was talking to my grandfather about Howie, but I couldn't tell him everything. I couldn't tell him about the thrill attached to my life's greatest sorrow, or my uncertainty over whether or not I could've prevented it. "What sad eyes you have, Big Boy," the expression on my grandfather's face would say. "Now I know why such sad eyes—sad and full of shame." Then my grandfather's lips would turn mute and pale, and the old man would turn away.

I envied the secrets of others. *"I got into college, Shakes, but don't tell anyone."* I would willingly take English's secret any day. I'd take anybody else's secret over mine.

77 ❖

FORGIVENESS

I loved Howie, no matter how many times I told him, "I hate you!" Sure, there were times he infuriated me, at times I wished him ill—but never *death*. Certainly never what happened. Still, questions plagued me: Was Howie's death entirely an accident? Why, for God's sake, did it have to feel so good, when I swung my bat? If my love for my brother had been stronger, would I have had the power to stop my swing?

"I *can't* change them, Grandpa!" I insisted. "The things I want to change back the most, I just can't."

"Welcome to adulthood, kiddo. Some things, Stephen, we just can't change. We just have to learn to like them how they are. We have just. . ."

"*Like* it? There's no way I am ever going to like. . ."

"You are right, 'like' is surely not such a good word here. Get rid of like. From mud you don't make cheesecake. 'Live with.' Maybe all we can ever do with some things is live with them and hope we will one day understand why they are there for us. Maybe they can even serve us somehow, someday. What else is there?"

"You think they take something away, and they do. But they also add," my grandfather advised. "Every scratch and dent on our lives adds dimension."

"Even death?" I countered. "Death's a pretty deep scratch, don't you think?"

"There is nothing that only takes away, Stephen. Not unless you make it that way."

"And Howie? How does his not being here add a single thing to my life, to any of our lives? Tell me that, Grandpa."

"Especially Howie. For you, *Tatella*, it may always be *especially Howie,*" my grandfather responded. "That is something you will be creating and recreating for many years to come—perhaps for the rest of your life."

"I know it's not easy to see," my grandfather acknowledged. "We are all blind. You, me, your parents, all of us struggling to remain on our feet as we stumble across black paths created by Howie's death. . . with me and my cataracts at the end of the line. But we have to keep moving forward. What else can we do?" Grandpa Oscar smiled, and then he added, "At least this is what your grandma says to me when I am distressed by the kind of sorrows troubling you now."

I wanted to smile, but I couldn't. All I could say was, "God forgive me," as my body shook with remorse.

"Of course he does, *Tatella*. It's His business to forgive," the old man said softly. "But He can't do it alone."

I couldn't look at my grandfather.

"Such sad eyes," he said, as he gently kissed my eyelids. "Howie was there the night I found you on the floor of that empty apartment," my grandfather reminded me. "I do not know how, but you have told me Howie was there. He will always be there when you need him, *kayna-horah*. Listen to him. Have your conversations. Let him be your *shoymer*, your secret watchman."

So many thoughts filled my mind. That night I transferred many of them to paper and, along with a poem I wrote for her, I sent them off to Diane.

She wrote me right back:

May 12, 1966

Dear Stephen,

Our Dutch friend held her painted breath for three hundred years and never looked our way. I used to think she was content being alone. Since returning to Baltimore last year I can only remember her as lonely, the way I felt since leaving Garrison City, the way you were sometimes, even when you were with other people. It was a part of you I never understood. Now I under-

stand. *What you just wrote to me explains a lot. I can't imagine what a shock your recent discovery must have been for you.*

I have continued working on the series of paintings I started in Garrison City, a series that has become a story. Your letter provides a fitting coda. Perhaps together we can add something good to the chapter's end. The series is based on your poems. I would like to think that what you said in your letter is true, and that your poems helped you cope with the loss of your brother. Maybe they even helped you arrive at the discovery you just revealed to me about your accidental part in his death, a memory which, no matter how painful, I'm sure you know you had to come to.

Perhaps you finally remembered what happened because you are now strong enough to face it.

I no longer want to be like the woman in our Vermeer painting who stands cornered and with her back to the world. I need to see you; I hope you still want to see me. Please call and let me know if we can meet this coming weekend.

Like our Dutch friend, I'm alone. You wrote in your letter that you are too. You don't need to be.

Thank you for confiding in me, Stephen. I'm sorry it took you so long. And I'm sorry it took me so long.

I love you,
Diane

Diane's letter gave me the added confidence I needed to communicate with my father. For the next few days I prepared myself to talk to him, but I didn't know where to start, so I finally decided to write out what I wanted to say. It came slowly. Even on paper I couldn't get going.

Father,
My dear Poppa PJ,
Dear Dad,
How could I have been so. . .
How can I ever. . .
What a shock. . .
What a fool I've. . .
Two wastepaper basketsful-later, this is part of what I came up with:

Dear Dad,
. . . There's a picture hanging in Grandma and Grandpa's living room of a girl on a ball and a man on a box. I've always viewed them as father and daughter. Perhaps because the girl is so involved with the balancing act that

life has presented her; in her eyes, the man is invisible, even though he is sitting just a few feet away. I guess a lot of times we fail to see what is right there in front of us.

I made up a name for the young acrobat, and sometimes when I look at the painting, I imagine who she is and who she will be. The stories I weave come easily because the uninhibited girl leaves herself open to so many possibilities. When she grows up she's going to be a star and tumble through the sky. Already her feet don't touch the ground.

Stories about the man come slower for me. I used to see him as distant, even though he sits up front in the picture. His charity is easy to overlook. Now I see a quiet but caring man content to sit back and give the child he loves the freedom she needs. If she loses her balance, he'll be there to make sure she won't get hurt, although she's so frail and wobbly you have to wonder.

If the strongman has anything to say about it, his child will enjoy a good and balanced life. That's all he wants, and he will do whatever is within his power to see that she is happy.

Like all true heroes, the strongman hides his heroism. He thinks he is invisible, but he is not. Although his deeds may long go unnoticed, eventually they come to light.

The strongman's name is Jacob. . .

 # 78

DREAM

"**Y**our move, Gramp."

In bed, I found myself within one of those Humpty Dumpty moments that confuses time by breaking it open. It is one of those moments that totter between the end of one day and the beginning of the next, between dream and awake time. I concentrated on keeping my balance.

Every night for the past week, a recurring dream, riddled by strange variations, filled my nights. Each night I returned as both an invisible spectator and creator to the same smoky, ten-watt-bulb background of Adriaen Brouwer's tavern, a place where Howie was still alive, where the likes of Hieronymous Bosch and Jan Vermeer vied for the affection of Mary Gustin, where Sidney Goodman played catch with Willie Mays, where a middle-aged Abby Lentz, who taught ballet to tutued pre-schoolers, went after work to unwind.

In my dream, Howie played checkers with Grandpa Oscar, and they talked. Howie learned to remind his opponent that it was his move, otherwise my grandfather would sit and wait forever, forgetting it was his turn. *"Nu, shoyn,"* my grandfather would complain impatiently; and Howie would either go ahead and move, or he'd try unsuccessfully to point out whose turn it really was. Each night they talked about my group of friends, but each morning I could remember details about only one of those friends.

This morning it was Mike. In the dream, Howie described him as a sad character, a guy who dropped out of high school a good ten years ago, but who still hung out at Take Five, where, besides Smokey the Bear, hardly anyone else was old enough to shave yet.

In the dream, Mike was a barber, a lousy one. Lousy partly because he needed glasses but refused to wear them, but more importantly, lousy because his drug abuse had finally caught up with him. Every couple of customers, he'd chop off too much from the top and leave a circle of scalp showing.

"Gotenyu! A vain drug addict. . . and a bad barber to boot," Grandpa Oscar would lament before recounting to Howie the story of his five-year-old brother's haircut with a hole in the middle.

As he spoke, the checkers changed form. Some nights Vietnam War medals might replace the traditional red and black disks. Most of the medals were simple circles, but one or two of them, I noticed, were shaped into purple hearts imprinted with facial features resembling one or another acquaintance from high school. Other nights the replacements might be red and black gobs of paint, or miniature toy railroad-set trees. In tonight's dream they assumed the red or black form of fallen nursery-rhyme statues topped by the artfully detailed facial features of, among others, Mary Gustin, Jan Vermeer, and Hieronymous Bosch, each of them with pieces missing here and there from shattered head to broken toe.

As I watched my brother and grandfather's game unfold, I saw, outfitted in a purple sequined leotard, tiny like the rest of the wooden-costumed troupe, Mary Gustin bidding, "All together now," as the bodies of Little Bo-Peep; Simple Simon; Jack Sprat; Tom, Tom, the Piper's son; Peter Pumpkin Eater's wife; the crooked man; Mother Hubbard; the black hen; the cat and her fiddle; and Little Tommy Tucker pirouetted in unison, their costumes catching the light like fireflies in a forest.

"Are you watching this?" my beaming grandfather asked his grandson. Mostly, he couldn't take his eyes off Mary Gustin. "The old girl's not bad."

"Your move, Gramp," Howie reminded the old man.

As Grandpa Oscar looked at the checker pieces and the squares they occupied, Hieronymous Bosch chased Mary Gustin around a table.

"Come back here, my little garden of delights," shouted the pursuer, as they ran out the front door, closely followed by all the other patrons who had filled the tavern except my grandfather and brother.

"Your move," Howie repeated. He waited. So did I. Grandpa Oscar studied the board. It started to rain. The sun came out, then the moon, then it rained some more. My sleep deepened beneath the mesmerizing beat of fat, countable raindrops.

Finally, the old man looked up into Howie's eyes. *"Nu?"* he said. *"Vos vet zein?"*

"Vos vet zein, Grandpa? I don't remember that one."

"It was one of your Great-Grandpa Izzie's expressions. He would come home from his tailor shop and see me quiet, sitting, reading a book, anything, and right away '*Vos vet zein?*' he would ask. 'What's going to be?'"

"Like 'What's happening?'" Howie offered.

My grandfather smiled. "More like 'What's happening *next?*'"

"Well," Howie said, "I'll tell you '*Vas vet zein.*' It's your move, Grandpa." "My move? I thought it was yours." My grandfather covered his smile with the tips of his fingers. "Oops."

I reached into my dream and moved one of the checkers, causing the pattern on the board to suddenly make sense. Then I became visible and sat down on the empty ladder-back chair next to my brother. Across the table from us, Oscar and Stanley suddenly appeared, the four of us, two sets of brothers embraced by time.

"Good move," Howie said. "Sometimes it's just a matter of connecting the right dots."

The four of us talked for hours, or maybe it was days. When Grandpa Oscar and Howie finished their drinks, I stood up and kissed them both on the top of the head. I shook my uncle's hand. "Grandpa told me so much about you," I said. "I never thought we'd meet." The sound of two empty chairs sliding back into the middle of a painting accompanied my departure.

"Come back anytime, stringbean. We're always here," a voice called out.

From the doorway, I saw my father, sitting in a shadow, smile and wave goodbye to me from his corner table. Had he been in my dream the whole time? I hadn't seen him there before. He held a letter in his hand. On the table rested a jar with a beetle in it. The lid was perforated so the beetle had fresh air and food holes where its caretaker could slip in tiny insects. My father had even bothered to coat the jar with a cushiony floor of sand to not only keep the beetle from slipping on the glass, but to absorb its secretions. I guess my father was privy to the tidy tip that "Piss on sand disappears."

Smiling gratefully, and waving back to the strongest man I know, I indicated, by my facial expression and where I focused my gaze, the letter in my father's hand. He closed both his eyes and pressed it to his lips. Then he carefully placed the letter back onto the table and gently slipped an insect into his beetle jar.

Even in shadow, my father stood out from his surroundings. To me, he looked like Yogi Berra—a trimmer, more refined version. There he was, solid and short (I must've inched him out in height several years ago without noticing), his well-matched clothes carefully pressed, his once-black, now silver-streaked and balding hair neatly cut and combed, his face clean-shaven. There was nothing in his appearance out- of-place or irregular. His eyes revealed no misalignment, like everyone else's did, his nose showed no traces of past injuries, none of his features were disproportionately bigger or smaller than any other. Maybe it was partly this, I thought, my father's lack of the kind of noticeable quirks that make us who we are to others, that made him invisible to me for so many years.

Intently, my father watched me approach him. Normally, such concentrated attention directed my way would have made me uncomfortable, self-conscious, but his gaze strengthened me.

"Dad." I could not recall the last time I had said that word.

"Sit down, son, if you'd like. Want to help me feed this poor little critter in the jar?"

I told him I'd rather just watch him do it.

We sat across the table from each other without speaking until the beetle finished its dinner. "See? Our little friend is happy now," he said. Then he reached his hand out toward me and traced a curve from my cheek to my ear, and came to a stop just below my lips. "Look at that!" he exclaimed. "You're developing a cleft in your chin, Stephen. I was the same age as you are now when I first noticed mine. It's a Schaech trait," he said proudly. "My father's cleft was so pronounced he used to complain that he couldn't get his shaver in there. I've always been grateful that I favored my father in the cleft department." Smiling and pushing his chin forward, he added, "My best feature."

Again, I focused my attention on my father's appearance. This time I looked more closely at him than I'd ever done before. His eyes were soft and inviting; they looked so different from how I grew up seeing them (or perhaps more accurately, *not* seeing them). He had a ballish nose, like Howie's, and a mole underneath his cheekbone, smaller and paler than Howie's, but in pretty much the same spot. Near his eyes and along his jaw, a lifetime of subtle wrinkles had nestled comfortably across the weathered landscape of his skin, creating a delicate, lacy design. His earlobes were even longer than Grandpa Oscar's.

"You have lots of best features, Poppa PJ. Lots." I couldn't stop looking at him. "It took me a long time, but I'm finally beginning to see that." Kindly, he didn't say, "It's about time," but if he had, he'd've been right.

"You protected me, Dad. What you did was an incredibly brave and generous thing to do." I could feel my eyes fill.

"Son, you don't need to say anything. Please don't. Not now. We'll have plenty of time for that." He paused, then added shyly, almost apologetically: "But as long as you brought up the subject of generosity, there is something you can give to me, if you would be so inclined."

I was thrilled by the prospect of hunting for just the right example of whatever it was he wanted. I would find a way to afford it.

"I'll tell you what I'd like." He paused again, even longer this time, and averted his eyes from mine. He ran his hand through the few hairs at the top of his head. Then he took his fingers and combed them nervously through the hair that grew more thickly above his ears. He did this over and over again as I waited for him to speak. Despite all his finger-combing, his hair remained in place, just as it was.

"I, I'm not an affectionate man, Stephen."

"Pop?"

"For years I've watched you sit with your grandfather when the family would all be together, and I would yearn to be him. I never sat with my father the way you two sit. My father would never allow it—so I didn't, well. . . I just didn't know how to make it happen with you. . . or your brother. I guess I'm not good at affection. Truth is, I'm not good at many things." As he said this, his hand knocked the beetle jar over. Sand spilled across the beetle's back, but the beetle hardly moved at all.

My father took his time trying to right the jar, which kept slipping from his fingers. When he finally returned his attention to me, he looked like a little boy, an undeserving one, afraid that what he was about to ask for was too much (a dog, a drum set, a handshake from Gil McDougal). "Stephen," he said, as I leaned toward him in order to hear, "Please, would you sit close to me, and place your hand in mine?"

I waited, expecting him to say more, but that was it. My father wanted to touch his son, and feel his son touching him back. That's what he wanted. *If I would be so inclined.*

His lips didn't move, but I could feel the smile within him when I did as he asked. I sensed that both our clefts stretched in delight ever so slightly. I was shocked by how inevitable it all felt.

❖

That's when my dream would always start to fade. Mercifully, each night it lasted a little longer.

"Gramp? Does that about do it, Gramp?" Howie would whisper, as my father and I would appear, as if out of nowhere, to join them at their table. Howie, my grandfather, my father, and me. And a checkerboard, empty except for a single train-set tree positioned in just the right place, thriving just so. "Does that about do it? For tonight, at least?"

"Let's ask your dad, Howie. I think we should leave it up to him."

"I guess it's about time," Jacob Schaech would reply.

And then I would wake.

It was time.

So much is about time.

I would have liked to reach back into my dream and move more of the checkers across the board, creating ever-new patterns, but there was nothing there to reach back into.

Or was there? My dream had not altogether vanished. It was within me now.

79 ◈

YOUR MOVE

A breeze cooled my cheek and stirred a curl of my hair. I pulled a blanket over my chest and looked toward the open window near my bed. Gradually, I became conscious of a pencil nestled in a crease of my stomach, and then, near my arm I noticed two sheets of paper cambering toward the breeze. I lifted Diane's letter. *Please let us be together again,* she wrote. She wanted to meet this coming weekend.

"This coming weekend sounds great!" I said out loud. "If that's what you want." Since she returned to Baltimore, that's all I had wanted.

Rubbing sleep from my eyes, I lifted the other sheet of paper. It was Diane's unfinished self-portrait that she left behind for me, the only visual trace that proved I hadn't made her up. *"What sad eyes she has,"* Grandpa Oscar remarked when he first saw the drawing. *"Such a pretty little thing, with such sad eyes. Don't you think?"* I probed the expression on her face. The sadness my grandfather saw—that I myself saw when I last looked at the picture—was gone.

I turned the drawing over. Across the top of the white sheet, written in clumsy capitalized letters followed by a looping question mark at the tail-end running off the page as if already a part of the future, I read, *VOS VET ZEIN?*

Beneath, was a string of letters. Illegible. A word, maybe two.

I turned the page back over and looked again at Diane. Her coming to Garrison City had been a stroke of luck. . . for me. . . but not for her. I hated her abrupt, sad return to Baltimore. Was I to blame? As if seeking through my fingertips to penetrate her thoughts (or maybe to transmit my own thoughts to her), I slowly traced into the air, just above her self-portrait, the lines of Diane's face.

I thought of Jerry and the paralyzed bowler—well-intentioned, perseverant, twelve-year-old Jerry, failing to cure the man's paralysis. I thought of Jerry's confession about taunting Warren into turning his headlights off, and how, on the brighter side of things, Jerry had helped save the day at that empty Forstops Village apartment by momentarily blinding Mike when he shone the flashlight in his eyes. His action had allowed me to stop Mike from hurting, or even killing, my grandfather. Jerry was full of both darkness and light. Just like me.

I thought of English's secrets; of Malcolm Bazzaz's parting words. . . *"Don't let me see you in here again, son"*, of Diane in Baltimore, *Alice in Wonderland*, blind beggars in a ditch, Willie Mays in centerfield, Goodman's batter in his nakedness, an owl in Hopalong underpants, the trainman in his train. Then, along with many others, came Mike and Felix, Sarah, Oscar, Jacob, and finally, Howie—all part of me, every one of them. *"All aboard,"* I whispered to no one in particular. *All aboard*. A few lines from an Israeli poet (a distant relative of Grandpa Oscar's) came to mind.

All the world is wrapped in silence,
As I sit here pensively;
One world have I—yea, no other
Than the world which lives in me.

"Throbs the Night with Mystic Silence." I liked the title of this poem by Hayyim Bialik almost as much as the poem itself.

Sliding out from beneath my covers, I placed the page upon my bed, tucking it gently under the cotton edge of my pillow to keep it from blowing away, the paper peeking out like a bookmark. Waving to me from the reverse side of the drawing, in sight, then hidden, then in sight again, as it curled in the wind, was the string of letters I couldn't decipher a moment ago. Now I could:

YOUR MOVE

Softly pressing between my thumb and forefinger the white paper Diane had covered with subtle lines and tones, I stroked the words as I watched blue and orange leaves dancing in a purple sky. Then I gently placed the page in a portfolio, where a beautiful face smiled at me in the dark.

Inside my bedroom, black and white; outside, leaves of every hue. Walking to the corner window near my bed, I press my hand against the casement molding, fill my senses with the tones of indoor daylight, and gaze outward at tarless trees whose roots are twisted but kind.

In a nearby museum, a Dutch maiden looks my way and exhales. Shimmering invisibly within itself, her painted breath disappears like heat on evening sand, her silence as enlivening as an unspoken, unwritten word set free to inhabit a page of heaven.

Suspended above the maiden's gaze, floats a hard-hit baseball. Like threads woven through the binding of a book, the stitches of the bruised but precious white sphere seam the heart of a great big exquisite design, as traces of past and present are joined by pages of times to come.

About the author:

Barry Nemett has exhibited his paintings in museums and galleries throughout the United States, Asia, and Europe. Since receiving a Fulbright/ITT International Travel Fellowship to Spain, he has lectured world-wide, curated numerous traveling exhibitions, and has been a recipient of resident artist grants in the United States, Japan, Scotland, Italy, and France. In addition, he has received many awards for his paintings.

Upon earning his MFA degree from Yale University in 1971, Professor Nemett began teaching at Maryland Institute College of Art, where he is Chair of the Painting Department. He has recently taught at Princeton University and, during the summer months, he teaches at the International School of Painting, Drawing, and Sculpture in Umbria, Italy. He has published essays and poetry for numerous magazines, and he is the author of a college textbook, *Images, Objects, and Ideas: Viewing the Visual Arts.*

About the novel:

Reality battles fantasy, and both sides win in this poignant novel set in the late 1950s and early 1960s. Anger, sadness, and shame lead Stephen to magically project himself into a wide range of paintings that serve as compelling hiding places where he tries to heal himself emotionally, while plotting to avenge his brother's death at the hands of his father. The characters created in paintings by Rembrandt, Vermeer, Goya, Kahlo, and other artists are every bit as fascinating as those Stephen encounters inside his own painted illusions; and they affect him while he is inside and outside his invented worlds.

We also meet Stephen's eccentric high school friends whose hilarity, loyalty, and unpredictability are corrupted by drugs and violence; his grandfather whose wisdom is tempered by senility; and his shy student teacher, Diane, who educates him about art, life, love, and himself.

Time and places shift and collide. Scenes are set in Renaissance Italy and Hackensack, New Jersey. Through Stephen's eyes, we see beyond historical moments and conventional minutes to focus on how we experience time in grief and joy. This heartbreaking, yet surprisingly upbeat, life-affirming story explores the influence of friends and family, the gentle force of romance, the challenge of redemption, and ultimately, the wonder of how a life can seemingly fall apart and come together at once, as it follows the crooked tracks of a youthful journey.

Credits:

Front cover art: Nemett, Barry; *Gatehouse with Battered Ball*, 2007; gouache on paper, 14″ x 9″; private collection, United States.

Back cover art: Nemett, Barry; Detail from *Crooked Tracks Installation #1*, 2000; mixed media, 410″ x 240″; private collection, United States.

Photograph of author (above photo) by Robert Salazar

Poem, "A Boy's Dream," Richard Kalter, *Crooked Tracks*, chapter 59, p. 220.

Interior design by Candida Robinson/Rainbow Graphics